THE LOST
LANGUAGE
OF CRANES

Books by David Leavitt

Family Dancing

The Lost Language of Cranes

Equal Affections

A Place I've Never Been

While England Sleeps

Italian Pleasures *(with Mark Mitchell)*

Arkansas

THE LOST LANGUAGE OF CRANES

David Leavitt

A MARINER BOOK

Houghton Mifflin Company

Boston   New York

I would like to express my gratitude to the National Endowment for the Arts and to the MacDowell Colony for support that aided immeasurably in the completion of this work. I would also like to thank Lynn Hart for first telling me about the crane-child, and Dr. Francois Péraldi, upon whose lucid account of the case, in *Psychoanalysis, Creativity and Literature: A French-American Inquiry* (Columbia University Press, New York, 1978), my own imagined version is based.

To Barbara Bristol and Andrew Wylie I owe a debt larger than I can put into words. They have my love, my admiration, and my boundless appreciation.

For information about permission to reproduce selections from this book, write to Permissions, Houghton Mifflin Company, 215 Park Avenue South, New York, New York 10003.

Library of Congress Cataloging-in-Publication Data

Leavitt, David, date.
The lost language of cranes / David Leavitt.
p.   cm.
ISBN 0-395-87733-4
1. Fathers and sons—United States—Fiction.   2. Married people—United States—Fiction.   3. Gay men—United States—Fiction.   I. Title.
PS3562.E2618L6   1997
813'.54—dc21   97-18297   CIP

Book design by Anne Chalmers
Typeface: Janson (Adobe PostScript™)

Printed in the United States of America

QUM 10 9 8 7 6 5 4 3

Grateful acknowledgment is made to the following for permission to reprint previously published material:

Epigraph from "Days of 1964" from *Nights and Days* by James Merrill. Copyright © 1966 by James Merrill. Reprinted with permission of Atheneum Publishers, Inc.

Excerpt from "It Will Have to Do Until the Real Thing Comes Along" by Sammy Cahn, Saul I. Chaplin, L. E. Freeman, Mann Holiner, and Alberta Nichols. Copyright © 1935 & 1936 by Chappell & Co., Inc. Copyright renewed, assigned to Cahn Music Co. and Chappell & Co., Inc. (Intersong Music, Publisher). International copyright secured. All rights reserved. Used by permission.

Paraphrase of an excerpt from "The Crane Child" by Francois Péraldi, from *Psychoanalysis, Creativity and Literature: A French-American Inquiry*. Used with permission of Columbia University Press.

In memory of my mother,

GLORIA ROSENTHAL LEAVITT

Forgive me if you read this...

I had gone so long without loving,

I hardly knew what I was thinking.

—James Merrill, "Days of 1964"

CONTENTS

PREFACE

Of the books that I have written, *The Lost Language of Cranes* is probably the one with which I am today most closely identified; at the time of its publication, however, the critics and pundits of the publishing world roundly dismissed the novel as a disappointment, or a case of "sophomore slump." I think it was taken for granted that a very young writer who had been greatly praised for his first book would necessarily fumble with his second, and in many ways *The Lost Language of Cranes* was something of a fumble. "Artful transparency" was the phrase Richard Sennett used to describe the stories in *Family Dancing;* "the people and the scenes evoked in them are so vivid, so immediate, that we are unaware of their creator." But by the time *The Lost Language of Cranes* came along, the detached observer of those stories —a little boy who had seen a great deal but done nearly nothing —had grown into a young man beginning to be implicated in human experience. The result is a messier if more intimate novel, less beautiful, I think, because more alive.

E. M. Forster, in his commonplace book, wrote that the novel "must have either one living character or a perfect pattern: fails otherwise." *The Lost Language of Cranes*, if it succeeds at all, succeeds on the first grounds. Rereading it recently, I was appalled by the naive clumsiness that marks much of the prose, and went so far as to correct what seemed to me the most glaring infelicities. And yet the central characters — Rose, Owen, and Philip — strike me as being as alive today as they were when I invented them more than a decade ago. Voyaging forth to contend with the consequences of heretofore unspoken desire and need, all three are versions of the mysterious crane-child who seesaws at the novel's center, struggling toward a sense of self in a world where *feeling* love is a certainty even if *being* loved is not.

Probably the question I am most commonly asked concerning this novel is what I meant in the first place by that crane-child. By way of answer, I think the best I can do is pose a further question: Does a love object, particularly an unconventional one, confer identity upon the person who loves it? (Or him? Or her?) When I wrote the novel, I believed that the answer was yes, that an erotic attraction to men was, as Philip puts it to his mother, by necessity "the most crucial, most elemental force" in a gay man's life. "Whatever it is that we love, that is who we are": this I still believe. And yet age has inclined me to define that "whatever" less in the ideological language of post-Stonewall gay liberation and more in terms of Forster's creed of personal relations. After all, an erotic attraction to men only becomes real once it has been translated into a love for one man or for particular men. Perhaps the line should read, "*Whoever* it is that we love, that is *what* we are."

Finally, this: as I write, AIDS has been around half my life — eighteen years. In 1986, by contrast, both I and the disease were young. *The Lost Language of Cranes* thus engages in a kind of denial of the epidemic's importance, even as it articulates the muddle of resentment and uncertainty that characterized the attitude of those years. Like Philip, most of us back then were slapdash in our practice of "safer sex"; superstitious in deciding what we were willing to do, and with whom; condescending to the John Malcolmsons of the world and to the odd mix of rage and nostalgia that qualified their recollections. Even more surprising to me—and in this case I can speak only for myself—is the memory of taking for granted that a "cure" was surely only a few years away. Now, in the age of protease inhibitors, no one talks about a cure anymore. Instead we talk about "maintenance." We talk about "long-term survival." The world has changed, and the result—strangely enough—is that at the age of thirty-five, I feel historical. Hard to imagine that "compound Q" should have become a footnote in a highly accelerated history, but it has.

I used to say that I wrote *The Lost Language of Cranes* to fill a gap: to provide for young readers the very book that I never found on the shelf in the gay section of my local bookstore, back in the days when the gay section of my local bookstore consisted of the collected works of Gordon Merrick. Well, in the years since then, that gay section has grown, and transmuted, and been subject to heated ideological debate; it has evolved into whole shops, canons, mail-order catalogues; it has become the subject not just of university courses but university departments, on the curriculum lists of which are featured not only my books but those old chestnuts of Gordon Merrick. And for this I am glad, even as I worry that to young readers weaned on Dennis Cooper and Dale Peck, *The Lost Language of Cranes* may seem ridiculously unsophisticated. Which, I cannot deny, it is: as unsophisticated as its author was, those cold afternoons in the early eighties when he pounded it out on an old IBM Selectric typewriter. Yet it is its sincerity, I believe, that makes this first novel, for all its flaws, live and breathe.

May 4, 1997
Rome

Voyages

EARLY ON A RAINY SUNDAY AFTERNOON in November a man was hurrying down Third Avenue, past closed and barred florist shops and newsstands, his hands stuffed into his pockets and his head bent against the wind. The avenue was deserted except for an occasional cab, which parted the gray water puddled in the potholes and sent it streaming. Behind the lighted windows of apartment buildings people stretched, divided the Sunday *Times*, poured coffee into glazed mugs, but in the street it was a different scene: A bum covered by soggy shopping bags huddled in a closed storefront; a woman in a brown coat held a paper over her head and ran; a pair of cops whose walkie-talkies blared distorted voices listened to an old woman weep in front of a pink enamelled building. What, the man wondered, was he, a decent and respectable man, with a well-heated apartment, good books to read, a coffee maker, doing out among these people, out in the street on a cold Sunday afternoon? He laughed at himself for still asking the question and pressed on. No matter what he pretended, he knew, he was going where he was going.

Only a few blocks uptown, on the twelfth floor of a once

inconspicuous white brick building that had been painted a conspicuous baby blue, a woman sat at a desk, patiently waving a red pencil over a manuscript. She was barely aware of the clacking of rain against the drainpipe as it cascaded down her window in sheets. Her lips moved without sound, repeating the words before her. On the television, which was turned on but without volume, an elderly cartoon dinosaur limped across a chalk-gray landscape, its hair a white mophead, a satchel tied to a stick it held between its teeth. Unaware of the dinosaur, the woman breathed in rhythm with the kitchen clock, and her pencil passed over the manuscript like a wand, healing all it touched. She did not think of her husband, who walked alone, fighting the sheeted rain.

Rose often referred to her neighborhood, with its pink and blue and bright red skyscrapers, as the Middle East. It was in fact full of dark-skinned men who wore sunglasses at midnight, and white-robed sheiks in limousines, and black-veiled women who haggled with the tired old proprietress of the Korean grocery store. Where she lived, she liked to explain, was too far west for Sutton Place, too far east for midtown, too far north for Murray Hill, too far south for the Upper East Side. According to maps it was Turtle Bay, but Rose, who had a copy editor's sense of exactitude, knew that Turtle Bay was meant to connote only lamplit side streets with lush trees and townhouses. Rose and Owen lived on Second Avenue proper. The master bedroom looked out over cars and cabs and street traffic. Sirens blared through the night, so that lately Owen had taken to stuffing wax plugs in his ears when he went to bed.

Twenty-one years ago, when they had moved into the apartment, the neighborhood had been the humble, resiliently middle-class domain of people who might have identified themselves with Lucy and Ricky Ricardo, except that they did nothing so glamorous as work in nightclubs. Over the years it had become more and more affluent. By the grace of rent stabilization, Rose and Owen continued to pay the rent of a perished age, while the future slithered past them, uptown and downtown, on Second Avenue. Little changed visibly in their immediate vicinity, but Rose knew it was the invisible changes that in the end would be the most damning.

For twenty years Rose had been a copy editor, possessed of the rare capacity to sit all day in a small cubicle, like a monk in a cell, and read with an almost penitential rigor. In moments of tension she calmed herself by thinking up synonyms: feel, empathize, sympathize; rage, fulminate, fly off the handle; mollify, placate, calm. It was an instinct to put the world in order that powered her, as sitting at her desk she put sentences in order, mending split infinitives and snipping off dangling participles, smoothing away the knots and bumps until the prose before her took on a sheen, like perfect caramel. Cooking was her other pleasure. She gloried in foods that in no way resembled their ingredients: miniature fruits made of marzipan; perfect, silky icings. (The cake was an afterthought, a triviality, an excuse for the idea.) Owen sat before the cakes Rose made and gazed, his face filled with a kind of awe, for he had grown up in a house without frosting, fed on dry, heavy nutbreads and fruitcakes. A quiet man, he ate Rose's cakes with a ferocity of which most people would not have thought him capable.

They had a son, Philip; he was twenty-five, and lived on the West Side. For him, one particular image of his parents had a kind of primal character: Owen and Rose are sitting across the living room from each other in the twin corduroy La-Z-Rockers they had once rented a car and driven all the way to Jersey to buy. It is late at night. Through the crack beneath the door to his bedroom, the light of four one-hundred-watt bulbs glares. There is no sound but that of pages turning, bodies shifting, an occasional stretch. "Two hundred pages to go," says Owen. He is reading a densely footnoted biography of Lytton Strachey. Then he moves into the kitchen and opens the refrigerator door. The cake is there, the icing gleaming in the light that goes on when the door opens, one or two slices already missing and the knife — coated with white silk and yellow crumbs — lying on the plate next to it. Rose joins him. She takes the plate out of the refrigerator, puts it down on the counter, and sinks the knife into its softness. He stands by, helpless, watching her as she hoists two pieces of cake onto dessert plates and carries them to the table. All without a word. Then they sit down, prop their books open in front of them, and eat.

One fall afternoon, in the elevator, Mrs. Lubin — a widow who had lived in the building even longer than the Benjamins — confided in Rose. The landlord, she suspected, was capable of dark treacheries.

A letter a few days later confirmed her worst fears. The building was going co-op. Because they were not rent-controlled and under sixty-five, they had an option to buy at a reduced price, but they could not continue as renters.

Of course there had been portents, rumors, finally letters; but the thing seemed to have been put off indefinitely, and finally they had stopped believing it could really happen. Now it had happened. "Can we afford it?" Rose asked Owen. He took off his reading glasses, put down the letter, and rubbed his eyes. "I don't know," he said. "I suppose we have enough money. I'll have to talk it over with an accountant. I've never imagined spending so much money before, not since Philip went to college."

"We have a few months, at least," Rose said. "Before we lose our option." She looked around herself. Give or take a few new pieces of furniture, and some re-upholstering, it was the same living room they had moved into twenty-one years ago. On the rug, a seventeen-year-old urine stain alone testified to the existence of Doodles, the poodle puppy hit by a car when he was only eight months old. They had lived there so long it no longer seemed like a place to her.

"The maintenance alone is going to be twice our rent," Owen said. "Still, from what I hear, even that's a bargain." He looked out the window. "You know, Arnold Selensky tells me that every other building on the block has already gone co-op."

"I don't want to leave," Rose said. Like old Mrs. Lubin, she panicked at the prospect of change, had heard the stories of the landlords who hired thugs and dropped pets out of windows, feared homelessness. Not everyone felt that way, of course. Owen's spirited friend in the penthouse, Arnold Selensky, rich and getting richer in the video rental business, invited them up for dinner one night, wagged his cognac glass at them across the plexiglass table, and applauded change. "I myself believe in keeping up with the times," he explained. "That music on the stereo, for instance. Eurythmics. Not The Eurythmics, just Eurythmics. Nice, huh? The latest thing. That compact disc player is also the latest thing. No reason just because one's getting on one should lose touch. So many of the old women in this building, they're killing themselves, it seems to me; they're still listening to Lawrence Welk."

Rose thought, Living in the past. Anachronistic. Bag lady.

"There is just no future in rentals," Arnold Selensky said. "And there is quite a future in co-ops. Think about it. We get a good deal, we buy, we sell for twice as much on the open market, and we're on Fifth Avenue. Well, maybe not Fifth, but very likely Park in the Thirties. Or in my case, Tribeca. Loft living, Owen, that's the way. More space than you've ever dreamed of. Like a ranch house in the city. Incredible."

That night Owen woke in a sweat. "What's wrong?" Rose asked him. He shook his head and wouldn't tell her that he had dreamed everything had slipped out from under him, and he had been forced to take to the streets. In the dream, he had no legs. He rode up and down the length of moving subway cars on a skateboard, shaking a tin can for change. Unlike Arnold Selensky, he was not in a job with a future. For ten years he had made a decent salary assessing the value systems and moral character and S.S.A.T. scores of the little boys whose parents wanted to enroll them in the Harte School, a private boys' school in the East Nineties. He spent his mornings reading letters of recommendation from chairmen of the board and conducting interviews with seven- to twelve-year-olds, and in the afternoons taught one class, a Renaissance literature seminar with three bright students. He had thick graying hair he kept cut short, and though he rarely exercised, his body was strung tight as a harpstring. It was as if tension itself had taken a physical form.

Rose always shopped at the little Italian grocery store on the corner, and now that it was a little Korean grocery store she continued to shop there. Twenty-one years ago she had bought at that store the ingredients for the first dinner she ever cooked in the apartment — an underdone chicken that she and Owen ate off of paper plates — and she had been amazed that vegetables could be so fresh, even in New York City. She and the lady behind the counter, whose name she had never learned, knew each other well; chatted in the afternoons about asparagus; grew middle-aged together. One day the lady changed race; that was how it felt to Rose. She went on as before with the Korean proprietress. Visibly, their little block was no different than it had been. And yet, Arnold Selensky had told her, every other building had gone co-op. It seemed traitorous.

The phone calls started. Real-estate agents, brokers, people who had heard from people who had heard from people. "Excuse me," the voice would say. "Am I correct that there is a five-room apartment available in this building?"

"No, that's not true."

"Ma'am, if there is a five-room apartment available in this building, we could be of service to you."

"No thank you. Goodbye."

The phone calls came more and more frequently, and later at night. If Owen was home, he'd answer sternly. Weekday evenings, when Rose got back from the office, the machine was full of little pleas.

One Sunday, seventeen people called. Rose was irate. "This apartment is not available," she said to the eighteenth caller. "We live here. Why can't you people leave us alone?"

"Look, listen here for a minute," the voice said. It was small and nasal. "Now I'll have you know there is a client who is looking for an apartment in your neighborhood, and will pay good money for it. But I don't care. I'm sick of being screamed at.

All you people do is scream and scream. Well, enough. I'm quitting this stupid job. I could make better money doing anything else besides making these stupid phone calls. I've got three kids and no husband and we're living with my mother in Queens. I call you people because I have to, to feed the kids. I don't enjoy it. The least you could do is have a little understanding, a little sympathy before you start yelling."

"Well, I'm sorry." Rose lapsed into guilt. "You must understand, though. We've been bothered very frequently. We're quiet people, and — "

"I'm sure you're real cozy up there on the East Side. Well, you may not be for long. I know the score. Born and bred in New York, and look what it gets you. A slap in the face."

Rose hung up, pushing the receiver down hard. She looked at the phone. Among the many things in the apartment that she took for granted, the phone suddenly seemed very special to her. It was a shade of gray you didn't see very often anymore. There were vultures out there, she decided, returning to her armchair and her reading; they were clutching the phone wires, eager to rip the phone cord out of the wall, knock the walls down, strip the apartment of its furniture and memories, re-paint it and re-make it for themselves, without a thought for the life that had been interrupted, the life that had been thrown into the streets.

Now they could buy the apartment; then they would have no savings, but they would have the apartment. That didn't seem like much of a deal to Rose, since in every way she understood they already had the apartment, had lived there twenty-one years of their lives, and continued to live there. She tried to imagine tying herself to the bed, as some elderly tenants on Central Park West had recently done, but found it impossible. Other people, she knew, were waking up at five on Wednesdays to get a first crack at the ads in the *Voice*, were meeting with brokers and scanning obituaries to see where deaths might create vacancies. Rose couldn't face it. She put off the task of looking for a new place to live the way she had put off week after week, for six months, a letter she owed her sister in Chicago. They knew they had "six months to a year," as the terms of the building's transition from rental to co-op were still being negotiated. It sounded like the answer to the question, "How much time have I got, Doctor?" Day after day Rose checked the mail and was relieved to find no threatening notices with firm dates, so that she began to hope that this vague grace period might go on forever. But always some stark letter arrived, reminding her that her days were numbered.

Some afternoons, walking home from work, she would look up at the multi-storied buildings that surrounded her and see them transformed, in the blink of an eye, to heaps of bodies, the live limbs wriggling among the dead. The thought of so much life, boxed in, piled seventeen stories high, made her nauseous.

Philip came over sometimes to stand with his parents in their shell shock. His heart was elsewhere these days, across town, in love for the first time, and hardly had space left in it for grief. Still, sitting with his parents in the living room, he felt a sudden longing for his childhood, and he imagined he might say "goodnight," and turn, and discover his old room as it was, his homework laid out on the desk. Most of his life he had eaten his dinner here, done his homework, washed his hands, watched television and read his books, and gone to bed. Thinking of these things, tears came to his eyes, and he felt a gratifying lump rise in his throat.

But what Rose and Owen felt, as they went to bed, was pain, pure and simple. It started in their stomachs, a hoarse growl, and rose to their heads and threatened to burst through their chests. There was nothing pleasurable about it. They didn't enjoy it. They wanted it gone. The selling of the apartment was the beginning of the end for them. It was the beginning of the beginning for Philip, who longed for something that would signal the irrevocable start of his adulthood. There was no part of his life he wanted to relive, and he was glad of it. He had no regrets except luxurious ones. He looked only forward, hungering for the future, while his parents, suddenly helpless in the face of change, looked back at all they had taken for granted. No matter what else might have happened, the neutral years, the years they remembered as painless, were over. At night they lay awake, far apart, each clinging to the extreme edge of the bed, and assumed the other to be sleeping. Cars passed outside, casting their shadows twelve stories high, and the shadows swept like swift birds over the carpet.

M OST SUNDAYS Rose and Owen spent apart. It wasn't a rule, it just worked out that way. For the first year after he was back from college, there was another Sunday tradition, that Philip come over for dinner, but recently his visits had become irregular. He would call and say, "I just can't make it this week. But how about lunch, Mom?" Since they worked in the same part of town, lunch was a possibility for them.

Rose had worked twenty years for T. S. Motherwell, a small

literary publishing house. She had her cubicle neatly arranged. In the morning she would have some coffee with her friend Carole Schneebaum, then disappear behind the door to do her methodical readings. Every hour or ten pages (whichever came first) she'd get up, stretch, have some coffee. Elsewhere in the office people were panicking about poor sales and bad reviews, but none of this meant much to her. At lunch with Philip she listened to him talk about packaging and product marketing, but none of this meant much to her either. He worked for a company that churned out paperback romance novels. She wondered somewhat at his enthusiasm for the job, but Philip's life had a different scale than hers. "The computer training is invaluable," he explained. "Everything at the office is done on a computer monitor, Mom. Not a typewriter to be seen."

Rose had a Royal which was thirty-five years old. It shouldn't have surprised her that the world had moved ahead of her, but it did. Philip lived on a dirty street in a part of town she had thought white people could not walk through. But no, he assured her, his once-devastated neighborhood was on the upswing now; it was nearly chic. The tiny apartment in which he lived was a jewel, even though it had only two rooms, and the tub was in the kitchen. One weekend when Owen was away at a conference he had invited her over for dinner, and to see the place. Rose didn't like the look of the street, the Puerto Rican teenagers with their radios slung over their shoulders, the stray kittens mewing on the sidewalk. There was graffiti on the buildings, empty rum bottles on the stoop. Inside, however, was exposed brick and mauve walls hung with framed posters. Philip had painted the outside of the tub bright red.

After they ate dinner, Philip put on his coat to walk his mother to Broadway, where she could catch a cab. "This is a very African area," he said as they maneuvered their way among covens of menacing children. "The hallways of the buildings smell like Berber pepper."

On the way out of the door they had to step over a man asleep in the vestibule. "Our doorman," Philip said, and laughed.

"Philip," Rose said, "is that man all right?"

"Don't worry," Philip said. "He lives here. Sometimes he just has trouble making it up the stairs."

"I see."

They walked down 106th Street. "How long do you think you'll stay in this place?" Rose asked.

"As long as I can. The rent's dirt cheap, and the landlord would kill to get rid of me so he can up it. But it can't go co-op. I checked. Some obscure footnote to the building code, having to do with pipes or something."

"This place? Co-op?" Rose was incredulous.

"Believe it or not, it's happening all over the neighborhood."

"My."

They kept walking. On Amsterdam Avenue, a man was urinating in the gutter. "Is this where you go out?" Rose asked, looking away from the man.

"What do you mean?"

"You know," Rose said. "What you do. With your friends."

"Oh no," Philip said. "Not around here. In fact, lately I've been spending a lot of time in the East Village. It's a wild neighborhood — full of punks and street people and bad artists dressed up in outlandish clothes."

"You're not any of those things," Rose said.

Philip's mouth opened at that statement, but he didn't answer.

Instead he looked away and wrapped his scarf tighter against his throat.

Rose had the sense that she had asked the wrong question. Or asked it in the wrong way. What she meant was, Will you please explain to me what happened, why your life is so different from mine? But Philip said, "Have you decided if you're going to buy the apartment or not?"

She smiled, and shook her head. "We're waiting to hear what the accountant has to say. And then what the lawyer has to say. But it's hard. Your father and I are so set in our ways."

"I can't imagine you living anywhere else, quite frankly," Philip said. He looked away from her. "I hope it works out for you. Look, here comes a cab. I'll get it."

Forget the cab, Rose wanted to say. Tell me something, anything. I am tired of living in the past. But the yellow cab had pulled up, and she had no choice but to get in.

Philip's hand was cold as it took hers, his lips cold as he kissed her on the cheek. "I'll see you soon," he said. "Maybe lunch next week?"

"Yes," she said, and wanted to say, No, not *lunch*. Then the cab door closed, and she was speeding downtown.

"Cold night, huh, lady?" the driver said.

"Sure is," said Rose.

"I like working nights. Lots of guys prefer the days, but nights, you get more interesting customers. The later it is, the more interesting. I took a lady home to Fifth Avenue the other night? She asked for change, right? It turned out she was a guy."

"Really," Rose said.

"You bet," the driver said. "But I say, 'Live and let live.'"

The driver was young. From above the glove compartment, a

photograph of a pitted face with a bushy mustache contrasted oddly with the long, clean-shaven neck Rose stared at. A triptych of little girls was taped to the sunvisor: Slavic faces, big smiles on two, the one in the center thin and dangerous-looking.

"Well, the world is changing, that's for sure," the driver said. "A lot of things you wouldn't have seen twenty years ago don't surprise you too much today."

"So true," Rose said.

When Rose woke up, late, on Sunday, Owen was already gone. As always, he'd be back in the evening. She wouldn't ask him where he'd been. It wouldn't be polite.

Still, she wondered. He knew perfectly well what she did with her Sundays. She drank coffee and read the paper, and then she took out one of her manuscripts, and worked until it was time for "Sixty Minutes." She enjoyed the quiet of the apartment, the luxury of having the whole place to herself. Owen was always out. Was he at school? Maybe there was a woman. But only on Sundays.

Today she sat at her desk and read the manuscript of a manual on how to take care of elderly parents. The chapters had titles like "Diseases of the Brain" and "Incontinence: Fact and Myth." She liked the book; it seemed to her oddly comforting.

On page 165, she attached to the manuscript a small yellow sheet of paper on which she wrote, "When one is standing up, one doesn't have a lap." She reread the sentence with some satisfaction and went on. Then, in the midst of "How to Say 'No!' — Nicely," Rose suddenly had a flash of suspicion that she had missed something a few pages back. She backtracked, and indeed, on page 172, found a misplaced modifier, unmarked. What had happened? She reread the paragraph again and did not recognize it. The paragraph described symptoms of senile dementia: forgetfulness, paranoia, compulsive hiding. She was certain she had never read it before. "The straying of the mind," she read. She put the manuscript aside.

She decided not to do any more work today. Her mind was full of anxious thoughts about the apartment and about Philip, and rather than let them interfere with her work, she concluded, she might as well give them free reign to work themselves out or do themselves in. So she put on her coat and gloves and went outside, to walk a bit and breathe the cold air and clear her head. It had stopped raining. She pulled her scarf tight and headed north.

Because it was Sunday, and mid-afternoon, most of the midtown shops and restaurants were closed. The office towers announced their emptiness with patterns of lit windows and fluorescent, lifeless lobbies. The world was in apartments today, behind warmly illuminated curtains. Only bums were out, and people who looked lost. Smashed umbrellas tangled around her feet; on the avenue cars roared by, splashing her with puddled water. Still, she walked. She came to the intersection where the F.D.R. Drive grazes Sutton Place so closely that cars roar within inches of pedestrians, and stepped back, astounded by the maze of skyscrapers thrusting at contrary angles into the sky. Here a white-brick apartment building jutted out over the highway, and she wondered what the cars must look like from the apartment windows as they were sucked underneath it. Beyond the highway and its traffic and speed was the wild, choppy river, and beyond that Roosevelt Island, and the churring tramway, and the Pepsi-Cola sign. Queens. All this hugeness made Rose feel extraordinarily tiny, so she turned around and headed back to

First Avenue, and made her way downtown. The sounds of the highway and the river were immediately muffled, as if the city had drawn its breath and was holding it in. She remembered an episode of "The Twilight Zone" in which an astronaut had run hopelessly through an empty town, trying to awaken life by screaming until he was hoarse. There was nothing there. It turned out that the town was his dream, that he was in an isolation tank, being tested for his eventual ejection into outer space. Godspeed, John Glenn. We're all with you.

Other people, Rose thought, were camouflage. If someone were to jump her right now, drag her into an alley, who would hear? The noise certainly wouldn't carry up to the apartments. Hadn't a woman once been raped under her window while she slept or read or just sat there, never bothering to look outside?

She ducked into the Horn & Hardart Automat at Forty-second Street. Christmas music chimed through the cavernous cafeteria, bouncing off Art Deco pillars and creating a stuttering chorus, the voices out-of-sync with one another. Behind that was a low hum of life, of talking. Rose stared at the little metal cubbyholes, each of which contained one discrete thing: a tuna fish sandwich with its accompanying mound of potato chips; a goblet of slick red Jell-O cubes. Most of them were empty. This place had entranced her twenty-five years ago, when it had seemed like something from the future. It had been featured prominently in a Depression-era comedy she had been taken to as a child in Chicago. Now she knew enough about the future to know that the Automat was an antique, an anachronism, a thing of the past. She got a cup of coffee from an elderly black woman with a stocking pulled over her hair and sat down and drank it. All the people in the Automat were old, and they were eating things like roast turkey with green beans or Salisbury steak. They ate slowly, and chewed each mouthful methodically, as Rose's mother had instructed her to do, to make it last. Most were alone, some in couples, and several looked as if they lived in the streets. What she wanted was a cheeseburger, a Whopper from Burger King, dripping with mayonnaise and mustard and soggy pickles. She indulged this secret vice only occasionally, and then with great guilt, wolfing down the criminal burger in a corner so she could get out as soon as possible, afraid of being seen, although she realized that anyone who saw her would probably be eating the same thing. Now, in the Automat, Rose saw herself, a tall middle-aged woman in a tightly buttoned coat, drinking a cup of coffee alone, and felt such pity for that woman that she drew her breath and put her hand on the table for ballast. Fifty-two years old, pensive-eyed, dark-haired; men called her "handsome." She gulped down what was left of her coffee and hurried out the door.

It was drizzling again, but she kept walking. In the low Thirties and high Twenties there was a sudden burst of life — busy delis and warm, noisy Chinese restaurants and big, busy buildings with couples standing in front of them, hailing cabs. Then a dead region around Fourteenth Street, which made her think about Philip. A gang of Hispanic boys huddled under the marquee of an abandoned theatre, watching her. She kept going. There was no stopping now, even though it was getting dark and the wind was fierce. The voyage had her now. She walked down Third Avenue to St. Mark's Place, and turned into what she knew was the East Village. There were signs of the weekend everywhere: broken bottles; splotches of urine on the walls; purple-haired girls sitting on stoops, rubbing white, freckled arms for warmth. The quiet of an aftermath. She kept walking, through the Ukrainian district, past the Kiev and the other twenty-four-hour restaurants, and turned down Sixth Street, where a flourish of Indian restaurants bloomed brightly, like exotic flowers: Ganges, Romna, Anar Bagh. What was here? She was going in circles now.

At the corner of St. Mark's Place and Second Avenue, holding her head down against the rain, she ran into Owen. It was like running into a friend from the office. The wind was blowing the tails of his trenchcoat up, and the ends of the red scarf she had knitted him were whipping his cheeks. He was walking very fast toward Ninth Street, his face pale and agitated, and then he was in front of her.

"Hello," he said.

"Hello," she said. "I took a walk, and — it just got longer and longer."

"Uh-huh," he said. He burrowed his hands in his pockets and looked over his shoulder, lifted one foot from the ground and then the other.

"I decided I felt like walking," Rose said.

"Yes," Owen said. "I felt like it, too."

"It's some day for it, let me tell you," Rose said.

They stood there for a moment in the rain and the cold, lifting their feet up and down. Rose's toes were numb.

"I'm thinking of going to that bookstore on St. Mark's Place," Owen said. "Would you like to join me?"

Rose smiled, shook her head. "That's okay," she said. "I should be getting back. I have that Alzheimer's manuscript to finish for next week." She faltered. "Are you coming home soon?"

"No, not quite yet," Owen said. "I have some things to do."

"Okay. Well, I'll see you soon."

Owen smiled. "Yes," he said. "Soon."

"Okay. Well, bye."

"Bye."

They stood facing each other for a few more awkward seconds. Then Owen lifted his hand tentatively — half a wave — and walked away from her.

She had to stay there on the corner a minute before she could move. She was stunned beyond surprise. They collided with each other every day in the living room, after all. Twenty-seven years of marriage, she thought, and this is the first time I've seen what he looked like when he thought I wasn't there, the first time I've stumbled on the life he leads alone. And what was he doing so far downtown? What was *she* doing? Why hadn't they had a cup of coffee together, ridden home together?

She turned and walked north. Her legs ached from the long voyage, and she hailed a cab, got in, was thankful that it was well heated. Inside her boots, her wet toes were thawing. She thought, Twenty-seven years of marriage, and I hardly know him. Riding in the cab she felt numb and stupid, cocooned by her life, for she had stumbled into her husband on a strange street corner, running some mysterious errand she knew nothing of, and they had spoken briefly like strangers, parted like strangers. What was surprising was that she hardly felt surprised at all.

Owen walked on Sundays. That was all she knew. Perhaps he had someplace to go. Perhaps not. And now it was as if this tiny fact of his walking was all she knew about him. The slate of his life was clean, emptied in an instant. Who had she been living with all this time?

It was snowing. The snow fell in wet gobs outside the cab's

windows. The city brightened as night fell, until, through the fogged windows of Rose's cab, it looked as if it were lit by candles.

Owen walked. It was not an activity; it was a condition. For miles, in thick boots, over the length of an island, he walked. He had no destination. His destination was a circle. He walked so that when he arrived home, to the warm light of the living room and the smell of dinner, these things would seem real to him, home would seem real. He walked to ward off the encroaching panic of a wet Sunday, an apartment about to be lost, a life nearing the beginning of its end. When he walked, he stopped only at newsstands. He observed the covers of the pornographic magazines, scrutinizing them without sentiment. It was a rotten day to be outdoors. Young men still wearing pajamas under their coats dashed from under awnings to grab copies of the Sunday paper. Others lingered on street corners or leaned against walls — prostitutes and hustlers, drug peddlers, hare krishna, anyone for sale or with something to sell — while the buyers wandered, circling their targets, searching faces for the proper nod, wink, smile. The signal. Owen was an expert at Sundays. He recognized the traps.

For years he had felt safe only in his apartment, only with Rose. But now everything had turned around. The apartment was the place where he was afraid. Unidentifiable dangers lurked in the corners, waiting to spring. Static electricity clung to the walls, the bedspread, the sofa. He could not touch his fingers to any surface without risking a tiny shock. Worst of all, the threat was obscure. It hid like a coward, refused to show its face. He could not name it. He grew so anxious he had to flee into the open placelessness of the city, where, if not safety, he found at least the company of other scared strangers. There was a broth-

erhood of middle-aged men who wandered on Sunday afternoons, looking at one another gravely across streets, never nodding. They shuffled past Owen on the sidewalks, the shoulders
of their trenchcoats brushing his. They emerged at dusk from
empty office buildings and hailed cabs. All of them had hats bent
over their faces, downcast eyes suggesting secrets. They all had
secrets. And yet Owen at least was getting tired of his. Yes, if
anyone asked him now, he'd tell all, though it would do him no
good anymore; he'd tell for spite. But no one asked him. Not
even Rose seemed to suspect anything of him; he had stood right
in front of her just this afternoon, staring her in the face with
it, and she hadn't seen it. He had thought he might have to
turn away from the stupid confusion in her eyes then, the way
they went blank and her mouth twitched. She had struggled for
words. Such effort, and all for nothing! Why bother? Why not
shout it out right then and there, in the street? After all, as soon
as they were evicted from their apartment they would be street
people anyway. Already they wandered the city separately, as if in
preparation for the oncoming solitary poverty in which they'd
soon start to run into each other: he unshaven, his clothes rot-
ting, sleeping in men's shelters, eating soup made from potato
peelings; Rose scraggly-haired and dirty, her legs covered with
sores. They'd be on line at the lice clinic, waiting to be sham-
pooed and shaved, and Owen, thinking he recognized her, would
say, "Excuse me — Rose? Is that you, Rose?" And slowly she
would emerge from her stupor, turn and look at him, her skin
sallow and smeared with filth, her lips cracked, as his were, hair
greasy; should he go on? He could go on, he knew, coloring in
the details of their ruin. To make themselves into such creatures
— that would be triumphant! That would be a spit in the face of
this life.

Rose looked at him; she opened her mouth. She was making noises in the back of her throat, preparing to say something to him; what was it?

He stopped and kicked at some muddy snow that had caked on the corner. If he were to walk into the Waldorf-Astoria today, no one would notice him in his tweed coat. A pity. He wanted to be thrown out into the gutter. He and Rose hadn't even begun to talk about the arduous task of finding a new apartment; perhaps it would prove too much for them. He thought about this: If he quit his job and took to drinking and lived in an expensive hotel room for a month, the money would run out. He'd be rid of it. It could be done.

"Lunatic ravings of an old man," Owen said, and was startled to find that he had spoken out loud. A middle-aged woman with bright blond hair, turning and looking at him, pushed the hand of her child tighter into the pocket in which she held it and hurried away from him. Oh, it was cold. He tied the belt of his coat tighter around his waist and moved on.

He went into the Bijou, a movie theatre on Third Avenue. The woman behind the glass partition took his money, let him through the turnstile as she had practically every Sunday for fifteen years. For a long time this place had terrified him, but now it only tired him. He usually sat in the back row with the other old men who wanted to jerk off and be left alone. Oddly, just as his apartment, that haven of peace and safety, had filled up lately with danger, this place had lost its threat. It was as if he saw it with the houselights turned up, as they never were, and all it was was a room with a lot of chairs stained beyond the point where one could name their original color. Nothing lurked here. There was no mystery.

Owen sat in the back row. On the screen was a close-up of a boy's face contorted with pleasure, the white liquid dripping down his cheeks, hanging off the ends of his eyelashes like snow, falling on his darting tongue. He seemed to be transforming into a tree in a winter forest.

Owen concentrated. He had to work hard to be aroused by these images. Indeed, he was so absorbed that he hardly noticed when someone sat down next to him. He turned once, then back again, to face the screen. The man appeared to be in his thirties, with brown hair, a mustache, small tortoiseshell glasses encircling bright eyes. He was wearing a brown sweater-vest. He was staring at Owen intently. Owen looked back at him, then resolutely fixed his eyes to the screen. On the screen the boy was being chained to a metal fence by one cop while another pulled down his pants, removed and stroked and massaged a big belt. Still Owen felt the stare of the man next to him, hot as breath.

He closed his eyes. He was angry that this opportunity should present itself now when he wanted more than anything else to be alone in his wretchedness and indulge it. Was there time? Was he too exhausted? Would he be able to muster an erection? Old questions woke in him. He had not done anything like this for months. And he was so tired.

He sighed loudly. As if absently, he put his hand on the man's thigh. His eyes on the screen, he felt his way up the denim to the warm knot of the crotch and labored there.

The man's breath was deep and erratic. His hand was on Owen's leg. And now Owen slowly pulled the zipper down, felt the thing spring with a flash of heat, lunge against the thin, warm cotton fabric of the man's underwear. He watched as the boy on the screen, though protesting, was once again taken by the cop, once again loved it. The man was breathing fire on Owen's shoulder. Cautiously Owen bent toward him, and an arm barred him from leaning over the armrest. Owen looked into the man's face for direction. It was a kind face, unblemished, worried. "Please," the man whispered. "I can't do it here. Please. Can't we go somewhere else?"

Owen's hand lifted spasmodically. He looked at the screen, as if for guidance. On the screen, the cop said, "Yeah, shit, yeah."

The man wanted to go somewhere else. He sat hunched in his chair, his fly open, an erection tenting his underwear. He looked at Owen. "I have a place nearby; we could go there," he said, and Owen opened his mouth and looked the other way. He imagined saying yes, imagined how they would have to walk out of the theatre, exchange names, perhaps shake hands; how they would have to talk about their jobs and lives on the way to wherever they were going (what could he say?); worst of all, how they would have to admit to each other in the broad light of day that they had come, each alone, to that dark room on Third Avenue, that heart of shame and lonely self-indulgence, and thereby acknowledge each other as human beings and not just shadows that float in a theatre and mimic, moment by moment, the flickering gestures of giants on a screen. Owen knew how to touch; with his hands he could be gentle, fierce, seductive. But in fifteen years of coming to this theatre he had never uttered a word to one of his partners; he hardly knew where to begin.

He shook his head. The man rustled nervously; Owen wouldn't meet his gaze. "Thanks," he said. "Maybe some other time." In an instant he was gone. Owen thought suddenly of getting up and following him, but he seemed to be frozen to his seat. He fell back, deflating. In a few hours his desire to make love to that man, to hold that man, would become so acute that it would be practically unbearable. He would lie in bed and remember every tiny touch, and finally he would have to get up, turn on the shower, lean back against the wall and feel the warm water moisten his skin. The next day only enough hope would live in him to allow him to feel regret. By evening, it would be dead; starved.

He pulled his coat tight around his waist and stood up. At home, he knew, there was cake; there was always cake. There were books, too. It was cold outside, so it would be warm inside. Home would sustain him for a single night, and by the time the panic set in the next morning, he'd be on his way to work. Survival was possible.

He noticed a small flash of white on the seat next to his. It was a piece of paper. He looked at it for a few seconds before picking it up and unfolding it. On the piece of paper was written, in a small, blue hand, "Alex Melchor." Then two phone numbers, one followed by a "W." the other by an "H." Underneath, underlined twice, "Please give me a call."

Owen read the note over again. He looked around himself, at the shadows in the theatre. He looked at his hands, at the empty seat, at the screen.

Then he folded the piece of paper up, stuck it in his pocket, and headed out the exit door.

Outside, the wind was heavy and snow was falling in the darkness. Owen walked quickly, his hands in his pockets, his toes numb, watching his breath form larger and more frequent clouds. He thought of his book, the cake in the refrigerator, and smiled. That man in the theatre with the brown hair and bright eyes, Alex Melchor, had left his number. He wanted to see Owen again. He wanted Owen. And thinking of the man, Owen walked faster, the beat in his veins quickening. Then he swore he felt his heart burst inside his chest. And it was as if some sweet ambrosial liquid were pouring from that broken vessel, flowing in his veins, filling him and warming him, from the center of his chest to the cold, faraway extremities.

P HILIP WAS IN love. He lay pinned under Eliot's body, and he couldn't move. His left arm felt like part of Eliot — alien and heavy — but he did not dare reposition it. He must have woken Eliot up ten times during the night with his thrashing (love made him thrash), and he wasn't about to risk doing it again. Instead he lay still, trying to flex his fingers to get his blood running, and watched a sliver of gray cloud pass between the curtain rod and the frame of his one window. Eliot's breath tickled the hairs under his arm. The radiator wheezed, the super's Dobermans barked, rain clicked against the roof. He tried to identify the room's generally unpleasant smells — dirty dishes, sweat, old socks — and wondered what time it was. Probably around noon, he guessed, but could not bend around to look at the clock.

Then Eliot snorted and turned over, freeing Philip, who slipped out from under him as quickly and quietly as an animal escaping a trap. He rubbed his shoulder, waiting for feeling to return. From behind, Eliot threw an arm over Philip — a pleasant arm, pale and sinewy, downed with dark brown hairs. With his eyes closed, Eliot stretched languorously, then pulled Philip closer to him, wrapping his arms more tightly around Philip's waist, his legs around Philip's hips. He lay still. His hand began moving on Philip, in a circle that widened, then moved gradually downward. Eliot's eyes did not open. He was playing a game, pretending he was still asleep, and as he pulled himself onto his forearms, Philip turned obligingly onto his back. Eliot's body settled on top of Philip's. His head fell behind Philip's shoulder, then lifted again. He opened his eyes, smiled, and kissed him.

"Good morning," he said.

Philip's arm throbbed and buzzed with life. "Eliot," he said. "Listen."

"What?"

"I have to go to the bathroom."

Eliot stopped what he was doing. "Oh, that," he said. Laughing, he rolled over to the other side of the mattress.

"I'm sorry," Philip said. "I'll be right back." He disentangled himself from the sheets and blankets and pulled himself onto his feet. All at once he was dizzy. He trembled as he urinated, and tried to calm his erection, which was sending the urine off at wrong angles, making it hit the rim of the toilet bowl and splash onto the floor. Finished, he flushed, wiped up what he had spilled, and went back out the door. The stench seemed to have intensified during his brief absence. "Christ," he said, "what is that smell?" It was coming from the sink, where three days worth of dishes lay piled, all encrusted with bits of rotten food and crawling with roaches.

Then he noticed the clock. "Oh God," he said, and put his hand on his forehead to steady himself. "It's four o'clock. Did we sleep all day? I've got to do these dishes." Standing before the sink, he ran water, squirted pink detergent onto a sponge, and started to scrub.

"Come back to bed," Eliot said.

"I think I have to do these dishes."

"Philip, come back to bed."

Philip turned, surprised to hear his own name, and looked at Eliot. He was sitting up on the mattress, his dark hair rumpled, a few days' worth of beard darkening his cheeks. Even in half-sleep, his eyes amazed Philip, and weakened him.

"Okay," he said. He stood there, naked, and Eliot stared at him.

Then — in a voice he had never heard before, a voice that belonged to Greta Garbo — he said to Eliot, "I am yours."

For three weeks now they had been lovers, and they had not spent one night apart. Eliot hadn't wanted to. He lived a life unconstrained by schedule, futureless, open-ended. At the dentist's office Philip had read in *Mademoiselle* that it was dangerous for newly formed couples to spend too much time together at the beginning, but when he asked Eliot about it, Eliot seemed unconcerned. "Why should we stay away from each other when we want to be together?" he said. "The only reason to stop, it seems to me, is if we stop enjoying it." Philip agreed. He had absolutely no desire to spend a night away from Eliot; he had slept alone his whole life. Still, he worried that Eliot might grow tired of him if they spent every minute together, might get bored, go to a different party, meet someone else. It seemed he could do that easily. Although Eliot had hundreds of friends, who called and sent him invitations to downtown art openings and parties, he had no Week-at-a-Glance, no crucial dinner dates to change or commit himself to. His days were his own, devoted to a variety of mysterious "freelance" projects. Philip, by contrast, was burdened with commitment, compelled five days a week to be at a desk in a midtown office building. His friends all worked as well. They formed a complicated network of petty betrayals and loyalties in which his participation was often demanded. During working hours they met for lunch at Amy's, and on weekends for long drowsy dinners in Ethiopian restaurants, after which they would divide the check down to the penny. It was not a life he relished, and he believed he would do a lot for Eliot, who had saved him from it; he had done more for boyfriends who deserved less, arranging his life around their more important lives, making his first priority men for whom he was fourth or fifth at best. These other boyfriends had made no pretense of loyalty or love and were always on the lookout for someone richer, or more handsome. Eliot at least seemed to delight in Philip; he like to rumple his hair like a little boy's, and say, "You're really cute, you know that?" But he never seemed to think more than five minutes ahead of himself, and this worried Philip. He insisted that he "lived for the moment," an instinct Philip did not trust. What happened when the moment that was *him* ended?

This cold afternoon they drank coffee as the sun set. They were going to spend the night at Eliot's place in the East Village. "It's too cold for the subway," Eliot said, as they put on their coats. "Let's take a cab." A beat of worry. "I'll pay, don't worry," Eliot added. He generally paid. If the pattern of the past three weeks continued, Philip knew, they would spend four nights downtown before shuttling back up for another three. Prepared, he carried with him several changes of clothes, his toothbrush and nasal spray, and the bioflavonoid tablets for his gums. Eliot had nothing; he never brought anything with him when he came up to Philip's. He used Philip's toothbrush; he wore Philip's clothes. Afterwards, Philip sometimes slipped on the shirts Eliot had borrowed and breathed in his smell, faintly redolent of honey.

They rode down Broadway, blocks lined with Korean fruit-stands and laundromats and newsstands. Men were struggling to cover piles of the Sunday paper with tarpaulins. To Philip's surprise, a few flakes of snow started to fall, then more and more. He remembered coming out of a movie theatre in the East Village when he was a teenager to find that a snowstorm had come and gone while he was inside. The streetlights reflected off the white carpet that seemed so suddenly to have covered the city, creating a light as brilliant as in a skating rink. No cars could pass. Philip had to squint as he walked out into the middle of Third Avenue, where prostitutes in sequinned skirts and fur-trimmed jackets were throwing snowballs at one another. "Come play with us, honey," they shouted to him — a joke, or a sincere invitation, since they had seen what kind of theatre he had come out of. "No thanks," he said. He looked up. The pale night sky seemed to have risen from this brightness like smoke from a white-hot fire.

Now, in the cab, he turned, thinking he might share this memory with Eliot, when the driver slammed on his brakes and they lurched forward. "What's wrong?" Eliot asked.

"*Ay dios,*" the cab driver said quietly.

Then Philip looked out the window and saw that the intersection was full of white mice. Thousands of them. They swarmed the street in panicked hordes, like tiny indistinguishable sufferers in a fourteenth-century vision of hell. They cascaded over the sidewalk curbs and plunged after each other into gutters. Against the new snow they were nearly invisible, small quakings of motion.

"My God," Philip said. The driver opened his door and got out of the cab, and Philip and Eliot followed him. None of the cars at the intersection were honking, nor were they making any effort to move. Even the passersby — mostly old women who might have screamed had they seen just one of these creatures dart out from behind a garbage can — hung back while the mice poured out of a small white truck that rested on a corner, its front wheels on the sidewalk, its hood bent around a lamppost. "Poor little things," Philip heard someone say — a voice emerging from the low hum of the crowd which seemed so disembodied that after a moment he wondered if he had imagined it. The mice ran in circles or huddled in clumps as horns began to honk and drivers too far back to see what was going on yelled, "Hey, will you move it?" But no one moved it.

The cab driver shook his head. Nearby, other cab drivers were conferring in Spanish. Then they got back in their cars. Philip and Eliot followed. "I hope no one was hurt," Philip said.

"There'd be ambulances if anyone was hurt badly."

In the distance, police sirens wailed. The driver swore, spat, honked his horn, and began to move the cab forward slowly, but without stopping. The cab parted the sea of mice, and turned onto Ninety-sixth Street. Philip closed his eyes, fearful that he might be compelled to look behind himself for small clots of blood in the snow.

"I guess they were being taken up to Columbia, to the labs there," Philip said a few minutes later, when they were safely deposited on the West Side Highway. "In some ways, they were lucky. Probably they've escaped having horrible things done to them." He was thinking of a book he read as a child about rats who escape from some sort of government institution.

"Mrs. Frisby and the Rats of NIMH," Eliot said. "It was one of my favorites when I was a kid. Derek used to read it to me. Yes, I think those mice were being transported up to Columbia for some horrible experiment to test their pain thresholds. They'd be injected with varying quantities of morphine and set on top of gas burners, and the researchers would measure how long it took each mouse to scream. Or jump. Or whatever mice do when they're in pain. That really happened, you know. Some scientists did it to freak out a group of anti-vivisectionists who were marching in front of their building every day."

"Jesus," Philip said.

Now the taxi driver turned and delivered to them, in bad English, his own private explanation for the event. They listened, trying to extract what they could. "The shit of the world" was all Philip understood.

"Well, in any case, we can read all about it in the *Post* tomorrow," Eliot said, as if in conclusion. "The *Post* will put this on its front page. MICE ATTACK UPPER MANHATTAN."

He lifted his arm and stretched it out behind Philip's head. A beam of light from a truck going the other way passed over Eliot's face, illuminating for a fraction of a second his pale skin, his eyes, the small hairs coming over his cheek like a grass. Philip reached over and stroked the cheek, a gesture that even now seemed to him grand and terrifying, though Eliot hardly noticed it. Such efforts of affection were nothing for *him*; his life had been full of them, pats and caresses and casual kisses, whereas for Philip to touch a hand to a cheek was an action of such magnitude that it had to be treasured, preserved. It radiated power; it demanded bravery. Philip understood that there were people in the world like Eliot for whom love and sex came easy, without active solicitation, like a strong wind to which they had only to turn their faces and it would blow over them. He also understood that he was not one of those people. Instead, he seemed always to be eking out signals, interpreting glances, trying to extract some knowledge of another person's feelings from the most trivial conversations. Nothing came easy for him, and more often than not, nothing came of any of his efforts.

Only three weeks before, at a dinner party at their friend Sally's, in a gesture of drunken self-confidence he still found hard to believe, he had slipped his foot out of his shoe and rubbed it against Eliot's calf. And Eliot — without even looking at him, without even breaking the flow of his conversation with the woman next to him — grasped Philip's foot between his legs and held it there, trapping him for the rest of the dinner. That simply, his life changed.

"Your face feels like Velcro," Philip said now, suddenly remembering a mouse he had stroked as a child — how oddly soft, almost synthetic, its fur had felt.

Eliot laughed. "Yes," he said. "I'll shave when we get back to my house." He was eager to see if he'd gotten any mail, and to check in with his roommate, a lanky black woman named Jerene who made Philip shy. There was no talk of their spending the night apart, and Philip wondered if he seemed overeager.

"Tell me the truth," he said now. "Do you want me to come down with you tonight? I mean, we could eat, and then I could go back uptown. It would be no problem."

Eliot looked at him. "Philip," he said. "What are you talking about?"

Philip was quiet for a moment. "I don't want you to get sick of me," he said at last.

"If I'm sick of you, I'll tell you," Eliot said, taking his hand away, and turned to look out the window.

Philip stared into the side of Eliot's face. He felt like one of those crazed vivisectors Eliot had spoken of, determined to know the exact boundaries of pain. How far can I go before I feel it? How long before something happens that hurts?

The cab was passing through midtown now, past warehouses and towering garages, and the sidewalks were dotted with tired-looking prostitutes in hot pants, rubbing their stockinged legs in the cold. A garbage truck pulled up to the curb, and three or four of the women approached its enormous door. The wind blew, but their hair stayed perfectly in place.

"I'd like to stay with you tonight," Philip said.

"Yes," Eliot said. He stroked Philip's hand, looking at the prostitutes. "That's fine."

PHILIP WAS TALL like his father, and gangly. More than anything else he resembled one of those awkward, loping dogs who seem always to be getting caught between people's legs. His face inspired trust in old women in elevators: even-keeled, the features all in proportion to one another and nothing too striking except the eyes, which were a brilliant blue. It was a face so well composed, so familiar-seeming, that people who had never met Philip before insisted that they had (although they could never remember where), then afterwards were unable to recall a single detail of his physiognomy. He had straight brown hair that turned wheaten in summer, a likable grin, a tendency to laugh too loudly at inappropriate moments. Something about his very ordinariness, the fact that nothing in his appearance betrayed his homosexuality, made him attractive to other young men; he was the childhood neighbor they'd dreamed of jacking off with in bunk beds, and usually that was all they wanted. Philip longed for passion and romantic gestures, not play-acting, but somehow the men he slept with found the idea of being loved by him laughable. Wide-eyed in his infatuations, he had made a fool of himself in college, proclaiming his affections too publicly and scaring away whoever it was he had a crush on. Rejection seemed his lot in life. Most Friday nights he ended up at the local gay bar, where graduate students smelling of hydrogen sulphide would lure him to their rooms with dirty talk, pull out old jockstraps, and go to work recreating the Urbana High School locker room, circa 1977.

In college he had come out late, but with a bang. He was earnestly political, and felt guilty for his years of closetedness, as if somehow he had been personally responsible for the oppression of untold numbers of gay men and women. To make up for the enormity of his cowardice, he told everyone he knew, sometimes approaching near-strangers on the streets of the campus and saying, "Hi — I just wanted to let you know, I'm gay!" to which the bewildered respondent, usually a serious-minded female graduate student who was still trying to remember his name, would stutter something like, "Oh — how nice for you!" smile, and turn away.

As a child, he had been solitary and quiet, and often — particularly on windy afternoons when the stores and the streets filled up with warm, yellow midtown light — New York itself had seemed his best companion. But now, when he and his friends got together, in dark candlelit West Side apartments, or Indian restaurants draped with tapestries, or huge, crowded nightclubs, he rarely felt that familiarity the city had once offered him. Instead he and his friends got together to be alone together, to smoke cigarettes and commiserate on their lack of boyfriends or girlfriends, to ease the anxiety of their solitary lives with talk and vodka. His evenings with his friends would run a predictable course, and then they would all say goodnight and go home alone to tiny apartments with one window, or big apartments full of closed doors, or perhaps (on particularly bad nights) to bars, where warmth or a human touch is cheaper. They travelled in loosely formed packs, friends from work and their friends and their friends, and roommates thrown into intimacy by ads in the *Voice*, two in one bedroom or three in two bedrooms or four in three bedrooms. They were all on the prowl, in the market, on the lookout, and had the thin, questing aspect of people desperate to find lovers. Often Philip wondered if this urgent need wasn't the very thing that scared lovers off. It seemed to him a grave injustice that in New York, to get what you needed, you had above all never to look hungry. Everyone was hungry; but everyone else was better at hiding it. Or were they? Soon, Philip believed, he too might look unapproachable, and then, he imagined, it would only be a few short steps to being that way.

His friend Sally was different. She was the first person Philip had ever come out to, and she had taken him in hand, sitting with him in the college dining hall and identifying who, among the men who passed, was gay (it was an astonishing number), while his leg shook violently beneath the table. Now Sally was a tax analyst. She made money and lived alone in a co-op apartment she had bought by herself, which to Philip was amazing. One night in late September she called him up and asked him to come to a dinner party she was having. "I'm trying to get a lot of people from school together," she explained. "The old gang. But there's also going to be a new person, a guy I just met. I think you'll really like him."

Philip began to make up an excuse, but Sally interrupted him. "I'm serious," she said. "His name is Eliot Abrams, and he's just your type — tall and thin, with curly hair. And he's had a very interesting life. His parents died when he was little in some awful car crash, and he was raised in a townhouse in the Village by — are you ready for this? — Derek Moulthorp — you know, the guy who wrote all those children's books — and his lover."

Philip knew. "Wow," he said. "I read all those books. My mother brought them home. She was his copy editor for a while."

"No shit. Well, you've got a great opening line. Apparently his parents — his natural parents — were important Jewish intellectuals or something. And rich, because he has a trust fund. Derek Moulthorp and his lover were their best friends. Anyway, he's a really terrific guy, and the minute I met him, I thought of you. So — can you come?"

"Well," Philip said, and changed his mind. "Sure," he said. Then, cautiously: "I didn't know Derek Moulthorp was gay."

"Philip!" Sally said. "Everyone knows that."

Philip was quiet. "You know, of course, what I'm wondering," he said.

"Yes, and I don't think it matters. I think what matters is that Eliot's a terrific guy, and that he's apparently benefitted from a terrific upbringing. And he wears the best socks. You'll love his socks. He collects them — incredible colors, weird patterns.

At this party last week he had some on that he was showing everybody — they had what looked like little root beer floats on them."

"Really."

"I don't know where he finds them. Anyway — can you be there?"

"How could I miss it?" Philip said.

But a few nights later, when he walked into Sally's apartment, he almost turned around and went out again. The room was full of distant familiar faces he hadn't seen in years. There was Joshua Treadwell, and Connie Moss, and Chris Fletcher, and a host of other people he had spent most of his time in college avoiding. Indeed, the only person he saw whom he knew and liked was Brad Robinson, who had been his friend in the Gay and Lesbian Campus Coalition. They waved to each other across the room, and then Sally ran up to him, smiling. "Philip," she said, "I'm glad you came. Come meet Eliot."

Then, from behind some plants near the sofa, where he stood admiring her view of the Hudson, she beckoned a tall young man with curly dark hair, a cigarette in his hand. Philip's eyes widened, and Eliot threw him a smile so intense and unwavering he had to turn from it.

He was standing with Eliot, close enough that the tendrils of wool on their sweaters were touching (a delicious, barely perceptible sensation). They looked each other in the eye. Eliot's were framed by round gold glasses. Philip's mouth was open and words were coming out of it, though he hardly knew what they were, and he had to fight to bring each sentence to the end. He felt as if something was blooming in him — a flower, a fire, a possibility that moment by moment became, unbelievably, more real, as they kept smiling, as Eliot did not stop staring straight into Philip's eyes. For the first time in his life there seemed no doubt. The answer was yes.

"Sally tells me you work in publishing," Eliot said. A slight shifting of the knees. Eyes unwavering. Philip was relying completely on peripheral vision to make out the tuft of hair emerging from Eliot's collar, the clean, close-cropped fingernails, all the tiny, erotic details.

"Well, actually I work for what's called a packaging company," Philip said. "We're in the romance field. What I do is edit and rewrite these terrible novels — all about desert islands, pirate ships, cruise ships; the line's called Wavecrest Books. Right now, for instance, I'm working on *Tides of Flame*, which is all about how hardy and tempestuous Sylvia falls in love with evil Captain Dick Tolliver."

Eliot laughed, and Philip was relieved.

"Are you living uptown too?"

"More uptown than this — 105th Street, off Amsterdam. How about you?"

"I live in the East Village."

"How's the rent down there?"

"Mine isn't bad. I was lucky."

"Do you have a lease, or is it a sublet?"

"Oh no, it's my lease."

"That's great."

"Uh-huh."

Then there was nothing else to say. They stood there, not looking away. Philip was studying Eliot's eyes. They were dark, almost black, but when he looked at them closely he could see pulsating rings of green and yellow encircling the pupils.

A minute passed without a word, and still they stared. Every now and then Philip let out a snort of breath, almost a laugh, and his smile widened a little, and Eliot smiled too and let out a thin stream of smoke.

"So what do *you* do?" Philip asked finally, mostly because there was no one else there to interrupt, no Sally, no dinner bell.

"I'm sort of self-employed," Eliot said.

"Doing what?"

"Oh, I write copy for ad agencies and publishers. And draw. I'm working on a book cover now. A jack-of-all-trades, I guess you could say."

"That's great," Philip said. He's rich, he thought enviously, but then, because he was trying to fall in love with Eliot, he changed his mind. Freedom, he thought. Integrity.

"You must like the freedom," Philip said. "It must be great not to be stuck in the nine-to-five grind."

"I love it," Eliot said. "And anyway, I doubt I'd be able to live any other way. I don't like planning things more than a few days ahead if I can help it. It's just not a comfortable way of being for me."

"You know," Philip said, suddenly remembering Sally's game plan, "my mother was your father's copy editor. Or, I mean, your stepfather. Or — I'm sorry, I'm not sure what to call him."

"Really!" Eliot said. "She copy edited Derek's books? Which ones?"

A new panic replaced the old one. He didn't know. "I'm not sure, exactly — " he said. "The ones that Motherwell published."

"That's fantastic," Eliot said.

"You think so?" Philip said. He sputtered out a little laugh. "I thought it was a pretty neat coincidence myself. Of course, they never met. Though Mom always wanted to meet him. She loved his books. I did too."

"Yes, they're great. Derek's a remarkable person, a real character. You'd like him."

Something in the way Eliot said "You'd like him" alarmed Philip. He wondered if perhaps he was all wrong, if Eliot was going to shake his hand and say, "We should have lunch sometime."

Then Sally was between them, flashing a tight smile. For the first time they observed the party. People stood around in nervous little groups. "You two sit across from each other," Sally said, ushering them to the table, then arranged the other guests according to some elaborate plan of her own invention.

The dinner was long. Philip hardly had a chance to talk to Eliot, who was caught up in a conversation about the legitimacy or fraudulence of certain East Village performance artists. Every now and then someone at the table would make a half-hearted effort at nostalgia but always ended up slipping back into the inevitable refrain: "I'll quit if I don't get a raise by next month"; "It's an illegal sublet, so unless the landlord finds out, I'll be fine."

Everyone drank to excess. At some point in the wine-and boredom-induced haze of the meal, Philip made his grand gesture of the foot, only to be topped by Eliot's grander gesture. It astonished him — that quick response, that firm clutch of Eliot's calves. Eliot did not look at him, did not break the stride of his sentence. It was as if such things happened to him at dinner parties all the time.

Dessert was David's Cookies and Häagen-Dazs. Still they did not talk. Philip wondered if his posture gave anything away. Cautiously his foot explored, wiggled as it could, and finally felt

warm flesh under the pants leg. He was thrilled. Could anyone see?

Then Sally got up, and everyone followed her to have coffee in
the living room. Eliot let go of Philip's foot, looking at him for
the first time during the meal. They walked into the living room
separately. "I know another party we could go to," Eliot said.

"Yes," Philip said.

The other party was at a club in Chelsea. They went by cab.
In the cab they did not touch, though their legs brushed. A long
line was forming outside the doors of the club, but Eliot had
a special invitation. The bouncer ceremoniously ushered them
past a velvet rope, and a woman nearby shouted in a hoarse voice,
"Hey! What's going on? We've been waiting here an hour, and
you let those fags right in?" Then they were inside. They
checked their coats, and Eliot led Philip into a big room where
loud music pulsed into the darkness. All around them were
Chemical Bank employees, complete with nametags, staring
dumbly at Philip and Eliot. "Do you like to dance?" Eliot asked,
and they danced — the only same sex couple on the floor, as far
as Philip could tell.

In the middle of "Like a Virgin," Eliot said, "I don't really want
to stay here. Let's go somewhere else."

Philip faltered. "Yes, sure," he said.

They slipped away, then, and went to Uncle Charlie's, where,
in the midst of a massive and undifferentiated crowd of men,
they ran into someone they both knew, Desmond, and his friend
Brian, and a dancer named Martin. It was too loud and crowded
to talk, so Martin suggested they go to the River Club to watch
the wet jockey shorts contest "as a joke," but when they got there,
it turned out the wet jockey shorts contest was on Tuesday night.
They danced some more, and in the middle of dancing Eliot

moved close to Philip, Philip thought, in order to suggest leaving, or deliver some whispered confidence, but when he bent his ear to Eliot's mouth, Eliot's nose hit his mouth. "Oh Christ, I'm sorry!" Philip said to Eliot, who was reeling against the wall, his hand over his nose. But Eliot said, "No, no, I'm fine. I was just trying to kiss you." "What?" Philip said. "Louder!" Eliot mouthed the words: *I'm trying to kiss you.* Then he kissed him. Philip was so surprised he almost laughed, but he caught himself, and kissed Eliot back, and put his arms around his neck.

They stayed a while longer at the club, until they lost Brian and Desmond, and Martin decided to go home, which was uptown. Philip noticeably didn't offer to share a cab with him. "Well," Eliot said, as they stood outside on the curb. "Would you like to go to Boy Bar?"

Philip smiled. "Sure," he said.

At Boy Bar, the bouncers, two tall, emaciated young men with shellacked hair under their bowler hats, were standing just inside the door to escape the cold. "Good to see you, Eliot," one of them said. He was reading from a large red sociology textbook. Philip told Eliot a story about the one gay bar in the town where he'd gone to college. The owner employed his mother washing dishes. When the bar closed at three, and you were waiting in line to get your coat, you'd see her in the back — a pasty old woman with a white apron twisted around her middle, putting hundreds of beer steins through a big industrial washer. Eliot laughed. They were standing in a room painted in Necco wafer shades of green and pink, and *The Exorcist* was playing on a video screen. A dozen or so men stood lined up against the wall, their eyes large and bright as those of nocturnal animals, and occasionally threw each other needful glances. Philip knew from experience that they didn't really expect to pick anyone up this late but were staying out of a simple fear of going home alone. He watched the movie. During the scene where Linda Blair masturbates with a crucifix, Eliot began to rub Philip's back and shoulders without ever taking his eyes from the screen. His hands bunched the tightened muscles together, and Philip's eyes closed.

"Let's go," Eliot said.

Then they walked silently together from Boy Bar to East Sixth Street, where Eliot lived. There were ten or twenty tiny Indian restaurants on the block, their names glared from all directions. Philip's clothes were thick with cigarette smoke from all the bars and clubs. He sneezed, and the phlegm on his handkerchief was black. They walked down East Sixth Street, and Eliot turned the key in the door to his building. Cumin scented the hallways. They climbed three flights of stairs to the apartment, and Eliot put his fingers to his lips. Inside the door a figure thrashed and breathed on a small cot in the kitchen. *Jerene*, he mouthed. *My roommate*. They tiptoed past Jerene, into the second room. A blue futon lay in the middle of the floor, clothes strewn around it. They sat down, and their arms went around each other, their lips touched. Eliot's breath was warm and faintly sweet. Philip's hand moved slowly down the length of Eliot's left leg, until finally it lifted the cuff of his jeans. His socks were brilliant, as Sally had promised: royal blue, with a ring of white snowflakes around the fringe.

They made love, that night, with passion and industry, then afterwards lay on the blue futon, Eliot asleep, Philip wide awake, his heart beating too fast. In the morning he realized that he must have been asleep for some of that night, but that his mind had been so full of Eliot that he had dreamed he was still awake, gazing at him; he was living, at that moment, the strongest wish-fulfillment fantasy he could muster; his dreams ran parallel to his reality. The radiator in Eliot's apartment made wheezing noises. Inside its world of pipes water sloshed and high-pitched whistles sounded, like wind in the country in winter. At one point Eliot woke to find Philip staring at him, wide-eyed. "You can't sleep," Eliot said. "Here, let me rub your back." Philip rolled over and Eliot's fingers began their tugging. "Imagine that inside that radiator is a tropical island," Eliot whispered, "and a hurricane, and a little raft. And on that raft is a little bed — our bed. The wind howling, the rain pouring. But we're safe on our raft. It tosses and turns, but it will never sink." A sound like rushing water came out of the radiator, as if on cue. Philip's mind was full of thunder-swept islands, boats, arms clutching for survival. Images from the novel he was editing. Or was it from that poem his mother used to read to him before he went to bed? What were the words? "Far and few . . . far and few . . . they went to sea in a sieve . . ."

> *Far and few, far and few*
> *Are the lands where the Jumblies live.*
> *Their heads are green and their hands are blue*
> *And they went to sea in a sieve . . .*

The voice was Eliot's. Philip opened his eyes, and turned over.

"I was just thinking of that poem," Philip said.

"You were?" said Eliot. "Well, keep thinking of it."

Philip looked up at him, puzzled. Then he closed his eyes. The raft rocked, but he was safe.

Three Sundays later winter started. The wind was so fierce that on a certain block of Madison Avenue, where huge buildings towered over brownstones and tenements and the street tilted upward at a sharp angle, two parked cars were blown whole across the street. Hardly anyone witnessed this spectacle except the bag ladies who had staked out territories for the night in the dark indentations of grilled and grated storefronts. Newspapers clutched to their chests, they sat back and watched the refuse of the world blow by — mangled umbrellas, lost gloves, a child's tricycle. At the intersection of Broadway and Ninety-sixth Street, most of the mice had died from cold or shock or from having been run over by cars. Caught up in a dust of snow, their carcasses blew down the boulevard, block after block, as if in flight. Philip, in the taxicab with Eliot, found himself, just for a moment, turning to notice the mosaic of bright yellow squares encrusting the horizon of skyscraper spires, and beyond it, the resonant glow of more distant East Side lights, flickering and splintering, as if seen through water. The snow fell before this vision of the city, and Philip imagined that he was inside one of those tiny globed worlds where the air is viscous water, and the bright snowflakes little chips of plastic that fly up when the globe is shaken, then slowly fall back to earth. He looked up at the sky and tried to make out the vast, transparent shell, with its faint hint of reflection. My God, he was thinking, I live in that thing.

ROSE TOLD PHILIP a story. A woman from her office had gone with her husband on a cruise around the world, a dream second honeymoon, and they had gotten off the ship to spend a day on the island of Crete. Somewhere in the course of that hot afternoon spent bargaining for trinkets and staring at ruins in the sun, a delivery boy rode a rusty Solex around a blind corner and into that woman's husband, knocking him against the street and killing him. In a split second, the husband, who only moments before had been worrying to her about the squat toilets, was dead, gone, out of the world twenty years too early, on a day trip they had debated not making, on an island they had no ties with and would never again visit in their lives. Then that woman was a widow, and she was being escorted by two policemen to a cool, dark office, sat face to face opposite the pimple-faced killer, a boy of fourteen who shook and wept and cried out in Greek, "Don't kill me! Don't kill me!" It was funny, the woman told Rose, but sitting there, her first instinct had been to go over and put her arms around the boy and tell him everything was all right. But she didn't. A man with a mustache that extended from earlobe to earlobe asked her questions in an English she could hardly understand. What could she tell him? Her husband had wanted to stay on the ship because his stomach was bothering him; that fish last night, she'd warned him against it. *She* was curious about the shopping. He came with her at the last minute, on the spur of the moment. Of course, somewhere she still believed it hadn't happened at all, because it shouldn't have; it was all too fast, and nobody's fault. His clothes were still in the closet of their cabin, the soap still wet from the last time he'd washed his hands. Only as she approached the ship that afternoon, escorted by the captain and the cruise director, and the whistle blew, a high, piercing wail against which she had to cover her ears, did the protective membrane burst, making her cry out as loudly (she thought) as the ship's horn cried out, announcing that departure was imminent, and she must leave him there forever.

Rose told Philip this story one afternoon when he was sitting in her kitchen, eating cake and looking distracted. She said that

the woman had told it over and over to everyone at the office, as
if by perpetual telling she might find some logic that would prove
once and for all that this death couldn't have been avoided. And
there lay the horror of it. All it had taken was one wrong move,
one wrong step. If they had browsed a bit longer at the little
store, if they had crossed the street a bit faster, it wouldn't have
happened. The boy couldn't have known; it wasn't his fault. If
anyone was to blame, it was the city, for not installing a proper
stoplight, but cities — particularly foreign cities — were generally indifferent to grief and sorrow.

Rose finished. Philip looked at her respectfully. "I hardly know
what to say," he said, and went back to the piece of cake she'd put
before him. What was there to say? In fact, the story didn't seem
nearly as awful to Philip as it did to his mother. Chance made
sense to him, more sense than cause. He believed that all the
turnings of life, including its turn into death, were purely arbitrary; and he felt wiser than Rose, who was as bewildered by the
meanderings that had led her to where she sat now, alive, as she
was by the leisurely steps that had brought a stranger to be hurled
against the ancient stones of that faraway street. Of course, such
feelings were a new phenomenon for him, and had entirely to do
with Eliot. Before Eliot, Philip had lived so long without physical
love that he believed it to be the only thing in the world he
needed. He had fluctuated from one extreme to another, and
this, he believed, put him in a very different position from that of
his mother, who had, as far as Philip could see, dwelled for years
in that middle ground between emptiness and fulfillment, a
realm where contentment and despair coexist as dual sensations
so similar, and so faint, that they become impossible to distinguish, like the hiss of the radiator and the hum of the dishwasher.

This Sunday, she arrived home from her voyage downtown wet and disoriented, pulled off her raincoat and clothes, stumbled into the shower, and stood there under the rush of steam and water until she was warm again. Then she dusted herself with lavender-scented powder, put on a long, loose bathrobe, and sat down in her favorite chair to read.

A few minutes into her book she looked at the clock. It was nearly dinnertime, and still Owen wasn't home. She could not quite believe that she had run into him this afternoon, that she had spoken with him as if he were a passing acquaintance. It was as if someone else had been living with her all those years, eating dinner with her, sleeping in her bed, and raising her child. Owen had been replaced; he had replaced himself, gone somewhere else. Or perhaps it was Rose who was gone, Rose who had been walking entranced or asleep for twenty years and was just waking up to discover, like an invalid emerging from a coma, how much time had actually passed. Twenty-seven years.

She put her book away, settled down on the sofa, and turned on the television. A nurse who was gentle and kindly the last time Rose had watched the series had become, over a month's interval, a psychopathic murderer. Rose was confused. She tried to follow the story line, to figure out what had happened to the nurse; but where was Owen? To her surprise, she found herself wishing more than anything that it had not happened, that she might relive the day and take another route, miss seeing Owen. But of course it had happened, she had seen him. The strangeness of the meeting altered things; she could not concentrate, and remembered the years of Sunday nights watching television, so taken for granted, as precious and rare.

The television show was getting out of hand, so Rose switched it off, stood up, and walked to the window. Outside, the wind blew the hat off a woman on the street, who ran after it, past a bus, a cab, onto the sidewalk. She thought, Really, you're exaggerating. It hasn't been *that* long. For the first fourteen years or so, anyway, Philip was growing up, they had a child to occupy them. Maybe five years Owen had been gone, at most. And certainly, there had been moments when a great desire for change welled up in Rose, moments when, as she had long ago read in Proust (and she always, always remembered), the heartstrings yearn to be plucked at any cost, the soul tires of contentment, the body craves any kind of change, even decimation, even death. During those rare episodes of wanting, Rose had always looked to someone else, not to Owen. Could that have been it? she wondered now. It had all happened years ago, and besides, he could never have found out; she covered her tracks. But what if he did know? What if he knew, and had decided, rather than leave her outright, simply to disappear, and see if she noticed? And had she noticed? Not until today.

There was a familiar rattling noise at the door. Owen's key was a copy of a copy of a copy and didn't quite fit the lock; he always had to fiddle with it a few seconds before he could get the door open. For years he had been muttering about getting a new key made, and for years Rose had had a joke with him about what a convenient signal the rattling noise was when she was in bed with the doorman and had to shunt him quickly out the service entrance. Owen never got the key fixed, enjoying a little, she suspected, the secret knowledge he had acquired of its quirks and nuances.

The door opened. Owen's raincoat dripped onto the carpet. He took his Totes hat and held it gingerly over the doormat, and bits of slush dropped to the floor. Only then did he look up and notice Rose, who had stood up from her chair and immediately sat down again.

"Hello," she said.

"Hello," he said.

"My God, you're wet," she said. "Did you walk all the way home?" Then she caught her breath. Without ever intending to, she had acknowledged their meeting, that strange, numb moment on the street which had seemed to take place on the threshold of another life.

"Yes, I did," Owen said. "I don't know why . . . I felt like it, for no particular reason."

"Give me your coat," Rose said. She began unbuttoning, and Owen's hand dodged into the coat pocket, closed around the small, well-creased wedge of paper, and pulled it out as the coat pulled away from him into Rose's hands. Surreptitiously he replaced it in his pants pocket. His hand remained there, fondling it, re-creasing the edges.

Rose was taking his coat. He felt a sudden stab of guilt, watching her, recognizing as if for the first time in years all the good she had done him, their comfortable life together, this home built to the precise measurements of their compatibility.

"Thanks," he said. He could hardly say, "I'm sorry," though he wanted to. He tried to think how many Sundays he had done just this — come back from one or another pornographic movie theatre, purged (for the moment) of a week's tension, a week's need, and imagined that in a single afternoon the hell had been flushed from his life. Safe at home, he would feel the sort of relief that a child feels when he commits some act of petty theft and is not caught. He would think of the risk he had taken, contemplate the danger of the situation, and nestle in the absolute safety of his chair, with his book, his cake. Yet each week, it seemed, the hell would begin creeping back a little earlier, after just a day, an evening, an hour. With it came desire of a sort he had never imagined possible, and the only thing that kept him from going back to the theatre during the week was his immense fear of being seen. He would wait until Sunday, a day he figured was somehow hallowed, and therefore safe. He allowed himself Sundays. Yet each Sunday night, returning home, he would wonder how much longer he could keep this up. First he had been satisfied with the films alone; then a quick hand-job in the back row; then, over the years, being sucked, sucking, fingers up his anus; once, a muffled attempt at penetration. Sometimes his repulsion at his own actions was so great that he would find himself spitting onto the sidewalk, over and over, desperate to get that taste out of his mouth. Each week he wanted more.

He stood in the hall while Rose hung his coat over the towel rack in the bathroom. He wrapped his arms around himself and thought: Alex Melchor. It amazed him to discover, after all this time, that he still had the capacity to feel joy, and his pleasure at feeling pleasure was itself such a remarkable sensation that in the end the actual note really didn't mean that much. Anyway, he reminded himself, things were as bad as ever. He and Rose still had to make a decision about the apartment. Nothing had changed. No, everything was as it had been. And as he repeated those words to himself, his hand felt inside his pocket and stroked the note. It had frightened him at first. On the way back he had had to duck into a coffee shop and wait until he was sure no one was looking before he dared unfold it and re-read it. It really did say what he thought it had said. There really was a phone number

— he had already memorized it in case he should lose the note — although still, the idea of actually dialling the number was inconceivable. He was taking great pleasure, as he stood there, creating mathematical patterns out of the seven digits, figuring out keys to memory, adding and subtracting and multiplying.

He walked into the bathroom and said, "Rose." She turned from where she stood, startled, and looked at him. He was smiling at her.

"My Rose," he said, and embraced her. He wanted suddenly to tell her all about this man, this Alex Melchor, this number the first three digits of which added up to the same sum as the last four digits. He wished she were his friend, his confidante. Such absurd urges to confess had come on him before, however, and he had learned to control them. She was his wife. And thinking of Alex Melchor, his hand, his eyeglasses, Owen was taken by sudden desire; he bent and kissed her. Then he pulled away. "It was nice running into you today," he said.

"Yes," she said. "Funny, wasn't it?" She went back to hanging his coat on the towel rack.

"I'll be in the living room," he said, walking away from her. Well, he thought, perhaps I've gone to that movie theatre for the last time. He smiled at that thought, remembering the first time — the horror he had felt, the sudden stab of realization that he was, as he had always feared, a homosexual. And what had he done? He had gone flying out of that theatre and straightaway practically raped poor Rose on the living room couch, trying to see her, only her, to force the images from that screen out of his mind. But when he came, it was men he was thinking of, even though he said, "Rose, Rose," and she answered him, "Yes, I'm here, I'm here. I won't let you go." That he had lied to her —

that he had built a marriage with her on the basis of a sexual lie —
was a regret of such magnitude that he could not get around it; it
was therefore one which, at this moment, he chose to ignore. For
years, after all, he had told himself that if someone were to ask
him, pursue him, if someone were to give him a chance, he would
take it. He'd never imagined it would actually happen; he was,
after all, a married man, completely heterosexual in the eyes of
the world. Now it had. The chance lay in his pocket. Someone
named Alex Melchor desired him. It would be simple. He would
call. He would call and say — oh, never mind what he would say.
He moved across the living room, sat down in his chair, took up
his book. He knew he could live off this possibility just as a
possibility for a long time; he knew it could keep him going for
days now, because a starving man has a different notion of plenty.

Rose sat in the bathroom, staring at Owen's coat. Across the
room her face, in the mirror, was obscured by mist. She put her
hand to the place on her cheek that Owen had just kissed.

JERENE, Eliot's roommate, was typing at the kitchen table
when Philip and Eliot got home. Her fingers flew across the keys
in a whirl of motion, faster than Philip had ever seen. To her left
was a pile of color-coded notebooks; to her right, a neat stack of
paper, dense with prose. This was the text of Jerene's mysterious
dissertation, on which she had been at work for seven years. The
current title was "The Phenomenon of Invented Languages,"
but Eliot had told Philip that it changed every month.

Jerene had been up since seven. In the course of the day she had done the dishes, worked five hours at her job at the library, read three articles, and typed twenty-seven pages. But even though the sun was setting, it was still morning for Philip and Eliot; they shuffled through the door like jet-lagged travellers, people out-of-sync with time. "Ah, the decadence of youth," she said, ripping a sheet from her typewriter with a dramatic flourish. Then she stood up, unbending from her sitting position like a crane stretching itself out to demolish a building. She was just over six feet tall, and her height was accented by her sinuousness. She had long legs, the muscles braided like rope. Short-cropped hair, dark and dense as algae, clung to her scalp.

She slept on a cot in the corner of the kitchen. It had a monastic look about it, the corners tight and angular, the covers smooth, but when Eliot sat down it softened, as if giving in to the temptations of the flesh. "I see you've been your usual productive self today," he said.

Jerene nodded. She had always risen early. A mental alarm clock rang through her nerves every morning, sending through her spasms of anxiety that only work seemed to alleviate. She worked all the time. When there was no work she invented it, or helped other people with theirs.

"What were you writing about today?" Eliot asked. He had taken a cardboard half-gallon of orange juice from the refrigerator and was drinking from it.

"Today?" Jerene said. "Today I've been writing my chapter on these famous twins who invented their own language. Little girls. I don't know if you've heard of the case, but after they were discovered there was a big debate over whether they should be separated and forced to learn English, or kept together so the language could be studied. As you can probably guess, the social workers won out, for the good of the children. I suppose it was the right thing. Still, when I think of what could have been learned . . . There are tapes of them talking, you know. The sounds are like nothing you've ever heard before, nothing you could even imitate. It makes me sad. It seems to me the world has enough lost languages."

"Is that what your dissertation is about?" Philip asked. "Lost languages?"

Jerene smiled at him. "More or less," she said. "More or less." She really did not want to explain about the seven years right now, or the dozens of topic and title changes. She had friends who encouraged her not to finish, urging process as more impor-tant than product — a kind of Marxist-feminist, anti-capitalist, non-goal-oriented academics, they said. She knew only that as long as the Philosophy Department gave her money to fill her life with work, she was going to do just that. Library work was the kind she liked most, the kind that best calmed her, kept her grounded. She could spend hours examining sociological ab-stracts, or browsing through back issues of arcane periodicals, or sitting in a brightly lit cubicle taking notes from old monographs. She needed work that would completely occupy her, that would leave no space for rumination on her own life or condition.

"Anyway," she continued to Philip and Eliot, "I've decided to focus this chapter not on the language itself but on the response, which is in a sense more central to my thesis: what it means that a private, invented language must be sacrificed 'for the good of the child.'"

"So I presume the little girls were successfully taught Eng-lish?" Eliot asked. He was breaking eggs into a pan, cooking breakfast.

"Oh yes. They were separated, and kept apart by the social workers. For days and days afterwards, of course, they probably cried, probably spoke the language to themselves and wondered why no one responded. After a while they lapsed into silence. And then they began to adjust. Bit by bit they started to pick up the new language. Now they're nearly twenty; they're probably in college. I wonder if they remember the secret language, if they still speak it in private, or dream in it. Probably not. Probably their early childhood is like a dream to them, the way it's supposed to be for children who are kidnapped and raised by different parents. Something they're not even sure happened, something they can hardly believe is real when people tell them about it."

"It must have had something to do with what they heard," Philip said. "The language, I mean. It couldn't have just popped out of thin air."

"No one knows," Jerene said. "But language can begin as a very arbitrary thing. A woman was committed to a mental hospital for something like forty-eight years because the doctors said she 'babbled.' And then it turned out she was a Ukrainian immigrant. No one at the hospital recognized that she was speaking Ukrainian."

"It seems like a shame that the twins' language couldn't have been somehow recorded or preserved."

"Yes," Jerene said, "it is a shame." The smell of eggs frying was making her queasy. She steadied her gaze on the window. "I would love to compare the twins' language with some others," she said. "With Basque, perhaps, or the dialects of Hunza, to see if people invent languages the same way, if in a different kind of world the twins' language could have flourished, could have become the language of a culture. But I've realized that's something I can never do. What's relevant really is that the only possible choice, in the case of these twins, was the choice that was made. The language had to die. It's the integration of those little girls which is pertinent — that, and what was lost with it."

She sighed, and Eliot slid the eggs from the pan onto a plate. Philip was looking at her with confusion and curiosity, and she wondered why she always ended up in this position, explaining herself to Eliot's lovers. How odd and foolish she must sound to Philip, the perpetual graduate student lost in the fog of her obscure interests, without perspective on larger matters of the "real world."

Eliot she loved. When her writing was going badly, he came to her, his voice that of a mother assuring her ugly-duckling daughter that love will soon blossom in her path. "It'll come," he'd say, rubbing her shoulders as she wept at the typewriter. "It'll come."

She herself had no lover. She considered her work enough of a lover — sometimes gentle and comradely, sometimes fickle, elusive, frustrating, sometimes bringing her to unimagined heights of gratification, or reducing her to rage and inarticulate despair. Occasionally, on the days of rage and inarticulate despair, she put on her leather jacket and ventured uptown to an elegant women's disco called Shescape, and there she stood against a wall, a lit cigarette in her hand, and waited. Usually the women looked at her first. Because she was both very tall and very black, they almost always expected her to take control, to do with them what she would, and this saddened her; once in a while she would have liked to have given up that control to someone else. Still, she fulfilled their fantasies, even binding one girl's small wrists with ribbon when she asked her to. And then in the mornings she would ride the subway home, tiptoe into the apartment, where Eliot lay utterly still in his close, fetid room. Nothing stirred him. She showered, changed her clothes, and headed to the library, where the work — object of her true passion — awaited her, and after a few hours came home to find the apartment steamy from the shower, and Eliot, wrapped in a towel, shaving.

"How did the night go?"

"Okay," she'd say. "Yours?"

"The same. I went to a stupid party in SoHo, and then to the Palladium. Danced a lot."

She enjoyed standing there on those afternoons, watching him shave. After he finished, they'd sometimes head downstairs to the Indian restaurant run by their neighbors and dip strange breads in hot curries. He was often and casually in love, and talked about it over these dinners. "His name is Philip."

"What's he like?"

"Oh — bright-eyed, eager to please. Very sweet, very unsure of himself. I met him through Sally — you know, that girl who works at Goldman, Sachs?"

"Do you love him?" Jerene asked.

Eliot smiled. "No, alas."

"But he loves you."

"Yes."

"Yes."

In the oncoming dark she walked with him through the streets of the East Village. Invariably he had some social engagement he had to get to. She kissed his cheek and headed home. During the evenings she read eighteenth-century novels no one had ever heard of, except on Saturdays, when without fail she watched "The Facts of Life" on Eliot's little television. She was asleep by the time he got home. Sometimes, in the mornings, she'd find strange socks in the bathroom, or contact lenses boiling on the kitchen stove, and know he had brought someone home.

Once she startled a naked young man in the toilet, and he practically screamed.

"Sorry," she said, backing away and closing the door.

In a few minutes he came out, sheepish, wrapped in a towel. "I'm Philip," he said.

"Nice to meet you, Philip. I'm Jerene, Eliot's roommate."

"He told me. He's still asleep."

"Go back to bed," Jerene said. "You look exhausted."

"We were out really late," he said, and smiled, pleased and surprised to be part of a "we." "Well. It was nice to meet you."

"It was nice to meet you, too."

"Good night, then — or, I mean, good morning."

"Bye."

He pulled back the Japanese door that separated the living room from the kitchen and disappeared from her.

In the kitchen, now, eating eggs, this same Philip stared at her. "It sounds wonderful, really fascinating to me," he said, and she smiled. "What?" she said.

"Your dissertation. I'd love to read it."

She looked toward the window, smiling away her life. "Just the tedious pontifications of a graduate student," she said. "Nothing earth-shattering. I wouldn't waste your time with it if I were you."

"Oh, I wouldn't say that," he said. He took another bite of his eggs and turned back toward Eliot.

Jerene was adopted. She believed that her earliest memory — of a swatch of light bisecting a pink rabbit-patterned blanket —

came from before her adoption, from some moment in the first three months of her life, if for no other reason than because she could find no such blanket among her baby relics, stowed for years by her mother in a cedar-scented trunk in the attic. Her adoptive parents were a wealthy lawyer and his wife who in 1957 held the distinction of being the only black couple to own a home in Westport, Connecticut. Jerene had a photograph of herself that was taken just after the adoption, her hair done up with pink velvet ribbons, posed between her father and her mother in front of an absurdly overdecorated, white-frosted Christmas tree. In the picture, Sam looks out at the camera, unsmiling, dressed as usual in a tie and black pin-striped suit, while Margaret, her hair piled on her head in puffed whorls, holds her baby daughter up on a table, clinging to her tiny knees as if for dear life. Jerene has just barely learned to stand, but she is standing in the picture. Her mouth is open, her legs buckling, as if she might topple any second. All three of them are stiff with discomfort, like people posed in costumes from another century for comic effect. When Jerene looked at the picture these days, she felt sorry for all of them.

If she knew anything about her parents' past, it was that they had fought hard to get to where they were. They told her so all the time, hoping, she supposed, to instill in her the kind of respect for hard work that would ensure that she never slip back into the poverty from which they had pulled her. About their own origins they were evasive, as if they feared that too much exposure to a less privileged world would lead to its engulfing her. Only rarely would they take her to visit her grandparents and aunts and uncles in the city, and then only for the afternoon. When Jerene was seven, Margaret's mother, Irene, came to visit them in Westport, and Sam and Margaret took her to tea at an elegant restaurant, where elderly black women in white aprons served crumpets and petits fours from silver trays. The four of them sat there not speaking, and Irene, dressed in an out-of-style velvet hat with flowers on it, eyed the pastries suspiciously and refused to touch them. Everyone — the waitresses as well as the other patrons — gave the family curious, condescending glances, as if to question whether they belonged there. Still, for two hours they stuck it out, sitting stiff-backed in their chairs, smiling, pretending enjoyment as if their lives depended on it, and in certain ways their lives did depend on it. And even though she was just a child, Jerene sensed how unfair it was, that after all they had gone through, her parents should still be considered outsiders at that restaurant and in the town. Sometimes, on weekends, Sam and Margaret socialized with other wealthy black couples they had sought out or met through business. They drove to Larchmont or Noroton Heights, or the other couples came to their own big Tudor house and exclaimed over the reproduction Louis Quatorze furniture, the wall-to-wall carpeting, the new washer and dryer. These elaborate, formal dinner parties, presided over by a maid hired for the night, and full of the clinking of glasses and the peal of shy female laughs at gruff male jokes, confirmed Jerene's impression, at the age of seven, that the world consisted of two parallel and more or less identical sets of people — one dark, one light — just as the dolls on the toy store shelves always came in two versions, one dark, one light. Only the black dolls were hers, she knew. And yet there were more of the white ones, and they were prettier. Black dolls, she would tell Eliot years afterwards, provided her introduction to the politics of race.

Jerene knew she was adopted, but from an early age she was instructed to keep this fact a secret within the family. "Just be glad you've got all the things you've got," her mother would tell her, when Jerene asked about her origins. "You would've grown up mighty differently if we hadn't come along." Defeated, she would return to her room, her refugee's good fortune choking her. She could not get over the accidental nature of her blessed life; it made everything else wrong. With frantic exuberance Margaret dressed Jerene up in pink, lacy blouses, curled her hair and tied it with ribbons, sometimes painted her tiny but perfect nails bright red, until she resembled the black dolls that sat on her bedroom shelf — Black Barbie, Black Baby Talks-a-lot, Black Baby Alive — all identical to the originals, but dark, darkened, *wrong*, just as she was wrong, just as her parents were wrong and their friends were wrong, clinking their glasses in the Parkses' living room. They were alone in Westport. Across the street was a house with a F O R S A L E sign that no one bought for a year, and Jerene understood, from conversations she heard between her parents, that somehow they were responsible not only for one family's leaving but for another family deciding at the last minute not to buy. Coming home from shopping with her mother, Jerene would see notes slipped under the door, notes her mother would snatch up and ball in her fist, unopened. Racism was genteel in Westport, she would later tell Eliot; it always came in an envelope.

Once she was roused early in the morning, put in the car, driven through familiar streets of green lawns and houses, then down a long, grass-lined highway into a region of small, lopsided buildings where children her own age played in earnest among garbage cans and cars. They parked beside a glass door shot through with cracks, above which a sign announced B R I T E V I E W L A U N D R Y, and went inside, into that hot room full of steam and the sweet smell of fabric softener that Jerene would never forget. Her grandfather wore a T-shirt browned with sweat and tobacco juice; she did not want to touch him. But her grandmother, a bandanna twisted around her head, glowed and shone like something newly polished as she hoisted huge dripping sheets from washing machines. She turned, smiled, knew not to embrace Sam and Margaret in their suits. And then, as they all left together, Jerene's grandfather pulled the heavy metal grating down over the steamy glass windows of the laundromat, and they got into the back seat of the big car with Jerene. "It's a treat, riding," Jerene's grandmother Nellie said. She held Jerene on her lap, whispering nonsense in her ear as Sam drove them to the tiny apartment of his childhood, with its cracked, impossibly narrow halls, and there they sat for an hour on stiff-backed chairs in the little sitting room, eating cookies and drinking lemonade. Jerene always remembered the hand-shaped splotch on the kitchen wall, which she thought was a part of somebody's shadow; on the way home she would wonder who it was, the poor person whose shadow was missing a hand.

Sam was enraged on the rides home from his parents' house. "Why won't they *do* something?" he said to Margaret. "They could retire to Florida. I'd give them the money." But they wouldn't take Sam's money because of pride. Jerene had trouble figuring out what pride was. In her schoolbooks, the proud boy was haughty and looked down on his friends, but that sounded more like her parents than her grandparents. To Margaret, pride meant you didn't take things that were offered, pride meant you suffered stupidly. She was not above admitting the many times she had swallowed her own pride, and done better for it. Jerene leaned back in her seat, wondering. She knew her father's childhood as mythology — scrubby lots to play in, not enough heat. He had no toys. The streets were full of toughs. "Just be glad you've got all this, my little honeybee," he'd say to her when she was little, pushing her in the backyard swing, and she would look around herself at the twilit green trees, the leaves on the ground, the little gazebo near the gardener's shed. None of it was hers except by refugee's luck. And then an extraordinary thing happened: Her father, pushing her on the swing, suddenly grasped the metal chains, pulled her back, held her suspended in mid-air, so that she thought she could see the world's roundness below her, and buried his head in her back to weep.

She knew certain facts. He had been, at the age of seventeen, the first black boy chosen Boy of the Year by the Bensonhurst Brooklyn Optimists' Club. He had been the first black editor of the paper at his college, and of the Law Review at his law school; the first black lawyer at one firm, the first black partner at another. All through his twenties he stood on podiums, and his hand was shaken and his back was patted. Jerene came along. Afterwards many large men smelling like gingerbread lifted her into the air. She'd stand with her mother in the ladies' room, and the wives would politely pass makeup tips to Margaret, then suddenly grow embarrassed and say, "Oh — I guess you people have your own brands, don't you?" Margaret always smiled.

Sometimes they would find themselves alone in the car with the statuettes and prizes, driving through dark suburban streets that became increasingly unfamiliar. From the back seat Jerene would stare at the backs of her parents' necks — her father's carefully shaved and trimmed, her mother's shiny and bare in the moonlight, caressed by the clasp of a necklace, a few pearls. They would get lost. Sam would pull the car over, and his neck would be soaked with sweat. "Look, Sam, we're in Noroton Heights," Margaret would say. "I know exactly where we are. There's that mall where I went with Jerene the other day." And slowly, exactingly, she would direct him home.

He was a Nixon delegate in 1968. Jerene was eleven and voted for Humphrey. She prayed that her Humphrey-supporting best friend, Jessica Hudson, and Jessica's Humphrey-supporting parents, wouldn't say anything.

Still, when the convention was on television, she watched with her mother and was thrilled to see Sam's face suddenly filling up the screen. "We're talking to Mr. Samuel I. Parks," the reporter said, "an attorney from Connecticut, and one of the few black delegates here at the convention. Mr. Parks, as a Negro, how do you feel supporting Mr. Nixon in the face of your race's overwhelming support of the Democrats?"

"I fully believe that Richard Nixon is what our country and our economy needs now," Sam said. He was sweating and looked rather uncomfortable, but his voice was sure.

"Mom," Jerene said.

"Hush up!" Margaret said. "How many times in your life are you gonna get to see your father on television?"

And indeed, Jerene could not help feeling a secret pride, for he looked so handsome with the microphone in front of his mouth.

She never talked about it with Jessica.

She grew up, grew taller and kept growing. By the time she was in junior high school she was already five foot eleven and the star of the basketball team. That year her school won every game, and Jerene was named Most Valuable Player.

She brought the trophy home and showed it to her mother. Margaret was cleaning the big house, which over the years had acquired an apparently insurmountable coat of dust. "Why do you have to play that game?" she asked when Jerene showed her the trophy. "It's so — unladylike." She did not approve of Jerene playing basketball; she had said it from the start.

Behind her, Margaret dragged the vacuum cleaner like an unwilling beast of burden. "Why?" Jerene repeated. "Because blacks play basketball? You're worried someone might confuse me for one of them?"

Her mother only shrugged. "That uniform," she said. "Really, Jerene, couldn't they give you something a little more feminine? And why do you always wear those ugly pants, when I've bought you so many pretty dresses?"

"Pretty dresses look stupid on me," she said.

"You never try," Margaret said. "You don't give yourself a chance to be pretty. Ah, there you are. Now I'm gonna get you." She was talking to the dust. She stuck the special vacuum-nozzle behind an antique mirrored table, and Jerene listened to the peculiar, pleasant sucking sound it made.

She slept over at Jessica's all the time now. Jessica's mother, who was a magazine editor, was mild and abstracted and thought nothing of it. Jessica herself was Jerene's best friend, robust, big-breasted, a discus thrower, and had taught Jerene how to make love with her tongue and fingers and hips. They did this most nights when Jerene stayed over now but were only just beginning to gain a consciousness of what it meant — that they were lesbians — a realization to which Jerene's first reaction was, "Of course. That's how it is. I've known it all along." Of course there was more; she realized, distantly, that this kind of love couldn't be easy, that she must suffer more than she had. The word "abomination" kept creeping through her mind — from a church sermon, she supposed, or perhaps from under her mother's breath when they heard about Billie Jean King and her secretary on the radio. Were they lovers, girlfriends, in love? Certainly they had never spoken about the quiet passion that took up most of their nights together. And Jessica was too busy thinking about Harvard in the fall to worry about such things.

Jerene, less ambitious and yearning for the city, went to N.Y.U. Separated, finally, from her parents, she started to attend meetings of the Afro-American Women's Caucus, the Lesbian Caucus, the Radical Women of Color Caucus. In imitation of Cornelia Patterson, a lesbian leader whose stage presence and nearly bald skull impressed her greatly, she shaved off most of her hair one day. "What have you done to yourself?" her mother shouted when she walked in the door at Christmas break. "My God, you've maimed yourself." She and Sam were so appalled they threatened to refuse to pay her tuition for the next term, and she only dissuaded them by promising to grow her hair back. At first that didn't satisfy them, until they realized it was the only choice they had. They relented.

Over dinner she told them about her new politics, and her involvement in the Black Women's Movement. Margaret, spearing small curlicues of potato with her fork, looked at Jerene warily. "And do you really think," her father asked, staring her down across the table, "that such isolationism will do anyone any good?" It was an old argument, one they'd had many times before. "First the black movement," Sam muttered, gazing disconsolately into his plate. "Now the black *women's* movement. I know it's not a popular opinion, Jerene, but I just don't see the point of all this separatism."

Then he told her again that you had to work through the

system to change it from inside, etc. "We're all human," he concluded triumphantly. Margaret looked on in approval. Jerene recognized that tactic — wrapping his snobbery and defeat in the guise of Christian good will — and considered it beneath responding to. She went back to her dinner, and the next morning found a mysterious check for fifty dollars by her bedside table. "For a nice wig" was written on the line where it said "Memo."

Six months later she made a special trip home to tell them that she was a lesbian. For years afterwards she would wonder why she did it — whether it was, as she told herself then, an act of political integrity, motivated by her real need to be honest with her parents; or whether it was revenge she was really after — revenge, and liberation. She had long since convinced herself that her lesbianism was a neutral thing, neither good nor bad in itself. But she also knew that this neutral fact of her life, when presented to them, would be as potent as a machete brandished in front of their faces, and would cut as deep. She had made many preparations, consulted many books. "Afternoon is best," Cornelia Patterson had counselled her, and so she marshalled her parents into the living room in the afternoon to give the news. Her father looked out the window at the oleanders in the garden while she spoke; her mother sat on the sofa and wept. "Are you finished?" Sam asked her when she had been silent for a few seconds.

"Yes, I'm finished."

"Then I will say to you this," he said, turning around. "I will say I would rather you'd told me you were dying of terminal cancer." His eyes did not waver from the flowers.

"Dad," she said. "How can you say that? How can you just stand there and say that to me?"

"You've been a disappointment all along to us, trouble every step of the way. And now to come home with this — this filth, this abomination. What do you expect me to do, just sit back and smile?"

"It's like a death," Margaret murmured softly from the sofa, between sobs. "As if she's died."

"Mom!" Jerene said. "Dad! I'm still me. I'm still your daughter, your Jerene. Please! I'm trying to be honest with you, to tell you the truth for once."

Her father turned from her, looked once again out the window. "You're not my daughter," he said. "Thank God for that, if nothing else. You're not my daughter."

Thus he pulled the machete from where it lay implanted in his heart, turned it around, and sliced her clean off.

Without saying another word to them, she left. She walked the two miles to the suburban train station, waited an hour on the empty platform, on a bench, her knees gathered against her chest, rocking. Back in the city, she wrote them a check for the sum total of all the money they had ever given her. It was something like three hundred thousand dollars. They never tried to deposit it, of course, but she burned the checkbook anyway. Years later, it pleased her to think that the money she actually had in that account — a little over five thousand dollars — might still be sitting there, accruing interest, untouchable.

Once, about a year later, at Eliot's insistence, she called them on her mother's birthday. Margaret answered. "Mom?" she said. "Mom, it's me, Jerene."

Margaret said nothing.

"I'm happy to hear your voice," Jerene said. "It's been so long. I've missed you — "

Still, silence. "Jerene?" Margaret said. "I don't know anyone named Jerene. I don't know any Jerene. You must have the wrong number."

Then she hung up.

A few years later, walking down Fifth Avenue, Jerene saw her. Margaret's hair was all gray now, and she had put on weight. She was peering at some shirts in the window of Bendel's. For a moment, it was as if the years of silence hadn't passed at all. How could they have, after all? It was ridiculous, embarrassing — three intelligent people, and all too stubborn to make a gesture. Her mother stood there, completely unaware of Jerene's presence, staring at the shirts, and then she pulled a tissue from her big pocketbook and blew her nose. It was the same red patent leather pocketbook she had always had, and seeing it, Jerene was moved to tears. She wanted to run up to her mother, to embrace her and refuse to let her go until she cried, until she gave in, until she admitted Jerene was there, admitted she had a daughter. Indeed, standing in the middle of the intersection, she was held back by nothing but fear. Then the light changed, and a crowd swept across the avenue, over the sidewalk. By the time it had passed, Margaret had moved on.

"How old were you when Derek and Geoffrey found out that you were gay?" Philip asked Eliot. It was four in the morning, and they were lying on the blue futon, nowhere near sleep.

"Oh, let's see," Eliot said, stretching his arms out behind his head. "I guess it must have been — but no." He smiled. "The thing is, with Derek and Geoffrey, I'd only have had to come out if I was straight. Come to think of it, I don't think I ever actually did come out to them. I just remember, when I was twelve or so, Derek walking into my room and finding me making out with Timmy Musseo. And he just said excuse me and closed the door."

Philip's jaw dropped. "You were making out with boys when you were twelve?"

"Eleven," Eliot said. "Geoffrey and Derek only found out when I was twelve."

"Then how old were you when you first had sex?"

Eliot shrugged. "I'm not sure," he said. "How do you define sex? If orgasm is the criterion, twelve. If anal or oral penetration is necessary, fifteen."

"And was that with Timmy Musseo?"

"No, no," Eliot said. "Timmy Musseo had a girlfriend by that time. My first experience was with a much older man, a friend of Derek's. He and Geoffrey never found out about it. Probably they still don't know."

"How old is older?"

"Oh, let's see," Eliot said. "When I was fifteen, he must have been twenty-nine, thirty. My age now. He came and stayed with me at the house whenever Derek and Geoffrey went away."

"Did he seduce you?"

"I seduced him," Eliot said, and laughed. "Oh, he wanted to for as long as I did. But I think he was afraid Derek would send him up for statutory rape or something. I was irresistible at fifteen. I kept asking him to give me massages, playing the little nubile waif. And finally — well, he couldn't hold back anymore." He sighed. "It was a wild night. We did everything."

Philip's mouth was dry. "When I was that age," he said,

" — well, I never would have dreamed, no matter how much I might have wanted to — " But he knew enough about Eliot's childhood in that rambling brownstone on West Thirteenth Street to know that it was about as different from his own as you could get. Eliot had been raised not by normal parents, after all, but by two men, by Derek Moulthorp, the famous writer, and his lover, Geoffrey Bacon. When Philip imagined him as a child, he was lying in a brocaded canopied bed, having stories read to him by Colleen Dewhurst, but now the fantasy changed, and it was a young man with long brown hair, dressed in an unbuttoned tuxedo shirt, who sat leaning over Eliot in his bed, running his hand languidly through Eliot's hair.

"I just can't imagine," Philip said, "having that kind of self-knowledge, that kind of . . . wherewithal, at fifteen. At fifteen I was just discovering pornography. I didn't have sex until college."

"Everyone's different," Eliot said, "depending on their background." He was staring up at the ceiling, onto which he had pasted glowing constellations from a kit. At night, sometimes, he liked to name them: dog, dipper, hunter.

"One more question," Philip said. "If you don't mind."

"Not at all," said Eliot.

"How old were you when you had your first real lover?"

"Seventeen," Eliot said. "At Jasper Ridge. My roommate, Ben Hartley, and I were secret lovers for an entire year. He was wonderful. A hockey player. He must have been six foot five. We spent a semester together in Florence, and when we'd walk by the fake David in the Piazza della Signoria, everyone would stare at Ben instead. He was the most amazing lover I ever had. But it was one of those secret things, so it didn't seem real."

"Was it always secret?"

"Unfortunately not," Eliot said. "One of the house monitors happened upon us one afternoon in the shower. Now this was Jasper Ridge, mind you, the hippie school to end all hippie schools, but homosexuality was still not exactly a thriving thing there. We had to talk to the Jaspers themselves, and Mr. Jasper, who was this old ex-Beat with a lot of money, he kept saying, 'Wow, that's really great. I can really relate to that.' He wanted Ben and me to go before the whole school and announce ourselves, because he thought it would be very consciousness-raising for the other kids." Eliot laughed. "Thank God we talked him out of it. Most of those kids were little thugs. They'd have killed us."

"Whatever happened to Ben Hartley?" Philip asked.

"He went to Colgate. We lost touch. Last I heard he was out in California, working as a carpenter or something."

Philip was silent. "My first love affair — if you can call it that — wasn't nearly so much fun," he said.

"You mean Dmitri?"

"Have I mentioned Dmitri?"

"Only in passing."

"Dmitri was a physics major," Philip said. "He was very dark, and he had these mad-scientist eyes that would kind of zero in on you and just not turn away. It was hard to resist. My first lover." He laughed. "You know," he said, "he hated the word 'lovers.' He preferred to say we were 'friends who had sex,' and of course only between us, because he was insistent that none of his friends or, God forbid, his professors ever find out he was gay. He made it clear from day one that if I mentioned our relationship to anyone, even to Sally, he wouldn't speak to me again. But even though he was so secretive, he was very promiscuous. He used to claim to be able to identify how much hair a man had on his ass by how much he had on his wrists. That kind of thing was very important to him."

"How long were you together?" Eliot asked.

"Six months, I guess, give or take a few weeks. The last semester of college. But he never loved me. He had an older brother, Alex, who was also gay, and also a physicist, and I think if he loved anyone it was him. Not sexually, of course, just in a sort of worshipful way." He smiled. "I remember at graduation I finally met Alex. He looked just like Dmitri, except he worked out, so he had muscles, and his boyfriend was a male model. They were there with their parents — the father was some sort of industrialist, and their mother was this very thin spacey woman from Texas — and also their grandmother. She was something. Maybe four foot eleven, and built like a tank. She had this little camera, and she was so proud she kept insisting on taking pictures of Dmitri — first alone, and then with Alex, and then with both of us. And standing there, it felt so strange to me, to think that this old woman worshipped them so much, and didn't have the slightest inkling, not the slightest idea about them. Of course, it must have been very hard, both of them being gay after all, and the only sons. I guess they really believed they'd be disowned if they told their parents, and probably they were right. But what amazed me was, it was as if they couldn't care less. They just made joke after joke about it. In fact, I thought I'd feel very nervous standing between them like that, I thought I'd be afraid every second the parents would see something. But somehow I felt safe, safer than I'd felt all that year. I think Dmitri and Alex protected each other, and it was as if their protection covered me as well — does that make sense?"

"Completely," Eliot said. His eyes were closed.

"After that," Philip said, "they walked over to their grand-mother and picked her up. Literally. Just put their hands under her behind, and paraded her around the campus while everyone watched, and she laughed and screamed and begged them to put her down. I just stood back with the parents and smiled, until my parents came back to get me."

"Was that the end with Dmitri?"

"Oh, more or less," Philip said. "I visited him once after that, in the summer, at his parents' place in Southampton. He had a whole filing cabinet full of pornography. And I remember I told him that my great fantasy of domestic happiness would be if we put all our underwear in the same drawer and got them mixed up so we couldn't tell whose was whose."

"What did he say to that?"

"Oh, just what you'd expect. He said, 'That's funny, because my brother Alex and I used to do that when we shared a room, but I always knew which was which.' Apparently Dmitri was secretly turned on by wearing his brother's underwear. It's funny, he had no compunction about admitting things like that, even though he would have murdered someone before anyone in his department found out about him. Anyway, after that the weekend just sort of dragged on, and we spent a lot of time sitting on the porch, and Dmitri and his father would talk about engineering, and Dmitri's mother would say things to me like, 'Well, Philip, I know how you feel — when the men in this family start talking science, I just feel left out at sea. The next time, we'll go into the kitchen and talk about literature.' But we never did. Then I went home."

The blanket pulled away, and Eliot turned onto his side, facing the window. Philip looked up at the stars on the ceiling, which were fading fast. Now streams of sunlight were beginning to pour through the window, keeping the little stars steady and faint. It annoyed Philip that after a night of happy sleeplessness, exhaustion would still punch him awake with the alarm clock in the morning; he would shave, dress, head off to work, while Eliot shifted in the bed and gave a small sigh of contentment. He never said goodbye. Once Eliot was asleep he was dead to the world. There was no waking him.

"Eliot?" Philip said.

"Yes?"

"I'm thinking of telling my parents. About us. Which of course, means telling them about me."

Eliot said nothing.

"I'm thinking of telling them this Sunday," Philip went on. "Do you think it's a good idea?"

"I don't know your parents," Eliot said.

"Well I do. And I can tell you now, I don't think this is going to be a big shock for them. They're going to think 'Of course.' Then they'll understand why I never had a girlfriend and all. I mean, my parents are liberal people. They won't be destroyed by this."

"Probably not," Eliot said.

Philip nodded to himself. "No," he said, "the problem is not going to be my being gay, as much as getting beyond that. Because it's not enough, you know, just telling them and shutting up and never talking about it again. I feel like I should let them know what it's been like for me — what it felt like, growing up, keeping this secret. I feel like I should let them know what it means, having the life I have, having you. They deserve to know."

"That's what Jerene thought," Eliot said. "Look what happened to her."

"My parents are not like Jerene's parents," Philip said, a hint of
anger in his voice.

"Oh, probably they won't disown you. But don't be sure it's
going to be all sweetness and light, Philip. It's hard for you to
realize how new this thing is going to be for them because you've
lived with it all your life. But they haven't. They probably haven't
even thought about it."

"Oh, I'm sure they've thought about it. They're not stupid."

"Even so, the fact remains that no matter how well you explain
to your mother why it is you like getting fucked up the ass, she's
probably not going to be happy about it."

Philip glared.

"Look," Eliot said, "I'm not saying you shouldn't tell them. I'm
just saying that you should think about it very carefully before
you do anything rash. And you should be sure you're doing it for
them and not for yourself. This is going to be a big deal. Be
careful. I know Jerene's case is an extreme, but think about it.
The terrible tragedy of all this is that she still loves her parents.
And they love her. And if she hadn't told them — well, they could
all still have that."

He yawned, closed his eyes. Philip stared at the ceiling. What
was his motive in telling his parents, he wondered, when for years
he had so successfully avoided this confrontation? Was it for
them that he wanted to make this revelation, because they deserved to know the truth? Or was it for himself, as Eliot had
suggested, to relieve himself at last of the burden of secrecy? It
didn't seem to him there was anything wrong with that. Anyway,
he had Eliot now. He could show his parents Eliot, scion of

Derek Moulthorp, and then how could they say he was throwing his life away? How could they argue he was making a mistake, damning himself to a life of eternal solitude? He wanted to stick Eliot in front of their distracted faces the way he used to stick finger paintings and cookie-dough Santa Clauses — only now they couldn't turn away from him, they couldn't absently say, "How nice." They would have to pay attention.

"Eliot?" he said. "If I tell them, would you come with me to meet them? Would you come to dinner some time?"

"Sure," Eliot said. He was falling asleep. "Sure." He shuffled a few times, settling. A half an hour later his breath was coming in even rhythmic waves. In only a few minutes the alarm clock would blare. Philip lay in bed, his shoulders rigid, waiting for it.

When Philip remembered his adolescence, he remembered the hidden parts. Hiding had been so important, so essential a part of his life, that even now — grown-up, more or less, and living on his own — he still kept every book with the word "homosexual" in the title hidden, even in his own apartment. These days, when he thought of himself at twelve or thirteen, he did not think of school, his friend Gerard, board games and playground injustice and gold stars in workbooks. He did not envision himself sitting in a classroom, or with his parents at dinner, or in front of the television. Instead, he saw himself always and only lying on the bathroom floor and masturbating, the steam billowing from the shower, the wallpaper curling at the edges. He could remember nothing else, nothing but this forbidden activity, as if his memory was now capable of creating only a negative image, exposing only those things which were then in shadow. Philip's sexual awakening had not been uncommon: a chance collision of penis

and thigh, the unexpected, intense terror of orgasm, the shock
of the white liquid squirting onto his bedsheet. But what was
different for him was that it never ended, this period when sex
was only masturbation, it never developed into another stage.
For his friend Gerard, there was talk of girls, and then there were
girls, sex, talk of love. For Philip there was only this solipsistic
stroking, by definition nameless. Of course he realized, from the
magazines he glimpsed at the corner newsstand and later bought
in profusion, that there were many other men in the world with
similar visions in their heads. But he did not think to seek them
out, to match himself to one of them, to make love to one of
them, because sex for him had never had anything to do with
anyone but himself, and certainly had nothing to do with his
life, through which he now stumbled, no longer the pensive little
boy who at six or seven had spent whole afternoons patiently
constructing sand forts or drawing elaborate imaginary subway
maps. In school, he laughed too loud and talked too much; his
hair, when blown by the wind, stuck straight up; and he had a bad
habit of scratching between his legs in public, which his parents
were too embarrassed to mention, much less scold him for. Other
boys routinely called him "faggot" or "fairy," though he hardly fit
the stereotype of the sensitive, silent, "different" boy who knows
how to sew, is friends with the teacher and subject to colds.
Rather, Philip epitomized what happened when that quiet, unusual sort of boy tried to plow his way back into the exclusive and
cruel society of children, becoming, as Philip did, a loudmouth, a
clown, foolish in his zeal to be likable, gullible in his need to be
wanted. At thirteen, when Philip was invited to a party and was
standing with his best friend, the ever popular Gerard, before a
feast of Doritos and Chee-tos and Barbequed Potato Chips, he
farted so loudly that the whole party of children began to shriek

with laughter, flung open the windows, and panted dramatically for air. And Philip, in shock, standing in the center of a crowd of children who ran from him in all directions, laughed too, figuring that this would be his lot in life, to fart at parties and win that peculiar furious attention which seemed perhaps as close as he would get to love. When the boys called him a faggot, curiously neither he nor they ever connected the word with any reality, or with his by-then highly evolved masturbatory life. The girls stared at him, some with their lips upturned in sneers, or their tongues out, the smart, quiet ones pityingly, in groups, at the library tables. He absorbed and steered right around their disapproval — it was attention after all.

One afternoon Gerard, his once-fat, dogged best friend since kindergarten, his beloved Gerard with whom he had stolen candy and stared at dinosaurs in the Museum of Natural History — one afternoon Gerard had a girlfriend. He had been teasing Laura Dobler for weeks, had scoffed when other girls brought messages that she liked him. Then, to Philip's immense shock and betrayal (for Gerard had sworn he would never do it), he "asked her," and they were going steady. At recess they sat hand-in-hand on a bench in the playground, and the girls came up to them, to flirt and smile, or to ask their solemn advice. In the afternoons, in math class, Gerard wrote Laura love notes which he signed "Love Always," in imitation of his sixteen-year-old brother, Stuart. Philip, in a panic of confusion, asked Tracy Micelli to go with him. He was desperately fearful of losing Gerard, who had been his faithful friend since infancy, and he imagined he and Tracy Micelli might double-date with Laura and Gerard, thus providing a reason for the friendship to continue. He asked Tracy Micelli to go steady in a long letter, written in red magic marker and complete with illustrations, which he slipped inside the grate of her locker. A few hours later, he saw her. She was with Laura and some other girls, and as soon as he came into their view, they ran into the girl's room.

After that, in the course of four days, Philip asked seventeen other girls to go steady with him, and they all turned him down. It became a minor scandal; even the teacher was aware of it. Finally Donna Gruber, who at thirteen was five foot ten and flat-chested, and as a result had a no-nonsense air about her, decided something had to be done. "You're making a fool out of yourself," she told Philip sternly in the library, her two best friends nodding on either side of her in corroboration. "You're a nice boy, but you're being stupid asking all those girls to go with you. And while we're at it, you've got to stop scratching yourself. It's very unattractive."

Philip's mouth opened in shock. He had never thought anyone had noticed.

"It's my underwear," he said meekly. "My underwear is too tight."

The girls on either side of Donna Gruber turned red.

"Do you think that's why they wouldn't go with me?" Philip asked.

"Oh, Philip!" Donna said. "You asked seventeen girls. *Seventeen*."

"Would you think about going with me?"

"Philip!" they all shouted, exasperated. "Boy, are you stupid," Donna said. "You really don't get it, do you? Well, I've put in my bit. The rest you have to figure out for yourself." And they left him.

It was after that that he threw himself against the wall. No one saw. He went to Central Park to do it, to an obscure wooded corner where he could have gotten mugged or beaten up. Again and again he threw himself, unsure which he wanted to crack more — the wall or his head — or if he just wanted to get to the other side, where he might take tea with hedgehogs and be king.

"Kid!" a voice said. "Kid! What are you doing?"

A hand grabbed him by the collar and pulled him away from the wall. Philip's eyes were red with tears, his fists red, little pieces of grass stuck in the creases.

"Nothing!" Philip said, and wondered if the man was going to kill him. He was a tall man, in his thirties, with a black mustache and very short hair. Although he was dressed mostly in leather, he didn't look dangerous.

"What the hell are you doing here?" the man said. "Do you know where you are?"

"Where I am?" Philip said. "In the park. In Central Park."

"Kid, trust me, go somewhere else — go play with your friends on the grass, go to the zoo. Don't stay here."

He let Philip go. Philip brushed grass from his pants and jacket, and started to walk away. Nearby, two or three other men stood among the trees, staring past each other, stroking erections that bulged from their pants. Philip watched them. They didn't scare him; indeed, he was almost drawn to them, to their lonely circle, the way they didn't look at but over each other. He watched the sad ritual of his kind and was not surprised. Then one of the men saw him. "Hi," he said. He smiled, unzipped his fly. "You like what you see?" Philip ran away.

Sometimes Philip thought about what would happen if his mother were to walk in on him one day and find him surrounded by the shiny magazines, mounds of them spread all over the floor, colorful as the toys and blocks with which, as a child, he had often built play castles to house himself. He imagined the look on her face — her eyes wide, her mouth open in confusion. Beyond that, he couldn't imagine. His life, he presumed, would end in a flash, as it had begun. If he was lucky, he would be born again without this need.

It was only many years later that Philip was finally able to face this possibility, to enact the scene that never took place, the scene where his mother walked in and caught him with his pornography. He imagined what it would have felt like to be forced to talk about it, to acknowledge the protruding erections and the "toys" in the ads and the sergeants in the stories, "planting liplocks" on willing recruits. His mother would probably have handled it relatively well, he decided. She would have left the room, let him clean up. Later, calmly, she would have brought it up with him, said something wise and never mentioned it again, imagining, he supposed, that this was a childish phase, something he'd get over. And he — what would he have said? His sexual life had been bred in secret; he had never spoken of it with anyone, not even himself. Could something so private be real, he wondered? Wouldn't he someday soon meet a girl, fall in love with her? Wouldn't there be some shifting in the hormones he was just learning about in science class, so that he could make love to a woman like any other man, marry her like any other man? He would be free of it, then, that other life, the secret life; it would fall away, unknown to anyone but him, and he would look back on it as a distant dream. Only if his mother found out, if she caught him — then he could never go back.

It wasn't until college that Philip finally made love with another human being, and it was a man. He was not altogether happy about this, but he felt compelled: Loneliness, horniness, the need to touch real flesh — these things conspired against him. He and a skinny medical student named Dean rolled on an ancient sofa in a dorm room, and Philip's hands grabbed for flesh, touched where they had never touched before, investigated the hardness of some things, the softness of others.

What disappointment he felt when, in the midst of sex, Dean took his own penis in hand and began, without compunction, to jerk himself off. He looked right at Philip as he did it, too, a look full of lusty encouragement, prodding Philip to join in, to pose, to become, for a moment, a photograph in a magazine. And Philip — disappointed, but more than that, dazzled by how much easier it was this way, and how exciting — went along with him, watching him, watching him watching him.

When Philip came, it was with such power that the semen flew across the bed and hit the radiator, where it sizzled and disintegrated on impact. Dean smiled appreciatively. "That was some distance," he said. "It must have been a long time since you had sex."

"My whole life," Philip said.

"Your whole life!" Dean said enthusiastically. "Really? Does that mean I'm your first?"

"I suppose so," he said. "Yes."

Dean put an arm around him, wrapped his long body around Philip's and kissed him on the cheek. "That's great," he said. "I've never been with someone their first time. You know, I wish you'd told me, because it would have been a big turn-on for me. Then maybe I could have shot as far as you."

"Sorry," Philip said.

And now Philip is seventeen, and walking in circles. He is used to this. When he goes to parties given by his friends from school, he tends to overestimate how long it will take him to get to the apartment or house where the party is taking place, and he arrives sometimes a full half hour early. So he walks in circles — wider and wider circles, first a five-block radius, then a ten-block radius. He walks until ten minutes after the party is supposed to start, and still he is the first guest.

Tonight there is no party. The place he is going has no beginning or end. It runs on an endless loop. He actually called the theatre week earlier to see when the feature started and the woman on the other end of the line laughed at him. The circle he is walking includes the crucial block of St. Mark's Place, with its haircutting salons and clothes shops; the Indian ghetto on Sixth Street; Third, Second, and First Avenues. He knows every inch of this territory by now. He has been walking for an hour.

He passes the theatre. The brick wall is painted red. Behind twin glass doors and a glass partition, a woman with peroxide blond hair sits and files her nails. She is the fulcrum of his circling. The first time he passed he almost went in, but then an old woman hobbled by, and he couldn't.

The feature film is called *Strap*.

Enough. He walks directly up to the theatre. No one is passing in front; no reprieve awaits him. He has his money counted out in his front pocket, no wallet in his back pocket. Nothing for pickpockets, no identity. He is no one. To the woman behind the pane of glass, he hardly exists. She has a large, artificial-looking mole on her cheek and is certainly real enough to him as she takes the money from his shaking hand through a slot in the glass. Then she reaches under herself — a gesture that in itself seems obscene, prophetic — and pulls at something. The turnstile loosens, and he passes through it, counted, a click, then through a curtain, into darkness.

Ahead of him is a screen, and on the screen a penis six feet long lunges at a back, over and over, seeming to miss the opening deliberately. It slaps the back. It bounces. There is jazz music. He can see nothing except the huge screen — no seats, no faces — and he gropes behind himself for a wall, for something to lean on until his eyes adjust. The wall is tattered velvet. He feels the soft, diamond-shaped mounds, as well as the bald patches worn down by years of leaning. He is blind and helpless. The wall is sticky. His shoes stick to the floor. He feels as if he has walked into a spider's web.

Slowly he begins to see. People are sitting in the rows of seats — most singly, some in pairs or trios. A number of young men lean against the side wall, themselves on display, as if in rivalry with the film. Most of the people in the theatre are pacing up and down the aisles, occasionally turning into the men's room, the door marked "Lounge."

He gropes for a seat at the end of the aisle. He thinks that this will make it easier for him to escape if need be. On the screen ahead of him, three of them go at it, wildly, violently. They are vocal, and that is the best part. They grunt out what they want and how good it feels; they scream words and phrases Philip must whisper even in his imagination. Ahead of him a pair of shadows grope, meld, separate again. Which is the film and which is real? One slides below the other. A third comes to watch, to join in, if possible. They push him away. Philip turns his head up, determined to watch only the screen.

The film has a plot. According to the plot, a young man about to be married sneaks into his brother's room, discovers a gay pornographic magazine, and begins to masturbate. The brother finds him. "Hey, I'm straight," says the groom. "Then if you don't want your bride to find out, you better do what I say and suck my cock," the brother says. The groom is hesitant, but complies.

Philip is fascinated by the film. He hardly notices, after a few minutes, that a man in his fifties — one of the pacers — has taken a seat in front of Philip, just to his right. Philip immediately feels his back tense up. Up until this point, he has assumed that the people pacing the aisles were employees of the theatre, there to make sure nobody did anything they weren't supposed to. He was grateful for this imagined protection, for he really only wants to watch. But now the man who has embodied security — who might hoist other men off their knees by the scruff of the neck and put them out the door — is sitting in front of him, and his hand is cradling the empty seat in front of Philip's seat, as if there is a person there, a date, a girl, and the man is a nervous teenager, making his first, tentative move. Once the man turns around, looks at Philip, then turns back. He looks him straight in the eye and doesn't smile. His face is chunky, stubbled with gray; he has some sort of cap on. He sits in front of Philip and his arm squeezes the shoulder of the seat, the imaginary date. Philip almost laughs, and then the arm dips down over the back of the seat and brushes his leg.

He gasps, and closes his eyes — not because he is surprised, but because it seems so inevitable, this first touch. The hand strokes Philip's thigh, back and forth, gently, and the capped head does not turn around. The hand goes in circles, larger and larger, over his lap, landing on his groin, but not resting there. Instead — to Philip's surprise — the hand reaches for his own hand, and coils around his thumb. He can see the forearm — watchless, thick. He can feel the tiny hairs brushing against his hand.

The man removes his hand from Philip's lap, gets up and walks to the aisle, where he stands right next to Philip. He gestures for Philip to move in one seat so he can sit next to him, and Philip does. He had not planned to; he had told himself, I'll just nod my head no; but now he is doing it, he is moving in one more seat. On the screen, the giant genitals are back, going about their business, and the strange man's hand unzips Philip's fly and burrows into him. How strange it looks there — rustling in his pants like an animal making a home in a tree. By the time the hand has found what it is looking for, Philip's mind is blank, his body is soaked in sweat, and his penis is soft.

The man gives a few tugs, and turns to look at Philip. "What's wrong?" he asks. "What do you want me to do?" Philip closes his eyes, and shakes his head. There are tears in his eyes. He feels as if he can't breathe.

The man removes his hand and zips Philip's fly, as his father zipped his fly after helping him to pee out of it when he was five. They were in Europe, then, on a mountaintop. All around was air and snow and green, green hills.

The man pats Philip's stomach. Keeping his eyes closed, Philip is still five years old, and he is still on the mountaintop near Lausanne, and his father is pointing to the distant village where they are staying.

He opens his eyes. Faces now. A man with a beard sits on a diving board and caresses the crotch of his blue Speedo. Nearby, a blond boy watches him and does the same. They stare at each other, their eyes never moving.

"Come to Daddy, boy," the bearded man says.

Myths of
Origin

Because he was a shy man, not given to self-advertisement, few people knew that Owen had a Ph.D. His dissertation had compared the ideas of history espoused by several English and Italian Renaissance poets most people had never heard of, and won him a post-doctoral fellowship and an adjunct position at a small women's college just outside Boston. This hardly pleased Owen's father, who had a different idea of success. "Why the hell do you want to waste two years and three hundred pages on some poets no one's ever going to read in the first place?" he'd cry to Owen, thrashing through the pages of *The Wall Street Journal* with a violence that had nothing to do with reading. "Just look at this," he'd say, and point to news of some catastrophe. "With the world in the shape it's in now, you want to go off and write about poetry." He was the sort of man who believed that to offer aid to starving peasants was to deny them the chance to succeed on their own. "Every man has the God-given, fundamental right to make his family proud of him," he used to say, while Owen sat across from him and pulled at his fingers until they cracked, a mute smile planted on his face. He had spent most of his life not listening to his father, and he hardly intended to start now. It was 1963. Rebellion was in the atmosphere, taking many forms; it took in Owen the form of a Marxist psychoanalytic reading of Spenser that meant little to his students at the Belmont College for Women and even less to Rose, whose main goal at this point was getting Philip to talk. He was almost one-and-a-half, and he still hadn't said a word, to the secret satisfaction of the other young mothers in the Belmont faculty ghetto, who seemed to be conducting a competition to see who could get her baby to speak earliest. Fortunately, Philip didn't keep her waiting. He surprised everybody by opening up his mouth one day, pointing to his teddy bear, and saying, "Gimme animal" — much better, she thought, than the "dada" Sandy Eisenberg's Naomi had uttered at eight months.

A few years later, Owen was offered a tenure-track position at a small college on Long Island. They moved to New York — to the city — because Rose was getting itchy just sitting around the house with Philip (who, in spite of his early burst of articulation, was turning out to be a rather taciturn child), and her cousin Gabrielle had promised that she could get her a job in book publishing. Every morning at seven on the dot, Owen left the apartment on Second Avenue and rode the train out to Long Island, the lone white male in a car full of black and Hispanic maids. From the beginning, the head of the English Department, an old man named Maxon who had read Owen's dissertation (and been principally responsible for hiring him), made it clear that he considered Owen's ideas juvenile and pretentious, the product of a young mind bent on making trouble and too influenced by what he termed the "fashionable" ideologies of certain youngsters up at Yale. He hinted that Owen had better change his ways if he wanted tenure; his mind, he said, was too good to be allowed to "spoil." It was characteristic of the kind of man Owen was at that time that he did not defend himself and his ideas against this attack, and at the same time did not (as Rose suggested) ingratiate himself to "the old fart" while privately pursuing his own interests in the classroom. Instead, six months into the year, after a particularly bad lunch in which Maxon had gone after him a bit more mercilessly than usual, he quietly and abruptly quit. Maxon was infinitely more angered by this action than he would have been by yelling and raging — he rather liked an "angry young man" attitude in his juniors, having once had one himself — because it left his already understaffed department short one basic composition instructor. Maxon told Owen in no uncertain terms that if he walked out on the college now, he would make sure that he never taught again as long as he lived. Owen was sufficiently convinced of Maxon's power to believe him. He slammed the door soundly. So ended his career in academia.

A few weeks later, he found out that he had won a fellowship he had forgotten he had applied for that would allow him to spend a year in Rome. The fellowship was to provide an opportunity for him to begin research on a new subject — attitudes toward Etrusciana in the Renaissance — an interest he had generated primarily in order to win the fellowship. Like fugitives, then — and they felt like fugitives — he and Rose sublet their apartment, took the money, and ran. Philip was five years old. He would remember this trip to Europe as the year of strange foods, strangely shaped pillows, three-tiered bunk beds on trains, and incomprehensible squat toilets. Philip was extremely important to Owen and Rose — more important than either of them probably could have guessed he would be. In those first years of marriage, following the fated double-date on which they had met, each trapped with the wrong partner, they had been a little like two casual friends who embark on a long and difficult trip together and are shocked to discover themselves thrust into a sudden, intense intimacy they are neither prepared for nor particularly desirous of. They longed for their child the way those friends might long to meet up with some jovial third party, amicable and unthreatening, who could add another voice to the endless conversation, and remind them that there were other people in the world, other lives outside the endless effort of travelling together. Rose was certainly in love with Owen, or so she assumed. She dreamed about him and longed for him and admired his messy hair and professorial absentmindedness and ability to make a point forcefully without raising his voice. But sometimes she would listen to her favorite scratched Billie Holiday record; she would hear that woman sing:

> *I'd lie for you, I'd cry for you,*
> *I'd lay my body down and die for you,*
> *If that isn't love, it will have to do,*
> *Until the real thing comes along . . .*

Then her heart would sink at such absolute assurance, and she would wonder if she could ever feel that way for Owen, and even if she could, if she would want to. In those songs, all that was sure was the woman's love for the man. The man certainly wasn't sure; the world wasn't sure. For Rose the situation was almost exactly the opposite. She could count on everything but her own feelings. As for Owen, sometimes she almost wanted him to become that hurtful two-timer in the Billie Holiday songs, traipsing along and never particularly caring that this woman was holding the world in orbit with her voice, and all for his sake.

Owen was steady, kind, attentive. In bed he always asked if he was hurting her. She appreciated that. But from the start he was distant. At dinner tables in restaurants, after they had finished eating, he would turn his chair out from the table and sit with his long legs stretched into the open space before him, his head slightly cocked in her direction, his eyes veering around to join his legs, and gently nudge a toothpick into his gums. There was never enough to say. The baby came as a relief. It was jubilant and sincere; it laughed or cried. Now there were no longer awkward gaps in their conversation. Philip filled every moment with his inexhaustible lungs, his desire for food, his efforts at affection and play. Suddenly they were happier than they'd ever been together, and Rose imagined (with relief and some shortsightedness) that perhaps it had just taken this baby to make them finally fall in love. They were lost in Philip. They spent hours by his crib. At night they pored over catalogues from Creative Playthings, trying to choose the best toys for him. They did all these things together, too; it was no illusion that during those first years after his birth they seemed to their friends happier, more self-contained and occupied, than they ever had before. And though he was just a baby, the innocent result of chance collisions during sex, they regarded him as some kind of minor deity, an angel sent down to save them, to bring light and color back into their lives.

In Rome, they fell in with a group of expatriate Americans, mostly academics. Their best friends were a couple named Rhea and Karl Mutter, both of whom were archaeologists. Karl was a balding, paunchy man of forty who had a fellowship at the American Academy. He had the kind of broad humor that made people like to listen to him, and a jowly face and body Rose found

repulsive and at the same time curiously appealing; he was like the Pillsbury doughboy, begging for a squeeze. Rhea, by contrast, had long, sun-bleached hair and cavernous cheeks and big eyes that were set oddly close together. Having (in Rose's opinion) no sense of humor to speak of, she was often the victim of her husband's. Every jovial remark Karl made, every peal of laughter he managed to prompt from a female mouth, seemed to plunge Rhea further into the abyss of sour depression where — lacking a fellowship herself, and having no reason to be in Rome (her specialty was Mexico) — she toiled most afternoons and evenings, nursing aperitifs in cafés, her wet eyes looking as if they were about to spill out onto the table. Rose suspected she would have liked to lead a less public life, but her husband's incessant cheerfulness not only made her glumness more visible, it aggravated it. One afternoon she and Owen and Rhea and Karl were sitting at a café with another couple, and Karl had said, "Hey, here's a good one. Now tell me: Why do mice have such small balls?"

The third woman — Rose couldn't even remember her name . . . Betty? Biffy? — let out a shrill laugh just upon hearing the riddle. For her, apparently, the punch line wasn't going to be necessary.

"I don't know," Owen had said. "Why *do* mice have such small balls?"

"Very simple. Because very few mice know how to dance."

He let out his famous laugh — a clipped series of squawks, each following the one before it with a confident regularity. There was something almost consoling about that laugh, like the sound of a car engine finally turning over on a cold winter morning. It put Rose at ease.

She had understood the joke at once, and laughed out loud to be polite. It took a few more seconds for the others to figure it out. Only Rhea didn't laugh. She looked at her husband pleadingly and said, "I don't get it."

He let out a thin, frustrated breath. "Rhea," he said, "come on, think. Balls. Balls. What do you do at balls? You dance, right? You go dancing at balls."

Her mouth opened in confusion, then shut again.

"Jesus," Karl muttered under his breath.

"I'm sorry," Rhea said. "I'm just stupid. I'm just a stupid moron, that's all." Her lips were pressed together, her eyes wide. On top of the table she tore a napkin in half, then in quarters, then in eighths.

"You're just deaf to puns," Karl said. Rhea didn't look up. Her lips trembled.

Karl shrugged his shoulders, looked at Rhea, and said, "What's a mother to do?" He leaned back in his chair. He looked again at Rhea, whose eyes were still pointing down. Very suddenly he formed his face into a cunning parody of hers — tongue stuck out, eyes bulging wildly, cheeks sucked in. Owen was taking a gulp from his drink and it spurted out the corners of his mouth. Betty or Biffy smiled broadly, then covered her mouth with her hand. But by the time Rhea had looked up, Karl was back to normal, red-cheeked, beaming, as harmless-looking as a little fat Bacchus. Rhea eyed him suspiciously. He leaned toward her and made the face again. Her eyes bulged in horror, and he took her hand.

"Rhea, honey," he said, "learn to laugh a little. Have fun. We're all having fun."

She looked around the table. Everyone was smiling uncomfortably. Rose was amazed, in retrospect, that Rhea had been able to keep her composure at all.

Those eyes. Rose would never forget them. Sometimes they opened so wide you could see the red, bloody edges. Years later, when she saw *A Clockwork Orange*, Rose was reminded of Rhea by the scene in which Malcolm McDowell's eyes are pried open and he is forced to watch hours of footage of Holocaust torture, mayhem and maiming. In their merciless openness, Rhea's eyes had that same nakedness about them, that quality of having witnessed inconceivable horror. Or so Rose thought.

Little about Rhea attracted Rose. She was sullen, indolent. She put up with anything from Karl, who seemed to abuse her primarily in order to test the limits of her adoration, to see how much he could get away with. He could get away with anything, it seemed. Rhea was possessed by a passion for her husband so complete and absorbing it overshadowed even her instinct for self-preservation, her need for dignity. By comparison, Rose's love for Owen seemed like nothing at all. Could a different man than Owen inspire in Rose a similar passionate devotion, or did it perhaps have nothing to do with the men at all? Perhaps it was a quality of certain women, women like Rhea, to live in the thrall of a man.

She wanted to understand Rhea. She invited her over for lunch and said, "You know, I can't believe you take all that crap Karl gives you. I wouldn't."

Rhea looked at her, surprised. "It's not crap," she said. "He's very funny. He's all right. It's me."

"You!"

"Yes," Rhea said. "He's explained it all very well. You see, he's got this real talent for making people like him, and he's very popular with other women. And I get jealous. He says that kind of love is too needy, too intense. He can't respond to it. As long as I refuse to relax, as long as I insist on feeling inadequate, or getting jealous every time he makes another woman laugh, he's not going to be able to love me. And he's right. I've got to relax. I've got to ease off. But it's easier said than done for me."

"Forgive me for butting in," Rose said. "But I don't think that's the whole story. Doesn't he have to give something too? Don't you think you'd be happier if he didn't flirt so much?"

"It's all in the eye of the beholder," Rhea said. "I see it as flirting. He sees it as just being friendly, just being nice."

At that moment Philip burst into the kitchen with Mira, the Mutters' little daughter. She and Philip were talking to one another in Italian, having picked up the language much more easily than their parents. Now they spoke with each other all the time in this private tongue of theirs, passing back and forth small secrets, going through complex verbal rituals. This worried Rhea; it impressed Rose, who found herself much less at ease in negotiating Rome than her little son, upon whom she often relied to translate when irate or confused shopkeepers threw up their hands at her, unable to understand her requests. Philip had, at some mysterious and crucial point when her back was turned, changed from a baby into a child. It seemed to have happened quite suddenly, sometime during his third year. All at once he had a face that she recognized as his face. The photographs she took of him now were the sort that people would look at years later and say, "You look just the same." His name was suddenly *his* name, marking him, and not just a testament to the hours Rose and Owen had spent choosing it. He spoke, and more alarmingly, did not speak, while behind his eyes a mind just beginning to recognize itself generated thoughts that had nothing to do with her. Soon he would be keeping secrets from her; soon after that lying. And then, of course, he would leave her.

It was already happening. As he grew older, Rose seemed to know less and less about him. He was industrious and diligent, and spent his evenings in his room, working on exhaustive projects. Early on he had his stuffed animals arranged in his room according to a precise and private geography. Later, he became fascinated by road maps and would draw elaborate plans for imaginary cities and suburbs. Then he created a whole series of subway systems with numbered, named, and color-coded lines and would toil for hours striving to make a perfectly proportioned map. He never shared these projects with his parents unless they asked him to. He seemed to have no real need for their attention or approval. He took care of himself.

In Rome, this independent-mindedness surprised Rose. She was used to Philip's babyhood, when he had liked nothing better than to sit on her lap and gaze at her face. Now, when he wasn't running around the neighborhood with Mira, he stayed by himself in his room, busy with some project. He hardly seemed to notice her. Perhaps that was why she didn't bother to close his door that afternoon, after Rhea left, when Karl came over. She supposed later that on some level she had been expecting Karl. He sat with her, talking, and she found herself, to her own surprise, wanting to touch his thick, well-fed body. With his rich laugh and quick eyes, he radiated the corpulent, easy good humor of a fertility god. He sat very close to her, so close that his breath, sweet as a child's, tickled her cheek. He had been admiring her breasts for a long time, he told her. She looked away, surprised by his frankness, by the lust in his eyes, which did not waver from hers. Then he told her exactly how he wanted to touch her, and what he wanted to do to her; how good it would feel. She felt his hand on her skirt. "Karl," she said, "I'm not sure what to say." But she knew what she was going to do. She was going to find out what made Rhea so hungry.

Two o'clock churchbells rang all over the city.

Near the end of their stay, the Benjamins went with the Mutters to spend a weekend at a friend's villa in the Umbrian countryside. It was an elegant villa, the halls dry and stony and lined with terra-cotta Madonnas. In the back was an old topiary garden, shrubs carved into the shapes of wild birds, curlicues, Romulus and Remus and the wolf giving suck. The Benjamins arrived first. While his parents unpacked, Philip sat on the stony gravel of the courtyard, staring up at the umbrella pines overhead, and the columns of noble cypress, and beyond them the walls of a tiny hill town where they were going the next evening to eat wild boar. Soon he heard the sound of wheels against the gravel. It was Rhea and Karl and Mira, in their ancient Citroën. They parked near where Philip sat, and as Rhea got out she called to him, "Philip, help me with some of this food." He didn't hear her. His attention had been caught by a fountain in the garden, and he ran off to stick his hand under the slimy water dribbling from the mouth of an ancient stone fish.

"Philip," Rhea called again. "Philip!" Her voice was suddenly, unexpectedly furious, but for what reason? He turned around to see. She was standing there, staring at him, her hands on her hips. Her huge eyes were red and swollen, her cheeks streaked with tears. She marched up to him, pulled him onto his feet, and slapped him on the hand. "Philip Benjamin," she said, "I have never met such a selfish, inconsiderate boy in my life! Did you hear me calling you? I said, did you hear me calling you?"

He looked up at her, dazed, and did not answer.

"Answer me!" she shouted. Her voice was hoarse with rage, nearly cracking. "Answer me when I ask you a question. Did you hear me calling you?"

He did not answer. He stood before her, and she raised her hand, as if to strike him. He screamed, and shielded his face with his fists. But when he opened his eyes again, her hand was still motionless in front of her face, and she was looking at it as if it was something inanimate, a flower or a stick she'd picked up.

Rose, who had heard the shouting in the kitchen, ran out to see what was going on. "What's happened?" she shouted. "Is anyone hurt?"

"I asked him to help me and he refused," Rhea said, her voice suddenly calm, distant. "He sat there and deliberately disregarded me."

"Philip," Rose said. "Is this true?"

He did not answer her.

"Philip, answer me," she said.

Still he said nothing. Rose grabbed him by the hand and pulled him toward her. "Is this true?" Rose said, and her voice was panicked. "You just sat there when Rhea asked you to help her?"

It was then that he started crying. Rose looked at him, looked at Rhea (her wild, enraged eyes), pushed Philip away. He pawed frantically, trying to get back to her. "Oh, God," Rose said suddenly. "Philip, honey, come here." But before she could catch him up in her arms, he had run to the back of the house and crawled inside a thorny shrub carved into the shape of a bird.

"What's going on?" Karl called, emerging from the side of the house. "What's happened here?" Owen followed him, coming down from upstairs. They stared across the garden at the bush. "Philip?" the men called. "Philip?"

He would not come out. When Rhea approached to apologize, he crawled farther in, farther back, and she walked off, shaking her head and muttering to herself, "Jesus Christ." The men lay down on their stomachs, reached in their hands, and he pushed to the back, keeping himself from them. "Philip, honey, come out," Owen said. "We understand. It wasn't your fault. Rhea's sorry she yelled at you."

It started to get dark. Rose sat down on the ground next to the bush. "I'm not leaving without you," she called into its murky interior. "I can stay here as long as you can." Crickets chirped, and the sky filled with stars. "I'll tell you what," she said. "I'll sing to you."

Half an hour later, in the middle of "Do You Know What It Means to Miss New Orleans?" he crawled out, dirty, on all fours. She was shaking violently from the chill on her skin, and she pulled him into her arms as much to calm herself as to comfort him. "I'm sorry, honey," she said, beginning to cry now herself. She stroked his back, bit his hair. There were small, dried-up tracks of blood on his arms and legs, where the thorns had scratched him. Bits of leaf stuck to his hair and clothes and she pulled them off. "I'm sorry, honey, I'm sorry, honey," she said again and again.

She carried him in, washed him, and put him to bed. The children asleep, the two couples slunk separately through the vast, dark halls of the villa, turning away at any sound of an approaching footstep, avoiding each other. Only late at night, when the men were asleep, did Rose and Rhea meet, as if by prior agreement, in the big cook's kitchen. They made coffee before they started fighting. Then they sat down at the table. "Why did you have to yell at him like that?" Rose asked.

"Why did you have to sleep with my husband?" Rhea shot back.

Rose was silent. She stared into her coffee cup. "He told me in the car on the way up," Rhea said. "As if it was nothing. As if it was the most casual piece of news in the world. 'And I won't apologize,' he said. 'That's just the way it's going to be. If I can't get what I need from you, I'll go somewhere else.' Then I started to cry, and he started the radio blasting and opened the windows so Mira wouldn't hear."

"He's a bastard," Rose said softly.

"Shut up about him," said Rhea. "You have no right to criticize my husband. You of all people."

"No, I guess I don't," Rose said, lifting her head from the table. "But you had no right to attack my son, and you went ahead anyway. Christ, *I* did it to you, not Philip."

"Don't act like you're such a great mother," Rhea said. "It's true I was hard on him, and I'm sorry. But you! You could have defended him against me. Instead you pushed him away. Your own son. Because you were scared of what I might have said in front of Owen, weren't you?"

Rose resumed her previous position, eyes focussed on the coffee cup. Rhea was right. She had done it to cover her own tracks. "There's nothing I can say," she said. Then she walked out of the room and headed upstairs, where Philip lay asleep, his mouth open, the blanket thrown across the bed. She sat down next to him and took him in her arms, hugging him fiercely, waking him. Her guilt was so acute and so painful that she imagined she would go insane if she did not obtain his forgiveness, and was willing to do anything — even hurt him more — in order to get it from him. She rocked him. "Philip," she whispered, "I'm sorry, honey. I love you, honey, I love you, honey." Philip lay there in her arms, neither resistant nor affectionate, his body as limp and unresponsive as a bag of wet laundry. It felt to Rose like a bag of wet laundry.

Of course, she broke off the affair — regrettably, since Karl was a skillful lover and had brought her to pleasures she had never approached with Owen. Still, her sympathy for Rhea was so acute, her rage at Karl so intense, that she momentarily forgot the extent to which she was implicated in her friend's suffering. They barely spoke throughout the weekend; hurt and hushed, Rhea stuck inexplicably by Karl's side, and the couples went about their business separately. There was no expedition to the hill town to eat wild boar. Rose made frugal cheese sandwiches which she and Owen and Philip ate outdoors, in a field far from the house at the bleakest hour of dusk. All through it, of course, Owen believed that Rhea's rage at Philip (the product of a generally unstable nature, he felt) was the true subject of the fight. The families went back to Rome separately. The Benjamins didn't see much of the Mutters after that weekend, for in a month they were returning to New York and they had a lot of packing to do.

Ten years later Rose got an unexpected phone call from Rhea. "I'm in New York for some lectures," she said. "Boy, I'll bet you're surprised to be hearing from me after all this time, aren't you, Rose? But I'm happy to hear your voice. I've thought of you a lot, all these years."

Rhea had a new husband now, she told Rose, and a teaching position at Arizona State and a fellowship to go to Mexico for the next academic year. "You might also want to know," she said, "that it was me who left Karl, and not the other way around. Six months after we got back from Rome, I just decided I'd had enough of his shenanigans. He really was the most selfish man in the world. And, Rose, don't think I hold any grudge toward you, because I don't. I was just crazy that weekend. God knows I understand what was attractive about him."

She said all this quickly, with barely a pause to take a breath.

"Where is Karl now?" Rose asked.

"In Rome again, actually. Teaching. Remarried. I never met her, but I hear she's beautiful. Younger, of course."

"Yes, that figures," Rose said. Ten years had passed — ten years of long workdays, two-week vacations, rising early and going to bed early — and Rome to her was a distant dream.

"And your life?" Rhea said. "Tell me about your life, Rose."

Rose thought about it for a second. What could she say? That they had returned to New York after Rome, returned to the apartment. That Rose's cousin had gotten her a long-promised job in publishing. That Owen, refusing to have anything more to do with university life, had started teaching at a private school on the West Side. She had advanced to copy editor. He was promoted to assistant principal, then hired away by the Harte School as its director of admissions.

"And Philip," Rhea said. "How is Philip?"

"Philip?" Rose said. "He's grown up. A junior in high school."

Two nights later she came to dinner. She was dressed in black, as gaunt and strange-looking as ever, and told long stories about her experiences in Baja California, about her new husband and his passion for pedigreed terriers, about Mira and her S.A.T.

scores and where she wanted to go to college. Somewhere along the road, Rose noticed, she had acquired . . . not a sense of humor, not quite, but a relaxed and pleasant affect, a conventionality at odds with her bizarre appearance.

She was particularly interested in Philip. All through dinner she asked him questions — about his school, his ambitions, his plans for college. Even now, Rose noticed a certain distance, a reserve in her son, who sat across the table from this sad-eyed woman and would not return her insistent, searching gaze. How much did he remember, she wondered, of that afternoon he had spent wrapped in the thorny wings of a topiary bird? How much had he understood?

"Well, that was quite a surprise, seeing Rhea Mutter again," Rose said to Owen in bed that night. "It made me remember a lot of things. I think I'd like to go back to Rome someday. Would you?"

From inside his book he nodded. She knew they would never go. They rarely spoke about Rome these days, or about Owen's brief shining hour on the limelit stage of Renaissance Studies. The work on the Etruscans, half-finished, lay in his desk drawer, abandoned.

"Owen," she said. "Do you ever wonder what our lives would have been like if you'd stayed in academia?" And added to herself, Would we have been closer? Would we have been happier?

Owen pretended not to hear her. Of course he did wonder, though he spoke about it to no one. His days as a scholar seemed so much a different lifetime that he hardly believed in them. When on occasion he thumbed through the yellowing pages of his dissertation, the elegant argument in which he had once taken such pleasure made so little sense that he could barely follow it. Sometimes the work seemed the product of another mind — one infinitely more precise and scrutinizing than his own. At other times he would feel a glimmer of recognition, and a wave of nostalgia for those lost days would ripple through him. It never lasted long. Soon enough he would fling the thing away and wonder to himself what kind of fool he must have been to have wasted two and a half years and three hundred pages on a bunch of poets no one was ever going to read anyway.

ELIOT WAS SITTING at the big drafting table in the living room of his apartment, his head bent over in concentration, his Rapidograph pen making scratching noises against the paper in the light of a two-hundred-watt bulb. He was working on a promotional flyer for the children's book division of Derek Moulthorp's publisher. He did not speak, did not even seem to notice that Philip was in the room, watching him. Then, after a few minutes, he put the pen down, cracked his knuckles, stood up and looked at the work-in-progress from several angles. "Not bad," he said. Philip gazed at him. He walked over to the futon, folded now into a sofa, and sat down on it. "What are you doing here on your lunch hour, anyway?" Eliot asked. "I missed you," Philip said. He sat down next to him. He put one hand on his shoulder and one on his thigh. Then he reached over to kiss him, and Eliot lowered his head down so that their foreheads collided and rolled against each other like ball bearings. Hands on shoulders, hands on thighs, Eliot slid back against the futon, content for once to let Philip do the work.

There was a peculiarly competitive aspect to their regular

nighttime lovemaking which was absent this afternoon. Usually Eliot insisted on controlling everything, on being the purveyor as well as the receiver of pleasure. He liked to surprise Philip by doing exactly what Philip wanted him to do before Philip even had a chance to ask. When they made love at night, Eliot always made sure that Philip came first and thereby assured his own status as supreme sensualist, expert lover. For a while Philip resisted this effort on Eliot's part, but no matter how hard he tried to make Eliot come first, no matter what tricks he employed to gain an advantage, no matter how subtly and skillfully he caressed and probed to make Eliot reveal his points of vulnerability, he simply couldn't do it. Eliot could always hold out longer, and thus always won the orgasm-postponement battle that underscored their otherwise zealously affectionate lovemaking. Today was the exception. Today, for whatever reason — time constraints, tiredness, affection, boredom — Eliot just lay back, fully dressed, his jeans opened and his underwear pulled back, and let Philip make love to him, taking in the sight of his closed eyes and open, breathing mouth, his bare white feet, the springy, erect penis jutting out from his open pants. And when, in due time, Eliot started to moan and his hips started to gyrate and his hands, instead of gently stroking, began to pull at Philip's hair, Philip thought he might die from loving him, and tried to record in his memory all the simultaneous sensations he was experiencing. Eliot pulled and pushed in and out of his mouth, which was a signal to reach up under his shirt and pinch his nipples. He let out a low heave, and without warning thick, salty liquid squirted into Philip's mouth — a slight disappointment, as he hoped for violent spewing, hosing the back of his throat. Eliot breathed deeply, his mouth open, and his hands embraced Philip's head.

Respectfully, in spite of health warnings, Philip did what with other men he had never done: he swallowed.

Then he stood up, kissed Eliot on the mouth, and went to have a drink of water. Eliot zipped himself up neatly, a package rewrapped, an envelope resealed. He followed him to the kitchen; he kissed him back. Once again they rubbed their foreheads together.

"Eliot," Philip said.

"Hmm?"

"Remember how you said when we met that you might introduce me to Derek and Geoffrey?"

"Yes."

"Well — do you think maybe we could have them over to dinner or something?"

Eliot took a sip of coffee and didn't answer. Philip drew in his breath, for he was convinced that every request he made of Eliot, every inch he insinuated himself into his life, would be one demand too many, one step too far, and Eliot would turn away from him.

But in fact Eliot put down his coffee mug and said, "I think that could probably be arranged."

"Really?" Philip said.

"Sure," Eliot said. "I'll tell you what. I'll call Geoffrey this afternoon."

"Thank you," said Philip. "Thank you, thank you." And hugged him. Then he said, "Eliot?"

"Yes?"

"How old were you when you were adopted?"

He breathed in and out, evenly. "Three," he said.

"So you don't remember much about your parents?"

"Not very much. I was pretty young." He pulled away from Philip. "Do you know what time it is?" he said.

"Oh, don't tell me."

"You told me to tell you."

"Yes, I know. But don't."

"You don't want to lose your job, do you?"

"Yes," Philip said. He walked up to where Eliot stood and wrapped himself around him. "Let's just stay like this a few seconds more," he said. More than sex, more than talking, it was this he loved — resting his head against Eliot's shoulder. In the background they heard the dull yowl of a badly scratched Jimi Hendrix album, along with the adolescent voices of Menudo coming out of a little girl's radio. The kitchen window framed an afternoon that was steel gray, sunless but mercilessly bright.

"You don't like to talk about your parents much, do you?" Philip said. "How come? You can trust me."

Eliot didn't answer. He let Philip go, walked across the room to the window. "Did I say something wrong?" Philip said, suddenly fearful that he had offended him. "I'm sorry if I said something wrong." He followed Eliot across the room, put his arms around him. Eliot's body was arched.

"You're getting sick of me, aren't you?" Philip said. "I knew it."

"Philip, please! For Christ's sake!"

"Oh God, I'm really blowing it today, aren't I?" Philip said. He buried his head in Eliot's shoulder.

"Just lighten up," Eliot said. "Don't be so worried all the time." He sunk his hand into Philip's shoulder, gave it a hard knead, and Philip winced with pain. "You worry too much," Eliot said. "Try not to."

"Okay."

They rocked back and forth on the old linoleum as if they were a couple in an old-fashioned ballroom, a mirrored ball twirling above their heads. It was like a cartoon Philip remembered from his childhood, where musical notes danced together and trumpets and saxophones played themselves with agile, white-gloved hands.

Eliot called Philip at work and said, "We're on for Saturday night at eight. Derek's house."

"Oh, that's great!" Philip said. "That's terrific! I can't wait!"

"It should be fun," Eliot said. "But listen. I don't think I can see you for a few days. It's this project I'm working on. They just called me and told me they want me to have it done by Friday."

Philip was in a cubicle on the nineteenth floor of a building on Lexington Avenue. Around him typewriters clicked, phones rang, someone giggled by the coffee machine. "Oh," he said, then realized he was obligated to say more. "Listen, don't worry," he said. "I understand. But . . . well, I have an idea. I have some work to do myself tonight. Some manuscripts to look over. Maybe I could come over and do my editing while you do your drawing."

"I don't think so, Philip. You know what happens when we try to work together. Neither of us gets a thing done. Up until now it hasn't been a problem, but I'm afraid that for the next few days I really have to buckle down."

"Do I distract you? I'm sorry," Philip said, and felt ashamed and inferior for having no project in his life of equal importance, no work he could put before passion.

For a moment they breathed silently. "Well, look," Eliot said, "we did have our little lunchtime antics, didn't we?"

"Yes, we did."

"You bet we did." He laughed. "Listen, I've got to get going. I'm really panicked about this project. But I'll call you tomorrow."

"Okay. But — Eliot?"

"What?"

"It isn't that you're mad at me — is it?"

"For Christ's sake, Philip!" He sighed in frustration. "Look," he said, "I'm not mad at you. I'll miss you very much."

"You will?"

"Yes. Now I have to go, okay? I'll talk to you tomorrow."

"Okay. Bye."

He hung up. Philip held onto the receiver until he heard the click and the dial tone start up again. He had fantasized the phone call Eliot had just made so often that it had become, for him, unreal, like something from one of his romance novels. He could not believe Eliot had really said what he'd just said, and for a moment wondered if he'd dreamed the call.

A few days, Eliot had said. Given that they'd spent every night together since they'd met, Philip had anticipated with dread his wanting just one night. Now he would have gratefully given him one night.

He sat upright in his desk. What was he thinking? Why couldn't he take Eliot at his word? Eliot loved him, was taking him to meet Derek and Geoffrey on Saturday night. He simply needed time to work. And he did have a point about the two of them not getting much work done together. Philip pretended to read. Eliot pretended to draw. One would tell a joke, or try to distract the other. Soon Philip would find he couldn't help giving Eliot a kiss on the neck.

Flushed warm by the memory, Philip went back to work on the manuscript he was editing, a novel called *Tides of Flame*. Sylvia, the brash and hardy heroine, had dressed up like a boy and joined the crew of the *Black Serpent*, Captain Dick Tolliver's pirate ship. She hoped to find out the truth about the disappearance of her fiancé, Steve Lionel, whose own ship had met its unfortunate end at Tolliver's hand. Now, to her horror, she was finding herself strangely attracted to the brooding, one-armed Tolliver. "He would not give her the time of day," wrote the author, Fiona Carpentier, who was also Jack T. Spelvin and Marlena McCoy, and was really Lynnea Seligman of Springfield, Illinois. Yet Sylvia would win in the end. She always did.

Half an hour later he heard a sharp rap on the side of his cubicle. "Philip?" a voice said, and he turned. It was Marsha Collins, the editor-in-chief famous for her twelve-toned hair, and she was standing with a pair of middle-aged women, both of whom were wearing enormous blue butterfly-shaped glasses and fur coats. "Philip," Marsha Collins said, "I want you to meet Laurene and Gladys Cooper, from El Cerrito, California. They're Vanessa Southwood. We're going to make you ladies a big success," she said, turning to the giddy women. "And Philip as your line editor is going to be very important in the process."

She plopped them down in plastic chairs and walked off.

"I enjoyed *The Serpent and the Flame* a lot," Philip said, and smiled.

"We're so happy to hear that, Mr. Phillips," Laurene Cooper said. "It's our twenty-seventh book."

"But the first that's got accepted," Gladys added. Both had bright red hair, and lips the color of Hawaiian Punch. Though he knew that they were mother and daughter, he wasn't sure which was which.

"It's terrific," Philip said. "I especially liked the Tahitian sequence, and that scene in the volcano."

"Mother spent a week in the library researching that one," said Laurene.

"But I think we may have to do a little work on the love scenes. That one between Mallory and Raoul, for instance — "

Laurene's mouth opened and didn't close. But Gladys nudged her and said, "Mr. Phillips, whatever you want is fine by us. We're just so excited to have our book accepted."

"The one thing is, we want to keep the romance," Laurene threw in. "Mallory's a passionate woman, and that's very important to us."

"Oh yes," Gladys reiterated.

"Well, don't worry," Philip said. "I'd never — "

"There isn't enough real romance in romance fiction, if you ask me," Laurene said. "Too much cheap sex and not enough romance. It's a gyp."

"That's why we started writing," Gladys said.

"I couldn't agree with you more," Philip said. "And I can assure you, we won't compromise any of the romance."

"Well, I'm glad we're set on that. Like I said, we're very excited to be working with an editor."

"Vanessa's excited too." Gladys chuckled.

"Vanessa is Mother's cat," Laurene said, and chuckled too. "Pure-bred Maltese. We bought her with the advance money and figured there wasn't a more fitting name. Don't you think?"

"Oh, absolutely."

"Having a nice chat?" Marsha Collins said, returning to Philip's cubicle. "Hate to break it up, but I've got to introduce these ladies to marketing. We'll talk soon, Philip."

"Yes," Philip said, as Gladys and Laurene stood and gathered their bags, "I'll be looking forward to it."

"Us too!" Laurene winked at him as Marsha led them away.

Philip returned to *Tides of Flame*. He was reading happily until the middle of chapter twenty, when his anxiety came storming back. As he read through that long chapter, which recalled Sylvia and Steve's first wild night together, it occurred to him that for the first time there was a schedule with Eliot, a plan to be made or to be broken. Of course, he had known all along the spontaneous passion that had carried him this far wasn't going to last forever. He had known that eventually they would have to talk about what "they" meant, where "they" fit into the larger contexts of their lives. Up until now it was enough that each night they seemed to consume each other, like Sylvia and Steve, "licked by white-hot flame, the fire of their urgent need." That was fine. That was how love affairs were supposed to begin, in the real world as well as the stormy seas of Fiona Carpentier's novels. But Philip knew that in his case the fire was burning out a cavern inside of him, an emptiness, a need where before there had been no need. He knew he was less than he had been before he met Eliot. A void now ached in him to be filled — so much so that the thought of even one night without Eliot seemed impossible to bear. And there lay the difference between them; for when it ended, Eliot would have things to return to, "projects," whereas Philip would have less than he'd started with, would have a gaping hole in him. Before Eliot, he had at least been self-contained, content with his aloneness, having known nothing else.

A sudden urge to call Derek Moulthorp's publisher — to confirm that Eliot's project was in fact due early, that he really was going to be working these days — stole over Philip, and just as quickly dissipated. It would be a ridiculous call. He was ashamed, suddenly, of his own suspicion, which seemed to him mad, excessive, and he cursed himself for doubting Eliot, who had never given him any reason, who had never lied to him about anything, who was taking him to meet his adoptive fathers, one of whom (and he felt a thickening of anticipation in his stomach) was Derek Moulthorp himself, whose books Philip had so loved all through his childhood.

He left work in the dark. A fierce wind flapped the flags in front of the Waldorf-Astoria, where doormen ushered fur-capped women out of taxicabs and into revolving doors. Ahead of him, an ungainly girl in a purple down coat pushed her way up Lexington Avenue, struggling against the wind. On any weeknight the East Side was full of women like her, straggling into small delis and grocery stores to buy diet Coke, Häagen-Dazs, chicken hot dogs. They had on blouses with complicated, frilly collars — big bow ties and ruffles of pink or eggshell satin — and carried enormous handbags, and tried to fix their hair in the convex spy mirrors that hung over the frozen foods. Giant buildings filled with luxury and pomp towered over blocks of crabbed tenements, and even this early, everything was plastered with Christmas decorations, as if the whole world were a pile of presents for somebody else: reindeer strung along laundry lines, Santa Clauses peering out of windows, bright chains of lights.

Somehow the thought of being alone in his apartment tonight was unbearable to Philip, and so he pushed his way across town to Second Avenue, to his parents' apartment. The doormen had been dying off lately. A new one stood resolutely inside the glass doors and did not recognize him, and Philip was annoyed to have to wait while he rang up. "I have a key," Philip said, irritated, his teeth chattering.

"See that sign?" said the doorman. "All visitors must be an-nounced." He read it slowly, like a third-grader. Into the phone by his stool he said, "A young man who says he's your son is here, Mrs. Benjamin." A pause. "Okay, go on up." Old Mrs. Lubin, wrapped in furs, waited by the elevator. "It's slow these days," she said, and Philip nodded. She smiled at him. After a few seconds she said, "Cold, isn't it?" and Philip nodded again. "I can't remember a November this cold," she said. "Not since the fifties."

"I wouldn't know. I wasn't born yet."

She laughed. "No, I guess you weren't."

The elevator arrived, and Mrs. Lubin got off on the second floor. He continued to the twelfth. His parents' apartment was at the end of a long mud-colored hall. Undoing the complicated series of locks, he went inside the apartment. His mother sat at her desk in the living room, bent over a long and messy manuscript, and, seeing him, she raised her head in the barest greeting. "Well, well, well," she said, taking off her glasses. "It isn't often we get a spontaneous visit from the likes of you." She stood, offering him her cheek to kiss. She smelled dusty, like pencil shavings, and more faintly, of lavender-scented soap. "What's the occasion?"

"No occasion. I just had a free night and thought I'd drop by."

She helped him off with his coat. "That's nice of you, Philip," she said. "But unfortunately your father's not here now. Tonight's the night he has to address the parents. He'll be in around ten. Anyway, I wasn't planning anything for dinner. I don't know what's in the fridge — "

"Don't worry, Mom," he said, following her into the kitchen, "I'll order out some Chinese food or something. I was just thinking that I'd like to go through some of my old books, and I thought tonight might be a good night to do it."

"Yes. Tonight." She seemed suddenly distracted.

"Mom?" he said.

"What? Oh, yes, tonight. Well, that sounds fine." She began opening up containers of pink Tupperware and dumping their contents into saucepans. "We've got leftover Stroganoff you can finish," she said. "And turkey Tetrazzini. You used to love that."

"Really, Mom, you don't have to — "

"But you're doing me a favor. No one's going to eat these leftovers if you don't."

"Well — "

"All right, then, it's settled." She stirred the contents of the saucepans with a wooden spoon while he sat at the kitchen table and read the paper. One of the models in a Bergdorf Goodman ad bore a strong resemblance to Eliot, he thought, and he almost mentioned the coincidence when he remembered that his mother knew nothing about Eliot, wouldn't even recognize his name. He would have liked to have said to her, "Mom, I'm in love." He would have liked to have told her that later in the week he was having dinner with Derek Moulthorp, that his lover was the adopted son of Derek Moulthorp, whose books she had copy-edited and loved so much she had brought them home for Philip to read. It was almost more than he could bear to keep from telling her. His mouth opened involuntarily, then closed again. He looked at the table. He had no more fear, as he had for years, that she would turn on him, reject him, deny he was her son. He was afraid only of the power he held to hurt her. And yet somehow the atmosphere of this cold night seemed too tender to bear such blows.

He ate his dinner quietly while she sat across from him, rubbing the tip of a pencil eraser against her teeth, her half-glasses hanging low on her nose. Then he went into his room. They had not done much with it since he'd left. The shelves were still filled with the books of his childhood, like all the books in the apartment, haphazardly crammed on top of one another. Off of the shelf he pulled an old gray and pink book with a slightly torn dust jacket. It was titled *Questa and Nebular.* All Philip remembered of the book was that there was a rich child who spent most of his time in a giant playhouse so ambitious in its scale and so accurate in its reproduction of adult reality that it might as well have been a real house. He opened the book to re-acquaint himself with the story, and soon it came flooding back. Of course it was not a real house, and the child's distracted parents worried that their son was "losing touch with reality." Clio, the rich boy's cousin (and the novel's heroine), appreciated her cousin's impulse to escape but didn't have such options herself. Determined not to expect too much, she expected too little; that was what all of Moulthorp's children were like.

Like a child, Philip sat cross-legged on the floor. On the jacket cover of *Questa and Nebular,* three of Derek Moulthorp's famous fat-cheeked emerald-eyed children — the little girl, Clio, and her two odd neighbors, Romaine and Godfrey, a.k.a. Questa and Nebular — stood in a room full of toy robots. Moulthorp had painted them in a style that reminded Philip of the Japanese cartoon shows he had watched after school as a child, Speed Racer and Gigantor and Kimba the White Lion. It thrilled him to think that he had once read this book merely for the pleasure of it, merely because he had enjoyed Moulthorp's other books, and had not realized that someday he would fall in love with a man who had been raised in the benevolent atmosphere of the same mind, the same imagination that had generated these words, these pictures. And yet his nine-year-old self had sat here, lost in *The Wish-Portal,* and not known he was being offered a prophecy of his own life it would take him years to recognize. Eliot had always been there, in those books, on those shelves.

Philip held the book in his hands now, away from his face, like one of those rare and ancient Bibles the mere touch of which is said to hold curative powers. He opened it, moved past the title page and the copyright page. There, majestic and grand, in bold, legible Jansen, was the Moulthorp canon:

OTHER BOOKS BY DEREK MOULTHORP
THAT YOU WILL ENJOY

The Original Mr. Olliphant (1955)

The Frozen Field (1957)

The Wish-Portal (1962)

Mr. Olliphant's Orphanage (1964)

Mr. Olliphant's Orangery (1966)

Questa (1968)

The Radioactive Erector-Set (1970)

So the career progressed. With the exception of the five-year gap that fell between *The Frozen Field* and *The Wish-Portal* — unquestionably Moulthorp's greatest work — a new book had come out every two years with clockwork regularity, all the way up to *Questa and Nebular,* the last Philip had owned, and beyond: He knew there were five or six more that had been published since his childhood ended. Philip wondered about that five-year gap. Perhaps it simply proved that a work of genius takes longer to gestate than a work of mere competent brilliance. Perhaps a long writer's block had occurred. And yet he could not help being conscious of the fact that the gap corresponded almost exactly with the death of Eliot's parents and his subsequent adoption.

It must have been an ordeal for two men, in the late fifties, to adopt a child, requiring, Philip imagined, a bravery and a self-assurance which could not have been easy for a gay man to come by. Had *The Wish-Portal* been born out of the crisis of those deaths? Certainly the novel exhibited a grand and generous pessimism, a cautious yet extensive knowledge of sorrow, but it hardly provided any facts that would enlighten Philip on the direction of real history. In *The Wish-Portal*, a boy named Alvin and his loud family take a trip in a Winnebago across country, stopping along the way at bizarre tourist attractions. They end up at "The Place Where Time Is Broken" — a house built on the line between two time zones where an old widow and her daughter have set up a makeshift Time Machine Museum. The surprise of the novel is that the Time Machine Museum hides a real "wish-portal," a gateway to other worlds of which even the old women aren't aware. Its wonderfully humane conclusion insists upon children's need for dignity, even in the most undignified situations. Was it because of Eliot, Philip wondered now, that Derek Moulthorp was able to understand this? He could taste the question on his lips; could taste the answer, the knowledge, salty with danger, for he knew Eliot would not like it if he were to ask Derek questions about that part of his life. Eliot avoided talking about his real parents just as he refused to explain the source of his income, changing the subject whenever it came up; he kept no pictures of them, no mementoes. And Philip had learned that it was risky to nag him about it; Eliot's silence on the question had a panicked edge he could feel.

He turned another page of *Questa and Nebular*, and the dedication leapt at him, even though it had nothing to do with Eliot or anyone else he knew or had heard about: "For my nieces and nephews: Sambo, Sousou, Joanna, Alexander, and yes, you too,

Margaret." He had never thought to look at the other dedications, and so, springing up from the floor, he began tearing the Derek Moulthorp titles from the shelves. He had to ransack the living room where his mother was watching television before he finally discovered *Mr. Olliphant's Orphanage* tucked between a couple of tourist guides to Venice. *The Radioactive Erector-Set* had fallen behind some home repair manuals. Soon he had them all. Breathless, he arranged them chronologically in a pile on the floor of his room and began to read the dedications. *The Original Mr. Olliphant* had none that he could discover; *The Frozen Field* was dedicated, but unrevealingly: "To the memory of my parents and grandparents." Then came *The Wish-Portal:* "To the memory of Julia and Alan Abrams." That would, of course, be Eliot's parents. And closing the book, Philip thought: They had names. They were real, and their names were Alan and Julia, and they died sometime in the fifties. Alan and Julia: the names conjured images in Philip's mind: a talkative, sprightly young man, thin, with a balding pate and small round glasses; a pretty, dark-haired woman, older, dressed in old clothes. Why old clothes? Who could say if they looked like that? Two people were dead, their car smashed and smoldering, and perhaps a little boy, alive, in the back seat, screaming for his parents. Or was that merely Philip's imagination? Was Eliot really in the car? Had it been a car? Philip didn't know.

He read on. *Mr. Olliphant's Orphanage* was dedicated, unmysteriously, "to G." *Mr. Olliphant's Orangery* even less mysteriously, "to G.B. with love." Only two left. Warily he opened *Questa* and read, "Once again, for Geoffrey" — a sequence that was in and of itself something of a history. And now only one book, *The Radioactive Erector-Set*, remained that he possessed, the only one Philip hadn't finished. It must be dedicated to Eliot. How could Derek

Moulthorp have not dedicated at least one book to his beloved son, who would have been by that time thirteen years old?

He opened the book and read the dedication: "For Eliot — if he wants it." No more, just those words. Philip closed the book. Well, he thought, that's what I was looking for. "If he wants it." He had hoped for too much from a dedication, he supposed; enrichment, assurance, prophecy, ebullient sentences that would corroborate the myths of Eliot's origins. "If he wants it": Was that true ambivalence? Was it a joke? He read the words again and again, until they stopped making sense. They were private words. Their meaning could not be unlocked without a special key. They closed Philip out. And after all, why shouldn't they? Dedications were not for readers; they were for the author's friends and family, his special inner sanctum, his loved ones. How dull his own life suddenly seemed in comparison to Eliot's, his lonely childhood which seemed to him now to have taken place entirely on stretches of blacktop, on cold afternoons when the hands ache, when children skid on ice and fall flat on their faces. Whereas Eliot, he was sure, had grown up very differently, in a house of clever jokes and made-up songs, a house where stories were told and pictures drawn, and doors to pantries were portals to lands where princesses rode unicorns, and doughy creatures laughed on the banks of rivers — the very lands, in fact, that Philip was reading about on those rainy afternoons, escaped into through wardrobes or holes in fences: Narnia; Wonderland; Oz. Fountains casting cold sheets of bright water, rainbows, nights on boats counting the stars. He had tried to get there once, that afternoon in Central Park, when he threw himself, again and again, against the wall. He had hoped it would happen as it happened in *The Silver Chair*, where the fence falls open, and

Eustace Scrubb and Jill Pole fall into Narnia, into heroism, and away from the indignity of their hated school. As Derek Moulthorp knew, children care more about dignity than most adults realize or remember. But Philip, no matter how hard he threw himself, got nowhere. Eliot, lucky Eliot; he was probably playing on the other side of the wall all along.

He lay back on the floor, trying to imagine Eliot's house. Perhaps it would be like the grand apartment in Tudor City that belonged to old Madame Duval, the French teacher at Harte. She had made a tea for her class there, and they had sat on velvet furniture amid shelves of old books while dust swirled like insects before their eyes. But Derek Moulthorp did not live in a highrise; he lived in a house, a grand and glorious townhouse with a fireplace. Philip envisioned the fireplace as huge, vast, the size of a room, another wish-portal in a house full of wish-portals. He'd push his way through; the embers would gradually turn green, turn into soft green ferns.

There was a knock on the door. "Philip?" Rose called. "Are you all right?"

As usual, she did not wait for him to say, "Come in," but swung open the door and walked in on him. He flew into the air so fast that the book he was reading leapt out of his hand, hitting a wall. Only after a few seconds did he realize that the worst nightmare of his adolescence was not coming true; that he had been caught in the act of nothing for which Rose might find him guilty; that he was sitting surrounded not by pornographic magazines, but by the books of his childhood, the most innocent books of all.

"I was just looking through some of my old books," he said, and although he spoke the truth, his voice was that of a liar.

"I see that," Rose said, and laughed. "Well, forgive me for acting like a mother, but I hope you're planning to put those back when you're done with them."

"Yes, Mom."

"Because even if you don't, your father and I still live here — God willing — and we use this room and want it to look neat."

"Yes, Mom, of course."

"All right, then." She looked doubtful. "Can I really count on you?"

"Mom!"

"All right, all right. I'll leave you alone." She backed away and closed the door, shaking her head, clearly grateful for the chance to behave like a mother again. Relieved, Philip sat back down on the floor. He knew, of course, that all the magazines were gone, long gone, thrown out ritualistically the day before he left for college. There really was nothing left here that might taint him, nothing she could hold over him.

But still he looked around himself, trying to find something to hide.

THE SUMMER Philip first read Derek Moulthorp's novels was the one summer Rose and Owen took him on a real vacation. He was twelve years old, not yet pubescent, anxious about the strange new school he'd be attending in the fall. Every summer since their return from Rome their holiday had consisted of two weeks at the Jersey shore, at cousin Gabrielle's house on Long Beach Island, where Philip, bored and lonely, spent most of his afternoons walking along the beach, bouncing a big red-and-white-striped beach ball. One day out of the two weeks, in response to extreme pleading from Philip, Rose and Owen took him to the amusements at Asbury Park, where he would ride the roller coaster and go through the Chamber of Horrors and on the Tilt-A-Whirl and the Trabant and the Lobster. There was a strange wistfulness about those afternoons, riding alone or with other single children (usually fat little girls in halter tops, gnawing taffy) in little cars designed to hold couples and encourage sexual intimacy. Owen and Rose followed him, tired and bored in the heat, shielding their eyes from the sun, while occasionally a barefoot child screamed, his soles singed by the blacktop. The rides made Owen sick and terrified Rose, who doubted she would ever recover from one in particular in which she was strapped upright to the inside of a thing which resembled a giant piepan and which turned on its side and twirled in the sky, its cargo of standing prisoners screaming. She lost her hat, and afterwards would only ride on the gentle twisting train that took them through Fairyland. Once or twice Philip's friend Gerard joined them for a few days, and Rose and Owen were freed; the boys went alone to Asbury Park, while they sat reading in an air-conditioned restaurant, and the melancholy ritual excursion from ride to ride was suddenly enlivened for Philip. In Gerard's company, he no longer had to wait for another single child to come along to share a claw with him on the whirling lobster. They rode together, and what he knew was centrifugal force pressed Gerard's body hotly into Philip's as he gasped for breath, feeling himself buried under the mass of Gerard. Gabrielle and Jack's daughter Michelle, who was a year older than Philip, came along sometimes as well and brought her friends, who absorbed Philip into their easy suburban cliquishness, until the Benjamins arrived one summer to find that Michelle had grown breasts and done her hair like Farrah Fawcett, after which Philip, still a child at twelve, stayed in his room, frightened by the big hoarse-voiced boys who came round to admire her potent, threatening pubescence. Michelle looked twenty at thirteen, went to bars regularly, and laughed out loud when Owen and Rose asked her if she would like to accompany them to Asbury Park, as if a hundred years had passed since last summer. Alone again, Philip rode the Hurricane and the Tumbler, and worried about the sparse hairs that were growing under his arms. Fearful of his mother seeing them, he kept his shirt on until the last possible minute when going swimming, then jumped into the water, his arms glued to his sides.

All that summer, back in the city, he was mopish. Rose blamed the weather. It was so muggy outdoors that coming home from work, she sometimes felt as if she were slogging through warm honey, the air was so hard to breathe, so crowded with heat. Gerard's parents were taking *their* children to Egypt this summer, Philip told Rose and Owen one night at dinner. "And last summer it was Atlanta — Six Flags." He put a forkful of salad in his mouth and said nothing more, but they got the message. "Well," Rose said to Owen that night, "why not? I have vacation time saved up. We could take the month of August, go west, rent a car."

Owen put down his book. "I suppose we could," he said.

"I've always wanted to do that."

"Yes."

"Yes."

But the trip was really for Philip. They flew to Tucson and

rented a car, and for three weeks drove through New Mexico and Arizona and all around California, staying in motels and eating in restaurants with gift shops attached to them in which women wearing Harlequin glasses sold "authentic Indian Artifacts." Though they hit them all, the big attractions had little interest for Philip. Raised with a View-Master, he was unmoved by the spectacle of the Grand Canyon, while at Disneyland the lines were so long and confusing that he never got to ride the Teacups or the Matterhorn, and as Pirates of the Caribbean was being renovated, he had to content himself with It's a Small World three times, in a boat crowded with elderly women. Instead it was the smaller tourist attractions that Philip would always remember. Around Santa Cruz, he began to notice a bumper sticker on many of the trailers and Winnebagos their rented car tended to get stuck between. It was yellow, with a great black circle on it, and it pronounced in great black letters: "I'VE BEEN TO THE MYSTERY SPOT!" And sure enough, as they headed north, signs began to appear on the highway, asking, "HAVE YOU BEEN TO THE MYSTERY SPOT?" or declaring, "TEN MORE MILES TO THE MYSTERY SPOT." And when they finally arrived at the Mystery Spot — a parking lot in the middle of a vast redwood forest — Philip was disappointed that there wasn't a vast black spot right there, as promised, a perfect charred circle of earth, perhaps a landing pad for alien spaceships. Instead, he and Rose and Owen and three other families were led up a path to a house where gravity was off-kilter and balls rolled up. When they got back to their car, they discovered that a big yellow sticker, just like the ones they'd seen, had been affixed to their bumper, so that it was nearly impossible to remove. They kept going north, and when they began to see stickers declaring, "I'VE CLIMBED THE TREES OF MYSTERY!" Owen shook his head. At Philip's insistence, they climbed the Trees of Mystery, and braved the Valley of the Dinosaurs, where giant plastic replicas of Tyrannosauri and Brontosauri lunged at nothing in a field of yellow grass. They visited Santa's Secret Hideaway Village, where there was Christmas all year round, and rusted metal dwarfs and cotton snow decked a few pathetic merry-go-rounds that turned emptily to piped-in carols in the heat. They stopped at the Giant Artichoke restaurant, and at Troutland, where for a dollar a piece you could fish from pools overstuffed with starving trout. And all this Rose and Owen bore stoically, knowing, perhaps, how odd they looked in their eastern clothes, Owen in his button-down shirts and black pants, Rose in her skirts and sandals and sleeveless buttoned blouses. Around them were mothers and fathers in Bermuda shorts and sunglasses, tennis dresses and sunglasses, Hawaiian muumuus and sunglasses. They had loud sticky children, and lots of them, and sometimes, while Owen and Rose were bickering over a road map in the parking lot, Philip would stare longingly as one or another mother attempted to restuff her brood into their Winnebago. The spectacle reminded him of the old woman who lived in a shoe.

In the back seat of the car, while Rose or Owen drove, Philip read Derek Moulthorp's novels. It was Rose's idea to bring them along. She herself had been moved to read of Dorothea's disillusion with Rome, in *Middlemarch*, while she was suffering great disillusion in Rome, and so believed that to read of an experience while experiencing it was necessarily a good thing. Philip sat in the back seat, *The Wish-Portal* on his lap, breathing through his mouth, lost in the story, and every now and then Owen would say, "Look at that tree!" or "Look at that mountain!" and he would dutifully look before returning to his book. At first Rose chided him as she knew mothers were supposed to. "You know it's not good for you to read in the car, Philip," she'd warn him, until it became clear that he wasn't suffering any ill effects. Owen drove, Rose folded maps, Philip read. In addition to *The Wish-Portal*, he read *The Frozen Field*, in which animals that have been awakened from their hibernation begin to appear, mysteriously, in a frozen Minnesota wheatfield in winter. He read *The Mysterious Mr. Olliphant*, in which a little boy becomes lost in a vast, dilapidated housing project on one of the moons of Jupiter. He read *Questa and Nebular*, in which a little girl meets a pair of peculiar neighbors, a very fat, red-haired girl and her adopted baby brother, who may or may not be alien emissaries in disguise. At night, they would stop at little motels off the highway, and Philip would lie on the cot set up at the foot of his parents' twin beds and read late into the night. The world of Moulthorp's novels — tourist-pocked deserts, forgotten extraterrestrial colonies, vast housing projects — was every lonely child's world, but transformed, heightened, made magical.

Lost as he was in his books, Rose and Owen wondered if Philip was having a good time on his vacation. They wanted him to have a good time. After six empty summers they felt guilty and wanted to make up for their absentmindedness. They themselves bore the vacation as well as they could, although they often felt stiff and ridiculous in the strange world of California, which was infinitely more foreign to them than Rome. In the one photograph Philip managed to save from that vacation — for like any good tourist, Owen brought along an Instamatic and snapped sights when he could remember to — his parents sat on a giant redwood stump, arm-in-arm, smiling, surrounded by a canopy of trees; under her skirt, Rose's calves were tanned — or perhaps the snapshot had just yellowed with age. Owen sat beside her, half of him cut off by the white border of the photographic paper because Philip, who took the picture, hadn't known how to frame.

Sometimes Rose and Owen surprised themselves (and Philip) by revealing hidden capacities for pleasure. Near the end of the trip, they were staying at a motel in Half Moon Bay right near the ocean. Philip didn't remember why they were in such a giddy mood that night — whether they had decided to have wine with dinner for a change, or whether they were simply invigorated by the cool, gentle wind, the salt in their hair, the sound of the ocean outside their window. Whatever the reason, at ten or eleven that night they dragged him out of the chair in which he sat slumped, reading, and pulled him out the door with them and ran up and down the empty beach, Rose laughing, her shoes in her hand. At some point she ran through the water and shrieked at how cold the little waves felt, lapping her calves. Owen took him to the tidepools, and when he aimed the flashlight at the little lakes left by the tide, live things crawled and wriggled in the blinding brightness. A hermit crab crawled on Philip's hand, and he got to stick his finger inside the mouth of a sea anemone, which closed instantly around it. Even though the sea anemone was stuck to the rock, Owen explained, it was an animal, not a plant. It lived by digesting whatever was unlucky enough to fall into it. Worried, Philip pulled his finger out, and the thing writhed with loss. All along the beach, little clumps of light shone where groups of teenagers had lit campfires. "Hey, buddy! Want some grass?" they called, and Owen pushed Philip forward, toward Rose, who was still running along the lip of the ocean, her feet skipping the water like stones.

Beyond the closed door to Philip's room a television was playing at a very low volume. Tiny gunshots rang out, followed by faint screams, the screeching of minuscule tires, bleating sirens. He assumed his mother was watching "The Rockford Files" — a show to which women of her generation seemed to be preternaturally addicted. The low volume, he knew, was for his benefit. He had fallen asleep on the floor, surrounded by his old books, and she did not want to wake him. Sometime during the course of the evening she had laid a blanket over him, stuffed a pillow under his head, and turned out the light. From this makeshift bed he watched the flickering of colored rays through the crack at the bottom of his door, and listened as the noises of violence gave way to the noises of domesticity — children in a commercial, joyful as carollers. "Cookies taste as good as Mom does," they seemed to be singing. Could he be hearing that right?

He pushed away the blanket and shakily stood up. The tiny lights on the alarm clock pulsed blood-red in the darkness. It was 11:38. He turned on the light, shielding his eyes; but when he opened the door to the living room, the volume immediately increased. Rose was sitting on the sofa, watching, in fact, "Mannix," an empty cup on the floor next to her. When she saw Philip, she turned and smiled.

"You fell asleep," she said.

"I know," Philip answered. "It must have been all that nostalgia."

"Would you like some tea?"

"No thanks."

He sat down next to her on the sofa. On the television, Mannix was interrogating a scared-looking housewife. "What's going on?" Philip asked.

"Drug ring. Her husband is behind it. The big industrialist."

"Isn't the big industrialist always behind it?"

"More recently, but remember, this is 'Mannix.' It's 1969 so it's not a cliché yet."

"Aha."

The windows, when he looked at them, were sheaths of black, shiny as patent leather. "Where's Dad?" Philip asked.

"I don't know. He was supposed to be home by ten. But sometimes these things run late."

"Did you find out anything more about the apartment, by the way?"

A pained expression, quick as a shudder, passed over Rose's face, then was gone. "Most of the tenants seem to be all for it. Because they can buy their apartments and then resell them."

"So you could do that too."

"We'd have to get a loan first — but I don't want to burden you with this, Philip. It's not interesting."

She took a walnut from the nutbowl, rolled it in her palm.

"I think I'll stay here tonight, if you don't mind," Philip said. "It's so late already."

"You know where the sheets are."

"Yes. Mom, I wanted to tell you — "

"Ssh!" Rose said. "Just a second." She bent over, focussing on the screen, where a man was running out of a house, past a swimming pool, onto a vast, green lawn. Another gunshot sounded.

From where he sat, on the opposite end of the sofa, Philip moved closer to his mother. He tucked his feet under his legs.

Cautiously, he let his head rest on her shoulder — so lightly only the tips of his hair touched her — then let himself sink in.

Her dress smelled sweet, like apricots. Underneath him he could hear her breathing, the beating of her heart, a faint gurgling from her stomach. She did not take her eyes from the screen, but her hand came up gently from where it rested and stroked his head.

"I wish we'd hear from your father," Rose said. "I hope he's all right."

FOR GENERATIONS, the rich boys of the Upper East Side had called the Harte School "the prison" or "the tombs." The nickname had nothing to do with the degree of discipline imposed by the faculty, which was in general lenient; it referred, rather, to the blackened, doomed aspect of the building itself. From where it loomed over the F.D.R. Drive and the East River, the school resembled one of those orphanages which in Victorian novels are the site of unspeakable horrors perpetrated by gaunt, evil mistresses. Its elaborately carved railings and rows of high, thin windows, darkened by soot, suggested beatings, rats, polio in the water. There were rumors that the building exerted an evil influence. An alarming number of car accidents took place on the stretch of the F.D.R. Drive over which it cast its spindly shadows. Most of the residents of the slumbering German neighborhood in which the school stood went out of their way to walk around it, remarking what an eyesore it was. Even the local historical society described it apologetically, in its pamphlet guide to local architecture, as "an unfortunate experiment in Neo-Gothic revivalism."

Given the imposing mythology that the school's architecture engendered, first-time visitors always found it a surprise, perhaps even a disappointment, to discover, as they entered the front doors, that the school's interior was quite ordinary, even pleasant. Carpeted hallways connected the high-ceilinged marble foyer with stairs, elevators, and classrooms. There were bowls of fresh flowers in niches in the stairwells, and a special bathroom with Laura Ashley print wallpaper for the female faculty and visiting mothers. There were no dimly lit garrets, no torn mattresses. Behind the school's spiderweb of wrought-iron grillwork lay small, well-lit classrooms filled with framed prints from the Museum of Modern Art, Apple Macintoshes, and high-resolution videocassette recorders.

It was, in fact, the Harte boys themselves who took the greatest pleasure in "the prison's" hideous façade, and who were responsible for the wild rumors about their school that circulated at Browning, St. Bernard's, and Collegiate. New students — particularly mid-term arrivals whose parents had just moved to the city from Houston or California — were treated to the spurious legend of Jimmy O'Reilly, who had "disappeared" one afternoon in 1959 while cutting gym class, only to be found in the boiler room six months later, his body decomposed and half-eaten by rats. Afterwards, the initiate would be taken on a harrowing tour of the school's labyrinthine basements during which he would be conveniently "lost" in a dark, windowless room below the gymnasium. After a while, if the boy screamed enough, he'd be let free. Halloween at the Harte School was, needless to say, a favorite and calamitous holiday. Boys arrived in class with hatchets buried in their heads, dripping blood, or with a third eye in the middle of their foreheads. Sometimes they terrorized the girls at St. Eustacia down the street, invading their locker rooms dressed as the living dead. The St. Eustacia girls were noted for their obtuseness and cowardice, but they were also, in general, larger and stronger than the Harte boys, and on more than one occasion little Harters came crawling back from these afternoon revels with black eyes, real blood mingling with the ketchup they had poured onto their shirts.

Philip was twelve when Owen started working at Harte. Up until that time he had attended an obscure, modest co-ed school on the West Side. When Owen took the job at the much more expensive and prestigious Harte, it was as much for Philip's sake as for his own; indeed, the waiving of his son's tuition was one of the chief lures with which the Harte administration drew Owen. But Philip hated Harte. He complained to Rose that he didn't fit in there, that the boys called him names and gave him funny looks. He found their tough, rich-boy cockiness scary, the way they stood in clusters on the stairs in their expensive sweaters and trenchcoats, smoking and hitting each other on the shoulders. They called one another by their last names, and some of those names were famous, recognizable. To make matters worse, Philip had not yet entered puberty and was scrawnier and younger-looking than most of the robust Harte boys. Of course, he realized later, a lot of his contempt and fear had to do with the fact that their camaraderie, their genial physicalness with one another (and his exclusion from it) generated in him such intense erotic longings. From the distance of the teased, Philip fell in love first with Sam Shaeffer, then with Jim Steinmetz and Christian Sullivan, though he never admitted it. Soon he could not bear it anymore. At Christmas break, he told his parents he wouldn't go back. When they asked him what he intended to do instead, he produced a folder of catalogues from other city schools and announced that he had chosen a co-educational academy on the West Side which resembled a giant television set and which was noted for its progressive educational methods. His friend Gerard was already going there and he loved it. Then Owen asked Philip where he expected the money to come from, and Philip's eyes widened, his lower lip shook.

"Owen!" Rose said then. "Can't you see how miserable he is? My God, all year he's been foundering. If Harte's not right for him, it's just not right for him. I'll pay his tuition, for God's sake, I'll take on extra freelancing, but it's not fair of you to make him stay there just so your reputation doesn't get hurt!"

Owen didn't answer her. The truth, although he wasn't about to admit it, was that the Harte School inspired in him the same fear and self-doubt that made Philip so desperately want to leave it. He felt isolated from the faculty, who were all rheumatic old men, intense young women from Seven Sisters colleges, effusive, aging homosexuals. (Owen never connected himself with this third group.) The parents, whom as director of admissions he was required to face and console daily, treated him with an almost imperceptible noblesse oblige, as if his status as a member of the underclass, a Jew, a servant, was something to be taken for granted.

He decided that if he could not achieve his own liberation from Harte, the least he could do was abet Philip's. The next fall, with Owen's sanction, Philip began at Riverside Preparatory Academy, from which he graduated, four years later, with highest honors. In fact, Owen paid most of the tuition; he wasn't about to let Rose kill herself with the extra freelancing. At Philip's graduation, he stood with Rose and watched as his son, full-grown and handsome now, took his diploma and with what seemed to Owen uncharacteristic exuberance threw an overblown, Eva Peron–style kiss to the world at large. He hoped that someday Philip would recognize how he had loved him — quietly, and from a distance — and appreciate all the unspoken ways in which his father, from behind the scenes and without ever making overt claims, had watched and sympathized and protected him, and perhaps made his life better. But the love of a silent father, he knew from experience, was hard to appreciate, even for the most empathetic son. The truth was, he was afraid that if he got too close to his son, things might rub off on Philip — things he preferred not to name. Thus the distance between them grew rather than shrank, as Philip got older. There was no tension, no suppressed anxiety; there was just miles and miles of nothing. And that was as it should be. For if they had been closer, then, if Philip ever found out the truth about Owen, he'd have interpreted his father's affection as something sick, something perverse. But if there was no overt affection, if he stayed at a distance — well, then what could Philip accuse him of? Only of staying at a distance. And there was nothing ignoble in that.

Owen remained at Harte for years, far longer than he'd intended. Because he received more parents than any other administrator, he was given an office that was slightly larger and better-situated than those of his coworkers. He had a new oak desk and three windows, and a whole wall where diplomas (including his Ph.D., prominently displayed at the principal's request) hung alongside pristine black-and-white photographs of Harte boys hard at work in a chemistry lab, laughing on the playground, looking up at a teacher, their eyes misty with knowledge. These photographs, mounted on thick styrofoam and handsomely framed, were extremely well posed fakes. The chemistry lab in question had never taken place. The photographer had set up the beakers and titration tubes in an arrangement she considered aesthetic and said to the boys, "Okay, now look fascinated. That's right. Good." They had done so obediently. If Upper East Side children knew anything at all, it was how to simulate pleasure for pictures. And though he was often tempted, Owen never revealed this tiny fraud to the parents who huddled over his desk, begging him to divulge their sons' chances at admission. Instead, he took out lists and statistical charts that showed how many Ivy League colleges would accept their sons, and what wonderful grades they would make at them, and what law firms and advertising firms and investment banking firms would employ them, should they be lucky enough to be among the select few admitted to Harte. The parents scrutinized the statistics, nodded. Usually he did not have to sell too hard. It was the parents who had to sell, and sometimes the children themselves. "I realize Greg's S.S.A.T. scores aren't the greatest, but he's got so much imagination and energy," mothers told him. "He started reading very young. He's always saying the wittiest things to company." Fathers boasted about their sons' intuitive know-how, the entrepreneurial instincts they displayed in starting businesses to deliver videotapes from the local rental shop to other residents of the building. The boys themselves arrived in his office well scrubbed and well trained. "Why do I want to go to the Harte School?" they would ask, carefully repeating Owen's question in order to give themselves time to remember. "Because I believe its combination of tradition and innovation in educational methodology would be consonant with my personal ethical system."

Hundreds of them passed through Owen's office; sat across from him, cowed and intimidated in their stiff black suits. Owen, himself dressed in a stiff black suit, sometimes had to fight the impulse to laugh at the ridiculousness of his position; that he, a grown man with a Ph.D. in comparative literature, was being paid to frighten little boys. Usually he flashed a smile to console them after the first five minutes. Sometimes he remained stern and watched their shoulders tighten. It was easy to cut past the spiel their parents had prepared for them. He liked to get them talking about what they liked, whether it was the Hardy Boys or chess tournaments or Twisted Sister. Some of them had long hair they had clearly refused to cut. Others had no instinct for rebellion and seemed eager to follow in the footsteps of their parents, to become exactly what would make everyone in their families most relieved and happy. Those were the boys Owen liked the least.

Sometimes he wondered what all those parents would think of him if they knew the truth about him. Already, when their sons were accepted, their attitude imperceptibly changed. Their original smugness returned, and they treated him with the same patronizing glibness that they lavished upon the faculty; now that they had gotten what they needed from him, there was no need to kowtow to this middle-class Jew. Sitting in his office across from a scared little boy, the door closed, he often pondered the implicit sexuality of the interview, which was somewhere between a rape and a seduction. The candidate was obliged to make himself as attractive as possible to the interviewer; the interviewer was expected to terrorize and dominate the candidate. If they found out about him, Owen quickly decided, the Harte parents would demand his resignation immediately, figuring that if he hadn't already, it was only a matter of time before he went off the deep end and started taking advantage of their desperate little boys, many of whom had been promised cars and computers if they got into Harte and might have done just about anything to get them. Which was doubly ironic, since Owen was not in the least attracted to boys and had little sympathy for men who were. His own taste ran to very masculine men with chiselled faces and hairy chests, although it was something of a joke to claim he had any "taste" in men at all. He knew which images on a screen or in a magazine excited him; that was all. None of it seemed to have much to do with reality, with the possible exception of Winston Penn, the new English teacher, whose blond hair and strong-jawed face and wire-rimmed glasses had more than once found their way into Owen's masturbatory second life. He liked Winston Penn, liked his slow, careful voice, liked his sweater-vests and bow ties. But he could never approach Winston Penn, except as a colleague. He had learned early on, in prep school, how much it hurt to grow close to men who would never return that closeness.

It was now ten-thirty on a Tuesday night, and Owen was sitting in his office, in the dark, alone, fingering a very creased piece of paper the numbers on which had long since been worn past legibility. No matter; he had them memorized. The scrap was a totem. Earlier this evening he had delivered to a group of prospective Harte parents a speech so familiar to him that he joked to Rose he could give it on automatic pilot. As he talked, his mind moved in other directions, in circles, endlessly recombining the two sets of seven digits and their letter equivalents, creating anagrams, creating a language.

The man was named Alex Melchor, and he was going to save Owen's life — that is, if Owen could only get up the nerve to call back. He had been sitting now for forty-five minutes, his hand cradling the black receiver, which was already slick with sweat.

Occasionally panic seized him. He would get up and pace the room, his mind gripped by a sense of the madness and danger of what he was doing so potent it could have been something he had only just conceived, not lived with for years. On his desk, pictures of Rose and Philip stared up at him with an almost pornographic intensity. Periodically he would sit down again at his desk, calmly dial the number (though his hands were shaking), then press down the two nubs on top of the phone with terrible violence and hold them there, to make sure he had actually cut the call off. His office was purgatory, a middle ground where rest was impossible. He knew he could not leave until he had made the call he could not bring himself to make. And yet, as the night wore on, he wondered, if he didn't make the call, which would be stronger: the feeling of relief at having resisted temptation and evaded potential danger, or the feeling of pain as he walked through the dark, empty streets of the Eighties toward the subway, the longing to touch and be touched by another man beginning again its wail inside of him. That longing pulsed stronger in him tonight than it had for years. He must make the call, he told himself. It was no longer a matter of choice. He must make the call, and for the first time in his life speak of these things, and he would not leave this room until he'd done it.

But what if this Alex Melchor wasn't home? Then the ersatz ringing in the phone's heart would go on and on, and no human voice would interrupt it. He could walk all the way home easily, propelled by the beat of a heart pounding in his chest, then decelerating, easing. No one could accuse him of cowardice, of not trying. (No one but himself.) He would wash his hands, and sit down in his favorite chair, and read, and eat a piece of Rose's apple cake. Or would he? He remembered Alex Melchor's voice, shaky with breath as he whispered in the dark theatre: "Please. I can't do it here. Can't we go somewhere else?" — words so unexpected, so unlikely in a place like that, so surprisingly tender. He was in love with Alex Melchor, with all he knew of him, his underwear and his voice and his telephone number, and as fiercely as fear pulled him away from the telephone, desire pushed him toward it. Hope had stolen into his life just as he was growing comfortable with despair. And why now? He didn't want hope. He didn't believe in hope. He didn't even think he needed hope. Yet he was in its grip.

He was imagining things that would have been unimaginable to him just a year ago, a month ago. It was the same fantasy that had carried him through prep school, only recast to fit his current life and shrunken expectations. Over the years, as it gained in intensity, Owen's desire had become less and less specific; now what was growing in him was simple, undifferentiated need. The man no longer had to have dark curly hair, or be over six feet tall; it no longer had to be perfect, enviable love of the sort that bloomed in the movies of his adolescence. All he wanted was a man to make love with — fully, exhaustingly, more than once — and perhaps a little companionship. And yet, even that was as impossible now as it had been then. He had a job, a wife, a son. Perhaps he could have pulled it off if he were younger and less established; but it seemed to him that each year he lived as a hypocrite, his identity as a family man, a husband, a professional hardened in the minds of those around him, not to mention those he loved. For twenty-seven years, after all, he had been Rose's husband; he held her fate like a hand grenade. To break out of that mold now — well, he would lose his job. He would lose Rose. He would lose Philip. And still he knew he would not leave this office until he had dialled that number, spoken to that voice; that if not tonight, he would come back tomorrow night, and the next night. It was out of his hands now.

So he sat there, his heart pounding, and the phone squatted shamelessly before him, offering to unlock for him the secret safe at its heart for which the seven long-memorized digits of Alex Melchor's phone number were the combination.

He picked up the phone. He dialled in a kind of delirium, and it was only when he was finished, and the ringing started, that he came to consciousness and realized what he had done so easily, and that there was no turning back. He could hang up, but he wasn't going to. He would let it ring five times. One. Two. Three.

There was a clicking noise. He took in his breath. A crash sounded. "Oh shit!" a male voice said. He heard music in the background — he couldn't recognize exactly what. For some unknown reason, relief flooded him. His pulse slackened. He wanted to laugh.

"Sorry, I dropped the phone. Hello?" The voice was raspy, slightly effeminate.

"Is this Alex Melchor?" Owen said. He was bent over in his chair, his feet tucked under his buttocks, smiling broadly and holding back laughter.

"No, just a second, I'll get him. Oh, who's calling?"

"You can tell him my name is Owen Benjamin. But he won't recognize it." He could hear the voice that said these words distinctly, although it seemed to have nothing to do with him.

"Okay, just a second. Al-ex! He's in the kitchen, hold on a minute."

It was Vivaldi. *The Four Seasons.* Owen closed his eyes and concentrated on the birdsong of the violin, the tiny pips of music as the bow darted back and forth. He tried to think of birds in trees in parks in summer, as his music appreciation teacher had taught him to do in fourth grade. Birds in trees in parks in summer. He had never forgotten that. Strange, he thought, how things come back. Things are not lost.

More crashing. Then the music was obliterated by a hand over the phone.

"Hello, Alex Melchor," said a new voice, this one deeper, more threatening. Some sort of muffling noise sounded. Owen, frozen, couldn't identify it. For a few seconds, he said nothing, expecting his other voice, the confident voice, to take over, but it had run off, leaving him high and dry and alone. Strings broke on a violin somewhere.

"Alex," he said. "This is Owen Benjamin. Owen. Oh — you don't know my name, do you? But you — we — met — you gave me your name and number and said I should call you, I should give you a call."

There. That was fine. That sounded fine.

"I did *what*?" the voice said. The muffling noise continued. Food. He was eating. And Owen thought, Don't destroy me, please, don't destroy me.

"You left it for me. Your name. You said to call."

"Um — Owen — I don't *think* so," Alex Melchor said. "Are you sure it was my name, and my number? That you didn't dial wrong?"

"Yes. Work and home." Owen repeated the numbers.

"Those are right. I'm sorry, but I really can't recall giving you this note. Where did I supposedly do it?"

Owen stammered, strangled. "A theatre," he said.

"At the theatre!"

"Yes."

"What show? I was at the theatre twice last week. We saw *Tango Argentino* and that new Sondheim thing — "

"No, no — not *the* theatre — *a* theatre."

"A movie theatre?"

Owen faltered. "Yes."

"Well, which one?" He sounded impatient.

"The Bijou," Owen said. He closed his eyes.

"Did you say the Bijou?"

"Yes."

Alex Melchor started to laugh. Hard. Loud. "Then, honey, that note must be pretty old, because I haven't been in that dump for ten years! Are you someone from my deep dark past?" he asked. "Hey, Leo! My deep dark past is on the phone!"

Owen was close to tears. "I'm sorry, there must be a mistake. I'm sorry. Something's wrong." He gritted his teeth, prepared to slam down the receiver.

"Hold on," Alex Melchor said. "Don't hang up. I'm curious about this. Now, you're saying that someone at a porno theatre gave you my name and number? Needless to say, I'm very curious to know who this person was."

"No. It was a mistake. I'm sorry."

"Don't hang up! You sound upset. What did you say your name was, Bowen? Listen, Bowen, don't mind me, my shrink tells me fifty thousand times a day my bark is worse than my bite. Now calm down. Just calm down."

"It's Owen," Owen said. "Owen, not Bowen." He laughed a little. Who would have the nerve to name a kid Bowen? he wondered. His voice shook. His throat seemed to constrict. But he did not hang up.

"Now, Owen, can you describe the man who gave you my number?"

"It was dark."

"It certainly was," Alex Melchor murmured.

"Anyway, I told you. I think it was a mistake. After he left, I found the note on his chair."

"You found the note on the — " There was a moment of silence. "Oh my God!" Alex Melchor said. "What day was this?"

"Sunday."

Suddenly the voice on the other end of the phone burst into a fit of hysterical laughter. "It was Bob Haber!" he said. "Hey, Leo!" he called away from the phone. "Guess who's been hanging out at the Bijou! Bob Haber!"

"I knew it. I knew it," Leo said in the background.

"Forgive me for leaving you on the hook like that," Alex Melchor said. "I think I've figured out the answer to this dilemma. You see, I gave my number and name to this actor named Bob Haber. He's an old college friend of Leo's — that's my lover — and I met him at this dinner party. I'm an agent, you see, and he had a lot of — well, to be perfectly honest, I liked his looks. So I gave him my number and told him to give me a call and we'd have lunch. That was on Saturday. And on Sunday — "

"It fell out of his pocket. I know."

"So the mystery's solved."

"Yes. I'm sorry to have — "

"Oh, don't worry. I'm sorry too. I mean, Owen, you sound like a very nice guy. But I am sort of married to Leo. And Bob Haber — well, I wouldn't recommend him to you. He's a real closet case."

"Sure," Owen said, and wanted to say, "Tell me, show me. Invite me to dinner. Introduce me to Bob Haber. Save me." But he did not.

"Goodbye," he said.

"Bye now." Then Alex Melchor hung up the phone.

Owen fell back in his chair. He could feel his heartbeat, a tiny persistent pulsing in his forehead. Sweat trickled down and dried under his arms. Through his half-closed eyes, he saw that it was past eleven. He realized, quite suddenly, that he had been breathing through his mouth. His throat was dry, his lips chapped to the point of bleeding.

He went into the bathroom. It was a classic boys' school bathroom, with a big trough instead of urinals and three tiny toilets for the first-graders. At one of a row of white enamel sinks he washed his face with a cake of industrial soap. The room smelled strongly of disinfectant. After he had combed his hair, he went back into his office, straightened his desk, put on his coat, and left. It was a cold night out, but windless. He pushed his hands into his coat and started off. The sky was still and clear and full of stars.

For the first twenty blocks he hardly knew what he was feeling. Fragments of the conversation replayed in his head, out of order, along with bits of *The Four Seasons*. Then, around Seventy-second Street, he realized to his great surprise that he did not feel bad. No, not bad at all. To his own shock, he discovered that his hope was still alive — greatly reduced in bulk, it was true, modest and a little ashamed, but there, alive, and fighting fiercely to hold onto him this cold night as he briskly marched downtown. It no longer had a firm grip. It crawled on him, rather, like a baby kangaroo that must struggle blind, in earnest, to find its mother's pouch. Hope breathed choppily but defiantly in Owen, searching for a place to grow again.

He pushed up the collar of his coat and walked faster. His

breath became visible in the dark and cold. He had done it. He had made the call. He had come through it alive, still himself. That mattered more to him than the fact that there had been no note, no last-minute offering. He had set a goal and carried through on it, as his father might have put it to him when he was a child, trying to build a model of a car, a Ford Model-T, and if it hadn't turned out quite perfect — Well, what of it? his father had said. You did your best. I'm proud of you, and you deserve a reward.

Owen did deserve a reward. Right now. So he walked into an all-night newsstand and bought himself a Hershey bar, with almonds.

THE EVENING of Derek Moulthorp's dinner Jerene stood with her foot on the edge of the tub. She was wearing a pale silk slip; below her knees, her legs were half covered with shaving cream.

"Wow," Philip said. "You look — "

"I know, I know," she said. "Don't tell me. It's ridiculous."

"Do you ever cut yourself?" Philip asked. "I cut myself a lot."

"Remember," Jerene said, "I haven't done this in six years."

The scraping noise of the razor against her skin made Philip wince. He sat down on Jerene's cot, being careful not to muss the dark blue wool dress splattered with wildflowers which had been carefully laid out next to him. He gazed at her. Jerene had a date.

She hardly knew what had driven her to the Laura Ashley store. But she had walked in, remembering her mother, the lacy dresses that had been foisted upon her as a little girl and the hand tightening her hair into ringlets. The salesgirl was Pre-Raphaelite, pale. Long blond hair swept her shoulders. If it had been Shescape, if it had been a Saturday night and she had had on her leather jacket, Jerene would have made her move. Thin like a snake, she was good at winding her way through dance floors, getting where she wanted to be. The girl would have been scared at first, then fascinated when Jerene asked, "Have you got a light?"

She said instead, "I'm looking for a dress" — anticipating surprise with a challenge.

The manageress — an older woman in a suit — lowered her ornamental half-glasses to give Jerene a frank, suspicious gaze. There she stood, six feet tall and denim and leather from head to toe, in a low room full of sachets and potpourris and wallpaper patterned with lilacs. The steel-gray manageress stared at her as if she feared Jerene might break something accidentally, or even on purpose. But the pale girl didn't flinch and showed her dress after dress, and when none of them hung right offered a gift of alteration. Her name was Laura (though not Ashley) and she lived with her mother on Park Avenue, and by the end of the afternoon Jerene had her phone number and a tentative drinks date when the dress was ready, in three days. Walking out of the store, she thought of a friend of hers — a gay man from Louisiana — who after coming out to his parents had honored their request for a new photograph by sending them a picture of himself with a girl, a friend of his named Lucy, standing under a broken piñata at a party. A week later they sent him a check for fifty dollars. At first he was shocked, and wanted to call them up, to challenge them. But in fact he was able to use the fifty dollars.

Now every time he needed money, he simply had his picture taken with a different woman friend. If he sent a series with the same girl, the checks got larger.

Jerene wondered what effect a photo of herself in a dress — a Laura Ashley dress — might have on her mother, whose one weakness was lace. Could that be all it would take? Of course she would never do it, although she found herself contemplating such actions often these days, imagining her mother at her door, tears in her eyes, crying, "You're cured!" And once again it seemed strange to her that six years had passed without even the slightest contact. What would her parents think if they received such a picture in the mail? Would it mean anything to them? Would they even recognize her as their daughter?

It seemed to Jerene funny that after all these years of rebellion she was now finding herself thinking so much like her mother. Buying shirts at Macy's one afternoon, she had been shocked to realize how naturally she applied Margaret's standards of taste and quality, the little rules she had been taught for rooting out the good buys from the sales table. A few years earlier she would have rejected that guidance on principle, bought only what her mother would have thought hideous. It was a gesture of political as well as personal rebellion to mock the taste of mothers. For a long time now it had been the fashion among her friends to be as unornamented as possible. Simplicity was sexy, because it was a rejection of male standards of beauty; what was left was something fleet and unadorned, pure form. She had known women in her first days in New York with whispers of beard, pale mustaches which they cultivated, almost as a challenge. Like the preened and oiled men who wore dabs of eyeshadow and had their muscular backs waxed, these women marched shirtless and proud on

Gay Pride Sunday — but of course it was a different kind of pride, one that had more to do with denying sexual attraction than flaunting it. All along, Jerene cheated in small ways. As her mother had taught her, she bleached the small hairs on her upper lip once a month, after which, during the course of a morning or an evening, she would wander around her apartment looking like a child with a milk mustache. No one ever knew but Eliot, who laughed at her for feeling so guilty about it. Jerene dressed every day for years in the jeans and lumberjack shirts that were the only wardrobe possible for a serious lesbian leftist, but anyone with an eye for detail would have noticed that there was embroidery on her sleeves. Now things were changing. These days her friends were wearing pink, wearing maid's uniforms, wearing nose rings. Many wrote stories in their spare times for women's pornographic magazines with names like *Bad Attitude.* Lust, like fashion, they were proclaiming, was a radical woman's prerogative, too — as long as it was *her* lust, her fashion; and over the years since her break with her parents — slow, painful years, years in which she had never let her hair grow thick enough to hide her scalp — she *had* found herself eyeing women in pretty dresses on the street in summer. She was eyeing the women, but she was also eyeing the dresses.

Tonight she had her date with Laura. In the bathroom, she washed the shaving cream from her legs, while Philip and Eliot stared, then slipped the new dress awkwardly over her head.

"Remember," Jerene said, "I haven't done this either for six years."

She stepped out into the hall, and looked in the mirror.

"My God," she said. "I look like a pinhead."

"Earrings," Philip said. "You need earrings."

"Yes. I guess." She turned and rummaged through her drawer, where she found a pair of spikes she wore when she wanted to intimidate one of her professors into giving her an extension on a paper. But these were not right for tonight. She dug some more and found an old pair from high school — two long strings of fired blue beads — and attached them.

"Yes," Eliot said. "Exactly."

They were ready. Philip stood in front of the mirror, playing with the knot of his bow tie. "I can't believe I'm finally going to get to meet Derek," he said as he put on his coat. "After reading all those books — to finally meet him — it means a lot to me."

"I'm glad you're so excited."

Outside, a light wind blew along the street. The ice from the previous weekend had started to melt, creating an illusion of spring, and Philip felt proud and happy as he walked — proud of Eliot, who looked so handsome, so self-assured in his pink shirt and sweater; also proud of Jerene, proud that he knew this strange, beautiful woman, so surprising-looking that people would turn and stare at her as they passed. From Sixth Avenue, Eliot had turned them onto Thirteenth Street, where dark trees shone in the blue haze of the streetlamps, and the subtle neon of a basement restaurant occasionally shone below the brick townhouses. They walked up steps to a dark walnut door with a brass knocker. The house was indistinguishable from the row of elegant brownstones in which it stood — boxy, many-windowed, hairy with vines. "Well," Jerene said, "this is where I say goodbye."

"Where's your date?" Philip asked.

"Café Luxembourg, if you can believe it." She shrugged her shoulders, cast her eyes to heaven, and Eliot bent to kiss her goodbye. "Good luck, honey," he said. She waved and disappeared down the street.

Eliot lifted the knocker and let it drop, then pulling keys from his pocket, clicked one easily into the door. They walked into a foyer, and beyond it into a living room illuminated by firelight.

"Hello, Geoffrey," Eliot said.

"Eliot!" A red-cheeked man emerged from the dark, holding out his arms in greeting. He was roughly pear-shaped, and wore the loose clothes of a father — a yellow cardigan sweater over an Oxford shirt, simple brown slacks, a macraméd belt that appeared to be left over from a child's arts-and-crafts class. "And you must be — " he said, clasping one of Philip's hands in both of his.

"Philip," Philip said.

"Philip, of course!" said Geoffrey. "We've certainly heard about you."

"You have?" Philip grinned.

"Oh yes," Geoffrey said. He leaned closer, as if to deliver a confidence, and Philip saw that the palest of blond beards covered his cheeks, so pale it was practically invisible. Geoffrey's eyes were small but bright, like a hunting dog's, and they held Philip in a reassuring stare. But there was no confidence to be given. "Let me introduce you to our other guest," Geoffrey said, and led them into the living room, where a sinewy man in blue jeans leaned against the wall, nervously shuffling through a book of Etruscan vase-paintings. "This is John Malcolmson, a noted gay journalist," Geoffrey said, and the man put down the book and looked at Philip briefly. "I'm sure you've read John's columns in the *Voice*."

"Certainly," Philip said. "They're terrific."

"John, Philip is an editor — right?"

Philip nodded.

"Good. Now, if you'll excuse me, I have to see to the muffins."

He had only soft backless slippers on over his socks, and the soles flopped noisily as he padded across the wooden floor and out of the room.

The three of them stood there.

"Where's Derek?" Eliot asked.

"In the kitchen," said John. "He's preparing one of his color meals. Blue tonight. Can I get you a drink?"

He was looking at Philip. He had an inscrutable, acne-scarred face and wore around his neck a single strand of black leather, like a noose. "Just a glass of white wine," Philip said. He was only now beginning to make out the shapes and the colors of the room. To his pleasure, what appeared to be an original colorplate illustration of Tintin, the French boy reporter, and his dog, Milou, hung over the fireplace. There were other pictures as well — Babar and Celeste, Curious George, Maurice Sendak's wild things — all signed originals inscribed with loving dedications to Derek. Then there were the clocks — at least twenty of them, including a gold-painted cuckoo from which a smiling mermaid occasionally emerged. A zooful of noises announced the half-hour — chirps, roars, barks, meows, and whinnies, along with an assortment of cuckoos, clucks, and clacks. Astonished by this concert, Philip looked at Eliot, who smiled, lit a cigarette, and blew a stream of smoke into Tintin's face. Beyond the dark living room and the lighted foyer, an ivory-colored staircase glowed.

"This is a great house," Philip said to Eliot. "It's hard for me to imagine growing up here."

"Oh, in a few days you'd get used to it. It's no different from any other house."

"How can you say that?" Philip asked, his voice rising slightly. "To have grown up here — it must have been wonderful." But before Eliot could answer him, John was back from the bar and handing Philip a small glass of wine. "So what kind of editor are you?"

"Romance novels. Or, as they're called in the trade, bodice-rippers."

"Aha," John said. "Those certainly are popular. I have a friend who's writing gay ones. What do you think those will be called? Codpiece rippers?"

Philip let out a spurt of laughter. "Maybe," he said. The stem of the glass he held was elaborately fluted; unconsciously he stroked its indentations. Then a flapping sound announced Geoffrey's return. "The muffins are perfect," he said, "just perfect." He grinned at Philip. His face, though now somewhat bloated, had clearly once been handsome; beneath the puffiness Philip could see the outlines of high-arched cheekbones, a square jaw.

The clocks ticked. A stray cuckoo let out an attenuated cluck, and Geoffrey said, "I knew I forgot to wind that one." Then he turned to Philip. "Why don't you come and meet Derek now? He's refusing to leave the stove tonight."

Gulping, Philip looked at Eliot, who motioned him to go on. "Yes, I'd like to. Excuse me," he said to John.

"Sure, sure," John said. He walked across the room and poured himself another glass of wine. Geoffrey took Philip's arm in his firm grip and led him into the kitchen — a vast room, gleaming and metallic, where a huge man presided over pots of varicolored blue paste.

"Derek," Geoffrey said, "this is Eliot's friend Philip."

Derek turned from the stove. He was at least six foot five; wild ringlets of gray hair fell over his forehead, which was damp with steam. He wiped his hands on his apron, said in a clipped British accent, "Philip, it's a pleasure," and offered a hand that was huge and hairy, but shook Philip's with extraordinary care — the handshake of a strongman who, if he wasn't careful, might crush the fingers of a child to dust. Philip smiled. "Boy," he said, "you're really cooking up a storm."

"Oh, don't think we do blue every day. Only for the most special company. Now this," he said, pointing to one of the pots, "is mashed potatoes."

"Is it dyed?"

"Oh, heavens, no. I just added some ripe plum skins. You'll be surprised by the flavor. Very — " He smiled, looking for the proper descriptive flourish. "Nouvelle Californienne."

"Sounds great," Philip said. "What's in the other pots?"

"Oh, let's see. That's blueberry sauce for the duck, and that's a Roquefort sauce for the pasta, and there, on the counter, that's blueberry butter for the muffins, which are Geoffrey's specialty."

"I am the family baker," Geoffrey said. He was leaning against the counter, kicking it occasionally.

"It's really a pleasure to meet you," Philip said to Derek, remembering the introduction he had rehearsed last night in bed. "I don't know if Eliot told you, but your books — well, I was practically raised reading them. In fact, my mother was your copy editor. At Motherwell."

"Well, isn't that a coincidence," Derek said.

"Oh yes," said Philip. "She started me reading them. They really meant a lot to me." He laughed, looked away. "But I suppose you hear that from everyone, don't you?"

Derek turned from the stove and smiled warmly at Philip. "Well, nonetheless, that's very sweet of you," he said. "Geoffrey, why don't you go get Philip a copy of the new book?"

Geoffrey nodded yes, and whistling, walked out of the room. "A new book?" Philip asked.

"Yes. Not one of my best, I fear. But that's really up to you to judge. At this point I just crank them out when the bank account becomes depleted, and my public demands."

Philip was surprised by this revelation. "What's it called?" he asked.

"*Archie and Gumba*," Derek said. "Archie is a child whose parents are anthropologists of the twenty-second century, sent out to check up on a planetary colony which has been left completely isolated for two hundred years, as an experiment. The people on the planet have developed a quasi-technological, quasi–Stone Age culture; that's what the book's really about — the culture. Gumba's a little girl Archie befriends."

Geoffrey returned, waving a small green book in his hand. "Are you going to sign it?" he asked.

"Of course, of course." Taking the book from Geoffrey, Derek leaned over the kitchen counter. "Let's see." He chewed on his pen, then scribbled something fast, closed the book, and handed it to Philip. On the cover was an illustration of two children with pots on their heads maneuvering their way through a space-age, alien-ridden bazaar.

"Thank you," Philip said. "I can't tell you how much I'm looking forward to reading it."

"Oh, don't bother to read it," Derek said. "So where's Eliot, anyway? Eliot!"

"Coming," Eliot called from the living room.

"Would you like to see some old pictures of Eliot?" Geoffrey asked. He led Philip across the kitchen to a large corkboard covered with snapshots. Philip immediately recognized Eliot, with hair down to his shoulders and black plastic-rimmed glasses, in what must have been a high-school graduation picture. His eyes scanned the board, settling on a snapshot of Derek and Geoffrey, much younger. Geoffrey had indeed been handsome in his youth; shirtless in the picture, his short wheaten hair wind-blown, he stood smiling next to Derek, who was dressed in a heavy sweater, stooped, gangly. Between them, Eliot, a little boy in a sailor shirt and no pants, leaped and grinned on a sandy terrain. "That was taken on the Lido in Venice," Geoffrey said. "Eliot was five."

"He was very cute," Philip said. Above the photo was another of Geoffrey, in a black suit and tie, his hair crewcut. It looked like a professional head shot for an actor. And above that, Derek, wild- (and at that point, black-) haired Derek, lifting a tiny, joyful Eliot into the air. He reminded Philip of the selfish giant (or was it the sleeping giant?) — that gargantuan who lived in a walled garden and was terrifying to all but one wise and innocent child. And who, after all, had invented that giant but stoop-shouldered, seven-foot-tall Oscar Wilde, himself so ungainly in his massive velvet suits?

There was one more photograph — an old discolored Ko-dachrome of Derek and Geoffrey seated around a table lit with red-net candles. Between them sat a thin, balding man with a broad smile and a girl with red hair, high cheekbones darkened by shadow, dark red lips. Her eyes had caught the light of the flashbulb and seemed to glow gold-green. "Are those Eliot's parents?" Philip asked, and Geoffrey nodded. "That was taken a year before they died."

Now Eliot and John stepped into the kitchen, and the room was suddenly filled with the commerce of greeting. Derek hugged Eliot. "You're just in time for one of my horrendous blue meals," he said. "I hope you don't mind."

"He's been making these for years," Eliot called to Philip from inside the warm circle of Derek's arms. "And I've always hated them."

"You never have understood the appeal of the cunning, Eliot." Derek grinned.

"Dinner will be ready any second," Geoffrey said, checking the pots. And Philip, unnoticed for the moment, stole a glance into his copy of *Archie and Gumba:* "To Philip," the dedication read, "if he wants it! With fondest regards, Derek Moulthorp."

At dinner, Philip sat next to Geoffrey and across from Eliot, and stared at the blue food on his plate — duck piled with thick berries, blue muffins, and the plum-flavored mashed potatoes. He avoided the pasta which, cooked, had turned an unappealing gray color. ("Every great experiment has its little failures," Derek apologized.) Every few minutes Geoffrey disappeared into the kitchen, returning with a basket of muffins or another bottle of wine. He was wearing a heavy gold ring which made scraping noises against the silverware as he spooned more potatoes onto Derek's plate, or tipped wine into his glass. Derek was telling a long, rambling story about an Italian poet who liked to make love to his dog. On his deathbed, he had finally "come out," as it were, and declared to a visiting interviewer, "There is nothing closer to divinity than the taste of a dog's tongue." Everyone laughed, and Philip, who as a child had secretly French-kissed his poodle puppy more than once, tried to remember the flavor: alkaline, he thought he recalled, with an aftertaste of metal.

Absorbed in the story he was telling, Derek hardly seemed to notice the muffins being constantly slipped onto his plate, or the fact that his wine and water glasses were never empty. Geoffrey attended to him watchfully, but with a certain stealth, as if his wifely purpose were to efface himself as much as possible, to create the illusion that food sprang from Derek's plate like fruit from a tree.

Derek had lived in Europe for a time, he was saying: in Berlin; in Barcelona; in Paris. He smiled as he told stories of dissolute European homosexuals, dalliances in the Faubourg St.-Germain, transvestite prostitutes who lounged in deck chairs along the big, tree-lined avenues of the Bois-de-Boulogne. "The clubs those days were piss-elegant," he said. "Not like now. But in the fifties, in Europe, elegance was so important to everyone, and to the homosexuals perhaps most of all. It was a way of propping up a shattered ego. They were always impeccable, those Parisian men I knew — even the cab drivers, even Falasha, sitting on her deck chair in the Bois, drenched in Chanel and drinking champagne from a crystal glass."

He leaned back in his chair, smiling. There was the famous French photographer, his dear friend, whom he had once accompanied to Tangiers in search of beautiful brown-skinned little boys. "It's easiest there, you know," he explained, "because the kids are on their own so early, and the parents, if there are any, aren't likely to make much of a ruckus. Also, the children are streetwise; they're sexual from a much earlier age than American or European children because there's nothing to hold them back. They really like it. So I would wait in a café and eventually Roland would come back with some little Mustapha or Hamid and buy him a Coca-Cola for his trouble — among other things." Seeing Philip's stricken face, he added as if in apology: "Of course, Roland never really did anything with the boys. He liked to caress them and sometimes give them baths."

"Oh, I wasn't thinking — "

"Of course. You young men today are *so* puritanical."

He laughed. Once again the wine bottle circled the table. Geoffrey spooned potatoes onto Derek's plate. There was a napkin around his neck, stained various shades of lavender and blue. Everything about Derek was hunched and constricted, even his gesticulations mere jabs at the air, diminished by years of conditioning to a world built simply on the wrong scale. Probably he had once punctuated a remark too emphatically and accidentally hit someone in the face.

Philip was still drinking wine. He was on his fourth glass, and Derek's lilting voice had long since ceased to have meaning for him, blending as musically as it did with the rhythms of the clocks. The wine had made him feel brave, so he turned intimately to Geoffrey, who was watching Derek, as though somehow still riveted by these stories he had probably heard a hundred times before.

"How did you and Derek meet?" Philip asked him, and felt Eliot's head turn.

"Meet!" Geoffrey's mouth opened in surprise, his head lifting from its resting place. "Well, it's quite a story. You see," he said, "I was married at the time."

"They called it *Paris bleu*," Derek was saying.

"Married!"

"Strange but true. To my high-school sweetheart, Adele Marie Probst. Morristown High School. Class of 1950. President and vice-president of the Drama Club, respectively. We moved to

New York, imagining we'd be Bohemians and get onto the stage, but I ended up working as an accountant and Adele was a waitress at the Proud Peacock. I didn't know Derek then. He'd just come back from Europe, you see, and was getting work as a commercial artist, and he was in love with a young Spaniard and was trying to earn enough money to bring him over, sending a little every week and all. And Julia — that's Eliot's mother, though of course she wasn't Eliot's mother then — she was going to marry this Pedro to get him citizenship, then divorce him, and then she and Alan were going to get married — "

"Alan?"

"Eliot's father. They were going to get married because there was no way this Pedro fellow could have stayed otherwise. It was the sort of thing Julia did. Anyway, that's how I met Derek. You see, I wanted to be an actor, but all I could get was night work doing the lights for these odd little East Village things, and Julia was a big actress at one of them. We got to be *intime.* I learned all about Derek and his Spaniard from her, and it was like a radio serial — each night I'd get a chapter. And of course Julia had her own motives for telling me the story. She had — how should I say it? — insight into me. Anyway, eventually she introduced me to this wonderful Derek whom I'd been hearing so much about, and my heart went pitter-patter. I suddenly knew what I wanted. But of course I was married."

" — and he positively insisted, insisted, that he *was* Linda Darnell — What are you two girls whispering about over there, Geoffrey?" Derek called across the table.

"Oh, never mind," Geoffrey scolded, "we're having a nice little private chat." Turning back to Philip, he lifted his wine glass and winked. "Well anyway," he said, "Derek's little Spaniard got into a brawl at the local cantina, and then he went off to jail and that was the last anyone heard of *him*. Julia and Alan went ahead and got married, and we were both at their wedding. Derek was the best man, but he might as well have been the maid of honor, the way he was dressed. We saw each other all the time after that, because we liked each other — just as friends. He was living on the top floor of a walk-up, and Anaïs Nin of all people lived across the fire escape from him — I could tell you stories about that! But I'm off the point. One thing led to another, and I started — experimenting. Not with Derek, of course; that was too close to home. Just with men I met. And finally there was a Cuban boy named Hector who phoned up Adele in a jealous rage and told her everything." He sighed. "The next thing I knew she was back in Morristown."

"What happened after that?"

"Well, I was a free man," Geoffrey said. "And once Derek knew it — it was only a matter of time. He knew I loved him."

"How old were you?"

"Oh let's see. It was 'fifty-five, so I must have been — twenty-three, twenty-four? And Derek was probably twenty-eight."

"I was twenty-seven, Geoffrey."

"Forgive me!" Geoffrey cast his eyes at the ceiling.

"That's an amazing story," Philip said. "But Eliot never told me his parents had introduced you." (Once again he felt Eliot's head turn.)

"Introduced us, nurtured us, carried love notes. Even supported us for a while when Derek was finishing *The Frozen Field*. That was after Julia came into her inheritance and began to spend it on her artist friends." Geoffrey laughed. "Their house became a veritable artists' colony — full of Julia and Alan's friends. Special, special people. And little Eliot, just two years old, with hair down to his shoulders, brown as a nut, a little Cupid running naked on the beach. Julia was still breast-feeding him, I think." He took another sip of wine. "Julia," he said, wiping his mouth with a napkin. "Julia. I remember — "

"You know, Derek," Eliot said loudly, "Jerene's had a really extraordinary twist in her dissertation. I think it would interest you a lot. She's come upon this story that could be the plot of one of your novels."

"Really," Derek said. "Tell me."

He told Derek the saga of the twins and their invented language. "Fascinating," Derek said. "I actually once started a novel on a subject like that — a brother and sister who invent a secret code between themselves and then suddenly start getting messages in the code through their television set. But it never came to pass." Sighing, he shook his head, and returned to his monologue.

"So how was it when Eliot came to live with you?"

"Oh," Geoffrey said, "it was very hard. It was terrible. But there it was. They were dead. We were the guardians." He leaned back in his chair, stretching his arms behind his head. "Eliot was such an amazing little boy. Brave, in his own way, when things were scary. It actually helped us. That's why we bought this house. Because we felt that we owed it to Julia and Alan to raise him the way they would have, even if we couldn't really afford it at the time."

"Geoffrey," Philip asked quietly, "I hope you don't mind my asking you this, but — how did they die?"

Geoffrey's eyes widened. "You don't know?" he said, and Philip shook his head.

"It's not very extraordinary," Geoffrey said. He was looking over Philip's head at one of the clocks, as if to make sure it was running properly. "After a party," he said. "They were driving home. Someone was drunk, but it was never clear who, or which car." He closed his eyes, opened them again. "And then," he said, "we were parents. I remember when we took Eliot to school the first day, to register him. I'll never forget the look on that woman's face when she asked, 'Father's name?' and I said, 'Which one?'"

"You know," Eliot now called from across the table, "that I just love being talked about as if I wasn't here."

"Oh dear, I'm sorry, Eliot," Geoffrey said. "Philip's just curious, and it is quite a story. So many things," he went on, ignoring Eliot's stare from the other end of the table, "were easier in the Village. We had quite a house in those days. People in and out all the time, sleeping on the living room couch. Never any shortage of friends for Eliot. Why, Anaïs Nin bounced him on her knee, Djuna Barnes read him bedtime stories, e. e. cummings played trucks with him. Even Mr. Malcolmson here. He used to babysit for Eliot all the time, stay with him when Derek and I were away." He wagged his wine glass across the table at John, who smiled, and Philip felt his mouth go dry.

"Yes," John said, leaning back in his chair and looking up at the chandelier, "Eliot and I did have fun."

The night before, Philip had conceived, in advance, a vision of this evening at Derek and Geoffrey's. In this vision of the dinner, the party engaged in dialogue so graceful it seemed to have been choreographed or scripted; food appeared in silver dishes, and was eaten delicately; and afterwards — Derek and Geoffrey having shown Philip their world, and Philip having drunk his fill of it — Philip showed them *his* world, took them out to a bar, or dancing. At first, of course, they were resistant to the glittering splendors of New York nightlife; but soon enough they lost their inhibitions and had a wonderful time, and were grateful to him.

Now they sat in Derek Moulthrop's living room, drinking coffee, and John Malcolmson, whom Philip had not counted on, explained why in his opinion Philip's was a generation of greedy cowards, without principle, and why, for him, the world had practically ended in 1977. And Philip, in response, recounted how, coming back, the gay alumni at his college were moved to tears by the sight of a thousand pink balloons released into the sky, and all the eager-eyed young people cheering loudly in pink triangle T-shirts. "Balloons," John Malcolmson said, sinking resignedly into the velvet couch, "what are balloons? I'm talking about revolution — real revolution. We gave you the chance to take over, and look what you did instead — just slid right inside the status quo."

That was Philip's opportunity. "I don't think that's entirely fair, John," he said. "Because in certain ways, things have changed — for the better. For instance, there's a bar in the East Village, called Boy Bar, that Eliot and I like a lot, and I think if you went there it would change your mind. It's a friendly place, very social, a place where people go who really are comfortable with being gay, and know it's a lot more than a matter of who you sleep with. In fact — well, I'd like to take you there, to show you gay men my age who are actually very decent and principled, and who I think you'd approve of."

"A bar!" John said. "Do you know how long it's been since I've been to a bar?" He laughed, and leaned closer to Philip. "In my day, we had bars compared to which — but never mind." He took another gulp from his coffee mug. "For three years I've been completely celibate, not even a kiss," he said, "and so far — God willing — no symptoms. But the other day, I was out for dinner with my friend Jake, and I ran out of water, and when he offered me some of his, I said, 'Jake, you think after three years of celibacy I'm going to risk getting AIDS from a water glass?' Me, I said that. Me." He looked away.

"Well, John," Philip said, "it seems to me the time has come for you to take a look at the world. Right, Eliot?"

Eliot, standing at the other side of the room, was suspiciously attentive. "Boy Bar?" he said. "Philip, I really don't think — "

"And maybe Derek and Geoffrey as well?"

Hearing his name, Derek turned warily. "What?" he said. "What's Boy Bar?"

"I don't think you'd like it," Eliot said.

But Geoffrey said, "I think it would be fun. I'll tell you what, John — I'll go if you go."

John looked skeptical. Derek shook his head no.

"Come on, you old lug," Geoffrey said, kicking him. "You have to get out sometime. We'll go," he said to Philip.

Clearly miserable at the prospect, Derek stirred his coffee. Finally he sighed defeat. "I'll just go change my shoes," he said and disappeared up the stairs. When he returned, he was wearing green high-top sneakers. His feet looked about size thirteen.

There was a hurried gathering of coats, a few last-minute expressions of doubt from Derek — "I'm not sure about this. I think I'm too old, and anyway I never did like bars. Boy Bar! We're not boys. What if they won't let us in?" Eliot, meanwhile, would not look at Philip, seemed to be simmering in silent rage.

"Don't worry," Philip said. "Allen Ginsberg goes there all the time."

"Allen Ginsberg!" Derek huffed.

They were out the door now, on Thirteenth Street, heading east. The night was brisker than earlier, but even in the windy weather a lot of people were out in the world, walking fast, grabbing the last hours of fall. Soon enough Philip and Eliot, quicker in their stride than the others, were half a block ahead. "That was a wonderful evening," Philip said.

"I'm glad you enjoyed yourself."

"Thank you for inviting me. Eliot?" Philip asked. "Have you ever been to a gay place, a bar or anything like that, with Derek and Geoffrey before?"

"Not in New York. In Provincetown once."

"Then I guess this is a first for you too."

"Yes." He did not sound happy about it.

They turned downtown, then east again, onto St. Mark's Place, where a teenage girl in serious punk garb said, "Excuse me, can you give me some money to buy drugs?" Philip looked blithely over her head and walked on. "Faggots," she shouted, spitting out the word, and he visibly flinched. "Hey, you faggots, you want to suck my cock?"

"Shut up, bitch!" John Malcolmson shouted, turning around, and the girl's arms dropped to her sides. She looked suddenly like what she — was a fourteen-year-old girl — and seemed about to cry. Then she raised her fist. "Yeah?" she shouted. "Yeah?"

Ignoring her, John turned and walked, along with the others, through the glass-doored entrance of Boy Bar. The door swung shut behind them, blocking out street noise, engulfing them in the gentle monotones of Philip Glass. "Hello, Eliot," the shellacked-haired bouncer said. He smiled vacantly. "Fancy running into you at a place like this."

"Hi," Eliot said. "Jesus Christ, John," he murmured as they traversed the long corridor into the bar, "she was just a kid!"

"So this is Boy Bar," Derek said, and gave the room a critical sweep. In the bar's dark interior stood clusters of young, young men, some with carefully manicured, dyed, trimmed hair, some in yellow shirts patterned with Art Deco–style toothpaste ads, white socks, and slinky patent-leather shoes, some in gray T-shirts and sweatpants. All small, streamlined, tidy. Derek stood a head taller than most of the crowd. He slouched more than ever, his huge hands hanging by his sides.

"I'd like to show you upstairs," Philip said.

"What?" Derek said, bending down farther. "I can't hear you up here."

"I said, I'd like to show you the room upstairs. Eliot, why don't we go upstairs?"

But Eliot had wandered away and was talking to some people Philip didn't recognize.

"Maybe we should wait for Eliot and *then* go upstairs," Philip said.

"I feel extremely old," John said. He pulled the collar of his jacket up over his jowls.

"Me too," Derek said.

"Me three," Geoffrey said.

"Oh, don't be silly."

"Is there a back room in this place?" John asked.

"Here? Oh no, nothing like that!"

"Well, times *have* changed," John said, and he and Derek and Geoffrey harrumphed with laughter. Again Philip looked over his shoulder. Now Eliot was talking to just one man — a tall blond with a braided ponytail snaking down his neck. Philip searched the room for familiar faces, someone to whom he might introduce Derek, but although it seemed to him that any of the young men in the room could have been his friends, none of them were, and so he turned once again to Derek, John, and Geoffrey, who stood in a judgmental triumvirate against the wall, and asked them, "Well, what do you think?"

"Fun," Derek said. "Definitely fun."

"Oh yes, I agree."

"Fine. Fine."

"Different from what you expected, John, isn't it?" Philip said, but John had gone off to get a drink.

Across the room Eliot was still in the throes of conversation, and Philip tried to think of a way of insinuating himself into his little group. Then, just as he was about to excuse himself, a voice behind him said, "Philip?"

He turned around and saw a darkly handsome, oddly familiar face. Philip's lips parted as he groped for a name, and the man grabbed his hand and said, "Philip, good to see you, buddy. Alex Kamarov. You know, Dmitri's brother."

"Alex!" Philip said, his voice sputtering with relief. "Of course. At first I couldn't place you. But now — "

"Sure, sure!" Alex said. "It's been a while." They shook hands. "I'm living in New York now," Alex said. "Just moved."

"Really, how great! What are you doing?"

"I'm working over at Rockefeller University. You know, in a lab."

"Oh, great," Philip said. "That's just great."

They were still shaking hands, and so they stopped abruptly. "Hey, I hear from Dmitri a lot," Alex said. "He asks about you, asks if I've run into you."

"Oh yeah? How's he doing?"

"Oh, he's doing just great. You know Dmitri. Right now he's taking a semester off; he's doing his tour of Europe thing. I gave him my old *Spartacus* guide as a going-away present, and I gather it's come in pretty useful, if you know what I mean."

"I'm sure, knowing Dmitri, he's made a lot of friends," Philip said.

"Yeah, that's for sure," Alex said. "The latest is this guy in Florence, someone he met in the men's room at the train station. He sent me a postcard all about it. It was a close-up of the David's cock with lipstick smeared around it. Anyway, now it's Matteo. Before, there was Ernst, Jean-Christophe, Nils. He's really running a one-man diplomatic route there."

"Yes, it certainly sounds that way."

They laughed for a good few seconds. "And you," Alex said, "how are you doing? Enjoying the fruits of New York?" He looked around the bar suggestively.

"Well, I've been seeing someone for a while now," Philip said. "I'll introduce you to him." But when he looked where Eliot had been standing, Eliot wasn't there.

"I don't understand this," Philip said. "He was there a second ago."

"Philip," Geoffrey said, "I think we're going to be going now. It's been fun, but it's a little past our bedtimes."

"Oh, really? That's too bad," Philip said. "Oh, Alex, I'd like you to meet Derek, Geoffrey, John." Once again his eyes roamed the room.

"Pleased to meet you," Alex said, shaking their hands.

"Have you seen Eliot?" Philip asked.

"He's upstairs," Derek said. "We just said our goodbyes to him. But as I said, we really do have to be going."

"Oh, sure."

"Well, it's been a pleasure, my dear," Geoffrey said. "Perhaps we'll meet again sometime." He bent over, kissed him wetly on the cheek; Philip held back from wiping away the wet imprint.

"Goodbye."

A few seconds passed. "Who were *they?*" Alex asked, laughing a little.

Philip grimaced. "Just — " He faltered. "Believe it or not," he said, "they are my in-laws."

"Uh-huh," Alex said, drumming his foot on the floor.

"Have you ever heard of Derek Moulthorp?" Philip asked.

"Derek who?"

"Derek Moulthorp," Philip said. "He's a famous children's book writer."

"No, I can't say I have."

"Too bad," Philip said. "He was the tall one. He's really great — a great writer, I mean."

"Yeah, I'm sure." Alex was staring resolutely into the dark. "Listen, Philip," he said, "I just made eye contact with this hunk I've been cruising all night, and I think I'd better make my move while it's still hot. But it was great seeing you." Once again he was shaking Philip's hand. "And I'll give your regards to Dmitri."

"Yes," Philip said, imagining the letter Alex would write: "I think one of these old guys was his boyfriend." Again, he grimaced. "Tell him to call me."

"Will do," Alex said.

And he was gone.

Alone again, Philip moved upstairs; the crowd was thinning out, he noticed. Eliot stood leaning against a wall, his eyes closed, drinking Perrier water.

"I lost you," Philip said.

"Yes, well — I was talking to some people and we ended up here."

Philip looked away. "Are you ready to go, or do you want to stay a while?" he asked.

"No, I'll go."

He finished his Perrier in one gulp; then they headed down the stairs and out the door.

Once on the street, they walked south, toward Eliot's apartment. They did not speak, and they did not hold hands. Occasionally Eliot's shoulder brushed Philip's, but it was casual, accidental — not like the first night they had made this walk, when every brush, every touch might have been a planned endeavor. Now, for some reason, Eliot seemed far-off in his small round glasses, like someone viewed through the wrong end of a telescope.

They crossed Second Avenue, and Eliot said, "You know, if you'd wanted to know about my parents, you could have asked me. You didn't have to get it from Geoffrey."

They did not stop walking. "I didn't mean to upset you," Philip said. "It was just conversation."

"It was a conversation I would have preferred not to have had to listen to. I don't enjoy having my life held up to public scrutiny, even if it is by Geoffrey."

"Eliot, it wasn't public scrutiny. It was just me wanting to know about your childhood. What could Geoffrey ever say that would make you feel that way? Geoffrey loves you very — "

"Don't tell me about Geoffrey," Eliot said. "I *know* Geoffrey. I'm talking about what *you* did to *me.*"

"I'm sorry," Philip said hotly. "I didn't mean to hurt your feelings."

"Don't patronize me."

"Well, I don't know what you want from me. You say I should have asked you instead of them, but you never gave me a chance. You made it very clear earlier you weren't about to talk about — "

"*I* have the right to be private about what I wish to be private about." Eliot was almost shouting, walking very fast.

Philip was silent for a moment. "Eliot, I'm sorry," he said. "I really am sorry."

They stopped suddenly, and Eliot shook his head, and sighed loudly. Finally he looked up at Philip and said, "I don't mean to throw a hundred things at you at once, but I really do have to tell you that I am having doubts about our relationship."

Philip buried his hands in his pockets. "What?" he said.

"Just that," Eliot said. "Doubts. Your need is frightening to me, Philip. Those nights we spent apart, all the way across the city I could feel your anxiety. Miles away you were clinging, you wouldn't let go."

Philip looked at the ground before him. Weren't pain and worry supposed to be private things? he wondered, affronted that he was not even allowed to suffer in silence. But he was too embarrassed to be angry.

"I'm sorry," he said. "I'm sorry that you think that. But I think I really love you, and I just get very scared." He looked up at Eliot, who had audibly caught back his breath for a second. It was a desperate move, saying those words, but he hadn't expected this from Eliot: at least not so soon.

They continued to walk, more slowly, and Eliot said, "What are you scared of, Philip?"

"Of having this conversation." His voice was trembling a little. "I've dreaded it so much. I've tried so hard to avoid it. I thought that my loving you — I thought it could keep it from happening."

"But, Philip," Eliot said, "that's been the problem, don't you see? You don't trust yourself enough to trust *us*. So I can't help but wonder, has it really been me you've been loving? Do you even really know me, know anything about me?"

"What do you mean?"

"I mean, sometimes it seems to me you haven't gotten to know me at all. You haven't even tried."

For a moment Philip just stared, astonished, into the intricate weave of Eliot's sweater. Then he turned clumsily. "I have to go home," he said, and began marching very fast toward Second Avenue.

"Philip. Philip, stop."

He stopped.

"What are you doing?"

"I'm going home."

"Why are you going home?" Eliot turned him to face him.

"Goddamnit," he said, "to say that to me — how dare you say that to me! It's just not fair of you to — "

"What's not fair?"

He frowned. "It's just — all right, maybe I *didn't* see you, maybe I *don't* really know you. But is that all my fault? Whenever I try to ask you anything, you just clam up or get mad. If I don't know you, it's because you won't let me know you."

Eliot laughed — a brief snort Philip had never heard before. "You know it's not that simple," he said.

"Then how is it?"

Eliot took a long breath, turned away from him. "I'm sorry," he said, "but the fact is, from the very start, this thing has been you and yourself, and I've just been a mannequin; I've been an emblem of the sort of person you could imagine loving, not a person you loved. I haven't hidden myself from you, Philip. But you have to learn to ask the right questions in the right way if you expect to get answers." He ground his fists into his pockets. "This is hard for me to say," he said. "But it's the way it is. You say you're in love with me, but clearly you don't know anything about being in love, because this is nothing — "

"Stop," Philip said. "Stop."

Once again, Eliot turned and looked at him. He was standing there, silent against a wall, his eyes closed.

"Philip."

"I don't know how true what you say is, but you have no right to tell me I didn't love you. I have felt it — here." And he punched his own heart, hard, like a paramedic trying to restart a life. "You can tell me I'm selfish. You can tell me I'm childish and self-involved and unaware sometimes. But you cannot tell me that what I feel isn't real. That's going too far."

Eliot looked at the ground before him. "I'm sorry," he said. "You're right. It is going too far."

"All right."

He turned and began walking.

"Where are you going?" Eliot called.

"Home," Philip said.

"Stop," Eliot said.

He stopped. Eliot walked up to him. "Philip," he said. He turned him around, arms on his shoulders. "It's late. Do you really want to go home by yourself now, in the cold?" He smiled, and his hands took Philip's face, one hand on each cheek. His hands were warm and sure against Philip's cold face, like the

Kamarov brothers that distant graduation Sunday, holding him in against danger. Or so it felt. Why, why did he have to do this? Philip wondered. Why now, when he needed so much to hate him, did Eliot have to be kind?

"I'm sorry I brought it up this way," he said. "I was just angry. Look, let's go home."

Philip was suspicious. "What about tomorrow?"

"Tomorrow is tomorrow. Tonight I want you to stay with me."

He tried to look down, but Eliot held his face up and would not let it wander. "You tell me I've been terrible to you, you tell me I haven't loved you, I've just used you, and now, suddenly, you want me to spend the night with you? I don't understand this."

"Look, I said what I wanted to say, what I had to say, because it's been on my mind, it's been bothering me," Eliot said. "I care about you. Would someone who cares about you as much as I do let you make that huge trip home, on the subway, at this hour? By yourself?" He moved his face closer to Philip's, so close that Philip could feel his breath. "I want to be with you tonight," he said. "Don't you believe me?"

He smiled again, even more sweetly. Philip looked at Eliot's sweater, at their feet facing each other on the mottled sidewalk, at the Indian restaurants still lit up at this late hour. There was nothing Eliot had said that didn't make sense to him, that didn't have the frightening resonance of truth. Yet when he imagined storming off, saw himself waiting forty minutes on the cold subway platform riding the rattling train miles uptown to the small, dark room where nothing awaited him, he could not bear it. The prospect of that uptown journey drowned out his desire for showy revenge. It seemed there was to be no dignity for him in any of this.

"I believe you," he said. Then he began to cry, just a little. Smiling, Eliot took him in his arms, held him and rocked him and kissed his forehead the way Philip's mother had kissed it when he was a child with a fever. And Philip let himself burst into a fit of real sobbing and buried his face in Eliot's sweater, murmuring inaudibly, over and over again, "I love you, I love you," until a little wet spot had gathered on the sweater, over Eliot's heart.

"Come on," Eliot said. "Let's go home."

And they began to walk, arm in arm, toward Eliot's apartment.

When they got back, they made love with a sweetness and clarity Philip would always remember, even long after his other memories of Eliot had faded. It seemed to him that in the strange pocket of that single lost night, the simple instinct to take care of someone he had hurt had generated a new feeling in Eliot, one that had nothing to do with the troubled, arguable love he claimed he could no longer abide.

"Eliot," Philip said later, when they were lying quietly in the dark, listening to the traffic, "I think I'm going to go and shave."

"Wouldn't you rather wait till morning?"

"No, I think I'll shave now. I feel grimy. It would make it easier for me to sleep."

"Well, it's up to you. Just be careful not to wake Jerene."

"Okay," Philip said. Naked, he tiptoed past Jerene's cot into the bathroom, and closed the door. He shook the bottle of shaving cream, turned on the tap, and began to splash hot water on his face.

After a few seconds, Eliot came in to pee. Philip listened to the gentle, almost musical tinkling, spread shaving cream on his face, and almost immediately cut himself.

"What are you doing," Eliot said, joining him in front of the mirror.

"I cut myself."

Eliot shook his head crossly. "Clearly you're doing it all wrong. Here, wash off all that shaving cream and let me show you."

Philip complied. "The trick," Eliot said, "is making sure your face is really drenched in good, hot water before you put on the shaving cream. Like this."

The heated, wet slap of Eliot's hand against his face shocked him. "There," Eliot said, satisfied, and spread shaving cream on Philip's cheeks, smoothed it over his upper lip, down below his ears. "You better let me do it," he said, "or you'll cut yourself again." It was true. When he did it himself, Philip always cut himself.

Eliot took the blade and began deftly to drag it down the length of Philip's face. In the blade's wake Philip's cheeks tingled, suddenly smooth, and he remembered distant comic scenes from the TV shows of his childhood, of fathers teaching sons to shave for the first time, awkward laughter, men and boys in flannel pants and T-shirts attacking each other with spray cans of shaving cream. His own father had never shown him how to shave, and he had been too embarrassed to ask. Such awkward bonding was unthinkable with Owen. He had taught himself, in secret, hoping neither his mother nor his father would notice the mistakes, the scabs on his neck and chin, and as a result, he had never really learned the tricks of wetting his face, angling the blade and arching his cheek with his tongue. But now Eliot was teaching him, and he thought how this intimacy — Eliot carefully maneuvering the razor around his chin, washing off the extra shaving cream, patting his face dry; this thrill of smooth, wet skin, shining — this belonged to men who were lovers alone. It seemed to him a kind of celebration.

Afterwards, while Eliot lay sleeping on the futon, Philip sat up, staring out the window. His fingers beat against the hard cotton futon; his leg shook as he counted the minutes till dawn.

THE NIGHT AFTER Philip told them, Rose kept dreaming that she was keeping a vigil outside a hospital room. After she woke up, though, she couldn't remember who was inside the door, dying — only the hazy yellow hospital light at the edge of things, and a child wandering the halls, clutching the decapitated head of a doll. How strange that child looked; she held the smiling, glassy-eyed head by the hair, like Judith with the head of Holofernes. When Rose asked the mother — no face, no hair, just the idea of mother — what happened to the rest of the doll, the mother hissed. "Be quiet. Don't mention it," the mother whispered, "or she'll cry and cry. She'll start crying and she'll never stop."

"Who was the person who was dying? Who was I waiting for?" Rose asked Owen the next morning, when there seemed nothing better to do than talk about dreams. It was drizzly outside their window, and though neither had slept much, they were filled with giddy energy simply from their relief at having made it through the night.

"It was me," Owen said. His eyes were wide and red this morning. "That's obvious."

"And the child?" Rose asked, taking a sip from her coffee cup. "The child?"

"Again, obvious," said Owen, who seemed to have all the answers. "It was Philip."

Into the dark, regular calm of their weeknight life Philip had come, unannounced. "We're watching 'The Jewel and the Crown,'" Rose said. "It's almost over."

"Dad's here?" Philip asked.

"Yes. Be quiet, something important's happening."

He looked at the floor. "Well, I guess there's no getting around it now," he said softly.

Rose was too eager to get back to the television to hear him, or at least, to extract the sense from what he said. He sat with them until the program was over. "Another week," she said. "Will I be able to wait another week?"

Philip unceremoniously snapped off the television. There was a pop and a hiss as the picture shrunk to a tiny nugget of light before disappearing. Rose and Owen looked at him oddly, wondering what had compelled him to turn it off. Then the room filled with an almost tangible silence.

"I have something to say to you," Philip said. "It's very important."

Rose looked up at him, surprised at the seriousness of his tone. His face was blanched, his hands curled into fists. He still hadn't taken his coat off.

"Philip," she said, taking off her glasses. "What is it?"

Philip didn't say anything, just stood there, huffing; finally he took off his coat.

"Do you want to sit down?" Rose said.

"I'd rather stand."

More silence. "Philip," Rose said again. "Is something wrong? Tell us, honey."

"All right," he said. "Here goes." He looked away from them. "I've been meaning to tell you for a long time," he said, "and I haven't gotten around to it, because I guess I've been afraid — "

"Well," Rose said, "what?"

He closed his eyes. "I'm gay," he said. Then again, as if they hadn't heard: "I'm gay." He opened his eyes, looked at them, but their faces were blank. "Does this come as a shock to you? Are you surprised?"

His words ran together very fast. "This isn't something new. I've been out at work and to my friends for a long time now. Just not to you. I don't know why. I guess I've been scared of disappointing you. I wanted to wait until I felt my life was good enough so that I could show it to you and not be ashamed. I wanted to wait until I could show you that a homosexual life could be a good thing." He was suddenly crying a little. Rose kept blinking her eyes, as if she had been sitting in a dark room and the light had just gone on. Owen was hunched over, his shoulders tight in his white shirt, his hands kneading together between his knees. Philip went on talking — about political orthodoxy, personal choice, about the children's book writer Derek Moulthorp (but why?) — then suddenly stopped, took a tissue, and blew his nose.

It all went past Rose. Oh, she was not naïve. She knew homosexuals. There were a number of homosexuals in her office. But up until this moment she had thought about their lives as occasionally and as casually as she thought about the lives of the doormen in the building, whom she passed sometimes and wondered, Where do they live? Do they have families? children? Now, suddenly, it was as if she had been thrown head-first into a distant, distasteful world about which she had little curiosity and toward which she felt a casual, unstated aversion. She blinked.

Does this mean, she wondered, that from now on, every time I read the word "homosexual" in a book, or hear it on the news, I will have to cover my ears?

She thought, suddenly, of AIDS and wanted to cover her ears.

Philip was talking, his eyes frantic, as if he were afraid to stop. "It's not just homosexuality," he was saying. "It's really a question of secrets. I know it must be a shock to you that so much of my life I've had to keep secret from you. I mean, I know all kids keep secrets from their parents. But usually those secrets don't make up such a huge part of their lives. Well, I decided it wasn't fair to any of us. No more secrets. No more." He was looking out the window now, at night traffic and stars. Suddenly he turned, looked at them in challenge, and said, "You know I kept pornography for years in that little suitcase, the one in my closet. I kept it hidden there. Did you know that?"

"No, I didn't," Rose said, taking up the challenge, and suddenly remembered how once she had caught a glimpse of something under his bed — a photograph of naked men, she now vividly remembered it — and had thought little of it, had thought, He must have found that in the garbage; one of his friends must have given it to him as a joke. The memory was vague, insubstantial, but it was the thing that shook her out of numbness. Why hadn't she noticed that detail? She of all people noticed the details.

"Well, now you know," Philip said. He seemed to be having difficulty swallowing. He stared at them, waiting for the worst. But Rose said nothing. Her face was a blank sheet of paper, her mouth closed up into a very small knot.

Then she stood up, her hands corded together, and walked in a small circle.

"Won't you say anything to me?" Philip said.

"I'm not sure what to say."

"Maybe — 'I'm glad you told me.'"

"I'm not sure I'm glad you told me."

"You'd rather I'd kept it secret even longer?"

"We all have secrets, Philip. I have secrets, lots of secrets. Does that mean they should all be revealed?"

"Sometimes it's better to be honest."

"Better for whom?"

He was quiet a moment. "For all of us," he said.

"I wish I could be so sure," Rose said. She fingered a dying flower in a vase on top of the television. "But I am not a woman without prejudices," she said, then thought, Where did that line come from? She wondered for a moment if she had read it in one of her manuscripts.

"Well," she said, "it's too late now. What's said can't be unsaid."

"Do you think you can't love me anymore? Is that it?" Philip asked softly, from the corner chair in which he had taken refuge.

She looked at him, surprised. Why was he saying that? Then it hit her that of course her approval, her "love," was what this was really all about. To reassure him as a mother was supposed to, she saw then, she should march over to him and hug him, but the best she could manage was a bitter little laugh. "Oh, Philip, of course not," she said. "Nothing like that." She turned away. "This is just very new for us. It's something we haven't had to confront before. You've explained yourself very well, but you will — you will have to give us time. Right, Owen?"

From the corner, where he sat crumpled, Owen nodded.

"Time," Rose said. "We just need time. You're right — this *is* news."

She looked out the window at the night clouds, and rubbed her hands together.

"Mother," Philip said.

She didn't answer.

"Mother."

Still she didn't answer. She was close to crying herself.

"So you're not talking to me now, is that it?" Philip said. "Well, that really helps, Mom, let me tell you." Enraged, he clapped his hands together, marched in a furious little circle. "Don't just stand there like that, like I'm not here," he said. "You can't do that."

"Don't tell me what I can and can't do, young man," Rose threw back, turning suddenly. "For God's sake, it is not fair of you to expect me just to take this lightly. To come into my house, thinking you can tell me how to act — well you can't. You've sprung this on us, we didn't ask for it."

She turned around again, her arms tight around her chest.

Philip looked down at the floor. "I'm sorry," he said. "You're right. I'm overreacting."

He sat down, slumped, in the sofa next to his father. Their legs crossed in front of them, they stared blankly ahead of themselves like a pair of glassy-eyed husbands lost in a football game. There was a long silence. Then Philip said, "It's just that it was an ordeal for me to come to you with this. I mean, I've been waiting years now, worrying, wondering. Afraid you might not love me anymore." Rose looked away. He stood again, approached his mother from behind, put an arm on her shoulder. "I just didn't think it was fair for you not to know such an important thing about my life, Mom, for you to miss such an important part of my life."

Her shoulder flinched at the touch of his hand, and he removed it. She laughed, shook her head. "Philip," she said, "there are things I could tell you. Things I've never told a living soul."

"Tell them," Philip said.

"No."

"Why not? I'm prepared."

She turned, looked at Owen slumped on the sofa. "Because I don't believe that just because something's a secret it therefore by definition has to be revealed," Rose said. "Keeping certain secrets secret is important to — the general balance of life, the common utility."

"Maybe," Philip said. "Maybe some things. But why should this be a secret? What I'm saying is, imagine you had to keep your heterosexuality a secret. Never tell anyone when you met Dad that you were in love with him. Never be able to live with him and invite your parents to dinner. It would be hard. It wouldn't be fair."

Rose turned away. "It's not the same," she said.

"Why not?"

She was silent for a moment. Facing the window, she saw the onrushing cars streaming down Second Avenue. "I was raised in a different world from you," she said. "In my day, people cared about more than just self-gratification. There were more important things. You did without for the larger good. You had a family. Nowadays, everyone has to gratify whatever little desire comes into his head, no matter who it hurts. And I'm not just talking about you. I'm talking about everybody, all you young people, out for yourselves. I read the papers. I know what's going on."

"But, Mother," Philip said, "being gay isn't just — gratifying some urge. It's a matter of your life." He slapped his hands

She had no idea what to say, what to do. She didn't think she'd ever seen him cry before. "Owen," she said, faltering, clumsy, "I know this is hard, but really, sweetheart, it'll be okay. He's a good boy. He'll take care of himself. He said so himself; it doesn't have to be the end of the world." But at those words Owen only wept more, louder and louder, as if there was nothing that could console him.

And now, very softly, she thought she heard him say, "It is the end of the world."

"What, honey? What did you say?"

He cried. She heard the percolator bell ring. "Owen, let me get the coffee," Rose said. Cautiously she removed her arm, leaving him hunched on the sofa, went into the kitchen, turned off the percolator. Above her, on a shelf, were the cups, the same white china they'd had for years, the same pots, the same glasses. Every detail of the world was the same. It shouldn't have been.

Rose went back into the living room, and he was gone. "Owen?" she called. "Owen?" but no one answered. Panicked, she hurried into their bedroom and saw that the bathroom door was closed and heard the shower running. The sound of water streaming against tile barely masked the noise of Owen's sobbing.

She sat down on the bed. At its foot were Owen's shoes, the socks neatly balled up and stuffed inside; tomorrow's pants draped neatly over a chair. From behind the bathroom door she could hear him weeping loudly, his breath heaving in guttural wails which rose suddenly to throaty whines. Did he actually think that the sound of a shower running could cover up such a noise? She stood, walked to the bathroom door, cautiously leaned against it. A thin tail of steam was escaping from underneath, like smoke from a pipe. She knocked once. "Owen?" she said, "Owen, please, honey," and tried the knob. He had locked it.

against his sides and looked toward the ceiling. "I mean, what do you want?" he asked. "That I should marry a woman I'm not the least bit sexually attracted to? who makes me feel nothing sexual, just anxiety because I'm feeling nothing sexual? Okay. Say I do. Maybe we *can* have sex once in a while, if I think about men while we're doing it. And maybe she won't notice when I stare at men in the street. But in the long run — think of the wear on that marriage. Is it fair to her, when she could be married to a man who really could love her sexually? And more important, would it be fair to me, when I could be with someone I did love sexually?" He shook his head. "If I were to wake up thirty years from now and look back and see I'd wasted my life — well, it would be awful. Because it's important, Mother. My sexuality, my attraction to men, is the most crucial, most elemental force in my life, and to deny it, to pretend it wasn't there because I was afraid of what people would think — that would be a tragedy."

"Most people," Rose said, "would consider a homosexual life a tragedy — the bars and all." She turned to face him. "What happens when you're my age? It's one thing to do what you want when you're young. But later. To be alone. No family."

"I don't intend to be alone," Philip said. "I intend to be with my lover. And anyway, gay people can have families too. More and more, gay men and lesbians are finding ways of having children, either through adoption — "

"And what kind of life would that be for a child?"

"A fine life," Philip said. "As I was telling you, Derek Moulthrop and his lover raised Eliot, the person I'm seeing now, and he's one of the happiest, most well-adjusted people I know."

Rose stared out the window. "I consider this a tragedy," she said. "I'm sorry, but that's the way it is."

"The tragedy," Philip said, "is that you insist on making it into a tragedy. You're creating your own tragedy; I'm not. I just want to make that clear."

At that, Owen stood up from the sofa. He had been sitting quietly all this time, his hands tented over his temples, his eyes closed, listening. He looked at Rose and Philip, his lower lip trembling a little, as if he was about to speak some revelation. But the impulse passed. He put his hand on his head, and sat down again.

"Were you going to say something, Dad?" Philip asked.

"No, nothing," Owen said. "I don't feel so well all of a sudden. Will you excuse me?"

"Dad," Philip said. "You haven't said anything at all about this. Are you okay?"

"Yes, I'm fine. I'm sorry, son. I mean — I'm sorry I haven't said anything. I think — I think it's o-kay." He pronounced the word oddly, drawing apart the two syllables and giving it great emphasis. "Yes," he said. "O-kay."

Then, suddenly, there were no more words.

"I should probably go," Philip said. "I need to get home." He walked to the closet and pulled out his coat.

"Are you healthy?" Rose said as he was putting it on. She turned to him, her eyes suddenly anguished.

He stopped in mid-sleeve. "Yes," he said. "As far as I know I'm totally healthy."

"I'm only asking," Rose said, "because I read the *Times*, I read those stories, and I — " Her voice broke. "I would hate to see you — "

He smiled, and put his hand on her shoulder. "Mom, don't worry," he said. "I'm fine. Anyway, I have no intention of ever taking any sexual risks. I'll be fine."

She smiled a little bit.

"Can I call you tomorrow?"

"Yes," she said.

"Good."

He kissed her on the cheek.

"Goodbye, Dad," he said. "I hope you're feelin[g]

Owen nodded. But his face was the same col[or] shirt, and as crumpled.

"Mother?" Philip said. "Please try not to be ang[ry]

"I'm not angry with you," Rose said softly. " anything at all — I'm feeling a sadness. A grief. A[s] all being so big on honesty, I just have to say that. [

She looked away.

"Well," he said. "I'm sorry too. But I do thin[k] You'll see. I'll prove it to you. This is nothing to [He moved nervously from one foot to the other. " derful new boyfriend, Mom. I want you to meet maybe this should wait. Anyway, goodbye."

"Goodbye."

Awkwardly, Philip put his hands on his mother's s[houlder] kissed her cheek. He hesitated for a moment before imagining, she supposed, that she still might take arms. That neediness was almost enough to break he[r]

"I'll make some coffee," Rose said to Owen after h[e] She went into the kitchen and started the pot brewing she came out again Owen was weeping quietly into h[is]

She stood against the wall. "Owen," she said. "Ow[en] not answer her. He wept the way the Watergate consp[irators] wept at their trials.

"Owen," she said. He wept and did not answer. Sh[e] his shoulder. His back was tense as a board.

"Oh dear," she said, and closed her eyes.

Then the truth hit her with all the irrevocable force of revelation. She felt for balance against the door.

Just as fast as it had entered her head, she hurled it out, overhand, like a baseball, a fireball, passing miles over the heads of the astonished, silent onlookers.

She moved out of the bedroom, back toward the kitchen; she poured out coffee. It was nearly eleven o'clock, she saw, nearly time for the news. Trembling, she tried to drink the coffee.

She went back into the living room. In the living room she picked the dead flower out of the vase, brushed some dust off a table with her hand; even here she could hear him.

Oh, would he never stop? She sat down with her coffee, tried to ignore it, the wretched wail, the thrumming jets of water.

Then, quite suddenly, the shower was turned off and all she heard was the drip of the faucet. It sounded almost human to her, like the voice of a small child talking to himself.

The
Crane-Child

JERENE FOUND IT BY ACCIDENT. She was working in the library one afternoon — wasting time, really — skimming through indexes of psychoanalytic journals and papers in search of something, anything that would give her a clue, a new grounding, that would illuminate the way out of the mammoth, unruly dissertation in which she was lost. Over a period of seven years its subject had changed a dozen times from child abandonment to the phenomenology of adoption, and onto lost languages, children babbling in their bedrooms. Still her fellowship had been renewed, and would be renewed indefinitely, it seemed, for many of the professors on the philosophy faculty thought her a genius in the raw, a great philosophical mind, while the rest feared she might go off the deep end if they turned her down for money, feared she might come in with a sawed-off shotgun and blow their brains out, like that deranged mathematics graduate student at Stanford. Scanning the index, a little bored, beginning to think about lunch, she read the abstract of a case history that intrigued her. It was in a collection of psychoanalytic papers, shelved in a distant stack. She followed the trail of the call number; took the book from a shelf; read the article quickly the first time, a little anxious, skipping sentences to find the thesis as she had trained herself long ago to do. She read it again, slowly. By the time she was finished she was breathing unevenly, loudly, her foot drumming the dark metal floor of the stacks, her heart pounding.

A baby, a boy, called Michel in the article, was born to a disoriented, possibly retarded teenager, the child of a rape. Until he was about two years old, he lived with his mother in a tenement next to a construction site. Every day she stumbled in and around and out of the apartment, lost in her own madness. She was hardly aware of the child, barely knew how to feed or care for him. The neighbors were alarmed at how Michel screamed, but when they went to knock at the door to ask her to quiet him, often she wasn't there. She would go out at all hours, leaving the child alone, unguarded. Then one day, quite suddenly, the crying stopped. The child did not scream, and he did not scream the next night either. For days there was hardly a sound. Police and social workers were called. They found the child lying on his cot by the window. He was alive and remarkably well, considering how severely he appeared to have been neglected. Quietly he played on his squalid cot, stopping every few seconds to look out the window. His play was unlike any they had ever seen. Looking out the window, he would raise his arms, then jerk them to a halt; stand up on his scrawny legs, then fall; bend and rise. He made strange noises, a kind of screeching in his throat. What was he doing? the social workers wondered. What kind of play could this be?

Then they looked out the window, where some cranes were in operation, lifting girders and beams, stretching out wrecker balls on their single arms. The child was watching the crane nearest the window. As it lifted, he lifted; as it bent, he bent; as its gears screeched, its motor whirred, the child screeched between his teeth, whirred with his tongue.

They took him away. He screamed hysterically and could not be quieted, so desolate was he to be divided from his beloved crane. Years later, Michel was an adolescent, living in a special institution for the mentally handicapped. He moved like a crane, made the noises of a crane, and although the doctors showed him many pictures and toys, he responded only to the pictures of cranes, played only with the toy cranes. Only cranes made him happy. He came to be known as the "crane-child." And the question Jerene kept coming up against, reading the article, was this: What did it sound like? What did it feel like? The language belonged to Michel alone; it was forever lost to her. How wondrous, how grand those cranes must have seemed to Michel, compared to the small and clumsy creatures who surrounded him. For each, in his own way, she believed, finds what it is he must love, and loves it; the window becomes a mirror; whatever it is that we love, that is who we are.

After Jerene photocopied the article, she left the library. There was a brisk wind outdoors; she turned her collar up. Some construction was going on nearby — cranes working, lifting beams to the hardhatted men who swarmed the precarious frame of a rising condominium. The cranes looked like a species of gigantic, long-limbed insect. Transfixed, Jerene approached the make-shift wooden fence that surrounded the construction site. There was a crudely cut peephole in the fence, and through it she stared at the vast pit from which the building would rise, watched the cranes lunge and strain. She stood in the deafening roar of the cranes. In the grinding, the churring, the screeching, in the universe of the cranes, the womb of the cranes, she stood there, eyes open, and listened.

Father
and Son

Pʜɪʟɪᴘ ᴀɴᴅ ᴇʟɪᴏᴛ may have been lovers, but they never got their underwear mixed up. Even if they'd tried, it would have been impossible. Eliot favored loose, soft boxer shorts patterned with things like crowns or roosters, while Philip was almost fetishistically attached to plain white jockey shorts. One of the signs he should have recognized, had he been less blind, less in love, was that Eliot never left any of his clothes at Philip's when he wasn't there. None of his underwear stayed after him in Philip's drawer; none of his shirts and none of his khakis; only a long time later, he discovered a single purple sock, its fringe fantastically garlanded with a pattern of dancing elephants. By that time, Eliot was long gone to Paris.

It happened abruptly. One day, a few days after the dinner at Derek Moulthorp's, Eliot's phone machine came on and didn't go off.

For three days Philip left messages, and Eliot didn't call him back. By the fourth day, the silence on the other end of the phone, when he spoke into it, began to terrify him. He stopped leaving messages, just listened hungrily to Eliot's calm voice on the tape: "If you leave your name and number, Eliot or Jerene will call you back as soon as they can."

When no word came for a week, he left Jerene a note in her mailbox, begging her to meet him at a coffee shop the next afternoon. She was late, but she came. In a back booth, on ugly red vinyl benches patched with industrial tape, they drank coffee for which Philip insisted on paying. Jerene looked as thin and nervous as ever in her black leather jacket and jeans. "I'm glad you got my note," Philip said.

"Yes, I got it."

"It's been a long time. What have you been up to?"

"Well," she said, "the main thing I've been up to is quitting graduate school."

"Really? Why?"

"I just decided it wasn't for me. I realized that I'm not finishing my dissertation because I really don't want to write a dissertation. So I quit. Instead I'm doing other things, better things." She smiled confidently. "I have a job as a bouncer at this dyke bar," she said. "I keep the men out. Isn't that a riot?"

Philip smiled. "After seven years, it must be tough," he said.

She nodded a vigorous no. "It was the easiest thing I ever did in my life. I just said, fuck it, and suddenly all the pressures were gone, totally gone. It's the best thing I could have done. Anyway, I'm much happier now. I have a nice new girlfriend — believe it or not, she's the one who works at Laura Ashley. And I'm volunteering, answering phone calls at the Gay Hotline. I can't tell you what it's like not to have to depend on a library for your sanity. I'm relaxed for the first time in seven years. I can think about my life and not just about that damned dissertation."

Philip smiled. "That's great," he said. Then: "I was afraid you wouldn't come."

She laughed. "Why wouldn't I come, Philip?"

"I don't know. It feels right now like the world's in a conspiracy to isolate me. Or at least Eliot is." He laughed again, and then his lips froze in a parody of a smile, and tears welled in his eyes.

"Philip," Jerene said. "Philip." She put down her coffee cup, rubbed her hands together like an insect. She did not seem able to touch him. "Look," she said. "I know how you feel. I've been let down, too. Anyway, I think Eliot's being a baby. I tell him every day what a child he's being."

Philip blew his nose. "You do?" he said.

Jerene nodded.

"What does he say?"

She looked away. "He says he doesn't want to see you. He says he can't face you."

Philip's eyes widened, and he leaned forward in his seat. "Can't face me!" he said. "Can't face me!" And cried harder.

"Please don't ask me to justify him," Jerene said. "He does this to people. He's done this to other boyfriends. He can be a real bastard at times."

But Philip seemed not to hear her. He was really sobbing now. Across the way, a long-haired woman wearing dark circular glasses, as if inspired by him, began to cry as well.

Then, afterwards, in the midst of the heaves and the tear-mopping: "He owes it to me."

"Owes what to you?" Jerene asked.

Philip stuttered. "He owes it to me — at least to — at least to talk to me."

Jerene took his hand. "Philip," she said, "I know. You should be pissed off. He's being very immature, very irresponsible. He's a very weak person; very few people realize it, but he's very weak. I'm not trying to justify his behavior, nothing like that — just pointing out that weakness in his case makes him cruel."

Philip, in angry tears, said, "You can't just tell me to hate him,

Jerene; it's never that goddamned easy just to decide you hate someone when they're the person you love." He pulled a ragged tissue out of his pocket, blew his nose again. "Tell him he has to talk to me," he said. "He owes it to me."

"I'll tell him, Philip," Jerene said. "But I can't promise it'll do any good. It's like when you haven't paid your phone bill. You just don't pay it and don't pay it. And then you get a letter. And then you get another letter. And still you don't pay it. And then, suddenly, your phone's been disconnected. Well, Eliot is somewhere in the stage just before he gets the first letter. I don't know what good it'll do, but I'll tell him you want to talk to him."

Calmer, Philip said, "Thank you." And across the way, the owl-eyed woman dried her eyes. "Jesus, where are we, Bellevue?" the waitress said to the cook. "Greenwich Village, land of fruits and nuts," he replied, and threw a hamburger patty onto the grill.

They paid their bill and left. Nervously, on the sidewalk, they hugged and parted, walking in opposite directions in the wind. Philip put on a pair of dark glasses he had recently purchased. He felt like one of the betrayed, beaten-down women he saw sometimes walking in his parents' neighborhood, wrapped in pale coats and scarves and with their eyes hidden behind night-black shades, as if all clothing were a bandage to cover unspeakable scars. He thrust his hands in his pockets. He did not want to think. Across the street a dark-haired young man with small glasses, wearing an old black blazer, sat on a bus-stop bench reading a newspaper, and Philip's heart leapt to twice its normal speed. But then he saw the man wasn't Eliot. He didn't even look like Eliot.

After that, Philip went to many parties. He called up everyone he knew, asking about parties. Eliot was never at any of them. He remembered his mother telling him about a divorced couple she knew who, finding themselves at the same party, were able to coordinate their movements so they were never in the same room at the same time. There was an element of graceful coop-eration to their mutual avoidance that impressed Rose. But Philip knew that if he ran into Eliot at a party (and this was unlikely, for Eliot had a talent for prefiguring where Philip was going to be and staying away), he would not be graceful; he would run up to him, grab him around the waist, not let go.

One weeknight, around eleven o'clock, he was sitting with Brad Robinson, an old friend from college, drinking coffee at the Kiev, a twenty-four-hour restaurant that blazed alive after mid-night, like someone on his second wind on late-night Second Avenue. It was indicative of Philip's depressed state that he thought nothing of travelling halfway across the city in the mid-dle of the night just to drink coffee. Now, surrounded by refugees from the East Village nightlife, packed into a down casement that made him look like the pupa of some rare and ridiculous but-terfly, he hugged himself against the chill wind that blew through him every time the door swung open, ate slices of hot babka drowned in cinnamon and butter, and talked about Eliot. The breath of the Indian waitress came in visible clouds as she poured refills of hot coffee for them. Squeezed-out tea bags sweated on saucers. The waitress, who had gloves on, brought more babka, and added figures onto their soiled green bill.

"I suppose what I miss," Philip said, "is the feeling of euphoria he gave me. Real euphoria. Because everything seemed so right, so comfortable, with Eliot. You never had to tell him anything, to embarrass yourself explaining. He always knew, and he always did exactly what you hoped he'd do."

Brad was not impressed. "He's a jerk," he said to Philip. "He thinks he's more than human. You speak of him as if he was such a supersensitive person, but I think he just took advantage of your sensitivity, of the fact that little gestures, things which are nothing to him, can mean a lot to you. And, in return, he receives reverence. But of course, reverence gets boring, or so he says. I know the type. Once they get bored, just like that — they cut everything off."

At twenty-five, Brad, like many of Philip's friends, could still count his lovers on one hand, but believed that density of experience compensated for quantity of experience. He remembered every detail of the seven nights of his life he had spent with his three lovers; indeed, his gift for scrutiny and analysis during as well as after was, he acknowledged, probably one of the reasons most of his "love affairs" hadn't lasted more than a few days. As Sally had often told Philip, people can smell panic a mile away.

"*Was* I too reverent?" Philip asked Brad now. "He always said that if he got sick of me he'd let me know. I guess he did. So I wonder — should I have been more challenging? Tougher? More independent? Should I have played hard-to-get?"

Brad shook his head. He was small, pale-skinned, compact; at twenty-five he still looked fifteen, always got carded at bars and clubs, even during the months he had a pale blond beard. "You could have been any of those things," he told Philip now. "But it's hard with Eliot. He encourages you to be totally dependent on him from the start. He enjoys that. You have to get over his initial impact before you can recognize that he's just another human being, even though he'd like you to think he's some sort of superior alien, some visitor from another planet or something."

Philip took a sip of coffee and looked at his reflection in the breath-warmed restaurant window. "I can't deny anything you say," he said. "I can't pretend that it doesn't make me feel better, in some ways, to hear someone talk who isn't in awe of him. But at the same time, you have to admit, he does have a talent, a huge one. He's a real sensualist, I guess you'd say, in that he knows how to make people feel — not different, exactly, but more intensely than they normally might. He did that for me. I only wish I could describe the intensity of it, the wonder of it — "

But he could not describe it. Eliot's influence was ephemeral; it grew brackish in memory. Already, when Philip visualized their days and nights together, the scenes had a greenish, unreal tint to them, like old film that has sat in a canister too long. They looked as if they were taking place underwater. And as he spoke the word "wonder" — well, he felt nothing now. The memory was fading. Like any samaritan, Philip knew, Eliot's own pleasure demanded that he give pleasure to others; but was that samaritanism, or greed for control? Had Philip been misreading Eliot all along, thinking he wanted nothing but to give? Every sensualist requires an object, after all, just as every magician requires a volunteer from the audience — some tame, trusting creature, full of earnest feeling and unexpected desire, immensely sensitive to his immediate surroundings, in other words, someone nearsighted, nearly blind. Even Philip's fantasies about how Eliot would leave him were blind, part of a private dream. He never thought of Eliot as needing anything.

And what might Eliot have needed? Was it surprise, someone to do something to him for a change, to read his mind, to act on his own secret desires? Perhaps. Yet when his phone machine went on and didn't go off, Philip (of course) assumed Eliot to be walking free, rid of a burden, gratified. How did he know Eliot wasn't in his own way searching as well?

After an hour, Philip and Brad paid their bill and headed out onto the street. Even at this hour, the sidewalk was full of people selling their lives — vast collections of magazines and paperbacks, old clothes, eyeglasses, shoes. They walked among the refuse, uptown a little ways, and Brad, tough and unflaggable as ever in his romantic pursuits, told Philip about Gregg, an actor he was in love with from afar. He wanted one thing in life, and he knew exactly what it was: to find someone he could settle down with, live with forever. Each time Philip saw Brad, it seemed there was another actor, another hope, and though they always disappointed Brad, his spirit never weakened; he never lost faith.

They wavered on the stoop of Brad's building. Brad stood in his trenchcoat one step up, so that he was slightly taller than Philip for once, and looked across the street, his hands in his pockets, his strawlike hair blowing. Philip could see the clouds of his breath as he shuffled from one foot to the other, whistling.

"Well," he said.

"Well."

They were silent for a few seconds, standing there, the outsides of their coats touching. "Around this time of night," Brad said, "I can't help wondering what Gregg's up to. He's just finishing up at the theatre, I guess; taking his curtain call, or changing clothes. Getting ready to go home, or to go for a drink with someone. Sometimes I want to go to the theatre and wait by the entrance until he comes out. But I'm afraid I'd be too scared to say anything, do anything. I'd just hide in the shadows and wait until he was gone down the street." He sighed. "I think I'm in love with him," he said, and Philip wondered if he was giving a hint, if he was letting him down gently.

"Well, then, you should do it," Philip said. "Be brave, Brad.

How do you know he's not just sitting there hoping against hope that when he walks out you'll be waiting for him?" But his heart wasn't in it, and Brad could tell. He shook his head sadly. "Well," he said, "I really have to get going now. I've got to get up early. But it was great seeing you. And bear up, will you, Philip? Call me anytime you need anything."

They hugged and Brad smiled down at Philip. "Anything?" Philip said. "Do you really mean that?" He smiled. It had just popped out of his mouth.

Brad stepped back a bit. "Uh — well," he said. "Pretty much. Well, goodnight." He patted Philip on the shoulder and headed inside.

Philip waited until a good few seconds after the building door had closed to turn away. It was just beginning to occur to him how ridiculous that "anything" must have sounded, how embarrassed he'd be by morning; for the moment, he was just numb.

He wandered down Second Avenue toward Sixth Street, walked down Eliot's block. Across the street from his building he stopped, and counted the floors to Eliot's window. The light was off.

Then he was stumbling down West Tenth Street at three o'clock on a Saturday morning in February. A thin sheet of ice covered much of the sidewalk. Every few minutes he would feel himself slipping and have to grab onto a lamppost to keep from falling over. Other patches of sidewalk were sprinkled with a thick, brown sawdust that somehow managed to break down the ice and leave puddles of dirty water in its place. This water had long ago seeped through his boots, which in the morning would be covered with a thin layer of salty precipitate, and was now soaking through his socks. He had not felt his toes for over an hour. He had no excuse to be wandering the meat-packing district at this late hour, on a freezing cold night. He thought about going to the Anvil, a bar he'd heard a lot about, to watch the legendary master-slave whipping that happened every night there. He thought about checking into the Hide Away Chateau — the motel above the Anvil, shaped like a piece of pie and occupying its own individual island in the middle of the West Side Highway — and renting a room by the hour. He had nowhere else to be. His Week-at-a-Glance was empty. He was expected nowhere for brunch the next day, nowhere for dinner the next evening, and so on into eternity. If it weren't for his job and his parents, he could quite well disappear.

He was heading toward Christopher Street, where streetlamps shined brightly and people seemed still to be out. His gloveless hands were getting numb. Snow was piled on the sidewalks. A cab roared past and nearly splattered him with cold, muddy water. He only barely jumped out of its way, twisting his foot, and went sliding along another icy patch of sidewalk. This time there was nothing to grab onto, and he fell and landed hard on his behind. Cold water seeped through his pants. He cried out in shock, but no one heard. After sitting cross-legged in the wet snow for a few moments, he got up, and stumbled toward a pornographic bookstore incongruously decorated on the outside to resemble a ladies' lunch restaurant, with elaborate latticework and pillars embedded in green walls. Inside, a few men milled around, looking at the plastic-wrapped magazines, and the videocassettes, and the giant veined dildos. His entire backside was soaked. Unsteadily he gave two dollars to a man behind a bulletproof partition. The man, who was wearing a T-shirt with the letters E.T. and a picture of Elizabeth Taylor on it, pushed a button, admitting him through a small turnstile. Instantly he was engulfed in darkness. A smell of urine assailed him. As his eyes adjusted to the dark, he became aware of two or three men standing around him, leaning against walls, caressing prominent erections through their pants. He headed past them into one of the booths. There was a hard wooden bench inside and a small television screen on which a large black penis was fucking a white rump to the sound of jazz music and moans. Philip fell back on the bench, which was sticky. He closed his eyes. Only a few weeks ago he would have been curled with Eliot at this hour, on the futon. In his memory the radiator whistled.

Well, at least here it was warm.

Eliot was really gone. "To Paris," Jerene told him. "Apparently he'd been thinking about it for a while. He was lucky to be able to do it. He flew to Rome, and now I guess he's making his way north. God knows I'd like to take off like that someday."

Since Eliot's departure, Philip had seen a lot of Jerene, a lot of many people he hadn't spoken to for months or even years. Suddenly he was calling Sally from work to make a dinner date. "I'm sorry I've been so out of touch," he said. "I've been busy."

"So I understand," Sally said. "Just let me check my book. Well, I'm free Tuesday the week after next. Is that okay?"

Philip, who had no plans for the rest of his life, said it was fine. Two weeks later, on Tuesday, at a sushi bar on Third Avenue, he was telling once again the story of Eliot's leaving. Sally shook her head in sympathetic agreement with every word he said. "Men are assholes," she concluded. "I could've told you that." She then asked him why he didn't fall in love with Brad Robinson, who was so nice and with whom he would make such a cute couple. Sally's social life still revolved primarily around their friends from college; it was natural she would think of Brad.

Philip tried to explain that he was hoping to branch out in his life.

"I don't see why that should stop you from thinking about Brad," Sally said, "who no matter where he went to college is a super guy, really the best. And I hear he's looking."

Philip thought about it. Brad was all right; Brad was wonderful. But in spite of the blush of lust that had come over him when he was with Brad that night at the Kiev, the thought of sleeping with anyone who wasn't Eliot was still more than he could stomach right now. He feebly explained this to Sally, who shook her head and said, "That'll pass in a week." He was giving up a good thing in Brad, she told him.

Well, he promised Sally, he would think about it. He would give it a try. He called Brad up, nervous, because he remembered the way he had said "anything" that night on his stoop, and they went for a drink at Boy Bar. The actor, Gregg, had taken another lover, Brad explained. They leaned against a wall, and Brad's eye roved the room, which had recently taken on a second identity as an art gallery and was filled with murals depicting the deconstruction of the smiley face. "Perhaps the boy of my dreams is out there somewhere," Brad said. There really was a boy of Brad's dreams. "Is the boy of your dreams out there somewhere, Philip?"

Philip surveyed the crowd, thought of Paris, and weakly shook his head no.

Sometimes, at night, Eliot really was the boy of his dreams. Together they rode a train through lush Alpine hills, past villages as tiny and perfect as those in Advent calendars. There was a smell of ginger in the cold air, a tinkling of chimes. Philip could feel the chugging of the train as it rolled along toward Zurich, toward Venice.

The next weekend Brad's phone rang and rang, and no one answered; Sally went away on business; there were no parties; he could reach no one. He was alone. He considered calling his parents, then changed his mind. Since he had come out to them, they had become more private than ever, avoiding the topic of his sexuality in conversation, rarely phoning him. And (he had to admit) he was probably avoiding them as much as they were avoiding him, for he had counted on Eliot's presence in their living room to justify all he had said to them, to justify his life. Without Eliot, Philip felt his mother looking at him, narrowing her eyes, tapping her foot. She could prove him wrong. And that he couldn't bear.

Bored, he made his way downtown. By midnight he was at the southern tip of Manhattan, where funny little nautical gift shops glinted like the seashells and model ships they sold among the huge towers of commercial and investment banking. He wandered back uptown, and it got colder, and still he could not bear the thought of going home. It seemed appropriate that at the end of the night he should find himself in a booth in the porno shop on Christopher Street, crying. As at the coffee shop with Jerene, no one seemed all that surprised that he was crying. A lot of people apparently came here to cry.

About a half-hour after he arrived, the door opened and a man in his thirties stood in front of Philip. He was wearing blue jeans and a brown leather jacket. "Howdy," he said. Then, throatily: "Are you coming or going?"

Philip, who was sitting with his elbows on his knees, nodded vaguely.

"Mind if I join you?" the man said.

Philip said nothing. The man entered the booth, closed the door, and sat down next to Philip on the little bench.

"Oh baby," he said. Soon his hand was kneading Philip's groin. "Yeah," he said, extracting a tube of K-Y jelly from his jacket, and unzipped Philip's fly. He began to jerk Philip off with one hand and himself with the other. Philip came all over his sweater; the man, more wisely, on the floor; on the screen, the young army private came while being strip-searched by his corporal.

Finished, the man wiped his hands off with a handkerchief, patted Philip on the thigh, and went out. Philip thought he might throw up, so he got up and went toward the door. The light of the bookstore interior blinded him at first. Outside on the street, he had to squint. Dawn was breaking. A surprisingly bright sun rose somewhere above the gray sky. It was like a giant egg that had cracked and was bleeding, yolk and white together, against the clouds.

In Eliot's absence, Philip found himself possessed of an unprecedented, raging libido. Unable to concentrate, acutely sensing his aloneness, he returned to his old habit of buying pornography, and wondered how he'd been able to manage it when he was a teenager, the magazines were so expensive. Every few nights, when he was sitting down to thumb through his magazines, he would find that the images had lost all their potency and then, like a junkie in need of a fix, he would have to head out to find fresh images to fuel his need. He avoided the back booths in the porno shops and the movie theatres only because he didn't trust himself, and because the news about AIDS was so frightening. But he did allow himself to make frequent nocturnal excursions to an Upper West Side bar that was decorated in a plumbing motif and that featured two video screens on which pornographic films were perpetually shown. The repertoire was the same night after night, and soon enough Philip had it memorized. One night — it was March by now, and the first tentative spring buds were cracking through the ice of Central Park — a fight broke out at the bar. It took place somewhere behind where Philip was standing, and he was aware of it only as a lot of shouting and a pushing in the crowd, the ripples of which nearly knocked him off his feet. When a pudgy, bearded man in a suit was carried out, blood dripping from his nose, eyes closed in rage, Philip found himself pressed against the wall and against an affable-looking young man with dark, straight hair, big brown eyes, wire-rimmed glasses very much like Eliot's. "Excuse me," he said.

"It's all right," the young man said. "Do you know what happened?"

"A fight, I guess."

"Jesus."

Philip stood on his toes to see if there were any police.

"I'm Rob," the young man said, and held out his hand to shake.

Surprised, Philip turned and saw that he was still pressed firmly against Rob's blue sweater.

"Philip," Philip said.

They shook hands. "Nice to meet you, Philip."

"Nice to meet you, Rob." Philip laughed.

Rob was a junior at Columbia. His declared major was history, but he was thinking of switching to English. He seemed to Philip to be terribly, terribly young, though in fact he was twenty — only five years younger than Philip himself. They talked some more, amicably, about being an English major, and how Rob's father was pressuring him to go to law school. The chaos that had been touched off by the fight subsided. Muscled men in white T-shirts mopped up the blood and glass. Then Rob just stood there, not moving, glancing at his feet, glancing at Philip, turning away whenever Philip's eyes met his.

"Well, it's getting pretty late," Philip finally said, after they had stood there for five minutes without saying a word.

"Yes," Rob said.

"I should be getting along."

"Yes. I should, too."

"Shall we walk out together?"

He smiled, grateful. "Sure," he said. "Just let me get my coat."

As they waited at the coat check, Philip watched Rob close his eyes once, twice, open them, turn, and say, "If it's not too late for you, would you like to come back with me to my room for some tea or apple juice or something?"

Why had Philip made him go through that? Had he enjoyed withholding the offer that would have been for him so much easier to make? Perhaps. "That would be nice," he said, and relief suffused Rob's face. Philip recognized that for possibly the first time in his life he was the more experienced, the older partner, expected to carry the show. He wasn't at all sure that he could live up to the expectations of a boy who was clearly very inexperienced, maybe even a virgin, who probably wanted to be taught what to do.

They took a cab uptown; Philip paid. Rob's stuffy single room was familiarly messy; there were clothes and underwear tangled among the bedsheets, copies of *Rolling Stone*, crumpled sheets of paper strewn on the floor. "I'm sorry this place is such a wreck," Rob said, frantically picking things up and pulling sheets straight. "I'm usually neater."

"Don't worry," Philip said. He sat down on the regulation college bed underneath a big poster, a variation of a famous *New Yorker* cover, showing Venice from an insider's point of view — there was San Marco, the Lido, Milan, Paris, San Francisco. Rob bustled about, picking things up, throwing things away. Then he disappeared into the hall and emerged a minute later with a hot-pot full of water, which he plugged into an overburdened extension cord. "Were you in Venice?" Philip asked.

"Yes," Rob said, "just this summer. Have you been there?"

"Not since I was a kid."

"Venice is beautiful," Rob said, arranging one tea bag in a Garfield mug, another in a mug sporting a picture of a comically ugly man in jail-stripes; it said underneath the picture, "Mug mug."

"A good friend of mine is in Venice right now," Philip said, although he actually had no idea where in Europe Eliot was at that moment.

"Really," Rob said. He poured the hot water into the mugs. "Here you go," he said, and handed one to Philip. Uncomfortably, he slid onto the bed next to him.

They sat for a few moments drinking tea, and then Philip moved closer to Rob, put an arm around him, put a hand on his knee. Rob was shaking violently. "Are you okay?" Philip asked.

"I think I probably just had a little too much to drink," Rob said. "You know, when it's cold, alcohol thins the blood."

"Lie down on your stomach and I'll give you a backrub," Philip said.

Rob obliged. Philip rubbed his shoulders, pounded his back, untucked his shirt and sweater and reached under to touch warm skin. Rob's shaking subsided. He turned over, and Philip kissed him. Rob hugged back and let out a little gasp.

He was right. He had to take the lead completely. Rob just lay there. When Philip's penis approached his mouth, he took it in, no questions asked. When Philip lifted Rob's hand and placed it where he wanted to be caressed, it caressed in a nervous circle, but never of its own volition. The night wore on toward dawn. Rob was enormously excited, much more excited than Philip himself. Philip thought this to be impolite on his part. In his opinion, when one made love to someone for the first time, one was obliged to exhibit a healthy erection and at least feign great enthusiasm. But he had masturbated twice today and could probably do neither. When Rob came, it was with incredible force. A drop landed on his chin; the rest pooled on his chest. Philip brought himself, by furious and concentrated masturbation, to a climax of sorts about ten minutes later.

"A football player lives next door," Rob whispered just before Philip came. "Try to be quiet."

By the time they had mopped themselves up, Rob was shaking again. "Do you want me to stay or go?" Philip asked.

"Don't go," Rob whispered, his voice edged with panic. "Please don't go."

"I'll stay then," Philip said. He rubbed Rob's back some more, then wrapped himself around him from behind and tried to go to sleep. But Rob was not sleeping. Philip could feel his heart throbbing against him. He was lying awake, astonished, and Philip was moved by the spectacle of this boy, who reminded him so much of himself only a few months ago, the first night he had slept with Eliot and hadn't been able to get to sleep the whole night. And he thought of the Jumblies, the rhyme his mother had taught him as a child, and how Eliot had recited it to him, urging him on toward sleep.

But he could not sleep either. Eyes open, he surveyed this unfamiliar Columbia dorm room where clothes draped over chairs threw bizarre shadows on the wall, where the smell of cigarettes blended with the smell of mildew to create an oddly sweet, oddly nostalgic aroma.

Then dawn was breaking again. He missed the days when he had slept through dawn.

He left an hour or two later, countering Rob's pleas that he stay for breakfast with his own insistent claim that he had work to do. He had slept only two hours, and as soon as he got home, he showered and fell instantly into his bed.

Around three he got up and went out for something to eat, and when he got back he found a message from Rob on his answering machine. He did not return it. There was another message the next day, and another; still he did not answer. The messages stopped. He was a little sorry that they did. At another point in his life, he realized, he might have jumped full-force into a love affair with someone like Rob. But Eliot — or rather, the ghost of Eliot, the shadow — had him by the scruff of the neck and would not let him go, would not disappear. It seemed to him ironic that he should be doing to Rob exactly what Eliot had done to him. The oppressed, once again, became the oppressor. Men were assholes, Sally had assured him, and now, for the first time, regretfully, Philip felt himself sinking into the ranks of men.

Owen, huddled in the dark claustrophobia of his office after eleven, cradled the phone in his lap like a baby, held the receiver tight against his ear, and dialled.

"Hotline," Jerene said. "Can I help you?"

"Uh, hello," Owen said. "I'm calling because — " He broke down. "I need some help," he said very quietly, sobbing, to the alert voice on the other end of the phone. He tried to focus through the tears screening his eyes: night, the dark window, the fifth of bourbon leaning like a tower on his desk.

"It's okay, I'm not going to hang up," Jerene said. "Stay calm now. Just breathe in and out. We don't have to talk until you're good and ready."

Owen followed her instructions; breathed in and out.

"Now tell me how I can help you," Jerene said.

All Owen could get out was, "My son — " Then he started sobbing again.

"Your son," she said. "Go on."

"My son — he told me and his mother that he's — "

"That he's gay?"

"Uh-huh," Owen said.

"And how do you feel about that?" Jerene asked.

"I don't know. I'm confused — very confused — "

"Well," Jerene said, "why don't we start by talking about exactly what's confusing to you?"

"You don't understand," Owen said. "These things — they're very hard for me to talk about. I mean, I've never — " He faltered.

"Listen," Jerene said. "It's okay to talk about them with me. I'm not here to pass judgments, just to offer some help, a little advice. We all need someone to talk to every now and then, don't we? And that's what I'm here for."

"My son — " Owen said. "I've never been enough of a father to him. Always involved in my own life. And I can't help but wonder — "

"If it's your fault?"

"Yes."

"Listen, you shouldn't worry about that," Jerene said. "It's not a question of fault. Your son is what and who he is. That's not going to change. Now the important thing is to make things as good for him as you can."

"But you don't understand," Owen said. "It's not him I'm worried about — it's me."

There was a pause.

"Okay," Jerene said. "Go on."

Owen hung up. He poured some more of the bourbon into his glass and drank it down. A little spilled on his suit. He took a tissue and tried to wipe it off. From the wall, Rose and Philip stared at him, his Ph.D. stared at him, all the posed Harte boys stared at him. He looked at them for a few minutes and then he picked up the phone and dialled again, this time a number he had long since memorized. After one ring, a frantic-sounding man's voice answered.

"Is Alex there?" Owen said.

"Just a second, I'll check," the voice said. "Can I ask who's calling?"

"Bowen," Owen said.

"Hold on."

Owen held his hand before his face, watched for shaking. After a few seconds, Alex Melchor picked up the phone.

"This is Bowen," Owen said.

"Bowen?" Alex Melchor said. "Do I know you?"

"We talked on the phone a while ago," Owen said. "Remember, I thought you'd left me your number? But it all turned out to be a big mix-up."

"Oh right, of course. Well, uh, what can I do for you, Bowen?"

"I was wondering if we could meet, have a drink, maybe," Owen said, his voice shaking. "A lot's been going on in my life. I'm very confused about some things and I just need someone to talk to. We all need someone to talk to sometimes, don't we?"

"Uh — sure. Gee, Bowen," Alex said. "I wish I could help you, but you know I'm awfully busy this week and next week I —"

"It won't take long," Owen said. "Please, even over the phone. My son, you see, he came home last week to tell me and his mother — "

"Bowen, you know, I'm sure this is very hard for you. Listen, have you thought of maybe seeing a shrink? Because it sounds to me like you may need some professional help, certainly better than I can give you, God knows. I've been seeing a shrink myself for twenty years now, and believe me, I'd be loony as a tune if I hadn't — "

"My son, you see, he's a homosexual. And I'm worried that it's my fault. I mean, it's not that I'm a homosexual myself. I am a bisexual. But you see, I've never been enough of a father to him and now I'm scared."

"Bowen, that's very unfortunate, but I really don't know how I can help you. Listen, why don't you call one of those hotline things? They have professional people who can talk to you about things like this — "

"I'm scared," Owen said.

"Listen, I'm looking in the phone book right now. Now stay calm. Here — the Gay Hotline. Bowen? Do you have a pencil? Can you write down the number?"

Owen hung up.

The next number he dialled was Philip's.

"Hello," Philip said. "This is Philip."

"Philip, it's your father."

"I'm afraid I can't come to the phone right now, but if you'll leave me a message when you hear the beep — "

"Fag, fag, fag, your father is a goddamned fag," Owen screamed into the phone.

" — happy to call you back as soon as I can."

"Fag," Owen said morosely.

"Thank you for calling."

"Fag father of fag son," Owen said.

The beep sounded.

Owen hung up.

Rose knew. He knew she knew. But somehow they never talked about it; they must never talk about it. Instead they talked, endlessly and obsessively, about the apartment which, if they didn't buy, they would have to vacate in August. If they didn't buy, there would soon begin an onslaught of prospective buyers, people who were rich enough to displace them. The ultimate shame, Rose felt, would be having to clean up for the arrival of those people. If they had to be out, she wanted it to be before that stage. Every Sunday, now, instead of going their separate ways, she and Owen scanned the "Real Estate" section of the *Times*, and on Wednesdays did the same with the *Voice*. It became apparent early on that they were not going to get anything for under fifteen hundred a month, an unthinkably high price, but one they could just barely manage. More than anything else, the immense downpayment a co-op would require boggled them. They had never owned anything, not even a car.

One Sunday there was an ad which read:

> *Lrg 1-bdrm, lux drmn bldg. Eat-in ktchn w/ DW.*
> *Sthrn expsr. A steal.*

They went in the afternoon to see the place. It was in a tall, dirty building on West Eighty-sixth Street, near Amsterdam. The agent, a small woman with blue fingernails, led them up in the cranky elevator to an old, crumbly apartment with a marble bathtub in the bathroom, no views, and a bedroom the size of Rose's closet. She told them that it was a steal at seventeen hundred a month.

"Now if you're interested," the agent said, "I'll really have to know by this evening, because, needless to say, there's a lot of other people who want into an apartment house like this, a big old-fashioned West Side apartment. These are hard to come by these days. I have a lot of clients who are very interested, but depending on how enthusiastic you folks are, maybe we could arrange something."

They promised to call her if they were still interested.

Outside, in the street, Owen could feel his arms shaking in the sleeves of his coat. It was a cold spring day, windy and bright. By evening there would be rain.

"What are we going to do?" Rose asked.

Without much conviction, Owen said, "Don't worry, honey, we'll find something. You just have to keep looking. Remember you said it took your friend Donna six months to find her place?"

Rose kept her eyes on the ground. "I'm a little scared, frankly," she said.

Owen looked away. "Don't be scared," he said. "Things will work out."

"I don't want to move to Queens," Rose said with sorrow and distaste.

"We won't have to move to Queens. We'll stay right here in Manhattan. Don't worry."

They approached the park, and Rose said, "Owen, are you sure we can't stay where we are? Are you sure?"

"I don't know."

"Have you tried to work out the finances? Let's try to stay, Owen, please? We've got good, long employment histories. We're such good credit risks, I'm sure they'll give us a loan. And maybe we can borrow some money from Gabrielle and Jack, some money from your sister — "

"I don't know," Owen said. His voice cracked. She took his arm as they entered the park, clinging hard to him. A few blocks downtown Yoko Ono was still building Strawberry Fields. Yoko Ono had four or five apartments in the Dakota, Rose had read. Did she really need them all? Couldn't Rose and Owen have just one of them? Or perhaps they deserved to be homeless.

From behind them, swift as a mugger, Philip leapt, a gangly dog in running clothes. Rose screamed. "What's wrong?" Owen shouted.

Out of breath, all arms and long legs, Philip reeled back. "I'm sorry if I scared you," he said. "I was running, and then, all of a sudden, there you were. I had to sprint to catch up with you." He wiped his mouth off on his sleeve, and smiled. He smelled of cold sweat, cotton, grass.

Owen looked around himself. Searching for signs, his eyes found the hill where, even on this cold spring day, men lay shirtless in the sun.

"I'll walk with you a little way," Philip said.

"Yes," Rose said. "Please do."

They headed east. "So where are you guys coming from?" Philip asked.

"We were just looking at an apartment on Eighty-sixth Street," Rose said.

"West Eighty-sixth Street?" Philip said. "Wow, it'd be great if you lived there, you'd be so close to me."

"I don't know," Rose said. "It's expensive."

They passed a playground where a group of black children walked strung together like paper dolls in a chain. "Everyone is so afraid of losing their children these days," Rose said. "So afraid of kidnappers. It's hard for me to imagine what it must be like to be a mother now, scared all the time."

"Or a child," Philip said. "Remember how free you left me when I was a kid? I wandered wherever I wanted, walked alone from Gerard's building, even at night."

"I was stupid," Rose said. "You couldn't do it now with a child. Look at them all. They won't let go of each other."

It was true. All the children in the park were firmly attached to their mothers, or linked together in chains. Rose wondered whose idea the chain was — the children's or the parents' — and decided it would be more like a child to believe that there was safety in numbers. The children, after all, were as scared, if not more so, than their parents. At school, they were being taught songs to "empower" themselves, songs with lyrics like "My body is my body . . ." Rose knew because she was at that moment copy-editing a book of such songs, and its companion volume, a comic book in which Batman taught children what to do if a stranger approached.

Among the frightened children they walked, a family. Philip at least had made it to adulthood. He was safe from kidnapping, from molestation. He could run or walk alone in the park. But of course, survival only meant graduating to other dangers.

"So how's it going, old man?" Owen asked his son, as they neared Fifth Avenue, the museum, the old world.

"Okay," he said. They walked a moment in silence. "I guess there's no point in my keeping this from you. Eliot and I broke up."

"Eliot — " Rose frowned. Then she remembered and fixed her eyes on the ground ahead of her.

"Oh, I'm sorry about that."

"I really wanted you to meet him, see how happy I could be with another man. Now I guess you're probably thinking all sorts of terrible things, like all gay relationships are very transitory and can't last and things like that."

"No, Philip," Rose said. "I wasn't thinking anything of the sort, to be frank."

"Because it isn't true." He looked at the ground. "I don't know about Eliot. I guess he's just afraid of commitment or something. A lot of people are afraid of commitment these days."

"Are you bearing up?" Owen said.

"Yes," Philip said. "But I'm sad all the time."

By now they had reached the East Side, and Rose turned around, as if the border of the park was also the border of their walk together, the border of the common ground between their sides of the city, their opposed lives.

"Well, you're young," she said to Philip, putting a hand on his wet shoulder. "I know it hurts now. But you'll get over it. Trust me."

"I guess," he said. He looked at her, for a moment, a little pleadingly, as if he was hoping she might ask him home for dinner.

"Thanks for walking your old parents through the park," Rose said instead. "We do appreciate it." And she reached out her cheek to be kissed.

"I've missed you," Philip said. "I feel like we hardly see each other anymore. Remember when I used to come home every Sunday night for dinner?"

"Oh, tonight's just leftovers anyway," Rose said, hardly believing how wicked she sounded. "But I'll tell you what. Why don't you plan on coming to dinner next Sunday? Wouldn't that be a good idea, Owen?"

"Oh yes," Owen said. "A great idea."

Philip smiled. "I'd like that," he said. "I'm just sorry I can't bring Eliot. You know, I had dinner with his stepfather, Derek Moulthorp? And I told him you'd copy-edited some of his books. He was very pleased."

"I'm sure he was, dear. A wonderful writer, a wonderful children's writer."

"Goodbye, son," Owen said. He shook Philip's hand. It was a gesture that radiated finalness, as if Philip were going off to Europe, or to war.

But he was only going back to the West Side, to his apartment. "Goodbye," he said. "I'll talk to you during the week."

Then he was running off, away from them, fast, fast, as if he wanted nothing more than to be as far from them as he could.

Owen watched him. He looked handsome in his shorts and too-big T-shirt, fleet. Owen had been tall and gangly too as a young man, and the resemblance pleased him. "You know," he said to Rose as they walked out of the park, "he still runs funny. Remember how we used to worry because he was always walking into things, always loping to the wrong side of the sidewalk?"

"I remember," Rose said.

"We certainly worried a lot about nothing," Owen said. "He looks good, our son. But then again, he's always looked good, in his own way."

"Don't start this," Rose said. "I'm in a rotten mood."

"Do you want a Tofutti?" Owen asked. "Tofutti usually cheers you up."

She shook her head no, silent in her wretchedness, and they walked on; but Owen continued to wave his secret pride in Philip, as if it were a flag only he could see.

R OSE'S OFFICE was a tiny cubicle, one-fourth of a swastika. Carole Schneebaum, with whom she sometimes traded information or had idle conversations through the thin divider, was kitty-corner to her in the swastika, and had been there ten years out of Rose's twenty. The other two cubicles never had the same occupants for more than a few months at a time. Copy editing was not a profession people often thought of as permanent; more and more these days, freelancers took on the bulk of the work, and Rose's job involved assigning books as much as actually editing them. The freelancers on her list drifted in and out of sublets, moved away, went back to graduate school, all of which confirmed Rose's impression that while the world moved on, she and Carole were destined always to stay in the same place, patient and dependable, never changing, never promoted. The publisher, on the rare occasions that he spoke to them, made them feel like national landmarks. Ambition for a better position would have been perceived as unpatriotic. Rose was always getting flowers, and cards that read, "What would we do without you, Rose?" They were needed. Editors called them up on the phone to ask questions about syntax, or because they'd forgotten the code for figuring out the cross street from an avenue address.

Roger Bell had been in the swastika for a year now; a British woman named Penelope with two last names for six months. They were friends of sorts. Roger was tall, with a careful, clipped beard; he worked out at a Nautilus center every morning before work, and arrived puffed up in a tight white T-shirt. Penelope always complimented him on his musculature. She used that word, "musculature." She was glamorous, irritating, with wild pitch-black hair and makeup caked on her cheeks. She had lived most of her life in Indonesia, where her American ex-husband was in the diplomatic corps, and was now in New York "on the run" from the ex-husband. Often she asked Rose to answer her phone for her in order to help her avoid the detectives she was convinced the ex-husband had set on her trail. She dressed in boldly patterned bright red and green Indonesian blouses and skirts with little mirrors embroidered into them, and was willing to talk loudly to anyone about anything, it seemed to Rose, but mostly about her ex-husband. She left him, she said during a lunch, because she had found him in bed one afternoon with three Indonesian prostitutes. "Darryl was nothing if not excessive," she added. To which Roger, in the middle of his Pork Kew, responded with a throaty guffaw that people could hear all the way across the office. Every day at lunch the two of them ate take-out Chinese food at a little table by the coffee machine and talked about their "personal lives" — an expression Rose had always found peculiar; what about life wasn't personal? Occasionally they would whisper in each other's ears, then laugh outrageously. Roger, it seemed, had once aspired to be a chef. Now no one invited him to dinner, he said, because he wouldn't eat anything he hadn't cooked himself. "Everyone gets real mad at me," Rose heard him explain to Penelope. "They decide I'm just a selfish crazy because I criticize their cooking. But the fact is, I *am* a better cook than they are, that's just the way it is. My friend Leonie made a vichyssoise? I'm sorry, it was sacrilegious. My therapist says I have to be honest about this, otherwise I wouldn't be being true to myself. So I don't get invited to dinner a whole lot anymore. So what? I'm too old to lie, too old to pretend about what's important to me." Where they sat in Rose's cubicle, eating modest sandwiches, Rose and Carole looked at each other and raised their eyes to heaven.

One Tuesday in March, Penelope confessed to Roger over lunch that her seventeen-year-old son, Miles, was gay. "I have no problems talking about it," she said. "Nothing like that." It was a little past one, and Rose, in her cubicle with Carole, was just closing her mouth on a bite of sandwich. "Oh, believe me, I was shocked at first," Penelope continued. "But now I've really come to accept it. He has a great boyfriend, very cute, who comes and stays over at the apartment sometimes, and we all have a lot of fun. And it's opened my mind. I mean, I've just never thought about the possibility of being attracted to women before; it just never entered my head. I'm very man-centered, very oriented toward men, you might say, because of my mother, who was married three times and had lots of affairs. I was raised by my mother to appreciate the male physique. But then, with Miles being gay, well, on one level, it gave us something in common, I mean, men, but on another, it made me think — why not women? And I realized I really was attracted to women sometimes, that I was probably in love with my best friend Fanny in comprehensive school. So you could say it's been a mind-expanding experience."

Rose, protected by the thin walls of her cubicle, held the half-eaten sandwich in the air halfway to her mouth, then realizing that that gesture — that ceasing to eat — might give her away to Carole, quickly took another bite. Soft bread and lukewarm tuna salad clotted in her mouth, gagging her. Carole shook her head, silently mouthed, "That woman," and Rose excused herself to go to the bathroom.

In the bathroom, Rose blew her nose and wiped her eyes. She looked at herself in the mirror. She did not look like Penelope. She had a thoughtful child's eyes, high cheekbones, thin lips. All in all a gentle, trustworthy, maternal face, but one, she thought, with an edge of impishness, an edge of sophistication. Her hair was graying, her eyes ringed with shadow. She wondered: Have I ever been attracted to women? then decided the question was absurd, an evasion. She was not Penelope. Penelope's situation was not her situation.

"My situation," Rose said to herself. Unacknowledged, locked inside her imagination, it remained unreal. She was determined to keep it that way. She wanted not to know the truth but to avoid it, to continue as long as possible under the delusion that she might just be imagining things. Like a sleeper whose blanket has fallen away on a cold night, she was always shivering, her eyes clenched shut against the reality of waking. Nothing had changed in her practical, day-to-day life, after all. She still went to work on the same bus, still cooked dinner for Owen, sat with Owen reading in the living room and sometimes watching television. Visibly, their lives were the same.

But it was the invisible that worried her. Did she bear some extra chromosome, she wondered sometimes, some bizarre, deleterious gene, emit some strange pheromone that made men love other men? Looking at herself in the mirror, she tried to see the flaw in her face, the gap between the teeth, tried to recognize herself as evil. Maenad, harpie, castrating bitch. Synonyms assailed her, the endlessly rich vocabulary of what evil women might do to men. When she thought of Penelope's husband, caught in bed with three Indonesian prostitutes, envy flared in her.

Sometimes Rose caught a glimpse of herself in mirrors or reflecting shop windows and didn't recognize herself. She was surprised by what she saw: a face that was startlingly normal, almost not hers, a face that could have belonged to anyone. Now, in the bathroom, she searched for that stranger's face and couldn't find it. Instead her face seemed so inexorably her own it made her choke; staring at herself in the mirror, she was overcome by the claustrophobia of selfhood, a suffocating consciousness of her entrapment in that face in the mirror — complacent, unemotive, ragged with worry, a face that would change, liven, deaden, according to nothing more or less than her own grief or joy, her mind, her will. She rubbed her cheeks, pulled at her eyelids, straightened her mouth into a thin line. Even the act of masking, of molding the face into studied normalness, was a matter of will. But at least she looked normal.

She headed out into the hall. By the copy machine, two editors greeted her with lifted coffee cups: "Hi, Ducky." She nodded to them and kept walking, circling the office with a pretense of purpose. She could not, somehow, sit down. She was remembering how Owen had cried so fiercely that night, and later. And anyway, where had he been, where had he been going every Sunday afternoon for twenty years? He was always silent during sex, never praiseful. Maybe he just hated her. Maybe that was all. She had had her own life, after all, as she reminded herself now, and it had had nothing to do with Owen, that secret life in which she had been so fiercely needed and desired by a man. Owen never knew that across the office, at the other end of a complicated circuit of hallways and doors, was an editor with whom she had had a five-year affair. She and Nick had met often on their lunch hour, and sometimes, when Owen was working late, in the early evenings, taking a room at a big midtown hotel, usually the same room, on the twenty-fifth floor. There was always the smell of room deodorizer and Carpet Fresh and Nick's aftershave in the air, while they made passionate noontime love. But then Nick's wife had gotten sick; it was not cancer. Relieved, he and Nadia had gone off to the Bahamas for two weeks, and when he came back, Nick was sorry, he couldn't anymore, he felt too guilty. Nadia had almost died. He realized how much he loved her. He worried about her finding out, about hurting her. Rose understood. No hard feelings.

All that had ended seven years ago. These days she and Nick nodded at each other in the hall or talked in editorial meetings with a surprisingly genuine casualness in which there was masked neither denial of the past nor particular good feeling. They had both gotten heavier, softer. Different bodies had conducted that affair, which was mostly a matter of bodies anyway — bodies, and the romance of making love at noon in a midtown hotel, then getting dressed, eating something quickly, like a hot dog, heading back (separately, of course) to the office. Nick always put his shirt and tie on before his pants, Rose remembered. She would help him tie his tie, and sometimes reach down in a friendly way between his legs. It had excited her, the sight of him like that, in his shirt and tie, naked from the waist down. These days, occasionally, when she saw him in the hall, she would wonder: What does his body look like now? It was a faint kind of curiosity, not unpleasant at all. It almost moved her.

And perhaps Owen knew. Perhaps he knew, and hated her. Peculiarly, the possibility was a relief to her, since at least it meant it *was* her he was crying for; at least it meant she had had a life, had mattered to him, was something more than an excuse, the victim of his lifelong lie. She was fifty-two years old. Her husband cried all the time, several times in a day, sometimes for no visible reason, and was drinking too much for the first time in his life. Her son — but why was so much of her anger directed at Philip? He was trying as hard as he could with her, called her often, clearly wanted to love her, to help her. Still, she could not look him in the face without wanting to slap him. He had to tell everyone; he had to break open that door in their lives which they would have been far happier having kept shut. Such anger was her right, she thought. Pain gave her the privilege of anger.

In the oncoming dark, around five-thirty, she wandered by Nick's office and lingered outside, looking at the framed book jackets that lined the wall. She did this sometimes, curious, she supposed, to see what he looked like. He was standing by the window, watching night settle like a fine, hovering mist over midtown. He was a tall, soft man who should have been dark, who should have bronzed on islands, but who had instead chosen the pale life (and acquired the pale skin) of the bookworm, the perpetual library-dweller, white skin at odds with his black hair and eyes. Languorously he turned, saw her, smiled. "How's it going, Rose?"

"Fine," she said. "I hadn't seen you for a while, so I just — thought I'd drop by."

They went out for a drink. He told her how one of his sons had won a major award in graphic design at college, how another was starting medical school at Downstate in the fall. There was a daughter somewhere in the background, but she was a problem: drugs, obesity, abortion. He laid out the woes like an agenda for a meeting. The daughter was living in Seattle, in a house so filthy her mother had felt obliged to go out and buy Pine-Sol and Lysol and Ajax — but he didn't want to go into it all here, and poured some more Perrier into his glass.

"How's Nadia's health?" Rose asked.

"Fine, fine. No problems since that first surgery. She asks about you sometimes, by the way." They had met only once, at an office party. Nadia was a kind, smiling woman who had aged faster than Nick, had had to suffer for years looking too old for him.

"And your family?" Nick asked.

Rose shrugged. "Not much to tell," she said. "Philip's still working at the same job. Owen — well, he's depressed a lot of the time. There are some hard things going on."

"Do you want to talk about them?"

Rose smiled tightly, shook her head no.

Afterwards, on the streetcorner outside the bar where they could not have gotten a cab if their lives depended on it, Rose said, "Nick, I just wanted to let you know, I think about you these days. Often. More often than I'd have guessed I would."

He smiled. "I think about you, too," he said. But she knew it for a lie.

Finally they found a cab. She climbed in, gave the driver the address. A triptych of little girls' faces stared at her from above the rearview mirror. Siren, witch, hag, Rose thought, and had a vague recollection of having ridden in this very same cab only a few months before.

At the corner she got out, overtipped the driver, and hurrying back toward where the doorman rubbed his hands together and whistled, caught a glimpse of her face in a store window — the face of a worried, older woman, someone she might pass on the street and feel sorry for, someone, at an easier time in her life, she might have felt grateful not to be.

From the depths of his office, at five o'clock, Owen dialled, listened to ringing.

"Hello, Macho Man, can I help you?"

"I saw your ad in Honcho. I — well — I — I'm interested — "

"Which of the men do you want to talk to?"

He paused.

"Bruce," he said.

"Okay, let me just check — yes, Bruce is available. Now, have you used Macho Man before?"

"No."

"Okay, then I'll just explain how it works. Our rates are thirty-five dollars for the first half-hour, thirty for the second half-hour. You can pay with MasterCard, Visa, or American Express. After you give your card number and your phone number, I'll call Bruce and he'll call you. We pay for all phone charges that way."

Owen took a gulp of bourbon. "Okay," he said. He read out his office phone number. He read out his American Express number.

"Okay, Mr. Benjamin, now I'll just get an approval code on that card number and Bruce will call you back. Is there anything special you want me to tell him?"

"No," Owen said.

"All right, you'll be hearing from him shortly."

Owen hung up, poured more bourbon into his glass. After a few minutes the phone rang.

"Yeah, this is Bruce."

Owen laughed involuntarily. "Hi, Bruce."

"What's your name, cocksucker?"

"Bowen."

"Asslicker. You want to suck my cock?" Bruce said.

Owen took another gulp of bourbon. "Sure," he said.

"You better do better than 'Sure,'" Bruce said. "'Cause I want it bad." He growled. "I'm sitting here in my hardhat, I just got off an asskicking day at the site. I've got on my oldest pair of jeans, my cock is aching, it's so hard inside my jock. My wife won't go near me. I ain't had a piece of ass for weeks. You know how that makes your cock feel?"

"Uh-huh."

"I know you know. So you'll help me out, buddy, won't you?" Bruce said. "You gonna take it out for me?"

"Uh-huh."

"Yeah, that's right. You're taking it out, you're licking it — oh yeah, that feels good, you fairy cocksucker. Better than my wife can do, let me tell you. Yeah, that's right. Suck my thick rod. Suck your hardhat daddy's thick rod."

Owen started to cry.

"Hey," Bruce said, after a moment. "Hey, easy there. What's wrong?"

Owen cried. "Hey, man, chill out," Bruce said. "Are you okay?"

Owen tried to control the sobs heaving through him. He blew his nose, noticed his wedding ring, burst into tears again.

"Are you okay?" Bruce said. "What's going on? Did I do something wrong?"

Owen cried. "I'm sorry," he managed to say. "Go on."

"Hey, I'm sorry. I didn't mean to upset you," Bruce said, and Owen cried.

"Bowen? Bowen?" Bruce said. "Is that your name? Listen, do you want something more vanilla? Do you want me to hang up or what?"

No answer.

"Bowen?" Bruce asked. "Are you sure you're okay?"

Owen hung up.

Philip had just come back from work and was in the shower when the phone started ringing. He leapt out, nearly slipping on the wet floor, terrified in case it was Eliot.

"Philip, it's your father," Owen said, surprising him with the familiarity of his voice. It had been a long time since they had spoken on the phone.

"Dad," Philip said, pulling a towel around himself, "how are you?"

"Fine, fine," Owen said. "I was just sitting here in my office after a day's work and I started thinking — it certainly has been a long time since I called my son. So I thought I'd give you a ring."

"Well, that's great," Philip said, "just great. I'm very happy you decided to." He settled himself uncomfortably into a chair. "So — are you well?" he asked.

"Let's not talk about me," Owen said briskly. "I called to tell you — well, I just wanted you to know, your being gay — is okay by me. I mean, there's nothing wrong with it, is there?"

Was he drunk? Philip sank farther into the chair. He could not be sure if he was drunk. His father never drank much — at least not as far as he knew.

Soapy water dripped from him, like cold sweat, and he realized he had to give an answer. "Well," he said, "as far as I'm concerned, the only thing that's wrong is hiding the truth. That's what I feel."

"Exactly," Owen said. "So I say, bravo."

"Bravo?"

"Yes. Bravo."

He *was* drunk. "Dad," Philip said, "this is a real surprise to me. I mean, it just never occurred to me you might call me like this. I'm very touched, very happy."

"I'm glad," Owen said. "Because that's why I did it."

"It's very important to me to have your approval. It always has been. But do you know — is Mom feeling any better about all of this?"

"Oh, your mother," Owen said, and Philip closed his eyes. "You know your mother. Creature of moods. I'm sure she'll be fine soon."

Philip was quiet a moment. "Yes," he said. "I suppose."

Then there was some sort of confusion on Owen's end of the line — a wet crashing, a gasp. "Dad?" Philip said. "Dad? Are you there? Are you okay?"

"What? Oh, fine, son. Just fine. I just dropped the phone for a second. Now listen — I want you to tell me something. Can you always tell when someone is gay, just right off?"

Philip gulped again. "Well," he said, "I mean — it's hard to say. Sometimes, I guess — "

"How can you tell?"

"Because gay people give off signals to other gay people, I guess — little signals that individually, maybe, aren't noticeable, or aren't noticeable to someone who isn't attuned to picking them up. I mean, it's like they give off a little sexual buzz around men but not around women. Do you see what I mean?" He himself hardly knew what he meant.

"The reason I'm asking," Owen said, "is because there's a young English teacher here — well, to be blunt, I can't tell *what* he is." He laughed strangely. "But he's very charming, very nice, and — well, if he is, you know — gay — I think you might like him."

Philip didn't answer.

"Philip?" Owen said. "Philip? Are you all right? Is that a bad thing of me to say?" His voice suddenly grew much softer. "Oh, I knew it was a mistake," he said. "Forget it, just forget I called."

"No, no," Philip said. "It's just — well, it's just a little bit of a surprise to find myself being fixed up by my father. I'm just a little taken off guard, Dad." He laughed, actually pronouncing the syllables: "Ha-ha."

"I knew it was a mistake," Owen said. "Just forget about it."

"No, Dad, I don't want to forget about it, really," Philip said. "I — I appreciate your thinking of me." He tried to steady his breathing. "What more can you tell me about him?"

"Not much. His name is Winston Penn. He's Southern, I think. Very handsome, charming — that is, at least he seems that way to me. I mean, the women here, they're all crazy about him, but he doesn't seem to have a girlfriend, which is why I wondered — "

"Well, you never can tell."

"No," Owen agreed. "You never can tell."

Again, there was some sort of catastrophe on Owen's end of the line. "Listen, Dad," Philip said, "I really appreciate your thinking of me — but if he isn't gay, it could be embarrassing, very embarrassing, for you as well as me — and anyway, even if he is, if he's so handsome and wonderful, I'm sure he has a boyfriend already."

"You're right," Owen said, still sniffling a little. "Which is why I wouldn't think of doing anything too deliberate. But it doesn't have to be an official date. I was just thinking — maybe I'd invite him to dinner one Sunday, when you come over — well, who knows. I'd like to do this for you. I very much like this young man, and — well, I'd be happy if you like him too. But I'll think about it. We'll see."

"I do appreciate your concern, Dad, even if it may not sound that way." Philip paused. "I mean, it's very special having a father who would do something like this — so special it's even a little surprising for me. But I feel very lucky to know my father cares so much. To be honest, it's more than I ever expected."

He smiled, as if Owen could see him.

"It's nothing," Owen said.

A beep sounded. "Just a second," Philip said, and pushed down the receiver buttons. Brad was on the other line. "Hold on a second," Philip said. "Have I got a story for you."

He clicked back to his father. "Dad," he said. "I have to take this call. Can I call you back tomorrow?"

"What's happening?" Owen said. "Where did you go? Why did you cut me off?"

"I didn't, it's just my call waiting."

"I don't understand," Owen said. "You were there and then you were gone. Did you cut me off? I don't understand."

"It's nothing, Dad," Philip said. "It just means I have another call. Listen, I'll talk to you soon, okay?"

"Okay. Goodbye, son."

"Goodbye."

He pushed down the buttons on the top of the phone, and Brad returned. "My God," Philip said.

"What's wrong?" asked Brad.

"I just had the strangest conversation with my father."

"What about?"

"Well, he was asking me a whole lot of questions — things like, 'how can you tell if someone's gay.' And then he suddenly announces there's this young teacher at the school he thinks is gay, and he wants to fix me up with him."

"You're kidding."

"No I'm not kidding. I mean, what should I think? I want to run away from him. I know that's terrible. Isn't this a good thing — doesn't it mean he's really taking my being gay seriously?"

"I guess it does," Brad said.

"You sound doubtful."

"I've just never heard of a parent doing anything like that."

"It's not something you could imagine your parents doing?" Brad spoke often and lovingly about his parents.

"I would die of embarrassment if they ever tried to fix me up," Brad said. "I think they would die of embarrassment, too. Which simply means, they have their limits, and they're happy to take advantage of my embarrassment since it means they can stick to them."

"There *is* something a little weird about it."

"Maybe your father's secretly gay and has a wild homosexual life," Brad said, and laughed.

"Brad!" Philip laughed. "He's my *father.* He's married to my mother."

"It's probably one of those mid-life things," Brad said. "Maybe he's just fascinated by homosexuality because he's bored, because it's something different that he doesn't know anything about."

"Yes," Philip said. "That's probably what it is."

Owen thought of Winston Penn as he wandered out of the Harte School into the evening street. He ran into Winston every day, if not in the lunch room, then outdoors, during sports hour. Most afternoons he was obliged to take prospectives and their parents on a tour of the school, and sometimes to the playing fields on Randall's Island, where Winston coached lacrosse. "Look at our lacrosse team," he'd say, in mock astonishment. "The coach this year is Winston Penn, one of the younger members of our English department. In general, the faculty volunteer to coach the sports with which they're well acquainted." Then the parents would look on approvingly at those ruddy, athletic boys and their handsome young coach. The boys followed Winston like puppies.

Owen often sat with Winston at lunch. Most of the younger faculty were snobbish about their youth and kept to themselves in cliquish circles, but Winston even sat through lunches with old Herr Klappert of the German Department, listening to his excruciating memories, waiting patiently through his coughing fits. It was no secret that some of the fruitier members of the faculty were besotted with Winston. In particular the calculus teacher, Stan Edersheim, was shameless. Owen felt contempt for Stan, with his ascot and Don Ameche mustache, and never for a moment drew any parallel between his loud, obvious infatuation with Winston and Owen's own more restrained admiration. Often when he arrived at the lunch room he was dismayed to discover that Stan had gotten there first and was monopolizing Winston, leaning close to him, loudly laughing at his jokes. Then Owen would slog through his lunch with the head of the History Department, sometimes catching Winston's eye to give him a conspiratorial smile. But Winston actually seemed to enjoy Stan's company. Once, in fact, when Winston was eating lunch with Owen and Stan came in, Winston got up from the table and shouted across the room, "Stan, my man!" and Stan came over to join them. Immediately Stan started in with stories about famous old actresses. "I said to her, 'So, honey, are you planning to work on Passover?' She said, 'Stan, you know I don't do game shows.'" Owen spooned his soup and felt sick — was Stan whom he was doomed to become? — while at the same moment a flash of heat passed through him as he remembered that under the table, wrapped in flannel, dry now, inactive, were those same blond legs he had watched with such admiration on the playing field. And thinking that, guilt flooded him as he realized he was no better than Stan, that indeed, Stan was better than he. For rather than making him unattractive, Stan's forwardness appeared to be paying off; he was now that much closer to Winston, that much more his confidant and friend, while Owen still waited miserably on the fringe, hoping for a secret glance he knew was never going to come. No one doubted that Stan was homosexual. And as a result, Owen supposed, he had nothing to lose. Why not be frank? Was restraint really such an admirable thing? Perhaps Winston was *suspicious* of Owen's restraint, saw stealth and plotting under the calm, steady surface of his paternal kindness. There was no stealth, nothing undercover in Stan's behavior, and Winston probably liked that about him, found his frank sexual interest stimulating or intriguing. Immediately Owen's perspective on the situation turned; now he was the slimy one, the cowardly snake in the grass, working under false pretenses, waiting to pounce.

He left lunch feeling pathetic.

Also elated. For he had one card he hadn't played; he had Philip.

The day after he'd called to tell Philip about Winston Penn he called again. "Philip?" he found himself saying into the phone. "I'm sorry to bother you, but I was wondering — Rose has a late meeting tonight, and — well, I'd like to buy my son dinner."

Philip again sounded surprised, but he had no plans for the evening. On his suggestion, they met at a Japanese restaurant on Columbus Avenue. The window was full of shellacked sushi and tempura. The real food also looked like toys, like food that aliens would eat, but Philip claimed to be living on it these days.

In the dark depths of the restaurant, where they sat, tiny flakes of dried fish writhed and curled atop a steaming broth, as if they were alive. Smelt eggs illuminated sushi like miniature lamps. Cautiously Owen tasted things. "Be careful with the wasabi," Philip said, "it's murderous."

Finally they got down to talking. "Ever since your announcement to your mother and me, son," Owen said to Philip, "well, there are things I've been wondering, wanting to ask you. I'm very interested, you see, in your experience growing up, I guess because we've never talked about it before. I know you must think I've been a distant father, not all there, really, but the truth is, I've always been observing you, always interested in you, although sometimes you probably couldn't tell. In certain basic ways, I suppose, I'm very . . . reserved." His hands twisted in his lap. "I've never been very good at expressing affection, much less asking personal questions, Philip. And then you come home with this news which really is news to me, though it shouldn't be — and I thought, damn it, enough of this. I'm tired of being so . . . restrained. I should ask what I want to know. I should take an interest in my son." He let out a breath of relief, as if he had gotten through something very difficult.

"I'm glad you feel that way, Dad," Philip said. "And I really don't mind. Ask anything you want."

Owen reached across the table for the little pitcher of sake and poured some into his cup. "Well," he said, "how did it start?"

"How did what start?"

"Your — sexual life."

Philip put his fingers to his mouth thoughtfully. "It's hard to say," he said. "I mean, well, to be frank, I've been masturbating with gay sexual fantasies for as long as I can remember — " He stopped, looked at his father cautiously. "Is that too much for you?"

"No, no," Owen said, even though it was. "Everyone does it." He laughed awkwardly, and Philip turned away, suppressing a nervous smile. "I'm not smiling for any reason," he said quickly. "It's just that this happens to me sometimes — I smile at the most inappropriate moments. It's like my brain is pulling the wrong strings. Sorry."

"Don't worry," Owen said. "I remember how hard it was for me to imagine my parents having a sex life. It's perfectly natural. I can't expect you to be entirely comfortable talking about these things with me." He hesitated. "God knows," he said, "I'm not too comfortable talking about them myself."

Philip nodded, pushed his rice around for a few seconds. "Well, anyway," he said, "as I was saying, there was no real start. I guess I had my first sexual experience with a man — but no." He took a deep breath. "See, it depends on how you define virginity. I mean, Gerard and I fooled around when we were kids, but it wasn't really anything. And after that, the first real adult experience — I don't know, Dad, do you really want to hear this? It isn't all that pretty."

Owen nodded.

"Well," he said, "I had a sort of quasi-sexual experience with a much older man in a porno theatre on the Lower East Side, when I was seventeen. Not much, really. Some groping. I got out of there as fast as I could, I was so scared — and then there was nothing till college."

Owen's eyes were like glass. He stared straight at Philip, nodding slowly.

"I had sex with a medical student my freshman year," Philip said. "Then nothing for a long time. Then a few other little things — nothing that counts. And then senior year, Dmitri — remember my friend Dmitri? You met him at graduation."

Owen nodded.

"He and I were lovers — boyfriends, I should say — I never know what word to use. We were involved for six months or so, on and off; we never officially broke up. There was an understanding, I guess — the thing would just sort of peter out. He liked to say we weren't lovers, that we were just friends who had sex. Except we really weren't friends." He paused. "I don't know what we were," Philip said. "It's not a relationship I'm particularly proud of."

"And all through this," Owen said, "all through this you were sure — you knew you were gay?"

Philip nodded.

"How old were you when you knew? Did you know as a child?"

Philip had answered this question many times. "Well," he said, "there are different ways of knowing. I mean, I wanted men, desired men, all through junior high school, but I guess I didn't figure out that that had anything to do with my life until I was thirteen, fourteen."

"And all through it, you were never at all attracted to women?"

Philip opened his mouth, was about to speak — then closed it. There was no question. He shook his head.

"And you've never slept with a woman?"

Again he shook his head.

The table was vibrating a little. Underneath it Philip's left leg shook with violence. Across the continent of the table Owen reached, and Philip wondered for a moment if he was going to take his hand. But his arm stopped at the sake pitcher, poured some more into his cup. "Forgive me for asking so many naïve questions," he said. "This is all new to me. I feel very ignorant."

"It's okay," Philip said.

"Let me ask you then — how could you be so sure, when you were so young? How did you *know?*"

"Well, it was very simple," Philip said. "It was nothing psychological; it wasn't a decision I reached. The fact was that I got sexually excited by the thought of men. I got erections. With girls — I felt nothing."

Owen laughed. "Well, I guess you really are gay then, huh?"

Philip's eyes widened.

"I was just wondering," Owen went on, "because — well, it seems to me, everybody's fundamentally bisexual, don't you think? At heart, I mean?" He poured more sake, stirred a piece of sushi in his dish of soy sauce.

But Philip shook his head. "No," he said. "No, I don't think everybody's fundamentally bisexual. I think some people are, and a whole lot more are basically one way or the other — either homosexual or heterosexual. I think this whole bisexual thing can become an excuse, a way of avoiding committing yourself, or admitting the truth. It means you can duck out when the going gets rough."

Owen looked blankly at Philip, clearly bewildered by his vehemence. "I didn't mean to offend you," he said. "I was just — well, looking for common ground." He cast his eyes toward the table. "I mean, I've had sexual feelings toward men sometimes, some sort of attraction."

"Which is fine," Philip said quickly, sitting up in his chair. "I know gay men who feel occasional attractions to women, too. The point is, you're basically heterosexual, and that should be what defines your lifestyle."

Owen didn't answer. He poured more sake into his cup — the flask was almost empty — and looked out the window.

"So," he said, after a few seconds, "are you still going — you know, to that theatre, that porno theatre you mentioned?"

"The Bijou? I've never been back."

"And Eliot," he said. "How did you meet him?"

Philip smiled, and dutifully repeated to his father the story (beginning by now even to bore him) of his introduction to Eliot. "I feel," he concluded, "like I'm in some sort of strange transitional period which I don't really understand very well. Like I'm still not sure what happened, and yet I have no idea what's coming next."

"Are you — seeing anyone now?"

"No. Too scared of AIDS, I guess."

"Oh yes, that," Owen said casually. "Waiter?" he called. "Can you bring us another sake?"

The waiter arrived with the flask. "For whatever it's worth," Owen said, "I've invited that young teacher — Winston Penn — to dinner next Sunday. He was very happy. He lives alone out in Hoboken, you see, above an old tavern, and he hardly ever gets a good home-cooked meal. I hope you'll still plan to come."

Philip smiled nervously. "Sure," he said. "I should check my schedule, but I can't see why not."

"Good, son. I'm glad. You'll like him."

"I'm sure I will."

After they paid the bill, Owen walked Philip to the subway. He was stumbling just a little, couldn't quite keep up with his son, and when Philip looked at him, concerned, he shrugged. "Just the sake," he said.

He was glad they had had this talk, Owen told Philip. He felt better about their relationship than he had in years. And falteringly, Philip agreed. It was a good thing. They should do it again.

At the subway, Philip said, "Dad? Will you send my love to Mom?"

Owen smiled. "Of course," he said.

"I miss her a lot," Philip said. "She doesn't call me. She doesn't

seem to want to see me. It makes me very sad. I call her sometimes — but she sounds so nervous, not at all like herself."

"Well," Owen said, "maybe it takes longer with the mothers.
She'll come around. She just has a lot to sort out. Give her time."

"I will," Philip said. "Or at least, I'll try."

Then he disappeared into the subway. Owen waited a few
minutes, watching him descend. From Broadway, he walked a
few blocks to the crosstown bus. The late March air was brisk.
Flowers bloomed in clay pots on fire escapes. The bus was filled
with couples — old couples and very young couples, middle-
aged couples, black couples and white couples, Japanese couples,
Chinese couples, Korean couples. Owen recognized among
them a pair of ex-Harte boys out with their girlfriends, but neither of them seemed to notice him. When they're applying, I'm
king, Owen thought bitterly, but once they get in . . . He laughed,
because he was drunk, anesthetized, his pain still palpable, but
numbed, exerting only the vaguest pressure. Somewhere in the
back of his mind a voice wondered if Rose might be worrying
about him, but this voice too was hardly audible, exerted only the
vaguest pressure. The bus stopped at Second Avenue. It was a
nice night, a night to walk, and he walked.

Philip was going to save himself. Philip was going to get Winston Penn and save himself, and save his father, too. He smiled to
think of it, and somehow that idea of Philip, as an extension of
himself, of his own desire, made perfect sense to him. They could
help each other or hurt each other. It would be easy either way.
And suddenly he wondered: Does Philip know? Could Philip
have seen? Perhaps he should have asked fewer questions. But
after forty years of evasion, he had no will left in him for hiding
things, for analyzing how much a remark might reveal, for

quickly changing the subject to avoid incrimination. Fear had motivated him to such evasion, and tonight he felt drained of fear. Perhaps there is only a set quantity of fear one can feel in a lifetime; if so, he was sure, he had done his penance, used his due.

Perhaps it was genetic.

On Second Avenue, he passed a bar called Bullets which for about ten years had been called The Squire's Pub, then for about five years Sugar Magnolia. Some sixth sense for these things told him that in its current incarnation it was a gay bar catering primarily to the moneyed crowd — older men, some married, many looking for younger boys. He had always hurried past it, his eyes focussed on the ground before him, but tonight, catching in his peripheral vision a dark Hispanic boy lounging in the door and the sleek red sign in the window, he stopped. He had imagined, before, that if he stood too long in front of this bar without moving, either Rose would come upon him or lightning would strike him dead. Neither of these things happened. People passed him in the street, oblivious, did not shout out, "Owen Benjamin, dean of admissions at the Harte School, what are you doing standing in front of a gay bar?" "Excuse me," a voice barked, and a man brushed past him, hands on his shoulder, but he was not the police, not a Harte parent, not Rose, not Philip. The problem was that Owen was in the way of the door. "Sorry," he said, and the man glided into Bullets as casually as Owen might have walked into his own apartment building. It seemed astonishing, daredevil, like walking on a tightrope across a moat of crocodiles. And as at the circus, nothing happened.

He turned to look inside the bar. Behind the smoky glass

window, figures lounged against wooden counters, talked, drank. A man in a business suit hurried in, a trio of pale youths in leather jackets hurried out, all oblivious to Owen. The obliviousness disappointed him somehow. In certain ways he wanted to be noticed as much as he wanted not to be noticed.

He thought of pacing around the block once, then decided to be braver than that and, marching up to the door, pushed through it. It gave gently as a curtain at his touch. A smell of cigarette smoke engulfed him. The room was dark, but not as dark as the theatre. He let his eyes adjust. It was not a large place. In the corner an old-fashioned jukebox played Tina Turner at a reasonable volume. Twenty or thirty men were milling around the bar, standing at the counters and sitting at the few tables, most of them Owen's age, their collars and ties loosened, their jackets around their arms. In addition, some much younger thin black men and muscular Puerto Ricans stood in trios and clusters, not speaking, their eyes roving the room.

Cautiously, still shaking a little, Owen made his way to the bar. "Gin and tonic," he told the bartender in a surprisingly normal voice. He looked around. No one was noticing him. He took off his jacket, loosened his collar and tie. The bartender, a huge man in a muscle T-shirt, handed him his drink in a tumbler. "Thanks," he said. It calmed him to talk, to have something in his hand. He paid and moved away from the bar, looking for a place to stand, and chose an empty corner where he could hide in semi-darkness, not quite invisible, and watch.

There was not that much to watch. Nearby, some men in their thirties were arguing loudly over the stock market. In the corner, near the jukebox, a young couple kissed, caressed, danced, gyrated, crotches grinding together. All of it was interesting to Owen. The men in the bar were relaxed; they might have been anywhere. That was the most interesting thing about them.

Out of nowhere, a man was suddenly standing next to Owen, against the wall. They turned to observe each other at the same moment. The man nodded; Owen turned away. A flash of lust seared through him at the mere possibility of contact. He turned again, looked cautiously. The man was in his early forties, dark, bearded. He had on a white shirt, no tie, a jacket, and he was drinking beer out of a bottle — a gesture Owen found, at the moment, astonishingly sexy. He turned away and could feel, like radar, the man's head turning, his eyes scanning him. Then he turned away again. Owen looked back. The man was drinking his beer, staring straight toward the bar. He looked strong; his legs, bound in tight denim and boots, moved slightly to the rhythm of the music.

Owen gulped from his drink, praying that the gin would give him confidence. Soon he felt braver. He turned, looked at the man, who turned and looked at him. They nodded slightly and said, "How're you doing?" at the same moment.

"Fine," they then said, again at the same moment, and laughed.

Then the man turned again to face the bar. His legs moved to the music. His head moved to the music. He took a swig from his beer bottle.

Owen looked at his feet, at the floor. But before he had a chance to make a decision about what to do, the man turned to him, holding out his empty beer bottle, and said, "Can I get you something from the bar?"

"Uh — sure," Owen said. "A gin and tonic?"

"Okay," the man said.

"Oh, let me give you some money."

"No, no," the man said. "This one's on me." Then he walked away.

After a few sweaty moments he came back, bearing another beer and a gin and tonic for Owen. "I'm Frank," he said.

"Owen," Owen said.

They shook hands. Frank's hands were enormous, enveloping.

"You come here a lot?" Frank said.

"Not really."

"Me neither. I just work in the neighborhood sometimes, and then I drop by after work."

"What do you do?"

"I'm a contractor," Frank said, and nodded to the rhythm of the music. Owen nodded as well. They nodded together. Frank laughed.

Then he turned around again, faced the bar. For another few moments, they stared at nothing.

"This bar used to have another name," Owen said.

"Did it?"

"Yes, it was called Sugar Magnolia."

"Oh." Frank turned, looked Owen straight in the eye.

"You married?" he asked, his eyes focussing on Owen's ring.

"Yes," Owen said.

"Thought so." Frank looked away again. "Me too," he added.

"Really?"

"Uh-huh. It's tough, you know?"

"I know."

Across the bar the gyrating boys had disappeared. "It's a good, stable stock, goddamnit," said one of the brokers. Owen closed his eyes, opened them again.

"My wife," Frank said, fingering the chain around his neck. "She's real naïve. Good Catholic background. We got married when we were eighteen. She — she just wants to take care of the kids, go to church. She doesn't want trouble, you know?"

"Do you live in the city?"

"Staten Island," Frank said. "But I have a friend's place for tonight." He looked at Owen.

Now Owen was confused. Was the friend also married? Was there some sort of brotherhood of married gay men in the world, loaning each other apartments, finding each other in bars? He began to fear for a moment that Frank just wanted to induct him, to be his friend. Maybe the rule was that they were only supposed to sleep with the younger men.

"The other night," Frank said, "some kids came in here. One of them shouted at the top of his lungs, 'Dad! What are you doing here?'" Frank laughed. "You should've seen these guys drop their glasses — like that." He snapped his fingers.

"Funny, I guess," Owen said, and Frank nodded. He seemed restless, shuffling on his feet like an adolescent boy. Finally he turned and his face bore down on Owen's, so that Owen could feel the bristles on his beard, smell the beer on his breath. "Listen," he said. "Are you a nice guy or what? Because what I really need right now is a nice guy, someone who knows what he's doing, not some schmuck. I mean, there are a lot of schmucks around, you know what I'm saying?"

"I know what you're saying," Owen said. "I need that, too."

"I want a man," Frank said. "You know what I'm saying? When I saw you across the bar, I thought — hey, there's a guy who looks — different. Sensitive."

Owen was dazed. "Yes," he said. "Yes."

Frank moved closer, so that their thighs touched. "So, like I said, I've got this place for tonight. Do you want to go there with me? I mean, it could be real nice. You know, like that song. 'We've got tonight, who needs tomorrow?'" He smiled. Owen smiled. "I don't know that song," Owen said. "But I certainly understand the sentiment."

"I'll just go get my coat from the check room," Frank said, and he moved away. Owen leaned against the wall, breathing steadily. He was surprisingly relaxed. He didn't feel like he was doing much of anything out of the ordinary. All he knew was that he yearned for Frank to get back from the check room as fast as he could, and when he did, Owen could see Frank was in a hurry as well. The place he had for the night was a studio apartment in the East Nineties, he told him. Owen nodded. He put on his jacket, and they walked out of the bar together, into the public street, full of people he might have known. Frank hailed a cab. On the way, in the cab, he held Owen's hand.

It was a small apartment in a walk-up building, decorated simply and sparsely, like a motel room. Almost as soon as they arrived, Frank turned on the overhead light, and Owen took his coat off in the brightness. Out of the dark bar, Frank's face was a little pockmarked. His stomach sagged over his pants. There was something faintly dirty about his clothes and hair. And suddenly the dreamlike prospect of this moment, nurtured in the bar, gave way to something different — two older men, both married, both a little out of shape, meeting to make love, to touch each other and make each other feel better. Not an unpleasant prospect. Besides, Owen had had his fill of fantasy. He wanted something real.

Still, when Frank embraced Owen and kissed him, Owen was overwhelmed.

They fell on the floor and made love, and like so many men

making love that night, were careful, respectful of rules. They did not do what they might have wanted to. At one point Frank quietly pulled a rubber out of its plastic casement, threw the torn packet across the room, eased the thing over himself. It seemed the most natural thing in the world.

After they finished, Owen dragged himself from where he lay on the bed up onto his elbows. "I've got to get home," he said. "Rose is probably crazy with worry."

Frank lay stretched naked on the bed, his hands behind his neck, and Owen was suddenly astonished by the two shocks of black hair under his arms. They stared frankly at him, like an extra set of eyes.

"What are you going to tell her?" Frank asked.

Owen shook his head as he pulled on his pants.

Frank got out of bed. At the kitchen table he scribbled something on a piece of note paper that said "P.&R. Contracting / Construction Company. Frank J. Picone, President." "Here's my work number," he said. "Call me?"

"All right," said Owen.

They kissed once, and then Frank let him out the door.

Out on the street, the sky was surprisingly still. A few kids were milling around on the sidewalk. It was then that he realized he was only two blocks from Harte, which seemed to him suddenly funny. And as after all longed-for changes, he himself felt changed not in the least. The Harte School loomed as always. It had loomed for years before he knew it, and would loom afterwards, oblivious to his tenancy. But he was somehow able to walk past it tonight a little easier. If anything, he felt lightened of a burden. He had done it. He had made love — real love — with another man. It was no longer a hurdle he had to get over, and for that he was grateful. Besides that, he thought to himself calmly, my life will continue as it has unchanged. I will continue as I am. Unchanged.

He looked at his watch and saw that it was two-thirty in the morning. Had Rose gone to bed? He prayed that she had as he hailed a taxi, wondered what he'd say to her if she were still up. Sure enough, the light was on in the window when he got back. He tipped the driver too much, said hello to the doorman, headed up in the elevator. Rose was reading in the living room, in her bathrobe. She did not get up when he walked in.

"Hello, honey," Owen said.

"Hello," said Rose.

He kissed her on the cheek. She did not raise her eyes from her book.

"I was worried about you," she said softly.

Owen walked to the window, opened it. He did not say a word. Several beats of silence passed, and he knew Rose was counting them. She had her eyes closed tightly, her hands squeezed together; the book dropped to her lap. No book; no lies; no excuses.

"I'm not going to ask any questions," she said. "I don't want to know anything. But I want you to promise me one thing. I want you to promise me that the next time you go out until two-thirty in the morning, you will call and warn me so I won't worry myself to death wondering if you're dead."

"You're right, honey," Owen said. "I'm sorry. I will."

After a few seconds Rose got up. "I'm going to bed," she said.

"Rose," Owen said.

She shook her head vigorously no, then disappeared into the bedroom, leaving him alone in the living room with the vast, silent expanse of New York outside the window. Unconsciously he cupped his genitals.

Then it all came back — the panic, the turmoil, the sense of the world flying out of orbit — and they were bag people again, roaming the ruined streets of their lives, looking for scraps to live on or live in. Owen closed his eyes and mouth tight against screaming, and the scream burst inside him, ricocheted off the walls of his body. What had he done? Good God, what had he said? How could he have been so reckless, so obvious? Panic exploded in him. He remembered Rose's expression, the pain in her eyes, the way she held her hands together on her lap, calmly, the fingers pulling at each other like cracking party favors. He wanted to comfort her, to reassure her; but how could he, when he was the source and cause of all her pain? No matter how much empathy he felt, he was what was hurting her, and it could not be stopped, even by him.

He sat down in her chair, still warm with her imprint, then stood up again immediately, like someone burned on a vinyl car seat on a scorching hot day. Then he walked to the window, pressed his face to it, and felt the cold air outside seep through, into his cheeks, his eyes, his mouth. He breathed, watched the patterns his breath made on the glass.

After that he stood quietly for a moment, waiting for the shaking to subside.

In the bedroom, Rose lay stiff and knotted. He started to undress, looked down at her. But he had made up his mind and only wished he could find some way to save himself without killing her.

In bed, he reached over from his side to touch her shoulder. A spasm racked her body at his touch, did not subside. She lay there shaking, but would not look at him.

"Rose," he said.

She wept softly, did not answer, would not look at him.

SPRING HAD COME LATE, and the ring of ice around Philip's heart finally cracked. Then it was as if something had been freed in him, though against his will or better judgment. He woke up in the morning not feeling bad; he couldn't help it. It seemed the small pleasures of the world, elusive all winter, were now conspiring to assault him, to beat misery out of him, and no matter how he tried he just could not hold them off. The sun on his face, waiting for the bus early in the morning, or the sight of the super's wife taking her little girl to school, a Cabbage Patch lunchbox clutched in her hand — these things brought an unexpected, even unwanted smile to his face on breezy mornings in late March — small, unnoticeable to anyone but him, really, but enough to make him realize that he was perhaps recovering, that Eliot's spectre had faded.

He was less lonely than he had been — or, perhaps more accurately, he had learned how to be alone. He found himself looking forward to the prospect of a night in his apartment with the manuscript of *Island Rhapsody* and a foil container of sesame noodles. Other nights he saw Brad. They had dinner together, went to the movies. "All I want," Brad said, as they leaned together against a wall of Boy Bar, "all I've ever wanted, is someone to settle down with," and Philip agreed, both of them surprisingly unconscious of the extent to which they had settled with each other. Often they stood like this, staring into the dark, shoe-smelling depths of bars, scanning the room for faces, trying to pick out which ones they could fall in love with. But the faces were familiar by now and looked as tired of looking as theirs did. Perhaps these faces were mourning the old days of catch-as-catch-can, free love, guiltless ecstasy, the days when you could wink at someone, smile, and that would be enough: You'd be off together to a room somewhere to make love. Now monogamy was in fashion, but it had taken on the status of a safety tactic, an unappetizing but necessary catastrophe measure, like one of those World War II recipes for stretching precious rationed meat. "Find ten buddies and agree to fuck only with them," Philip had read in a porn magazine early on in the crisis. Then ten was reduced to five, five to two. Men found themselves stranded in couples, reduced to a choice of living alone or continuing with a person who, if he was going to infect you at all, had already done it, so what was there to risk? Thus couples formed; fear became an indirect route to monogamy and, sometimes, to happiness.

One Friday night, Philip and Brad took the subway uptown to Columbia, where the Gay Student Union was sponsoring a dance, and there they danced wildly, exuberantly, until sweat showed on their faces and their clothes smelled like tar. Afterwards, they ate cheeseburgers at an all-night diner on Broadway, and at six in the morning hiked the length of Manhattan to its very tip, marching through sleepy-eyed, hung-over Harlem, heedless of the dangers, until dawn found them at the fortlike Cloisters, triumphant as mountain climbers. After which they went separately home. As a matter of principle, as well as fear, they never slept with anyone, not even each other. They had never known that time when sex existed without the threat of disease yoked to it, and the fear of sickness was at the root of their consciousness — something of which they were seemingly unaware, yet which ruled them, formed their attitudes and determined their behavior.

That Sunday they spent the early part of the afternoon at the movies, watching cartoons. Afterwards, when the sun came out, they wandered through the zoo in Central Park and the Museum of Natural History. Philip loved that afternoon, with its faint whiff of childhood. On springy rainy mornings, he would wake up to hear the drizzle of water splashing against a drain, and wish for nothing more than the coziness of being ten years old and home from school with a cold, watching hours of game shows on television — "Match Game," "Wheel of Fortune," "The Twenty Thousand Dollar Pyramid." Around noon on those distant dizzy days, his mother would come home and prepare him chicken noodle soup for lunch, and then, after she left, as morning gave way to afternoon, the incomprehensible soap operas would come on, and fade, and it would be the time of old science-fiction movies like *The Day the Earth Stood Still*, *Forbidden Planet*, *Godzilla vs. The Smog Monster*, movies that, if you changed the channel constantly, you could watch simultaneously with Popeye, Tom and Jerry, Speed Racer, Gigantor, Kimba the Heroic White Lion. Lying in his bed on wet mornings in his own apartment, Philip could still recite to himself the exact sequence of shows. If only he had a color television, he'd think; if only he had a cold. And then he would remember that no cold could be just a cold for him anymore; no cold could be enjoyed or indulged. A cold meant anxious countings of how many times he'd been sick that year and a frantic prodding of the glands in his neck. And remembering this anxiety of colds, remembering the threat of pain, fast decline, and death, he'd bound out of bed, leap in the shower, and practically run to work.

One afternoon he came home from work and found a letter from Eliot in his mailbox. At first he put it down on his desk and tried to ignore it, but finally he could not help himself, and he opened the envelope and read what was inside. The letter, sent from Paris, was on blue airmail stationery.

He skimmed the first two paragraphs. Arrival in Italy, funny little pensions, a medieval church happened upon. Undiscovered beauty, untouristed countryside. Then Paris, and Roland Le-Clerc, a photographer friend of Derek's, "a 'bohème' of the old school," Eliot wrote, "always dressed in paisley and ascots. He lives in a big, ugly apartment in the Fifth, high ceilings and hideous furniture, everything dusty. But it's wonderful. In the morning I can smell that Paris smell, coffee and croissants, sweet jam and cigars and car fumes rising up." There was an afternoon tea party attended by very, very old gay men, and a woman who Roland insisted was a former lover of Colette's.

"I feel like I owe you an explanation for my sudden departure," the letter went on,

for not saying goodbye. You're perfectly right to think me cruel. But it was very hard for me, Philip. Ridiculous as you may think it is for me to say at this point, I did love you, in my own particular way. The problem is, loving someone is not the same as wanting to spend your life paired with him. That kind of compatability is a rare thing, and frankly, I just didn't feel it. Is this cruel of me to say? Perhaps. But I think you deserve the truth from me. My strong feelings for you made it that much harder for me to ease things off. The more I loosened the grip, it seemed, the more you tightened. And I've said it before: your need oppressed me. I began to feel it was something I had to escape, and when you start thinking in those terms — well, it's only a few steps to lies, to cruelty. I didn't want to let myself go that far, Philip, but it seemed there was no way I could not hurt you. I wanted you, at least, to have the benefit of being able to be angry at me, to hate me a little, because I know that makes it easier.

Here I feel renewed, revivified. I feel as if I can start my life over. I've met a young Frenchman, a student — he is droopy-eyed and handsome and given to bouts of depression, and I think we will be good for each other. I've gotten some connections established, have some possibilities for work. Thierry lives across town, near the Alésia metro, and I'll probably be moving in with him for a few weeks while I look for an apartment.

And you — I am sure your life is going well. If there's one thing I know about you, Philip, it is that you *are*, whether you like it or not, helplessly optimistic. No matter how much you may want to remain in a stupor of depression, you'll rise up from it. Sometimes I think you are doomed to happiness.

Please write me c/o Thierry. I miss you.

Eliot

Philip read the letter over twice, pacing the tiny confines in his room. Then he folded it carefully in thirds, replaced it in its envelope and stuck it inside his desk drawer. Outside the open window, at the far end of an alley full of garbage cans, a bunch of little girls jumped rope double-dutch, chanting in Spanish. He watched them. He thought: I can smell that New York smell — frying grease and sesame oil, *menudo* and beans and bus exhaust. He thought: I hardly knew him. Little chips of old paint were stuck inside the window frame — dirty white and red and blue fragments of the apartment's past — and methodically he scooped some up in his hand, a fine powder interspersed with jagged-edged chunks, like puzzle pieces. He examined them for a little while, curious about their age, their hardness. Then, experimentally, he dropped some out the window. The bigger pieces fluttered down, crashed silently on the ground. When he opened his hands to the air, the powder blew into the wind, whirling for a few seconds before falling like a last, late snowfall to the garbage-strewn landscape below.

A few days later, Jerene called Philip up at work. "It's been a long time," she said. "The last time we talked you seemed so upset. Are you feeling better?"

At his desk, Philip smiled. "Yes," he said. "Much better." He was quiet for a moment. "I told my parents," he said.

"Oh, Philip," Jerene said. "How are they taking the news?"

"I don't know," Philip said. "I saw my father this week, and it was pretty weird. He'd been drinking, I think, and he asked me all sorts of questions about myself, which was okay, but it really surprised me — I mean, he's always been very closed. It's a big change."

"Well, that's good," Jerene said. "Any interest is good."

"I know. As for my mother — well, things aren't so good. She hardly talks to me. I'm supposed to go over for dinner on Sunday, and believe it or not, my father's invited this teacher from his school he says he wants to fix me up with. That'll be peculiar, to say the least. I don't know if my mother knows anything about it."

"You mean a man?" Jerene asked.

"Yes. A man. I know, I know. My friend Brad thinks it's weird too. Some sort of mid-life crisis, I guess. But enough of that. How are you?"

"Good," Jerene said.

"Still working at the hotline?"

"Yes. But I quit the other job. I got some teaching work at N.Y.U. — freshman comp. Nothing great, but I was getting sick of being a bouncer." She paused. "The good news is, Laura's just moved in, and we've been fixing the place up. And we were wondering if you might be free for dinner tomorrow night. We want you to be our inaugural guest. And this friend, this Brad of yours — bring him too!"

"I'm not sure," he said.

"But Eliot's gone, Philip. The place is completely changed, a different apartment, thanks to Laura."

He closed his eyes. "All right," he said finally, although the prospect frightened him. "What time?"

"Eight o'clock," said Jerene.

Brad lived in a pleasant, dark apartment into which his parents had delivered intact the furniture of his childhood bedroom in New Jersey. There was a pair of big lacquered bunk beds, a white activity table, three beanbag chairs. "I'm almost ready," Brad said when Philip came by to pick him up the next evening. He pulled off his tie and shirt, and Philip could not help noticing his chest — white, well formed, and covered with pale, downy hair. Brad took a jersey from a white child's dresser which, like all the furniture in the apartment, was made for a boy, completely stripped of ornament, of anything that might be even mildly construed as frilly or feminine. "Are you nervous?" he asked Philip, as they headed out, once more, into the street. Philip thought about it. "Yes," he said finally, "a little. But not too much." He had not yet mentioned the letter from Eliot — indeed, he saw no reason to mention it. Lately he had been practicing restraint as a general policy, and had mostly forgotten the letter, except for that last annoying remark Eliot had made about his being "doomed to happiness." What could it mean to be doomed to happiness? The phrase made it sound as if happiness was some kind of imprisoning lie, a form of brainwashing; as if a valiant life made miserable by knowledge was necessarily better than one that was happy but ignorant. It infuriated him, the tyranny implicit in Eliot's smug, cynical tone, with its cryptic hints of foreknowledge, its wry psychiatrist's wit. And yet he could not deny that he could imagine no more pleasurable life than the kind led within the cozy confines of a half-hour situation comedy, that he really wanted each day in his life to collapse into a neat dot of light, to end the way an episode of "The Brady Bunch" ended, with everything in its place, all the gentle, soft conflicts put away or stuffed under the bunk beds, or smoothed like frosting on a birthday cake.

Eliot's building was unchanged when they got there, except that the name under the mailbox had been altered, the little tag of paper now reading FINLEY/PARKS instead of ABRAMS/PARKS. They stood there for a moment, Philip examining the pink linoleum walls of the foyer, the dirt caked into the mailboxes, Brad watching Philip for warning signs of emotional upheaval. But Philip only sighed loudly. They rang the buzzer and were duly admitted. Up the stairs, Jerene's new friend, Laura, was waiting for them at the door.

She was extraordinarily pale, with hair so thin and wispy it might have been woven out of sand. "Now let me get this right," she said, and her voice had grain, was sandy. "You're Philip," she said, pointing to Philip. "And you're Brad."

"That's right," Philip said. He worried he might call her Sandy.

She smiled and reached out her hand. "Well, I'm glad I got that right," she said. "I'm Laura. Come on in."

Inside, the apartment was much changed. New blueberry-patterned curtains hung on the windows. A matching tablecloth covered the table, and a bright, overstuffed couch perched where Jerene's spartan cot had once been. "I'm glad you could make it," Jerene said, parting herself from the stove to kiss Philip on the cheek and introduce herself to Brad. "We're making couscous."

The strains of a melancholy song by the Roches wound through the room, along with a faint smell of incense. "My recipe," said Laura, pointing proudly to the boiling red sauce. "Taste?" She reached a wooden spoon toward Philip, and an acrid sizzle touched his lips. "Fabulous, isn't it?" Laura said. "I got the recipe from a bunch of Algerians I used to live with in Paris. But then I lost it. For years I've been trying to get it back, get it right, and tonight — " She kissed her fingers dramatically, then returned to stirring the tiny buds. She was wearing a knee-length linen dress the color of blueberry yoghurt and had a row of tiny pearls studded into each of her ears. A girl who was almost transparent in her appearance, whom you would imagine would be allergic to everything and live in a Victorian house, and spend her days doing things like rubbing sandalwood oil into the faint freckles of her skin, or crocheting flowers into curtains.

"It's wonderful sauce," Philip said. "I'm glad Jerene's got someone to cook so well for her."

"Oh, she's not so bad herself," Laura said. "Anyway, I owe Jerene a lot more than meals. I don't know if she told you, but before I met her I was living with my mother in abject misery? And every day I had to listen to her have nervous breakdowns about me — you know, 'Why don't you marry a nice boy, it just breaks my heart?'" She turned to Jerene and kissed her on the forehead. "I'm very happy to be out of there, to have a new home," she said, and Philip nodded.

If Laura's looks were Laura Wingfield — fragile and transparent as a tiny glass animal — her temperament was pure Amanda: loud and brash and indiscreet; full of hype and bombast; good-natured, loving, easy to hurt. "So how are things going with your parents, Philip?" she asked, as she handed Philip a glass of grapefruit juice. "Have they come around at all?"

Philip gulped the grapefruit juice. How did Laura know about his parents? "Well," he said.

"Up and down, huh? I know." Laura chewed a piece of ice. "The same thing was true with mine, at first. One minute all curiosity, the next they won't talk to me. I think it's a mid-life thing, ultimately, don't you?"

"I suppose so."

"I wouldn't worry," Laura went on. "I told my parents three, four years ago, and it was a rough road for a while, but now things are really fine — well, at least with my father. He's even given Jerene and me our own set of keys to his place in Bridgehampton for the summer. And that really pleases me. I mean, it makes me feel like he really cares about me, more than he cares about my being a lesbian. As for my mother — she's a different story."

Jerene and Brad now moved across the room to join them by the stove. "Jerene's just been telling me about her work on the Gay Crisis Hotline," Brad said.

"I've thought about doing that kind of thing myself," Laura said. "I think I'd be a pretty good counselor-type person; in fact, I'm thinking about it as a career. But as Jerene can tell you, I have this phone phobia. I mean, I'm terrified of the phone. I guess it's because my first stepfather, when I was little, was kind of a sicko — he never molested me or anything, but he used to make me talk to him on the phone while he masturbated sometimes." And suddenly a look of mortification came over her face, and she slapped her forehead. "What am I doing?" she said. "I always do this. Just interrupt and stuff myself into a conversation. I'm terribly self-involved, just Miss Self-Centered. Please forgive me. Jerene, go on and finish what you were saying."

They moved toward the living room, each bearing a steaming bowl of food. Like the kitchen, it had been transformed. Flowers hung in pots before the windows. A big brass bed stood where Eliot's futon had been curled, and next to it, a big vanity table full of makeup and perfumes and scatterings of lace. There was an Oriental rug on the floor, stuffed animals thrown here and there. The gray walls had been painted sky blue. The only thing that seemed to be the same was the old ugly radiator, silent now in the warm weather. All through the dinner Philip kept looking around the room, expecting to see something that would spark strong feeling in him, but even the most potent of his memories refused to surface. Nothing was left. Everything of the past had been buried under all the strong frippery of Laura's presence.

She told them everything. It was as if she hoped that by dumping the whole mess of herself onto them at once they might be struck, almost against their will, by the good mixed in with the nonsense. "Since I dropped out of Hampshire I've just been travelling," she explained, while Jerene scurried about, spicing things, getting salt and pepper. "I was in Morocco, in Paris, in Tangiers. Then I lived in San Francisco for a while. I was working in the women's music industry out there. I knew some sign language, so I got this job interpreting for this singer named Melissa Swallow — you know, for the deaf?" She laughed. "You should've seen me. I wore nothing but turtlenecks and hiking boots, to the dismay of my *très sophistiqués* New York parents, and lived in this communal women's house in Mill Valley and smoked a lot of grass. It was fun, but it wasn't for me, so I headed back East, and my mother — my blessed heart of a mother — got me the job at the Laura Ashley store, figuring that was one place I'd be safe. Little did she know," she said, looking up at Jerene, "who'd be walking in."

Jerene blushed.

"You know," Laura said, "when I told her, she said, 'I can't believe it. I set it up myself. Why did I get you that job?' As if it was her fault. And you know what? Sometimes I believe her. I get so sucked up in her paranoia I start to regret it myself and blame her. You see, I'm basically still a very insecure person, still searching a lot, which is what I was doing then, in San Francisco, and what I'm still doing now, I guess, which is why my mother is such a terrible influence on my life. But I feel very happy, very secure with Jerene. Almost as if I'm settled." Then she leaned confidentially toward Philip, and said, "So have you heard from Eliot lately?" She spoke in such intimate tones of "Eliot" that for a moment Philip forgot what Jerene had told him on the phone: that Laura had met Eliot only once, for about five minutes. She smiled now, eager for his confidence. It was as if, by this intimacy, she hoped to bulldoze her way into what she must have perceived to be a pre-existing group of friends — he and Eliot and Brad and Jerene. Although her impression of them as a group could not have been farther from the truth, her eagerness not to be left out touched Philip.

"Well, I got a letter," he said.

"You did?" asked Brad. "Why didn't you tell me?"

He shrugged. "I didn't want to make a big deal out of it, that's all," he said. "It wasn't a big-deal letter. He just said he'd been travelling, but now he's settled in Paris. He says he has a nice, depressed boyfriend with a strange name. I can't remember what."

Laura swallowed a bite of couscous to clear her mouth for talking. "Thierry," she said.

"Yes," said Philip. "That's it. How did you know?"

She smiled. "I set them up," she said proudly.

Philip gazed at her. "You set them up?"

"Well, sort of. Remember I told you I used to live in Paris, with a bunch of Algerians? Well, Thierry was lovers with one of them, Mustapha, for a while. He lived with his mother in Neuilly or someplace like that. Anyway, we got to be friends, and we stayed friends even after he and Mustapha broke up and I'd moved out of the apartment. So when Eliot told me he was going to Paris, of course I gave him Thierry's number, never in a million years expecting — " She gestured vaguely with her hands, and swallowed another mouthful of couscous.

"Oh," Philip said. He looked at the table, and Jerene, seeing his crestfallen face, added, "I don't think it's really all that serious, Philip. I mean, Eliot doesn't even know how long he'll be in Paris." She looked at him earnestly. He appreciated that she cared. Still, he was embarrassed to be caught mooning like that. He no longer wished to call attention to his old grief, now that he was finally getting over it — especially in front of Brad.

"Jerene," he said, "you're very sweet to be so kind to me. But it really isn't necessary. You can tell me the truth, I'm not going to freak out. Eliot told me himself that he was going to be moving in with Thierry for a while, and I think that's just fine. I hope they're very happy, I hope it works out. He's getting on with his life, and I realize, now, that I've got to get on with mine."

"It looks to me like you're doing that already," Laura said. She glanced significantly at Philip, then at Brad, then at Philip again.

"Married life," Laura said, "is the greatest." And taking Jerene's hand, she held it on the table. Jerene was sitting straight up, her back like a board. She looked like the tin woodsman of Oz. "For Jerene and me, it's been a healing kind of process. For instance — I'm trying to convince her to go and talk to her parents. We've even done some research. Tell them, Jerene."

Jerene laughed nervously. "Well," she said, "I went and saw my grandmother the other day — it was the first time in years."

"Oh, Jerene," Philip said. "That's wonderful. Was it okay? I mean, was it a good thing, was she happy to see you?"

Jerene nodded. "It was very sad," she said. "Of course, she didn't know anything. She's pretty out of it to begin with, and besides, she hardly speaks to my parents, hardly has any more of a relationship with them than I do. She barely knew anything about me, she's been in this nursing home so long. It isn't a bad place, but I think she's lonely." Jerene smiled. "You can't imagine how scared I was going in there. It was the first time I'd had contact with my family for six years."

"The next step," Laura said, "is going to be a letter, from Jerene to her parents, telling them she's seeing her grandmother and insisting they come and visit her. Because you see, in this case, it's not just Jerene and her parents — it's the whole family. A whole history of disownment, of children rejecting parents and parents rejecting children. I think about this a lot, because of my plans to get my degree in family counselling. For instance, I've been reading up lately in systems theory, and I really think there's a lot to it. What's happened to Jerene — well, it's all part of a family system which is unique. In my family, disownment wasn't even something people thought about. But damn it, here I go again, blathering on about myself. Please forgive me. Let me ask: Did you ever worry about being disowned?"

"Oh, no," Philip said. And Brad said: "Certainly not in my case. My parents are very supportive."

"Which means," Laura said, "that we've all got to be supportive of Jerene in this, because she doesn't have that support. And she needs it."

They all looked at Jerene, who got up, went into the kitchen, and returned with a large multi-hued salad. Laura tossed and distributed it. "So how long have you two been involved?" she asked casually as she finished, and Brad and Philip both choked.

"Well — "

"I mean, we've known each other — "

"The fact is, we're not really involved, in a traditional way. We're just good friends," Philip said.

"Aha." Laura leaned back in her chair.

"Friends," Philip repeated.

"I understand," Laura said. "Of course. But — romantic friends, perhaps?" For this last phrase, she affected a clipped, mock-British accent, batted her eyelashes, stretched her lips thin.

"You might say that."

"So," Jerene said, "has anyone here heard the new Ferron album?"

Everyone had. They discussed it as, for a half an hour or so, the dinner wound itself down. It was like a ride through an amusement park fun house, lurching along through narrow corridors of frenzied display, then suddenly finding yourself at the end, ejected, dizzy on the cold street, a little sick to your stomach.

"She is something," Brad said.

Philip nodded.

"And your friend Jerene seems nice, too, though I guess she didn't have a chance to talk much."

"Oh, she's like that," Philip said. "She's always very quiet with company. Listen, do you want to have a cup of coffee or something?"

Brad was silent. In the light of Laura's coy questioning, anything could sound like a proposition. Anything. And, miserably, Philip remembered the evening last month when he had tried to say "Anything" seductively, and made a fool of himself.

"I mean at the Kiev," he added.

Brad shrugged. "I think I'm probably too tired," he said. "I kind of want to get home."

"I understand," Philip said. "I'm tired, too." He paused. "You know, I couldn't believe it when she asked us how long we'd been seeing each other. I felt very embarrassed. I'm mentioning it only because I don't want you to think that I said anything to her, that I suggested — "

"Philip," Brad said. "Of course not. Don't worry about it." He seemed annoyed.

"No," Philip said. "Of course not. I shouldn't have said anything."

Silently they moved on toward Brad's building, Philip remembering that uncomfortable night back when it had still been winter. Now a warm breeze blew. They walked ungloved, unhatted, without umbrellas. And Philip thought how nice it must be to be able, like Eliot, just to take off from a place you've come to call home, to eject yourself from the complex and dangerous network of friends, lovers, apartments, to sever all ties and leap into the startling newness of the unknown. Sometimes he tried to imagine doing it, just buying a ticket somewhere, say, to Paris, and going there, and he could almost feel the shock, the relief of knowing no one, smelling strange smells, feeling new breezes. But then he would remember that he hardly knew the language, that he had no friends to stay with in Paris; he would realize that once there, he'd have to begin again a ceaseless cycle of worrying — about laundry, about eating out alone and being mistreated by the waiters, about finding a boyfriend. Such concerns apparently didn't faze Eliot. He knew people everywhere, always had places to stay. And once again Philip envisioned Eliot in a trenchcoat, riding on a fast-moving train through some unspeakably beautiful landscape, with no luggage; he was standing on a sort of old-fashioned caboose balcony, the wind blowing through his hair. Probably he was going to Venice. Philip imagined Eliot and his lover, Thierry, riding a gondola through a jade-colored canal, strange, barnacle-caked towers rising above them on all sides. Some people left, some were left; it seemed the world required the two extremes, for balance. There would be no refuge in travel for Philip; he was too much of a coward for adventure, too yoked to routine and familiar comforts. Doomed, Eliot had said. Perhaps that was what he meant, as he sat writing in that dusty room in the Fifth, smelling "that Paris smell." Perhaps he was simply thinking of his own good fortune, and he had written "doomed," and added "to happiness" to cut the cruelty.

They arrived at Brad's building. Once again, they were standing on the stoop, and Philip found himself facing the trial of saying goodbye when he would have so much rather gone upstairs with Brad, settled himself into one of the bunk beds, and watched television or talked. Then Brad said, "Why don't you stay down here tonight? There's no point in your making that trip uptown when I've got plenty of room."

Philip's cheeks reddened. "Well — okay," he said, and laughed, he was so surprised, so thankful, so nervous. Clearly Brad was nervous too. "Okay, then," Brad said, and tripped on the stoop, and was short of breath as he climbed the stairs to his apartment. It had taken only a moment for everything to change.

Once inside, Brad flipped on the light, took his jacket off, and headed straight to the answering machine, which was pulsing red with enthusiasm to tell what it had to tell. There were messages from his mother, from Sally, from his friend Gwen at work, all of which he jotted down disappointedly. "The boy of my dreams didn't call," he said, and Philip turned away, almost but not quite brave enough to ask, "Will I do?"

Brad was reaching into his closet to fetch linen. "Do you prefer the top or the bottom?" he asked.

"Oh, I don't care," Philip said. "It's up to you."

"I actually kind of like to sleep up top, so I'll put you on the bottom." On his knees inside the crawlspace of the bottom bunk, Brad shook out a sheet. Philip sat at his white desk, his leg shaking. For once, it seemed they had nothing to say to each other.

They undressed modestly, trying not to notice each other's bodies. Climbing into the bottom bunk, Philip considered for a moment all that was implicitly sexual in this ritual of boys undressing, all that underlay that careful pose of disinterest. Then Brad turned out the light. Streetlamps shone up and through the thin gauzy curtain on the window. From where he lay on the bottom bunk, Philip watched Brad, also in his underwear, scurry up the little stepladder to the top bunk, his legs scrambling for a second before they disappeared. There was a soft thud as he landed.

They were quiet. In the dark of the apartment the only sounds came from the street. He could hear Brad breathing above him, hear how his body settled on the top bunk. This same anonymity had titillated him in college; sometimes he'd masturbated quietly while fantasizing that his very straight roommate was doing the same right above him. He felt a little bit now as he had then — distrustful of the dark, fearful of getting caught doing something or saying something Brad would misinterpret or resent.

"Brad," he said, when he was finally able to find words.

"Yes?" His voice was surprisingly hollow, as if the room itself were speaking.

"Can I ask you a question?"

"Sure."

"Why did you ask me to spend the night?"

There was a long silence. "I didn't see the point in your going all the way uptown this late," Brad said.

"But I've come down here a million times and you've never asked me to spend the night before."

Brad shifted in his bed. "Well," he said, "you know that I'm a shy person, a very private person in a lot of ways. I don't trust people easily."

"I know."

"I consider my apartment my refuge, my haven." He stopped, as if to choose the proper words, which made Philip nervous. "I'm safe here," he said. "I guess before you, there was never anyone I trusted enough to have here with me without spoiling it." He paused. "It just took me a little while to get up the guts to ask you up."

For a second, Philip's heart seemed to stop. "Really?" he said.

"Really."

"Thank you, Brad," he said. "I think I can say I feel the same way about you — even though my apartment isn't really very much to protect."

They were quiet for a few moments. "Does it bother you," Philip said, "when people assume we're a couple?"

"Aren't we?" Brad asked, and laughed, and Philip laughed too.

"I suppose so in some ways. It's nice, isn't it?"

"Yes."

"Brad?" Philip said. "Forgive me for asking this — but do you ever think about the possibility of us becoming a couple — really?"

"Sometimes," Brad said.

"Good," said Philip. "I do, too."

Above him Brad shifted again, and Philip imagined he was turning to face the window. Moonlight was streaming through the venetian blinds. Philip thought of Venice, and suddenly connected these blinds, these common things he had grown up with, with that mysterious, aquatic city he had only once visited, and hardly remembered. Did light shine through blinds like this in Venice? he wondered. Were lights shining on Eliot in Venice? He pretended that he was in Venice right now, that gondolas were passing on a canal below the window.

Then he noticed Brad's hand, dangling from the top bunk, apparently without intent. Illuminated by the moonlight, it seemed to glow.

Cautiously he reached up and took the hand. Brad's fingers were warm, as he'd imagined they would be, and Philip remembered how long it had been since he had touched someone. Gratefully he squeezed, and Brad squeezed back.

They lay like that, holding hands, for several minutes, until finally Brad said, "You know, we probably won't be able to get to sleep this way."

"I know," Philip said. He gave Brad's hand a last squeeze. Then they let go, and, saying goodnight, each curled toward the wall to fall asleep.

LATE AT NIGHT, in bed, Laura clung to Jerene, could not sleep until her head was curled in her lover's breast, and, when she was sure Jerene was asleep, whispered like a charm, "Never leave me, never leave, never leave me." Everything frightened her: supermarkets, large dogs, men. Not to mention phones. When Jerene — finally convinced to seek out her grandmother — asked Laura to do her the favor of making the initial phone call to the Briteview Laundry, Bensonhurst, inquiring as to the current whereabouts of the former owner, Mrs. Nellie Parks, Laura shook her head wildly, and dissolved in a babble of apology and self-loathing. She was a wreck on the phone, she explained. Jerene had had to swallow her twenty-five years of fear and make the call herself. She was relieved when a child answered.

"May I speak to the owner?" she said.

"We don't deliver," the child said.

"No, I'm not calling about that," Jerene said. "I'm interested in some information about the former owner, and I need to speak to the present owner."

Then there was silence on the line, followed by a stern female voice with a Jamaican accent.

"I don't know about the lady was here before," the woman said. "I been here three years now and I don't know nothing."

"Her name was Nellie Parks," Jerene said. "Please. It's important. I'm her granddaughter, and I have to find her."

"I'm very busy," the woman said. "No time. What you want it for?"

"I'm her granddaughter," Jerene repeated. "There's a family emergency, and I must get in touch with her."

The lady sighed. In the background Jerene could hear dryers churning. "Well, maybe I have something," she said finally. "You just hold on."

She left Jerene holding the phone for about five minutes, and then she got back on and said, "Eighteen fifty-four South Forty-fifth, and that's all I know. Goodbye."

"Is there a phone number?"

There was. The woman recited it and hung up.

"I'm really sorry," Laura said. "I can't believe it, but there's just panic shooting through me, just at the idea of it. Feel my heart." She sat paralyzed on the sofa.

Jerene dialled the number. A voice that reminded her of the computer on "Star Trek" picked up and said, "Pinebrook Home."

She breathed deeply and asked the question.

Mr. Parks, the voice was sorry to report, had passed on last year, but Mrs. Parks was still a resident.

Jerene asked for visiting hours. Every day between ten and five, the voice said.

"Thank you," Jerene said, and hung up.

She went on a Friday, riding through Queens on the Long Island Railroad into the very first fringe of suburbs. It was a brisk, sunny day — the kind of March weather that seems somehow fraudulent, hinting at the possibility of a snowstorm the next afternoon. Children were jumping rope and riding bicycles enthusiastically on the small, quiet streets she walked to the nursing home. There were even some sunbathers lying on chaises on the small lawns, their skin white with cold, braced against the breeze, diehards determined to enjoy this first sunny day even if it killed them.

It surprised her to be walking through a neighborhood of houses. So many years had passed since she had last gone home, so many months since she'd stepped off the island of Manhattan, that she had practically forgotten that smell of grass she was smelling now, the tender, green gentleness of a suburb after school lets out. Here, residential streets formed a grid with big avenues filled with supermarkets and little shopping malls, and nothing was taller than a few stories. Red brick houses, all alike, lined South Forty-fifth Street like sentries, and at the end was the Pinebrook Home for the Aged. When she entered, a whoosh of circulating air was sucked out of the automatic doors. The smell of vomit did not surprise Jerene. At the front desk she asked for Mrs. Parks's room, and a vacant-eyed girl in a nurse's uniform looked it up: room 2119.

She took the elevator. A hallway whose pale yellow walls were illuminated by pale yellow lightbulbs stretched before her, full of elderly women in their bathrobes, some in wheelchairs, some with walkers. They gave her frank, suspicious stares. In a little lounge area, others, fully dressed, almost elegant-looking in their outmoded finery, watched a rock video on a big television screen. With the help of a floor map attached to one of the walls, she made her way to room 2119. A television blared through the open door. Inside were two neatly made beds, two bureaus, and two armchairs, both empty. An elderly woman in a darkly patterned housedress, a black patent-leather purse slung over one arm, was sitting in a small desk-chair in the corner, watching television.

"Get it through your head, Mother," said a voice from the television. "Holly and I are going to be married, and that's final."

There was a cascade of music, the slamming of a door. Another voice whispered, "Over my dead body." Then more music. "I don't give my cat any old cat food," declared a new, different voice, and Jerene nervously crept into the room.

"Hello?" she said.

The old woman started, and stood up from where she sat. "Excuse me," she said, her voice high with offense.

Jerene stepped back. "I didn't mean to startle you," she said. "I'm sorry. I — Grandma, it's me. Jerene."

From where she stood, the old woman looked up, her mouth closed tightly.

"I came to visit you. I thought I'd surprise you."

"Jerene?" the old woman said.

"Yes. Your granddaughter."

Her grandmother's face melted. Tears came to her eyes. "Jerene," she said gently.

"Don't cry, Grandma," Jerene said, coming toward her. "Sit down here, in this chair."

"I'm just so surprised. Thank you. You can't know. I — I never expected to see you again. Sam only calls the last Saturday every month, and — goodness, I can't remember the last time he and Maggie came to visit."

Jerene had never heard her mother called Maggie before.

"I thought you'd gone away," Nellie said. "I thought — oh, it was ages ago that — you'd gone off to Africa, joined the Peace Corps. And then they told me you'd married someone there, you weren't coming back."

Jerene smiled. "Well, I'm back now."

"Did you have a good time in Africa?"

Jerene nodded.

"And how are your children?" She closed her eyes. "Oh don't tell me — let me remember. I know Maggie wrote me all about them. Let's see: Sam Jr. And what was the girl's name? Elizabeth?"

Jerene nodded. "Yes. Elizabeth."

"Are they with you?"

"No, they're there. In Africa."

"With their father?"

"Yes. He's taking care of them."

"Well, it's too bad. I would have liked to have met my great-grandchildren. Oh," said Nellie, "I — I wish I could offer you something. A cup of tea. Some cookies. But I don't keep much around, not since Sam passed on. You know, of course, your grandfather passed on last May, don't you?"

"Yes, I heard. I was very sorry."

"He was so sick," Nellie said. "It was a blessing, really. Tell me, how's your father and mother? They haven't been to see me since I can't remember, and when they do come, it's like they're not even here. To tell you the truth," she said, leaning toward Jerene confidentially, "I feel like I haven't known them in years. Ever since they moved to Eastport, or wherever it was." She looked Jerene sternly in the eye. "When was the last time I saw you? I wouldn't have recognized you. That haircut you've got — is that the fashion in Africa?"

"Yes."

On the television set a couple was kissing passionately. "My program," Nellie said, and reached for her glasses. "Do you get the soap operas?"

"No, I don't watch much."

For a moment, their attention was focussed on the screen. "Just think," a young, dark-haired man was saying to a pretty blond girl. "Only two more days and you'll be my wife."

"It won't happen," Nellie said sullenly. "The mother's out to stop it. Too bad. I get so worried when something bad's about to happen. A woman down the hall, she wrote to the network and asked them to tell her if everything was going to turn out all right for Steve and Kitty, in case she died before she found out? They sent back a form letter. Now she's worried all the time. But I say, it's a way to stay alive, right? It's something to live for."

Now the young couple were embracing again. A door blew open. Another young woman walked in, and the couple pulled apart.

"The last time you saw me," Jerene said, "I think it must have been my eighteenth birthday party. Remember? But what's most special to me — I visited you in the laundromat. I remember you let me put the quarters in the machines and push the levers in myself."

"Oh, all the little girls liked that," Nellie said. "Not me. It was a hard life. Not like the life you had, growing up in that big house with all those nice things. Look, there's the mother. She is out to make trouble for everyone else. No joy herself, has to take everybody else's away, I guess."

They watched the mother scheme for a few minutes. Then Jerene said, "Grandma? Do you think Daddy and Mommy will be visiting you soon?"

Nellie turned and faced her. "I don't know," she said. "Could you bring them?"

Jerene smiled. "We aren't getting along too well these days," she admitted.

"That's too bad," Nellie said. But her eyes were veering toward the television and finally, after giving Jerene a knowing, mischievous grin, she gave herself up wholly to indulgence until a commercial came on.

Now Nellie re-arranged herself in the armchair. "I'm grateful to have my program," she said to Jerene. "I don't have much of a life here anymore. But this — this is just like a life. It happens every day — except for the weekends. The weekends are hard, especially when they've had a big cliff-hanger on Friday. Usually I can tell when a big cliff-hanger's coming up as early as Tuesday. You know they're building up to something bad. The weekend that Jenny was on the operating table I couldn't sleep a wink."

When the program started again, Jerene said, "Grandma, I have to go now."

"Oh so soon? But you just came."

"I don't want to interrupt your program," Jerene continued. "Now that I know, I'll come back to visit you at a more convenient time."

"Oh, I feel so rude," Nellie said. "But my program is so important to me. Now tell me again — when are you going back to Africa?"

"Not for a while."

There was a loud crashing noise. On the television a car swerved to avoid collision, and then the screen went dark and a phone was ringing — whether on the show or in the real world Jerene couldn't tell. "Oh dear," Nellie said. "What's happened? Who was in that car?"

"Goodbye," Jerene said. But Nellie was lost in private anxiety and did not answer. Quietly Jerene moved out the door, leaving a vase of flowers and a box of candy on the bureau.

Her eyes felt heavy as she rode down in the elevator, as if caked with scrapings from the yellow walls of the hallways. She thought she might throw up from the smell of the food, and ran toward the exit. But when she moved through the heavy glass doors and out onto the street, it was as if the wind blew the scrapings away, bruised her alive again.

She did not think as she walked to the train station. She did not think as she changed trains at Jamaica, and changed trains again at Woodside. Indeed, only when she was under the familiar ground of Manhattan did she allow herself to remember the hidden fact, the tiny grain of knowledge. Maggie. Never in her life had she heard her mother called Maggie. It was a name from that dead time Jerene had never been allowed to talk about, that ugly origin which, when she brought it up, her mother shooed away like a fly: "Just be grateful for what you have," she'd say, as if in scolding, and immediately insist on buying Jerene a dress. No joy herself, has to take everyone else's away. Her mother was Margaret now. And when the ladies asked about her daughter, she invented a husband in Africa, and two beautiful grandchildren, Sam Jr. and Elizabeth. Elizabeth was Jerene's middle name, and sometimes, when they were alone, Margaret had called her Elizabeth. Jerene had been her father's idea, the name of his own grandmother, and she wondered if he had given it to her as a last offering to the pyre of his past, his part in a bargain that would guarantee her protection from everything the name meant.

When she got home, Laura was waiting for her on the sofa in the kitchen, chewing gum, one stockinged leg curled under her buttocks. "There's tea," she said. "I've made some really wonderful cookies."

"Just tea," Jerene said.

She poured the tea herself and sat silently on the sofa.

"What happened?" Laura said.

"I saw her."

"Oh wow," Laura said. "Was it okay?"

Jerene smiled and touched her hair, which was of course such a popular style in Africa.

"Yes," she said. "It was okay." She looked like she was about to cry. "Oh sweetheart, come here," Laura said, and taking Jerene into her embrace, held her there, silent, while the afternoon drained away.

I N   T H E   D A R K of her Sunday afternoon living room, cool through closed curtains, Rose searched a giant atlas for a six-letter Indonesian island known for its dragon lizard: blank-blank-blank-O-blank-blank. So far she had found "Tidore" and "Misool," both of which, once fit into the crossword puzzle, created more problems than they solved. But there were still many tiny islands to the north left to explore. She pressed on. She imagined herself a little cartoon captain maneuvering a crossword-patterned boat through a sea of words. She had finished the regular puzzle and was now doing the acrostic. Slowly, as she worked, a quotation was beginning to appear in the diagram, like a photograph emerging from darkroom fluids. Words that a moment ago made no sense were blossoming into comprehensibility, as when the G from GEORGE ELIOT transformed M — PI- into

MAGPIE. At the end, she knew, she would be presented with a whole thing — a coherent quotation, the title and author of which could be found by lining up the first letters of all the answers to the clues — and it was this she longed for. The meshing of meanings, the knitting of one set of words into another: It all made sense as a curative principle. And she wondered, suddenly, if all copy editors, encyclopedists, cartographers, crossword puzzle editors, were people who had stumbled into their careers because they desperately needed to forget things all the time. "The vultures of the thinking world," Owen had once called them, feeding on the leftovers of thought, on what remained after the great documents of history and science were pared down to reasonable size. As Rose was learning, such carrion was better than alcohol. This benign, useless activity literally tied up the brain; it blocked panic. In a burst of bitter energy, Rose thrust Thomas Mann and Timon of Athens into the fray. She fired out synonyms like bullets. But at the end her head ached horribly, as if her skull were a swollen, empty thing. The neatly completed puzzle had absorbed all order; her life remained as it was.

It was four o'clock. Owen, out somewhere, doing something, had invited a young teacher from Harte home for dinner. Thursday, at breakfast, he had said to her, "Rose, I forgot to tell you — I invited that young English teacher to dinner Sunday night, remember the one I told you about? He's lonely, I think, and needs a home-cooked meal. Do you mind?" What could she have said? The invitation had already been extended. And anyway, she was in some ways grateful to Owen for inviting the teacher. The presence of a stranger, she knew, would let her off the hook with Philip. He could not give her those pleading looks across the table — looks she could not bear.

She went to D'Agostino's. The air-conditioning blew her hair and numbed her face. She pushed her cart down the bright aisle of vegetables, arranged in fancy wicker baskets to reflect the market's new upscale image. As always, the place was full of women picking among the mounds of papayas and mangoes, their little babies' legs sticking through the slats of the carts. As a little boy Philip had loved it when she rode him in her shopping cart, had kept begging her to do it as late as his sixth birthday, when he was far too big, and it would have embarrassed her to be seen pushing him. She had not been an indulgent mother, not like some women she knew. One day she simply said, "No Philip, you're too big, and that's that." He looked at her, dumbfounded at first, and dragged at her leg as she maneuvered the aisles of the supermarket, trying to kick him off. This very supermarket.

But she was not going to think about Philip. She concentrated on pulling cucumbers, tomatoes, and squash from the bins, then turned the aisle, where a little girl was frantically trying to reconstruct a pyramid of toilet paper that she had accidentally toppled. "I said all of it," her mother commanded. Nearby, stuck in a corner, a haggard-looking woman not much older than Rose droned, "Free sample of low-calorie cheese spread, have a free sample of low-calorie cheese spread." She was wearing a stained hound's-tooth dress made from some sort of shimmering material. Across from her, a younger black woman, a girl really, dressed in tight spandex pants, was demonstrating a new kind of quick-cooking bacon at a little frying-station while a group of women watched desultorily. Rose stopped and gazed for a moment as the girl inexpertly turned the red strips. She would have liked to join the women, would have liked to have been able to absorb herself in so innocent a thing as bacon-frying. But it was too late for that now. She moved on to the checkout stand, where an electronic eye automatically calculated the prices of her purchases.

Having arranged for the groceries to be delivered, she went to Barnes & Noble. In the self-help section were many cozy books on self-assertion, how to put the zest back in your sex life, the Cinderella Complex. She looked through them feverishly. A couple of young women stood at the rack, absorbed in a book called *Go For It*. They were in their twenties, chewing gum; secretaries probably. They were genuinely interested in improving themselves. The sight of them made Rose feel fleetingly good, as she remembered the doldrums of her own life, those not-too-distant days when she too had had the luxury of worrying about whether she was going for it or was a victim of the Cinderella Complex. Those days had passed. What she needed now was a book telling her how to live in rubble.

Once, about five, maybe seven years ago, she had had a cancer scare — a mysterious lump in her back which, as it turned out, was nothing, a knot of fat. Still, in those first, terror-stricken days, she found herself perpetually drawn on her lunch hour to the "Health" section at Dalton's, where she flipped frantically through a book of symptoms, looking enviously at everything that was not a mysterious fatty lump embedded in the flesh of the back, covetous of fatigue, a sore throat, a mysterious exhaustion after meals. She would have embraced hypoglycemia if it meant she didn't have cancer. And indeed, she didn't have cancer, or hypoglycemia either. Thus she walked out of the doctor's office breathy with joy, shaking, and felt that classic surge of appreciation for the smallest things — for a tree bending toward the sun in a patch of sidewalk grass, for a woman crossing the avenue with twins in a carriage. But not for long. Those moments of the most intense pleasure, those moments for which she felt nostalgia at the same instant she was living them — they were brief indeed. Soon the business of life caught up with her, caught her up. Years passed. It was as if she'd been asleep. She looked once again at the symptom book. And once again she remembered who it had been, walking through her door on a normal night, full of news, eager to wake her.

Furtively, because she knew she was becoming addicted, she made her way to the aisle marked "Games and Puzzles." On the bottom shelf were neatly stacked books of acrostics. She thumbed through the first one she picked up, opened it randomly. The clues included: "French anthropologist, author of *Tristes Tropiques* (2 wds.)" and "mull, think over, consider." She thought: "Lévi-Strauss." She thought: "ruminate."

It was a good start.

Nearby, across the bookstore, the two girls were still entrenched in *Go For It*. Probably they worked for realty offices, read *Cosmopolitan* or *Mademoiselle* on their lunch hours, faithfully and honestly filled out the self-help questionnaires. She did not feel sorry for them. At that moment, she would have given anything to have their lives.

She grabbed the book of acrostic puzzles, and hurried to the cash register to pay for it.

Even though no one was home, the television was on to discourage burglars when Philip arrived at his parents' apartment. Fred Flintstone floated in a sea of cooked rice that spilled out the windows and onto the lawn. He and Wilma had reversed roles for the day on a bet. It seemed eerie, to Philip, the way the program played cheerfully to the empty apartment, to the chairs and sofa perched in a circle around it. He watched Fred battle the rice until a commercial came on: An unhappy-looking man was trying frantically to light a birthday cake, but the candles kept sinking into the frosting like periscopes.

Then there was a small commotion at the door, and Rose walked in, carrying the groceries the delivery boy had left with the doorman.

"Hello, Mom," Philip said.

"Philip," she said. "This is a surprise." She kicked the door closed and, staggering under the weight of the groceries, moved toward the kitchen. "Let me help you with that," Philip said. He took a bag from her arms and followed her through.

"You're earlier than I expected."

"Well," Philip said, "I didn't have much to do today, and I thought I might as well come early."

"That's nice," Rose said. She was putting vegetables in the refrigerator.

"Can I help you put things away?"

"Sure."

Dutifully he began to unpack the groceries — canned tomatoes, pasta, ground beef and veal. Seeing a cereal box, he was tempted to root through with his fist for the dusty paper envelope that contained the prize. He still longed for prizes. But the cereal was Familia — healthy stuff, no toys. Gone were the days of Cap'n Crunch and Count Chocula.

"You're making spaghetti?"

"Owen's bringing home someone from work, a teacher he says needs a good home-cooked meal," Rose said. "And there's nothing more home-cooked in this house than spaghetti."

"True," Philip said. "I'm glad. I've missed your spaghetti."

She was silent for a moment, as if distracted. "Well, I'm certainly happy to make it," she said, getting down on her knees before the refrigerator to put away the meat.

"Mom," Philip said, "do you know this teacher Dad's bringing home?"

She shook her head. "I haven't met him, but your father's talked about him a lot. He's from the South — Georgia, I think. He coaches lacrosse. This is his first year."

"So Dad told me."

Rose stopped where she knelt. "He told you?"

"Yes. When we had dinner together earlier in the week."

"You had dinner together this week?"

"Yes," Philip said. "Didn't Dad mention it to you?"

"No. I guess he forgot. What night was it?"

"Tuesday."

From where she sat, hunched, she hoisted herself up and walked back to the kitchen counter. The grocery bags were nearly empty.

"You work fast," she said.

Philip shrugged. "I know where things go in this kitchen."

"Yes," Rose said, "but how do you know things haven't changed since you moved out? How do you know your father and I haven't completely reorganized the kitchen?"

"I don't," Philip said. "I just assumed — why are you asking me that?"

Rose smiled tensely. "Just teasing," she said. "Thanks for your help."

She began to arrange pots and pans and cutting boards for cooking, and Philip returned to the living room. Wilma Flintstone was giving a speech about how a woman's proper place was really in the home. He watched for a few seconds, then switched off the set. Back in the kitchen, his mother was chopping garlic with a small paring knife.

"It hurts me when you're so cold to me," he said.

Rose paused in the midst of chopping, then resumed. "Cold to you?" she repeated.

"I come home, I haven't seen you for a while, you treat me like you'd rather I just jump out the window," Philip said. "Come on, Mom. There's no point in kidding around, or pretending what's happening isn't happening."

She stopped chopping. She put down the knife, moved across the kitchen, leaned her head into her hand. "Is that how I make you feel?"

Philip didn't say anything.

"I'm sorry, Philip," she said. "I'm having a hard time right now. You can't expect me to be all sweetness and light and maternal warmth all the time. Sometimes your own life preoccupies you. Warmth can be more of an effort than you're capable of." She rubbed her fingers together, went to the sink and washed her hands. "You're a grown-up now," she said. "You can't expect me to treat you like a child all the time or to pretend I'm feeling good when I'm not."

Philip ran his hand through his hair. "Mom," he said, "it seems to me something isn't being said here. What isn't being said is that you're mad as hell at me since I came home and told you I was gay. You can't get over it and you're furious. And I think you should just say it outright instead of pretending — "

"Don't put words in my mouth, young man," Rose shot back.

"I'm not putting words in your mouth. I'm telling you what I've observed."

"Then don't just assume you're the center of everything," Rose said. "I have a lot of other things in my life besides you." She returned to the garlic, chopped at it as if it were something she wanted to kill.

Philip was quiet. "Look, Mom," he said, "all I know is, whatever's bothering you, I seem to be bearing the brunt of your rage. It's not just today. For weeks now I've called you, I've tried to talk to you. When I see you, you act like you'd rather be anywhere else than with me."

"If you'd stop to think about it," she said, "you'd realize I haven't done anything to you, Philip. It seems to me you're not complaining about what I've done, you're complaining about what I haven't done. It seems to me you're mad because I haven't been your textbook liberal mother, going off and joining some organization, or wanting to talk to you all the time about your sex life, or spending all my mental energy trying to understand you. I'm not warm to you, I'm not kind, you say — well, right now I'm not feeling very kind, I'm not feeling very warm. And I have enough problems in my own life that I'm just not prepared to put out all the energy it takes to ease your guilt."

Wearily she scooped the garlic into a frying pan. "*My* guilt?" Philip said.

"Yes," Rose said. "You call me up, and all you want to hear is, 'It's all right, it's all right, all is forgiven, I love you.' Well it's not that simple. It's never that simple."

Philip sat down at the table. "You don't have to be cruel," he said.

"If you don't like it, don't badger me."

She switched on a burner. The garlic let off a hiss, a sharp bloom of aroma as it started to fry.

"Mom, I'm sorry you're having problems," Philip said. "And you're right. It's selfish of me to assume I'm the cause of them. But — well, maybe if you told me what was going on, what was upsetting you so much — "

"You seem to believe," Rose said, "that talking about it necessarily makes something all better. You seem to believe that confessing and opening up is always the answer. But I'm not so sure." She returned to the counter, where some onions waited to be chopped.

"I was hoping I could help you," Philip said softly.

Rose laughed.

"Is it Dad?" he said.

Rose stopped chopping. She stood silently over the onions.

"Mom," Philip said. "If there are problems between you and Dad, maybe if you told me, I could — do something."

She put the knife down and looked him in the eye. "I told you," she said, "I don't want to talk about this right now. Would you please just leave it alone?" She turned, fetched a larger knife from a drawer, and went back to her chopping. The odor of the onions filled the small kitchen, bringing a welt of pain to his eyes. He did not say anything, did not move. Finally Rose sighed loudly and said, "Look, if you want to help me, why don't you go set the table. That would help me a lot, okay?"

Philip nodded. "Okay," he said. He collected plates, silverware, and napkins and headed back into the living room. From the kitchen he could hear nothing but the blunt sound of chopping, an occasional tiny explosion as things were thrown into the pan to fry. The dishes set out (he still could not remember which side the fork went on), he returned to the kitchen. Rose poured the canned tomatoes into the frying pan. The sauce calmed.

Thick red bubbles burst its surface as it simmered, and Rose went to the sink to wash some lettuce.

"Did Dad tell you why he was inviting this Winston Penn?" Philip asked.

Rose shrugged. "To be nice, I guess," she said. "To give him a home-cooked meal."

"More than that," Philip said. "He told me that he — he was thinking of trying to fix me up with him."

Rose dropped the lettuce in the sink. "What?" she said.

"Just what I said," Philip said. "He thinks that Winston Penn may be gay, and since he knew how unhappy I'd been since Eliot left, he thought it would be a nice thing to introduce us."

Rose stood over the sink, closed her eyes.

"Didn't he tell you?"

She scooped the lettuce out of the sink and threw it into the salad bowl. "No," she said. "He didn't tell me."

"I'm sorry, Mom," Philip said. "I just assumed — "

"I want no part in this," Rose said, and stopped where she stood. "I want no part in any of this."

"Mom," Philip said, "please — I'm sorry I said anything. I shouldn't have said anything."

Rose tore at the lettuce in the bowl. "Fine," she said. "Fine."

Suddenly, fiercely, she closed her eyes, as if against tears, which surprised Philip. Awkwardly he stayed put. He hadn't seen her cry for years, hardly knew what to do. "Mom, please," he said, "don't be so upset. It's not such a big deal. Please — "

Then it was over. "It's all right," she said, and her lips heaved once. "It's all right. I've just got to finish this meal. I've got to get it cooked." She blew her nose and returned to the salad.

"Mom," Philip said, "we'll call Dad. We'll tell him not to bring Winston Penn."

"Too late for that now," Rose said. "They're on their way." She tore a piece of paper towel off a roll, wiped at her eyes. "Anyway, it's all right. I'll be fine. Now please, Philip, what I really need is to be alone just a little bit. Why don't you go out into the living room, put on some music or something?"

He hesitated. "All right," he said. "If you're sure you're okay."

She nodded. He walked into the living room and got down on his knees before the stereo cabinet. All the records from his childhood that he was too embarrassed to admit owning were there — albums by the Carpenters and the Partridge Family he had bought when he was eight or nine. He looked one over nervously — the Partridge Family in their black outfits, on their bus, with their saintly, beautiful mother, Shirley Partridge — then opted for the *Chipmunks' Christmas Record.*

"Philip," Rose called from the kitchen, "I really don't think that's appropriate!"

"All right!" he shouted. He took the record off. He was not used to Rose exhibiting strong emotion in his presence, had hardly ever in his life seen her move outside the middle ranges of ordinary worry and annoyance. Why did he put such value on revelation? she had asked. Why indeed?

There was the sound of keys in the door, a rustling of conversation. " — we can beat Dalton any day," Owen was saying, and blustered in, carrying with him a smell of outdoors — wet wool and exhaust.

"Hello, son," Owen said, and his smile was broad, too broad.

"Hi, Dad."

Behind him a tall young man in a trenchcoat grinned in greeting.

"Philip," Owen said, "this is Winston Penn. Winston, my son, Philip."

Winston Penn flashed at Philip a smile full of large white teeth. "Philip," he said, "good to meet you," and took his hand in a tight grip. His eyes were small and intensely blue.

"My father talks about you all the time, Winston," Philip said.

"I'm not sure I want to know what he says," Winston answered, laughing.

"Oh no," Owen said. "Only the highest praise for you, Winston. And you should hear what I say about the rest of the faculty! Ha!" He hit Philip on the shoulder, making him cough. His smile was terrible, undercut by the scent of liquor; he looked slightly unshaven; his tie was loosened, and he held his jacket over his shoulder. Winston laughed too — that same, unfamiliar locker room laughter, the laughter of men with men, slapping shoulders, validating affection with violence. Winston was perfectly shaved, not a nick on him. He wore a bow tie and a blue striped shirt just tight enough to suggest the tone and definition of his body, the build men in lower Manhattan gyms work years to attain, but in this case, a little slack, a little soft, making it clear it was naturally acquired in hard, hot adolescence, not purchased along with expensive weight-lifting equipment.

"Would you like something to drink?" Philip asked.

"Just a Coke would be good for me," Winston said. He sat down on the sofa. "I'll get it," Philip said before his father had a chance.

In the kitchen, his mother was violently shaking a vial of salad dressing.

"They're here," Philip said.

Rose smiled tensely. "Good, good," she said. He took a glass and a Coke from the refrigerator and followed her out into the living room.

"Hello," she said. "I'm Rose Benjamin."

Winston stood up to shake her hand.

"Rose," Owen said from where he sat, near Winston, on the sofa. "Rose — "

She looked away from him, wiped again at her eyes. "Onions," she said. "Just onions."

Owen was winning Winston. From Frank, his lover of one night, he had learned to affect the poses of macho camaraderie, and to his surprise had found that Winston, approached with such an attitude, responded with great enthusiasm. After the parents' day activities this afternoon, they had gone for a drink at a crowded Irish pub that Winston liked, "a real working-class place," he said, where the television blared sports shows, and everyone knew everyone, including the old Irish bartender, who waved a generous greeting to Winston and immediately handed him a beer. "Isn't this place awesome?" Winston had said. It was his favorite adjective of praise. He revelled in the pub, he told Owen, in the idea of pubs, in the idea of the intellectual as a true working man, the voice of the people. Tall steins of beer bubbled richly between them, and they talked about Bruce Springsteen, about the voice of the people. It was all very sexy to Owen. He kept imagining they might go work out on the lacrosse field and afterwards take a shower together.

Now they sat at the dinner table. Rose had made an unnatural amount of spaghetti, so much that it had to be served in the lobster pot, and all through the dinner the pot was passed back and forth between Philip and Winston, who took huge portions each time, as if he was afraid it would empty. "This is great spaghetti," Winston said the third time, and told a story about how, when challenged, he had once eaten three pizzas rolled up lengthwise at S.M.U. "That's good," Rose said. "A good appetite is something I like." She smiled and watched Winston eat. They all watched him eat.

"Tell us about your family," Owen said.

Winston's mouth was full. "Well," he said, wiping sauce off of his chin, "I grew up on a farm with my three brothers and my dad. My mom died when I was little, but then my dad remarried. I'm close to my stepmother." He tore a hunk of bread from a big loaf at the center of the table.

"Did you milk the cows every day?" Philip asked. "Did you feed the pigs?"

Winston laughed. "We had farmhands. My brothers and I just went to school and took cornet lessons once a week."

There was a moment of awkward, smiling silence, which Winston filled by filling his plate — "I think I'll just take a little more of this salad here," he said, and Philip hoisted the huge bowl over to him. They watched him as he served himself, and he smiled again and said, "This is really great salad." He looked at each of them in turn, then looked at his plate. Like most handsome men, he was used to being looked at, not at all used to being scrutinized. What did he make of this family, all eyes upon him?

"Philip," Owen said, "Winston's very big on Proust; aren't you big on Proust?"

"Well, I've read him, if that's what you mean," Philip said. "But I'm hardly an expert — "

Owen laughed. "I thought you were. Shows how much I know."

Then there was another gap in the conversation, and Winston took some more food. Philip gazed at Winston's moving mouth, until Winston, catching his gaze, smiled back at him, his eyes bright, and Philip had to turn away. He looked at his mother, who looked at Winston, and at his father, who looked at Winston. He could not escape looking at Winston. Owen and Winston talked about the school lacrosse team, and its star player, Jack Davidson, who was going to receive a special scholar-athlete award at graduation. And suddenly Winston winked at Philip; or at least, Philip thought he did; in any case, he looked right at him and smiled in a way that suggested a camaraderie of youth, an invitation to brotherhood. Thrilled, Philip laughed, smiled back, and suddenly wondered if his father's insistence that he liked Winston and hoped Philip might like him as well might not after all have been genuine. It seemed such a good, such a generous intention to Philip that a kind of euphoria suffused him, deep gratitude to Owen, who was suddenly revealing himself to be the dreamed-of perfect father. And once again he wondered what that smile (and possible wink) might mean.

As for Rose, across the table from him, she too smiled at Winston. From her vantage point — and she had the ultimate vantage point, the secret agent's longed-for anonymity, that of the nearly invisible, the unnoticed, the undesired — she observed how Philip and Owen mooned over Winston. They worked together in her mind, twin oafs from a thirties comic strip. She observed their mouths, always moving, smiling when they weren't talking. She observed their eyes, which was easiest, since they almost never focussed on her, although they blinked brightly, lowered, cast up and down in a perpetual flurry of response and observation. She betrayed no feeling; indeed, she thought she had none. She was numb, a copy editor, scanning coldly with an eye for detail, until, for a moment, she found herself wanting to stand up and topple the table, let the spaghetti and sauce and water glasses fall over all these men. She closed her eyes and counted to five. The impulse passed.

It seemed unlikely that she would be able to hold back from confronting Owen much longer; probable, now, that he would leave her or that she would leave him. As the wronged one, she supposed, the choice would be hers. But what would she choose? Oddly enough, the thought of leaving the apartment, of losing the apartment, no longer terrified her. Indeed, she was almost eager to get out of it. But where could she go? Probably to her cousin Gabrielle in New Jersey. And yet she knew Gabrielle was a bargainer. She would not accept no questions asked. Intimacy would be the price Rose would pay for being put up, even for a short while, because Gabrielle would not let her go until she had told her. And now she tried to imagine telling her, tried to imagine what the words would sound like, how she'd phrase it, the perverse freak accident of fate, the terrible coincidence (or was it a coincidence?): her husband and her son. Either, separately, had been the subjects of books, television movies, talk shows; both together was the stuff of tabloids, with headlines blaring above ugly lime-green and red photographs of movie stars: N.Y. WOMAN DISCOVERS HUSBAND AND SON SHARE SICK SEXUAL SECRET. Gabrielle would nod with concern, almost smiling, pity and delight firing in equal portions behind her eyes; and then disbelief; and the shocked, lewd thrill of the horrible, passed back and forth in whispers over the phone to her friends, other women, other wives, preceded by, "You'll never believe" — the delight in someone else's tragedy undercut only by gratitude that it isn't your own. "Can you imagine what it would feel like?" she'd say, and the answer, always — "I don't want to imagine it. I don't have to." And then they would go back to their lives, those wives, those friends of Gabrielle's in New Jersey, a little more grateful, a little less dissatisfied than they'd been before, and soon enough forget her. Rose raged at the looks she imagined receiving from Gabrielle, from women at work, from Penelope and Roger. They would fix her up with divorced men and kind widowers still mute from grief. But what men would want her? What if she did it to their sons, too? Oh, she did not want it, did not want to have to deal with any of it, did not want Gabrielle or offers of a new life or to leave this apartment or Owen. For how could Gabrielle understand? It was true that she was angry with Owen, furious with Owen. It was true that it had not been a great marriage. It had not even been a particularly good marriage. But it had been her life.

She looked across the table now, her mouth weak, her eyes wet. Like boys, the three of them laughed together, and she remembered suddenly, vividly, her youth, the feeling of her youth. She was a junior at Smith when they met. The youngest of four daughters, she had watched her sisters battle and make up with her parents, watched them become trapped, even as they moved into adulthood, in an unyielding knot of power and disappointment. All her sisters now lived near one another and near her widowed father, in Chicago, and continued to lead their lives with and around one another, acting out again and again the ancient griefs and jealousies of their childhoods. Rose, the baby, born seven years later, had withdrawn herself from this hot atmosphere early on, made it clear she wanted nothing to do with it and planned to leave, and in doing so had brought down the wrath of her parents, who demanded loyalty from their children as fervently as if the family were a war-weary nation they were devoted to defending. Even now her father considered her something of a traitor for having moved away, for refusing to come home for family holidays. When she met Owen she had thought, "Here is someone who can save me. Here is someone who can care for me." Owen too was a youngest child, his parents too had been old when he was born, and his father had recently died. He had lived through his adolescence being bullied by an army of older brothers and sisters; perhaps that was why he had seemed so gentle, so much gentler, at least, than the other men who had courted her. They dated for a time, and after two months made love in his little stuffy room in Somerville. Unlike the other men, Owen was not in much of a hurry for sex, and even seemed a little frightened, so that she wondered if he was a virgin and in the end had had to seduce him. But it was all right. He was so grateful, so surprised by her face above his when they made love that first time, that there were tears in his eyes, and she stroked his hair and kissed his forehead. For weeks after that he bought her gifts of rock candy and saltwater taffy from candy kitchens by the beach. And when they married, three years later, in a hotel in Boston, with the cheap band playing and the cheap little hors d'oeuvres being passed around, marching down the aisle on her father's tentative arm, she had looked at Owen as he came closer, as his bright, handsome smile, his thin face, came into focus, and she had thought she saw there evidence that everything was going to be right, that all her decisions were the right ones. What should she have seen? she wondered now. What had she missed? Wasn't Owen's gentleness evidence that no passion burned beneath his devotion, his gentlemanly love for her? "Save me, Rose," he sometimes murmured in bed, when they made love, in those early years, and she had wondered what he'd meant. Now, of course, she understood it all. He wanted her to guide him to the kind of life he longed to have, a family life, with children. But how could she have known that then? Homosexuality was a peculiarity to her, a condition to be treated in hospitals — not a way of life to be embraced or saved from. She had marched down the aisle, and now it seemed to her ironic that she should have seen in Owen's face assurance, a sign that she was making the right decision, when in fact she was making the first and largest of a series of mistakes that would carry her out into her life like an undertow, then cease, leaving her stranded, fifty-two years old, with nothing to look back on but a chain of wrong decisions carefully made, blindly made, an exam failed because the student has made one essential, thoughtless error over and over. Oh, why hadn't he told her? Why hadn't he let her know? Perhaps he imagined that those secret feelings he harbored would go away, fade with time; perhaps he thought he could cure himself, or that she could cure him. No, even if he'd told her, she realized (and it was a vague consolation), she would have married him anyway, would have believed, as he did, that marriage would provide the cure for the disease. The secret was thus buried, but even from underground it had its influence. A single lie, twisted and preserved, riddled the fabric of their lives together like a flaw in silk, so that a single rip might tear everything apart. They were not, and never had been, what they seemed; that she had somehow known all along. But how shameful that she had lived this life for more than twenty years, and never known, not even secretly, what it was they were.

She was the mother. She sat at the head of the table, her hands clasped tightly around one another, and watched her son and husband dance around the flame of Winston Penn. She served, and watched them eat a fruit salad with ice cream. Then she got up and began to clear the table. "Let me help you, Mrs. Benjamin," Winston said at once, and to her surprise, she said, "Yes, that would be nice." She headed into the kitchen, and Winston followed her, and she smiled to herself, relishing their frustration at having Winston taken away from them. They piled the plates in the sink. "I'll wash, you dry," she instructed. And removing her rings, she pulled rubber gloves over her hands, filled the sink with warm water. "That's a beautiful ring," Winston said, pointing to her Rome ring — a delicate, bejewelled thing she had found in an antique store off the Via Cavour.

"Oh, that?" she said. "I remember the morning I bought it. We were living in Rome for a year. Owen and I were out walking with Philip, and we saw this ring in an antique store window, and I loved it, I just loved it, the way you sometimes love a thing, even though you can't say why." She smiled. "It was expensive, but Owen said, 'Come on, Rose. Let's get it.' We had some money that year, from a fellowship Owen had won. But I'm talking too much — "

"Don't be silly, Mrs. Benjamin."

"Call me Rose — " She turned, and smiled up at him. "Rose," he said, and looked away, and suddenly she knew. It had taken her three minutes to determine what they had been struggling to figure out all night. She wanted to laugh. All through dinner she had stared at Winston warily, suspiciously, thinking him the embodiment of her fate. It wasn't true. He alone was her comrade, her kind. And somehow it thrilled her, this knowledge that even now Winston could belong to her in a way that he could never belong to either of them.

"Winston," she said, and felt herself running the name over

her teeth. "Winston. That's an awfully old-fashioned name for someone as young as you."

"I used to pretend I was named after Mr. Churchill," Winston said, "but the truth is it's a family name."

"I like it," Rose said. She handed him a pot hot from the bath of suds, steamy, and watched his rough, pinkish hands work the towel over its surface until it shone. A spot of moisture from the sink was spreading over his stomach. There was sweat on his forehead. He had wrists so thick that she imagined she could slip both of her arms through his watchband.

Suddenly he snapped his fingers and said, "Now I know. All through dinner, Mrs. Benjamin — "

"Rose."

" — Rose. Sorry. All through dinner, I was trying to figure out who you reminded me of, and now I've got it. You look like Gene Tierney."

Rose laughed. "Gene Tierney? You know Gene Tierney? At your age?"

"Gene Tierney is the woman of my dreams," Winston said. "She's the greatest. I've seen every one of her movies. And you look so much like her. You've got that same . . . charged quality. That's the only way to describe it. Charged."

"Ha!" Rose tossed her hair out of her eyes. She knew he was watching her rubber-gloved hand move in a slow circle over a skillet.

Owen and Philip came crashing through the swinging kitchen doors then, grinning. "Mom," Philip asked, "can I help?"

"Let me dry, Rose," Owen said, "don't make Winston do it."

She looked at them both, and suddenly smiled. "You're right," she said. "Winston shouldn't have to do this. Owen, you wash. Philip, you dry." And she led Winston into the living room, leaving Owen and Philip bewildered before the sink full of pots.

"You're the best cook, Rose," Winston said in the living room. "I haven't had a meal that good in years."

"Thanks." Suddenly, to her own fury, there were tears in her eyes. She kept smiling as if her life depended on it, turned away so he couldn't see.

"Rose," he said. "Are you okay?"

"Yes, I'm fine," she said. "Just fine." She pulled a tissue from a box, blew her nose. "Just don't mind me, Winston. Just — don't pay any attention. There," she said. "I'm fine. We have coffee. Would you like some?"

Winston shook his head. "Actually, I should probably be going soon. I've got to get ready for my classes tomorrow." He looked at her, worried, and she said, "You're a charmer, Winston Penn," and smiled, and blew her nose again.

He smiled back. "You are, too, Rose," he said. "You are, too." And suddenly, swiftly, he bent down and kissed her on the cheek.

Then Owen and Philip re-emerged, drying their hands on their pants. "I'm afraid I've got to go," Winston said, putting on the coat Rose held out to him. "Philip, could I give you a lift somewhere?"

"Sure," Philip said, and also put on his coat. "Goodbye, Mom." Then he bent to kiss her cheek, and to her own astonishment Rose found herself reaching out her arms and pulling him toward her, into an embrace he at first resisted out of sheer surprise, then gave in to. "Goodbye, Philip," she said, and looked at Winston.

"Goodbye," he said.

And now Winston turned to Owen, who stood, his hands still balled up in a towel, a look of vague disappointment in his eyes. "Goodbye, sir," he said in a tone of mock formality. "I'll be seeing you tomorrow."

"Are you sure you have to go so soon?"

"Afraid so."

"Well, I'm glad you could come tonight, Winston, certainly glad you could come."

"I am, too. Thanks for inviting me. Goodbye."

"Goodbye," Owen said.

Together the young men walked out the door. Rose closed it behind her, did up the locks. When she turned, Owen was sitting on the sofa, his eyes shut, his hands on his forehead.

"Your mood certainly changes fast," she said.

"I'm just tired, that's all."

She took a cloth and began sponging the kitchen table. In the table, her face emerged, clear as in any mirror: a face on the verge of panic. Winston was nothing. It was Owen she had chosen, Owen she would always end up coming back to, no matter how far awry things went. He was her husband.

He got up now from the sofa, and walked over to her. He was himself again, quiet, slightly absent, and he said to her, "Rose —"

She smiled. Unexpectedly she reached up and touched his face. He had aged well. This man in his fifties was really not so far from the boy she had loved. They looked at each other, each holding back for the sake of affection the words that must now be spoken, each desperate to prolong this last moment of innocence.

Then it was over. He sat down on the sofa, and she followed him, walking on to the window, looking out.

"Well," he said. "How much have you figured out?"

She closed her eyes, let the silence stretch out as long as she could bear, and then she turned to him and said, "Everything."

OUTSIDE, on Second Avenue, pieces of garbage clung to the corners of the building before being swept downtown by the wind. The doorman was helping an elderly woman get out of a cab. One hand clinging to the hat on her head, the other to his arm, she warily stepped into the wind, as if she were afraid it might blow her away. "So you really have a car?" Philip asked.

"Sure," Winston said. "Remember, I live in Hoboken."

"It's very nice of you to offer me a ride," Philip said. "But I really don't want to take you out of your way."

"No place is out of *my* way," Winston said, and Philip laughed, not sure what he meant. They walked down Forty-third Street, where Winston's car, a small red Toyota, was parked. "This is a nice car," Philip said, and Winston nodded. "It's little — but once you let her rip, this fucker could beat any Jaguar going around curves." He turned the key in the ignition, let the car warm up. "Where do you habitate?" he asked.

"I live on the Upper West Side," Philip said. "But I wasn't actually planning on going straight home — I was going to visit a friend of mine, in the East Village."

"That's cool," Winston said, pulling out of the parking space. "You're sure?"

"Sure I'm sure. Like I said, I love to drive, and I don't get enough of a chance to, now that I'm living here in the greater New York metropolitan area."

He honked like a taxi driver, maneuvering the car through the tight side-street traffic. "Are you in a big hurry?" Winston said. "I think I'll take you on the scenic route."

"No, I'm not in a hurry," said Philip.

"Good," Winston said. They turned onto Park Avenue. Winston dodged through a red light, and Philip settled back, grabbing onto the armrest for support. There was a stack of student papers on the back seat, a box of cassettes, and several copies of Milton. Above Philip's head, taped to the sunvisor, a pretty, dark-eyed girl smiled out of a snapshot.

"Who's she?" Philip asked.

"My girlfriend, Nancy," Winston said. "Or, I guess I should say, my ex-girlfriend, Nancy, at the moment." He laughed.

"Why at the moment?" Philip said.

Winston shrugged. "Mostly because I'm here and she's in Dallas," he said. "Long-distance is hard, you know?"

"I know."

"Well — Nancy's a nice girl. But I don't know — Hey, fuck you, you asshole!" he shouted to a taxi, which was attempting to cut in front of him.

"What's wrong?" Philip said.

"Yeah?" said the taxi driver, a thin, scraggly-bearded man wearing a bandanna. "Well, fuck you, buddy, you can just go fuck yourself far as I'm concerned."

"And you can eat shit, you shit-wiping moron!" Winston closed the window and put on the gas. "You've got to learn to speak the local language," he said to Philip. They edged in front of the taxi, zooming through a yellow light. "Anyway, as I was saying, Nancy's a nice girl, but we've been together since we were fifteen. Fifteen! That's a long time. I don't know; I'm ready to meet someone else, maybe."

Philip, still a little dazed from the shouting match, simply nodded. This man-to-man confidence made him uncomfortable. It had been a long time since he'd been in the company of someone who didn't know or assume he was gay, and he wasn't sure how to behave. Was it deceptive of him not to tell Winston outright? Would it be construed as a seduction tactic?

"If you ask me," he said finally, "I think you're lucky. A lot of people would like that kind of permanence, a relationship to last their whole lives. I certainly would."

"I guess," Winston said. "But Nancy and I — we were just kids when we started going out. We've been together so long I don't think we could even say what it was we see in each other. See, we're very different. She's not really an intellectual at all. Tennis is her thing."

He took a sharp left, carrying them west into Harlem. On either side of the street, bits of life glowed from the shadows — a child's face staring into a garbage-can fire, an old woman doubled over with shopping bags — all in sharp contrast to the sedate East Side streets, which were chill and empty by nine.

"My secret route," Winston said, "is New Jersey. I go over the George Washington Bridge and down the other side of the river. That way you not only get the best stretches of driving, you get to see New Jersey. I love New Jersey. I've discovered most New Yorkers don't know the first thing about the wonders of the Garden State. But when I met you, Philip, I said to myself, here's a guy who can appreciate New Jersey."

"Why'd you think that?" Philip asked.

Winston shrugged. "I could just tell. New Jersey's not sights. It's not Ho-Ho-Kus or Lake Hopatcong or the Paramus Mall, though those are all awesome places. No," he said, "New Jersey is a *state of mind*." He revved his throat like an engine. "Just to be in New Jersey, to feel New Jersey, is to experience . . . true cosmic oneness with the universe!" He laughed loudly. "So now," he said, "I've told you all about Nancy — it's your turn. Come on, 'fess up."

"My turn?" Philip said.

"Yeah, your turn. Come on. Tell me what *your* relationship status is, as they say out west. It's no fun if you don't too."

Philip looked out the window. "Well," he said, "I *was* seeing someone very seriously for a while. But it ended."

"Oh yeah?"

"Uh-huh."

"Okay," Winston said, "come on. Tell me about it." Again, he revved his throat.

"Not much to tell," Philip said. "He broke it off and went to live in Paris."

"They do that sometimes," Winston said. "What was the guy's name? I'll beat him up. Hey, eat shit, asshole," he shouted to another taxi that was trying to wriggle by him onto the approach to the George Washington Bridge.

"So go on," Winston said.

Encouraged, Philip went on. They were passing over the George Washington Bridge now, a rage of lights suspended high above the dark river. "Maybe I drove him away," Philip said. "Or maybe he was just sick of the relationship. Or maybe he really was a selfish jerk. I don't know."

He sighed loudly, and Winston shook his head. "You can never tell," he said. "Stupidly, somehow, you both end up being right and wrong, in different ways, every time. "Now," he went on, "now, we are *in New Jersey*." Like a man possessed, Winston looked around himself, his eyes aflame with what they were absorbing, but in the dark Philip could make out not a single detail. He guessed they were driving through trees.

"You just feel better in New Jersey," Winston said, pushing hard on the gas pedal. "And you can drive like an American — fast." Again he laughed. Reaching behind himself, he pulled a tape cassette from a box on the back seat and plugged it into the stereo. Bruce Springsteen sang "Born in the U.S.A."

They sped up, coming dangerously close to the back of a truck. Casually, at the last minute, Winston swept past it, and Philip closed his eyes and grimaced, prepared for death. Winston chuckled. "Did I scare you?" he said.

"A little," Philip admitted.

"Sorry. I get carried away when I listen to the Boss." They were slowing to a red light. It seemed they had reached a more populated area now — an ugly strip of motels, coffee shops, discount shoe worlds. "Here's where I eat dinner most nights," Winston said. "Now you can understand why I enjoyed your mom's spaghetti so much."

"She makes a mean spaghetti," Philip said. He was silent for a moment. "I hope you had fun tonight," he said finally. "My parents can be — to say the least — a little strange."

"I thought they were great," Winston said. "Anyway, I think your dad's great to start with. He's really one of the awesome bright lights of the Harte School."

Philip smiled. "Really?" he said. "You know, I went to Harte for a while."

"Oh yeah?"

"I hated it."

"Socially, it's a tougher place than anyone probably guesses,"

Winston said. "The kids are mean and smart, which is worse than mean and dumb, because they play tricks. And almost always it's the older against the younger."

"Do they still tell that story about the kid locked up in the basement?"

Winston smiled. "Every year. And it's hard to punish them. Because unlike most schoolkids, they do not believe in the God-given, terror-inspiring authority of the teacher. They're all so rich, they've been raised by their dads to know they're going to run the world, so what's a schmucky little peasant of a teacher got coming down on them? They just sit there and don't say anything, like they aren't even listening to you, like they own the world. And you know what? They're right. They do own it. That's the terrible irony of the place. They really do own the world." He shook his head.

"Do you like teaching there?"

"It's okay. I'm not planning to make it my life's career. But they're smart kids, and if you approach them the right way, they'll do good work for you. I figure I'll stay a year or two more, then probably go back to Austin and get my Ph.D. It's good for the moment. For a Southern boy like me, it's a real trip to be living in New York, let me tell you."

They were now descending into the greenish depths of the Holland Tunnel. "Isn't this unreal?" Winston said. "Isn't this totally unreal?" Philip nodded. Once, he remembered, as a small child, coming back from Gabrielle's, he and his mother and his father had gotten stuck underground in traffic for a half an hour, and when he had asked when they'd get out, his father had said ghoulishly, "We'll never get out. We're trapped forever." Philip had believed him and started crying right then and there. "Philip, honey, what's wrong?" his mother had asked, turning, alarmed, reaching her hands into the back seat to comfort him. But he did not want to be comforted. This time there was no delay. They sped through the tunnel, emerging suddenly from the green brightness into the dark, cool Canal Street night. "Back in Manhattan," Philip said, and Winston smiled. "Yes," he said. "I could tell. That great New Jersey feeling" — he snapped his fingers — "just like that. Gone." He sighed. "Now where did you say you were going in the East Village?"

"Tenth Street," Philip said.

They turned uptown. The wind seemed less violent down here than it had in his parents' neighborhood. Outside an unmarked nightclub, a row of white Mercedes limousines hummed, while a crowd thronged to be admitted. "I'm really glad you came to dinner, and that we got to meet," Philip said to Winston. "My father was very eager for us to get to know each other, you know. He thought we could be friends."

"So he told me," Winston said.

Philip was quiet for a moment. "My father — well, sometimes I'm a little embarrassed, you know, the way he tries to fix me up with new friends." He laughed nervously. "I just hope — I hope you didn't feel — "

"Like a blind date?" Winston said. "No, I didn't think of it that way at all. I had a great time. I really like Owen, he's a good guy, and believe me, there aren't that many really good ones on the faculty. Now where on Tenth Street?"

"By Second Avenue," Philip said, relieved. "Though actually, I wasn't thinking of a blind date so much as the gentleman caller in *The Glass Menagerie*. I imagined you must have felt like the gentleman caller, you know — just a normal person coming into a family madhouse."

"Really?" Winston laughed. "I suspect all vaguely intellectual families are secretly worried that they're the Wingfields. It's a universal American condition."

"Maybe," Philip said.

"Now my family," Winston said, "my family is the genuine article." But before he had a chance to elaborate, they were there, at Brad's building.

"I guess we're here," Winston said, pulling the car up in front of a fire hydrant.

"Yup," Philip said. "Well. Thanks for the ride."

"Hey, any time," said Winston. "And let's get together sometime, go to a movie or something, okay?" He hesitated. "I don't have that many friends in New York. I spend a lot of time by myself, which is fine. I do fine by myself, reading and exploring the Garden State. But I do miss socializing every once in a while."

"Fine," Philip said. "Maybe next week we can do something."

"Yeah, that would be great," Winston said. He reached out his hand, and Philip shook it warmly. "Well, so long, Winston. And thanks again."

"So long, Philip. Take care."

Then Winston rolled up the window, waved again, and took off down the dark street. It seemed a strange, anticlimactic farewell. "Oh, well," Philip said aloud, and turned to face Brad's building. The wind was calmer now. Seeing the light on in Brad's apartment, he climbed the steps up to the entrance, feeling strangely heavy, and rang Brad's bell.

"Who is it?" Brad said after a few seconds.

"Philip."

"Hold on."

There was a loud buzzing noise, and he was admitted into the inner foyer. Brad was waiting by the open door when he got to his apartment, in his bathrobe, smiling. "This is a surprise," he said, and Philip knew he was glad to see him.

They moved inside the apartment, which was warm with the smell of cinnamon toast and the low hum of Brad's tiny television set. "I just thought I'd drop by for a visit," Philip said. "It turned out this Winston had a car, and he offered me a lift home, and I just thought — well, as long as I can get a ride, I might as well come down and say hello."

"I'm glad," Brad said. He sat on the lower bunk and turned down the volume on the television. From Philip's angle, the tiny box seemed awash with silent, senseless progressions of light. "I was actually hoping you might come by tonight."

Philip smiled, sat down next to Brad on the bunk bed. From under the hem of Brad's terrycloth bathrobe, a lithe, well-tanned leg brushed Philip's jeans.

"So, how was it?"

Philip bit his lower lip. "Strange," he said finally. "Just — strange."

"How so?"

"Well," Philip said, "my mother was angry, so angry. I more or less confronted her when I got home about the way I felt she'd been treating me, and she really lashed back. She said I was being very selfish to assume that I was what was bothering her. And then, when I told her about Dad's wanting to fix me up with Winston, she almost started to cry, said she didn't want any part in it. And then Dad and Winston arrived, and she completely changed her mind. All of a sudden she was the model hostess, all smiles and nice remarks. She really put on the charm for Winston. And my dad — I've never seen him behave the way he behaved tonight. I mean, it was really bizarre. It was as if he had a totally different personality. He was loud, gregarious, for God's sake, which may not sound like much, but for my father it's a revolutionary act. Do you have any orange juice?"

"Of course," Brad said. He got up to pour some, and Philip lay back to stare at the mute television screen. "Star Trek" was on; Captain Kirk, dressed in a toga, was being forced to kiss Uhura on what looked like a giant chessboard. For a moment Philip thought he must be dreaming, but then Brad, who knew all the episodes of "Star Trek" by heart, arrived with the orange juice and said, "This is definitely one of the strangest 'Star Trek' episodes ever. The idea is that the Greek gods were really aliens, and they're still around, only they've gotten very evil. It's called 'Plato's Stepchildren.'" He handed Philip the glass of orange juice, and Philip propped himself up on his elbows to drink it. "I seem to have appropriated your bed," he said. "It's okay," Brad answered. "I'm small. There's probably room on it for both of us." He sat down on the edge, as if in hesitation, then hoisted himself onto the bed, so that he lay parallel to Philip, and Philip could feel the warm side of his body.

"So go on."

"There's not much more to tell. The dinner itself was pleasant, if uneventful. I mean, nothing happened in particular. But everything, everything was strange. And strained. I could tell that underneath her smile my mother was watching me like a hawk, and watching Dad, while the whole time he was trying to pretend she wasn't there."

Brad lifted himself onto his side, propped his head in his hand. "But you haven't told me the best part," he said. "You haven't told me about Winston, or your ride home."

"Oh, that!" Philip laughed. "Well, Winston was smart, and very nice. A little bizarre. He had this whole spiel about New Jersey being the center of the universe, or something, and I could tell he thought he was really funny, but also, on some level, I think he believes it. What I like about him is that he seems perpetually enthralled by the world. For instance — did you ever find when you were a kid that when summer vacation ended, and the back-to-school sales started, you would suddenly just want to beat your head against a wall because the vacation had passed so quickly, and you hadn't appreciated it? And you wished you had just a few weeks to live over, so you could sit there in your room knowing you had over a month until school started again, and savor that fact, sit there and relish it?"

"Of course," Brad said. "But you never could have done that. It's Zeno's Paradox all over again."

"Maybe," Philip said. "Still, I think Winston's like that. I mean, I think he savors every moment while he's living it the way the rest of us can only appreciate moments when we remember them. Which is a real talent."

Brad shuffled impatiently. "Was he really all that handsome, like your father said?"

Philip yawned. "Yes. Very handsome. And very, very straight. He took me on a tour of New Jersey on the way down, none of which meant anything because it was so dark. And he made a big show of swearing at cab drivers and going too fast. It was fun."

For a few moments they lay there, not speaking, and then Brad said, "I think I'm going to switch off the light now." He paused. "Would you like to spend the night, Philip?"

"If you don't mind."

"No, not at all."

There was no mention of the top bunk this time. Philip closed his eyes and felt Brad get up from the bed and switch off the light. Quietly, in the dark, Philip pulled off his shirt and jeans and got under the covers, delighting in the strangeness of new sheets. After a few seconds he felt a rustling, and Brad got into the bed as well. They lay there, not touching for a moment, and then Brad cautiously put his arm around Philip's chest, and Philip took his hand and held it. Brad's heart was beating violently, so violently he was almost shaking, and Philip gently rubbed the skin over his knuckles and wrist to calm him. "You know," Brad said, when he had relaxed a little, "I was once in love with a straight man. In college."

"Really? Who?"

"I don't think you knew him," Brad said. "His name was Richard, and he was in an art history seminar with me. He'd just transferred from the University of Virginia, and he really didn't have any friends at first." Brad laughed. "God, I loved him. He was always confiding in me his worries about the fact that he just wasn't as good as some of the other players on the soccer team. We used to sit in his room at night, and he would read aloud to me homosexual passages from Proust."

"Brad!" Philip said. "I never knew any of this."

"You didn't really know me in college," Brad reminded him. "Anyway, you can imagine how excited I was, only I was so naïve then, so unsure of myself, I hardly knew what to do. But the best part — and this is the reason I remembered the story — was his car. He had a car, and once or twice a week he'd call me up before dinner and we'd drive to the outskirts of town, where there was this fantastic Chinese restaurant, sometimes alone, sometimes with a few other people. Anyway, this Chinese restaurant — the parking lot was on a hill, and going down the hill you had to go over this big dip which was made by a bump in the road. It was like a roller coaster. After we'd eaten I'd always say to him, 'Richard, go slowly, you know that dip really scares me.' And he'd laugh, and of course he'd take it as fast as he could, so fast the car would heave and screech, and we'd lift off our seats, and when I screamed he'd laugh hysterically and then drive too fast all the way back, just to scare me even more. I think I loved it."

"Of course," Philip said. He lay very still, gently tracing pictures on Brad's back with his finger. "Did anything happen?"

Brad sighed. "One day I couldn't stand it anymore. I remember I was sitting in my room listening to this song by the Tom-Tom Club, and — I swear this is true — just as they sang the lyrics, 'Make your move,' the doorbell rang. It was Richard. He said he was just passing through and thought he'd stop to say hi. He saw I was upset, and he asked me what was wrong. And I told him. I just up and said, 'I'm in love with you.'"

"You're kidding."

"Nope. I knew I just had to say it. It was the bravest thing I'd ever done in my life."

"And what did he say?"

Brad smiled wistfully. "He was wonderful about it, really. He told me he felt very blessed. And then he went on to tell me he was converting to Catholicism, and this was going to be a significant part of his transformation — because faith is love, and he'd never really believed anyone could love him. Then he told me he loved me as well, and was only sorry he couldn't do anything about it physically."

"That was very nice of him."

"Yes," Brad said. "It was."

"Did you stay friends?"

"Oh — more or less. Except that soon after that he got a girl-friend, and then — well, he was busy. We didn't see that much of each other. And then he went off to Russia for the summer, and then to Germany for the year, and then — well, I don't know what happened to him. He's still in Germany for all I know." He was silent. "I think he was kind of fascinated by my loving him so much. If I'd been older and a little smarter — but I wasn't." He turned to look at Philip, his face awash with color from the television. "You know," he said, "I've almost never talked about this. Just because — well, it's always been kind of a sacred experience for me. I didn't want to taint it by talking it up to every-body."

"I'm glad you feel you can trust me."

Brad moved a little closer to him. "If I didn't feel I could trust you," he said, "I don't think I'd be lying here with you."

"I'm glad to be lying here with *you*," Philip said, since it was Brad's bed, and Brad smiled. They were still in the same position, Brad's arm pulled over Philip's chest, holding hands. Then, with his toe, Brad switched off the television set, and the room was dark. They lay silent for a while, matching their breathing to each other.

"I wish we'd done this sooner," Philip murmured.

"So do I."

They turned, so that Philip's mouth was in Brad's hair, his stomach against Brad's back, and Brad gave out a small, needful moan, closed his eyes, and gathered himself closer into Philip, like a mollusk pulling into its shell. Outside the window Philip could hear the sounds of nighttime mayhem and revelry. He listened.

Eᴇʏᴇs ᴄʟᴏsᴇᴅ, Rose faced the black window, shredding a tissue. She was not crying. She was not going to cry. Owen sat on the sofa, one leg hoisted over the other, his left hand stroking his own hair gently as a lover's, while the right, buried in his pocket, clasped and unclasped a set of keys. He talked into the pillow, as if to no one, but he knew she was listening.

"It was only a matter of time," he said. "I knew we'd have to talk about it, only I wasn't sure you wanted to. I thought maybe you wanted to just let things be, let sleeping dogs lie."

Ever the perfectionist, Rose said, "Nothing's sleeping here."

"Not anymore," Owen said.

It was astonishing, Rose thought, how quickly the tide of warmth, of love that had ridden her into this confrontation, had passed. She treaded cold water now; indeed, as soon as Owen spoke those first acknowledging words, she felt herself tighten and shrink, the way the skin of the thumb shrinks in the bathtub. Probably somewhere inside she had still secretly wished she might be imagining things, still hoped he'd say, "What are you talking about, Rose?" But of course he had not. He remained motionless on the sofa, his face as resigned and toughened against crying as that of a child brought before the principal for reprimand.

"I suppose you should know that Philip told me," she said, "about your reason for inviting Winston tonight. He wanted to know if I was in on the plan with you."

"I didn't give him any reason to think that," Owen said. Rose laughed. He looked up at her, confused. "What's so funny?"

"I was just thinking about how many times I didn't notice things," she said. "How many times I averted my eyes, how many times I drew ridiculous conclusions just so I wouldn't have to face the truth. Now, suddenly, all these things are making sense to me. All the gaps are filling in. It makes me laugh."

From where he sat, Owen lifted his head — rather, Rose thought, like a cartoon rabbit taking a peek at the world outside his hole. For a moment he rested his gaze on her face, then returned it to the darkness of his armpit. "Yes," he said, "I guessed it would be like that for you. It was for me, the first time I — " He paused. "Anyway, the reason I invited Winston was that I wanted to do something nice for Philip, to help him. It would be good for him to find someone, I think, don't you?"

Rose was grimly silent. She seemed to be concentrating intently on something out the window, although there was little to be seen — a woman across the street washing dishes; traffic; sky.

"Do you want me to talk about it?"

She shrugged.

"I guess that means yes. All right. I suppose I should begin by explaining about the Sunday when we ran into each other. By telling you where I was going that Sunday, and every other Sunday. I was — "

"I wish you wouldn't," Rose said. "I really don't think there's any point in your sharing the gory details with me, Owen, I really don't see how that's going to do either of us any good."

"I'm sorry. I just thought I should make things clear for once. We're talking about twenty-seven years of secrets, Rose. Things I've kept bottled up my whole life."

"Just because you want to say them doesn't mean I want to hear them." Her voice was thin and quiet. He looked up and saw her before the window, not facing him, the tissue reduced to a heap of blue in her hand.

Owen swallowed. "Okay," he said. "I can accept that. But then what should we talk about? Should we talk about the apartment? Should we buy?"

"Why do you act like it depends on me?"

"Because it does."

Grimly she bit a piece of cuticle off of her thumb.

"You can leave me, Rose, if that's what you want," Owen said. "Or I'll leave. If that's what you want, I'll do it."

"And what if it's not what I want?"

"Of course then I'll stay."

"What does that mean?"

"It means what it means," Owen said. "I want to stay, God knows, Rose. I'm not going through some mid-life crisis; I don't want freedom. Everything I know, everything I feel safe with in the world is here, with you. But I feel like I have to be honest. No matter how hard I try to convince myself I can just cut it off, no matter how hard I try not to think about men — " He shook his head. "It's no good. Even if I wanted to, I couldn't stop now. I'm too far gone. It's become too big a thing, bigger than I can con-trol. Even if we weren't having this talk, I'd still feel it, I'd still be lured into things I wanted — and didn't want at the same time. It's so hard to explain." He closed his eyes. "The other night," he said, "I met someone."

"I don't want to hear it," Rose almost shouted, shut her eyes, then got control of herself again. "I told you before," she said. "I don't want to hear about any of the details, so if you're going to insist on sharing them, we might as well stop right here. It's too much for me." She turned around again and looked intently into the mirror of the television screen, her arms wrapped tight around her waist. Owen groaned, lifted his head. "Rose, you're going to have to face them sooner or later," he said wearily. "For Christ's sake, please, don't shut me up anymore; it'll just be bad for both of us if we go on pretending."

"How you can say that to me," Rose said calmly, almost in a whisper. "How you can say that to me — I just don't understand." Her back, the only part of her he could see, was subtly shaking, her arms clenched even more tightly around the pale flowers on her blouse.

"Rose —"

"Because it isn't pretending for me. I am your wife. I have made my life with you."

"I know you have. And it's been a fine life. And it will continue to be a fine life for us. But we have to face the facts — "

"Don't you see how it kills me, how it absolutely destroys me to hear you say that? Pretending? All our marriage, everything with me? Just pretending? Don't you see? Even if it's true, what it means for me — "

"But it wasn't *all* like that. Rose, you know I love you more dearly than anything on earth; I always have and I always will. Still. There are facts to be faced here, for me as well as you. Sexually — I am more attracted to men. It's something I've been hiding, suppressing for years, only letting out — "

"Not that part," she said. "Not that part."

He sighed in frustration. "All right. Not that part." He paused, choosing his words carefully. "I want to stay with you, stay married to you. I feel like that's the bottom line."

"And will you continue — these exploits?"

He was silent for a moment. "I don't know."

"And how do you think I'll feel?" she said, turning to face him. "Think about me for once. A marriage which is a sham, a pretense. My husband *and* my son, both, both — for God's sake, my life is like the punch line to a stupid joke."

Inadvertently, she started to laugh, and Owen laughed, too. Then they stopped suddenly. Once again Owen looked grimly at his lap. "Rose," he said, "forgive me for pointing this out, but you haven't exactly been faithful to me."

She raised her head.

"I'm sorry to bring it up. I never wanted to. I know you thought I didn't know. But I did. Not that I minded. The truth is, it made me feel a little better, a little less like I'd wrecked your life. Because I thought you deserved that — real love, from a man who really felt what men should feel for women. I sat back and didn't say a word; I never made any ultimatums even when I felt jealous. I figured I was getting what I deserved — as punishment."

She was silent. "Is that all?" she said.

"Yes."

Then, very quietly: "I don't think my having relationships with other men is in any way comparable, in any way like — "

"My having relationships with other men?"

"Don't interrupt me. No. And not for the stupid reason you think I'm thinking. Because I was very careful, Owen. I made sure I never disrupted our lives together. It was a separate thing, something I needed — for reasons which are now clear and obvious. But with you — what you're saying is that the whole premise of our marriage has been a lie, a sham. And that's bigger than cheating on someone. Because it means for you that our marriage was the cheat, your — other life, that was the real thing." Her voice grew suddenly softer. "With me," Rose said, "you were always the real thing."

"I don't know what you want from me," Owen said quietly. "An apology? Okay. I'm sorry I married you. I'm sorry I ruined your life."

She laughed, turned to face him. "You're determined to turn your guilt around on me, aren't you?" she said. "You're determined to make me the guilty party. Well, okay. You want pity? I'll give you pity. It broke my heart, you looked like such an idiot tonight, salivating over that boy you'd brought home for your son to — to — "

"Rose, that's going too far — "

" — slobbering over him like that. I felt such pity for you. Jesus Christ, I thought, does he have no dignity at all?"

"It wasn't like that," Owen said. "It was nothing like that."

"Do you know what it felt like for me to just sit there and watch you with him? Embarrassed by you? Knowing you didn't even know what an ass you were making of yourself?"

"Rose," he shouted, "enough!" and she was quiet. "I told you," he said. "Enough."

"Good," she said. "Enough. So go call up Philip. I'm sure the two of you will have tons to talk about." And she turned away again, her throat dry, astonished at the electricity, the venom running through her.

Owen got up from the sofa. She could tell he was behind her from his breathing against her neck. He touched her, and her shoulders flinched. She wanted, suddenly, to throw him out, to tell him to leave and never come back. But the anger in her was burning off as quickly as alcohol. Soon it would all be gone.

Owen was silent behind her. Then he walked to the closet,

pulled on his coat. "I'll go for tonight," he said. "We both need some time. But I'll call tomorrow. Okay?"

She said nothing.

"Okay, Rose?"

"Just leave me alone," she said.

"Christ, Rose."

Then the door opened and closed again.

For a few moments she stood there, hugging herself, listening to the newfound silence. Then she turned. His imprint sagged the sofa. The radiator buzzed comfortably; traffic went by. It was 11:24.

She walked into the kitchen, poured herself a large glass of milk from a carton with the picture of a missing child on its cover, and sat down at the little table. The cold white liquid went down her throat in a series of chill gulps, making her gag, causing, like ice cream eaten too fast, an intense, sudden ache at the back of her neck. She felt as if she had just vomited; her throat and stomach were raw with the aftertaste of upheaval. It was Sunday night. It felt to her, suddenly, as if there would be no Monday, no breakfast, no return to work, as if the rest of her life would be an eternal, sleepless night spent waiting impatiently for dawn, knowing the rest of the world was enviably sleeping.

The milk was gone. She looked at the glass, coated still with white droplets, and almost couldn't bear its emptiness. Terrified, she opened the dishwasher, shoved the glass into its blue interior. She craved beginnings. There was "The Honeymooners" at eleven-thirty. Things would be starting up all night, but they would also be ending.

In the living room she turned the television on low; its hum soothed her. She opened the acrostic book; read, "Find fault with"; thought, Criticize? Disapprove? Upbraid?

A RIOT OF TELEPHONE RINGING drummed through
the night, tore the thin membrane of Philip's sleep. He was
dragged awake, his eyes opening to a darkness in sharp contrast
with his bright dream. Confused, he lifted himself onto his elbows, trying to figure out what could be making this strange,
shrill cry. All he could see in the dark were the glowing blue
diodes of Brad's alarm clock. It was 1:17 A.M. The phone
screamed, blared, wept. Beneath him he thought he felt the full
weight of one of his own limbs, the circulation cut off, until he
realized that what he was feeling was Brad's arm lodged under
him. "Brad," he said. "Brad."

"What?" Brad shouted, bounding, leaping out of sleep like a
gymnast.

"The phone."

"The phone? The phone?" Brad said, his voice edged with
panic. "But it's the middle of the night. Jesus, who could be
calling?" He reached back, snapped on a light, grabbed for the
phone. "Hello?" he said. A few beats of silence passed. He looked
at Philip. "Yes, he's here," he said. "Hold on."

He handed Philip the phone. "For me?" Philip said. "Are you
sure?"

"Of course I'm sure."

He put the phone to his ear.

"Philip, it's your father," said a voice made ghostly, distant, by
static and traffic noise.

"Dad! What is it? What's wrong?"

"No one's hurt," Owen said. "Everyone's fine." Something
roared in the background. "You're probably wondering how I got

this number, aren't you?" he said. "But it wasn't hard. When I couldn't reach you at home, I just called your friend Sally — her number was in your room — and she told me to call here. I hope I'm not waking you, or — disturbing anything."

"No, nothing, Dad," Philip said. "Look, what's going on? What's wrong?"

"Nothing's wrong," Owen said, then started to cry.

Philip knelt in the bed. Brad put an arm on his shoulder.

"Dad, where are you?"

He could not answer.

"Just calm down, now, Dad, and tell me where you are."

"I'm at a pay phone outside the Burger King on Cathedral Parkway," Owen said finally. "It just closed. I was sitting there until it closed. I came up here, to your apartment, but you weren't home. I'm sorry. I don't have anywhere else to go."

"Did you and Mom have a fight? Is that what happened?"

Owen blew his nose. "I suppose," he said, "that what has happened is your mother and I have temporarily separated."

"Dad — I don't understand — what do you mean, separated?"

"I'm sorry to be bothering you, but I was hoping I could stay at your apartment. I know I'm interrupting, I know it's late. I'll just go to a hotel."

"No, Dad, don't be ridiculous," Philip said. "I'll come up. Just wait for me outside the building. I'll get in a cab, I'll be there in twenty minutes, okay?"

"Philip, I don't want to drag you away from your friend, I don't want to do anything like that — "

"Dad, don't worry. Look, just meet me outside my building in twenty minutes."

Again he blew his nose. "All right," he said. Then, as an afterthought: "Thank you, son."

"Don't worry about it. I'll see you soon. Goodbye."

They hung up. "What happened?" Brad asked, putting his arms around Philip in the strange light.

"I have to go," Philip said. He pulled himself out of the bed, grabbed for his clothes.

"What's wrong?" Brad asked. "Where's your father?"

"He's at a Burger King. All he told me was that he and my mother have 'separated,' whatever the hell that means at one in the morning."

"Separated! "

"That's what I said."

"Jesus."

Philip pulled on his pants, reached for a shirt. "Look," Brad said, "I'll go with you."

"Brad, you don't have to do that."

"I don't care, I'll go with you."

"I think," Philip said as he put on his socks and shoes, "I think I should go there by myself."

Brad sat back on the bed, against the wall, and closed his eyes. From the top of the dresser Philip gathered his wallet, change, and keys and stuffed them in his pockets. "Do you need money for a cab?" Brad asked.

"No, I've got it."

Brad stood up, put on his bathrobe, and walked Philip to the door.

"Well," Philip said, "goodbye," and laughed, still not quite believing that ten minutes out of sleep he was leaving Brad and going uptown to save his father.

"Goodbye," Brad said. Spontaneously, without thought, they kissed for the first time, long and lovingly, then stood there in the doorway, embracing, their eyes shut tightly. "I don't want to leave," Philip said. "I feel safe here. I really want more than anything else to stay here with you, Brad."

"I'll be here," Brad said.

"Thanks," Philip said. "If I don't come back, it's only because I can't. Well, here I go, out into the wild blue yonder." He zipped his jacket, kissed Brad again. Then he unlatched the door and slipped out through the crack of the opening. He moved quietly on the stairs, not wanting to wake anyone.

Outside the street was empty, dark save for the light of a single lamp.

In the cab, speeding uptown, Philip felt strangely giddy, almost drugged. He hugged himself for warmth and leaned back against the stained seat, forcing his eyes wide open to wake himself. He was remembering a night early in his childhood when he'd woken up sweaty and retching, and his parents had had to take him to the emergency room. A fresh snow had fallen, and sitting in the cab he recalled how strange he'd felt as he was carried from sleep out into the world, still in his pajamas, wrapped in blankets. Rose, wearing her nightgown under a coat, held him under the awning of their apartment building while Owen raced up and down the silent, bright midnight avenue, searching for a cab. Snow fell perpetually through that memory, even in the little examining room in the hospital where the doctor gave him a suppository; snow, and with it an unspeakable dread. He didn't believe the world would ever be the same again after that; and he assumed that every night of his life, snow would fall in huge drifts, and death would be close at hand. Tonight it came back — that fearful sense of unreality, as if he was a spectre in someone else's dream. His own capacity for feeling was so heightened that he felt like one of those children bruised into allergic shock by the mere touch of the natural universe. Everything frightened him. Turning to look out the window, he was confronted with the familiar West Side skyline — darker now, since almost every light was out. The city had always seemed huge to him from this vantage point, and it still seemed huge, but now it was not so much a place where anything might happen as a landscape he might get lost in, disappearing forever the way people seemed to be constantly disappearing in this city. Posters were put up, rewards offered; people posited theories, claimed to have seen their friends wandering, ghosts, on West Street. A divinity school student, a secretary, a Korean immigrant who spoke no English — all gone without a trace. He imagined himself among them now, his own face staring, like theirs, from the makeshift posters on café walls, in the subways.

The cab turned up Broadway, where neon-lit signs still blazed above closed stores, and a few men huddled under awnings. A huge streetcleaning machine was crawling along the other side of the avenue like a strange nocturnal animal, blackening the pavement with water. The cab turned again, then came to a stop outside his building. "Thanks," he said, paying the driver, who roared back downtown without a word. Now he was alone. Only a few lights glowed, dim and yellow, in the windows of the tenements, the only sound the distant humming of the streetcleaner, blocks away.

He walked slowly up the steps into the squalid little entryway and found Owen there in his trenchcoat, squatting on the ground, his eyes closed. "Dad?" he said.

Owen jumped up. "Philip," he said, "I must have fallen asleep." He smiled. His eyes were red, swollen. A tiny track of dried blood ran from a crack in his lower lip down his chin.

"Thanks for coming, son," Owen said.

"Let's go inside," Philip said, and fished for his keys. "You must be cold."

Again Owen smiled. They went in, climbed the yellow flights of stairs to Philip's apartment. He hadn't cleaned the place up in a while, and a fusty odor of dirty clothes hung in the air. "Let me open some windows, air the place out," Philip said.

But Owen said, "Don't do anything on my account." He took off his coat, hung it up on a hook in the kitchen. "Take anything you want from the refrigerator," Philip said as he pulled sheets off the bed to re-make it.

"Oh, don't do that. I fully intend to sleep on the floor."

"Dad —"

"No," Owen said. "I insist." He walked to the refrigerator, opened it, and took out a cardboard carton of orange juice. "Check the date," Philip cautioned. "It could be bad."

Owen opened the carton and smelled it. "I'm afraid so." He laughed. Then he pulled off his jacket and tie and sat down on Philip's sofa to remove his shoes. Then he pulled off his socks, and Philip saw his father's pale ankles, lined with thick red grooves that mirrored the pattern of the socks. They were blue socks; a few inky spots of sweat stained Owen's toes. "I should have thought to bring a change of clothes," he said. "But I'll just go back and change after I know Rose has left for work."

"That seems like a good idea," Philip said. He took a pair of pajamas from a drawer and carried them modestly into the bathroom to change. When he came out, he saw his father leaning over himself, with his head close to the ground, staring at the floor.

"Dad," he said.

Owen didn't answer.

"Are you feeling bad?"

Owen lifted his head, gave a weak smile. "I don't know, son," he said. "I guess I'm just confused. This is the first time in years I've spent a night anywhere besides with your mother, at home. Sometimes — I just don't know myself anymore."

Philip looked at the ground. "I'm sorry the orange juice is bad," he said. "But I have some very good apple-apricot juice. You'll like it."

"Thanks, son, no."

"Okay." Philip turned to look out the window. "So — do you want to tell me what happened?"

Owen didn't move. He sat on the old sofa, breathing audibly. "I'm not sure," he said quietly, "how much you've figured out this last week about me."

"What do you mean?"

He was quiet. "I'm a homosexual," he said. "I'm a homosexual, too."

Philip stared at the neat rows of garbage cans in the alley, listened to the hiss of the radiator.

"Does that news surprise you, son?"

"No, not really," Philip said. His eyes began suddenly to tear. "It's just I — I guess I never let myself see it before."

"We said the same thing to you, remember, your mother and I?"

"Yes." He was shivering violently, but he could not bring himself to move from the window. He wrapped his arms around his waist, ground his teeth to keep them from chattering, tried to will himself into stillness.

"Did you tell Mom tonight? Is that what happened?" he managed to ask.

Owen shrugged. "More or less. She's had it pretty much figured out since the night you came home to tell us about yourself. So it was just a matter of talking about it."

"And how does she feel?"

"Confused," Owen said. "And angry." His voice grew soft. "She said she thought I made a fool of myself with Winston tonight, that I embarrassed her. Did you think that?"

"Dad," Philip said, "I hope you don't think because I told Mom what you'd said about Winston — that — "

Owen shook his head. "Don't worry. She knew already." He looked away. "I really hope I didn't give myself away like that. If so — I don't know how I'll ever be able to face — how I'll ever —"

"Winston wasn't embarrassed at all. He told me in the car on the way home that he had a wonderful time tonight."

"He did?"

"Yes. He likes you a lot, Dad; he thinks you're great. So don't worry."

Owen smiled in spite of himself. "Well, that's a bit of a relief," he said. "But Rose." He sighed. "I don't know what's going to happen, Philip — if we'll stay together, if we'll separate. One minute she's so angry, the next so — sad, so weak."

Philip hugged himself tighter. He counted the garbage cans out the window, counted the windows of the tenement across the alley.

"You're probably wondering," Owen said, "how long I've known. And the answer is, like you, all my life. But when I was growing up, things were different, Philip. Oh, some people managed, I suppose, even though it meant sacrificing your family, your career — everything. It was a disease, you see. So I married your mother and hoped it would go away. I really did hope that. Those first few years I tried so hard. But the problem was sex. I — I couldn't have an orgasm without fantasizing about men, and I had to have an orgasm, or else your mother, she would have — do you mind me telling you all this?"

Philip shook his head, kept counting.

"And then," Owen said, "we moved to New York." He paused, took a breath. "Suddenly there was this huge homosexual world, open and enticing. Or maybe it had always been there, and I was finally ready to start looking for it." He gave a long, low sigh of pain. "I've never talked about this, do you realize that? Fifty-two years old. This is the first time in my life I've admitted it that's not over the phone. My God. My God."

He was silent. Philip closed his eyes and prayed he wouldn't cry, that his father wouldn't cry. He braced himself against the window, knowing he must keep control, knowing he must not stop his father no matter how much he wanted to. What had started had become inevitable; it was as if Owen were giving birth to something with his words, something that was determined to fight its way out of him.

Owen began to talk then, and it was as if he couldn't stop. "I started going to the Bijou and other porn theatres when I was thirty," he said. "Boy, was I scared the first time I went — but also excited. Because what those men were doing on that screen — that was what I wanted to do, what I'd always wanted to do. And they did it so naturally, so willingly. They weren't shy or scared. They weren't worrying about whether it was wrong. It's strange, but those porn films were kind of healing for me. Everyone thinks pornography is alienating, and I guess it is, but for a man who's as scared as I was — well, it was telling me what I felt wasn't so wrong, and that I wasn't alone in feeling it. They were saying, Don't push it out of your mind. Revel in it. Celebrate it." He smiled. "The way those men made love," he said, "there was rebellion in their eyes. That meant something to me, Philip, it really did. So I got braver. I started to meet men at the Bijou, have sex with them. Not much at first. But then, over time, more and more until I'd done everything — or at least, everything you could do in a public place. And all without a word, without an exchange of names, isn't that incredible? Not once. Afterwards I'd feel so guilty I'd just run out of there and swear I'd never go back. I'd go every Sunday and every Sunday I'd come back and see Rose and just want to kill myself, I felt so bad for what I was doing to her. All week I'd swear I wouldn't go back. But then Sunday would roll around again, and I just couldn't control it. Do you see?" he asked. "I really couldn't control it. That was why I was so curious when you told me you'd gone to the Bijou. I thought, What if we were there at the same time? If I'd ever run into you there, Philip — well, I don't know what I would have done. I just assumed from the beginning that you would hate me, renounce me as your father if you ever found out. Maybe that's why I was so distant, as a father, all those years. Maybe I was thinking, If he doesn't really know me that well, it won't be so much of a blow when he learns the truth." He laughed bitterly. "It was horrible, really, what I was feeling, the sense I had that I was running a terrible risk every minute of my life — risking my family, my career — but not being able to help it; somehow just not being able to help it. I was thinking every day how I had to change my life, how I couldn't go on this way; but I knew the more I thought that, the farther I was getting from where I thought I should have been. It was as if I was fighting the wrong thing, fighting my life with Rose when I should have been fighting the homosexual stuff. But it was out of my hands by then. The more I thought about the possibility of loving a man, the more I couldn't go back to my life with Rose, and yet I couldn't bear the Bijou anymore, just couldn't bear it. And then you came home, with your news." He smiled. "I was so shocked," he said. "I'd never imagined you might be gay, I guess because I was so caught up in thinking how I'd tell my straight son the truth about me. Everything you said terrified me, but it also inspired me, I guess, gave me incentive. That night, I realized I couldn't go back to the way things were. Good or bad, I was too far gone. And after that — well, it was just a matter of time before Rose saw it. I'd let my guard down. I guess subconsciously I must have wanted her to find out, because I stopped covering my tracks. It was so easy, not having to cover my tracks. So blissfully easy."

He was silent. "I'm sorry I'm talking so much," he said. "I know it's very late. You probably have to go to bed. I won't talk anymore."

"Dad, don't be silly," Philip said. He looked at the clock and saw it was already close to three. Sleep was no longer a possibility anyway.

Carefully he turned to face his father. "Are there things I can do?" he asked. "Are there ways I can help you?"

Owen shrugged. "I met a man the other night," he said. "I think I may see him again. Also married, younger than me, but not much. I like him very much."

"That's good," Philip said. And again, for emphasis: "That's good. But what about Mom?"

Owen sighed. "I don't know," he said. "I just don't know."

"I'm sure everything will be fine," Philip said. He turned from the window and walked over to the closet, knowing his father was trying to catch him with a stare. He gathered blankets and sheets and began to make Owen's bed on the floor. "I'm afraid it won't be too comfortable for you," he said. "Are you sure you wouldn't rather have the bed, and I'll sleep on the floor?"

"It doesn't matter much," Owen said. He stood and walked to the window. "Jesus," he said. "I can't believe this is happening. I can't believe this is really happening to me."

"Dad," Philip said, "you're doing the right thing, talking about it. Don't ever doubt that."

"I know," Owen said. He laughed. "It's funny, I'm shaking all over, just like on my wedding day. I feel so strange, so alone and cut off, like I've done something irreversible, and things will never be the same again and nothing will ever feel normal again, feel good again — " And again he was on the verge of tears.

"It feels that way tonight," Philip said. "But tomorrow will be different." He wished mightily he could summon the courage to embrace his father and knew he could not. "You *will* feel good again. I promise. Give it time." And Owen nodded.

He had laid the blankets and sheets on the floor. "Are you ready to go to sleep?" he asked, and Owen turned, wiped his eyes. "Thank you," he said, looking at the makeshift bed Philip had created. "That looks very comfortable." Absently he began to unbutton his shirt, and Philip turned away, turned out the light. But the apartment was bright with moonlight, and in the shadows he could still see his father's heaving chest, his small brown nipples with their rings of gray hair. He looked for a few seconds, then averted his eyes. Owen undid his belt, unzipped his pants. With a crash of keys they fell to the ground and he stepped out of them. He looked forlorn in his big white boxer shorts, lost. Carefully he picked his way across the floor, lay down on the nest of blankets, gathered himself into a ball. The sheet did not stretch far enough to cover his feet. He shook visibly, screwing up his eyes as he tried to will himself into whatever sleep this night might offer him.

Philip stepped past him into the kitchen. He brushed his teeth, watching the brush move back and forth in the mirror. Then he rinsed his mouth and stood in the entry to the kitchen before his father's prone body. He would lie awake for a long time, he knew, looking at Owen's white ankles in the bright moonlight.

To my loving parents,
Anthony and Bessie Storey

ACKNOWLEDGMENTS

My thanks and gratitude to:

Glen and Berna Swodeck for helping me lay the foundation for this book;

Iann Schonken for his research contributions to this work;

Barbara Dycus, my editor, and the talented team members at Creation House for bringing it all together;

and a loving God who is willing to share His ideas with His children.

CONTENTS

Be the Best

Jim Storey

STEPS
ORDERED
BY GOD

G OD, WHAT do You want me to do?" It's a question we all have asked — even after we've repented of our sins, surrendered our wills and committed our lives to letting God have His way.

We often find ourselves wondering: Have I really heard from God? It looks like a great job, but is that what God wants me to do? Colorado Springs looks like such a beautiful place, but would it be God's idea to move there? I think I'm in love, but is this God's choice for me? Is this where I should work?

According to the Bible, "The steps of a good man are ordered by the Lord" (Ps. 37:23). That verse means it is possible for every single step a good man takes to be ordered for him by God. Therefore, if you are a good and righteous person who is walking with the Lord and listening to the Holy Spirit, you are probably making decisions every day which keep you right smack dab in the middle of God's will.

Still there are times you wonder (so do I!). How can

we have an unshakable confidence that we are doing exactly what God wants us to do — regardless of how things may appear? How can we trust the Lord completely and not rely upon our own logic and reasoning?

For many of us, the I-can-do-it-myself attitude of childhood invades our adult decision-making abilities. Self-sufficiency and independence are much-sought-after adult attainments. We become filled with good ideas to make our lives better. "I can take this self-help course to get a better job," and "I can pull myself up by the bootstraps and go on from here" become our pattern for living.

This isn't true for the Christian. The believer has been born again and must learn to step back into childlike faith and trust in a Father who knows best how to lead our lives. Our good ideas are no longer adequate; we need God ideas for our lives. The God ideas for our lives are the steps which have been ordered by the Lord.

Do you remember how Nicodemus struggled with being childlike? This highly educated Pharisee crept to Jesus by night, asking, "How can a man be born when he is old? can he enter the second time into his mother's womb, and be born?" (John 3:4).

Even Jesus' disciples did not always recognize the God idea that Jesus was trying to show them. They thought it was a good idea for him to eat supper when the only *meat* He wanted was to do the work of His Father (John 4:33-34). When Jesus tried to share the God idea with them about His coming death, Peter actually rebuked Him, saying, "Be it far from thee, Lord: this shall not be unto thee" (Matt. 16:22). Even when Jesus demonstrated the God idea by casting a demon out of a child when His disciples couldn't, their only response was, "Why could not we cast him out?" (Matt. 17:14-21). They were still attempting to use human logic and reasoning to explain what only childlike faith could comprehend.

You may have to forsake your *good ideas* for the purpose of finding His *God idea* for your life. If your trust is based solely on what you have been told by other people or by what you have read in books, you will have difficulty discerning the God idea for your life. True trust in God is based on a personal relationship and divine encounter. Not just *knowing about* God, but *knowing* Him intimately and trusting Him completely.

God longs for us to trust Him with every part of our lives. I was at a transition point in my life after I finished pastoring a church in Texas. We were considering several options for our future, but I needed to know the God idea as far as where my family should live.

I thought of moving to California, where I have close relatives, or to a different part of Texas. But I was leaning toward a decision to move my family to the Phoenix-Scottsdale area of Arizona. There are so many nice things about Scottsdale. It is a beautiful tropical environment. I love sports, and the Phoenix Suns were having a pretty good year.

I decided to take my wife and mother to the Scottsdale area to look for homes. We looked at some lovely, well-built houses. As we walked into the backyard of one particularly nice home, I saw a swimming pool and a view overlooking the cliffs around that area.

Now this is beginning to seem like a God idea, I thought to myself. I was caught up in the surroundings, the weather and the location of that house.

But as my wife and I talked about the decision to relocate to Scottsdale, the Lord showed us this was not a God idea — it was just our own good idea. Even though I liked the Phoenix-Scottsdale area, that was not the place for us.

Our God idea does not affect just us. It affects many people around us. It was God's idea for my family to move back to Southern California. There are many people whose lives could be touched for God if I was obedient to His God idea for my life.

The lives of many people have been changed through a Bible study I do for friends in my hometown. If I had not come to Southern California, they wouldn't be touched. I have been able to reach celebrities in Bel Air with a Bible study. They might not have been reached for God if I had been disobedient to the God idea of living in Southern California. A local outreach program in which I have been involved called *Hope 4 L.A.* has now expanded into *Hope for the World*. It might not have had the same impact without my obedience.

It was crucial that I discern the God idea for this time of my life. With God's help I did — and so can you.

How is it possible to distinguish between what I want and what God wants? How can I tell the difference between His voice and my own?

It is my earnest desire that the ten principles in this book will help you find the God idea for every circumstance of your life. God wants to share His plans for every step you take. He will bring order and direction to your path — and set you on the way to fulfilling His destiny for your life. ◊

INTRODUCTION

GOD'S PEOPLE
NEED
GOD IDEAS

BROTHERS CHARLES and John Wesley were two of God's people with a God idea. Though they attained great achievement and influence, their God idea consumed them with a desire that the doctrines of salvation be articulated by the preaching of John and the hymns of Charles throughout the world.

A glimpse backward at their beginnings shows us where this burning commitment to a God idea began.

Charles Wesley was born prematurely in 1707 — more dead than alive. He was wrapped in soft wool in the hope that he would survive. He did. In 1709 a fire destroyed the rectory in Epworth where the Wesley family lived. Charles was rescued from the Epworth fire by his nursemaid. John Wesley's face was seen at an upstairs window, and he was the last to be snatched from the flames by two brave villagers. It was a scenario John never forgot. He thought of himself as "a brand plucked out of the fire" (Zech. 3:2).

Both brothers knew they had been spared for a purpose which became clear to them when, within the space of three memorable days in 1738, they each discovered the reality of saving faith. They knew that God had given them a God idea — raised them up to do a work for Him in evangelizing Britain.

John and Charles became partners in the shaping of Methodism. Fired by their God idea and their own experience of saving grace, the Wesleys traveled the length and breadth of the land with unquenchable zeal to offer Christ to all. Their vision and goal were nothing less than a mission to the nation.

John Wesley reportedly once said, "I look upon all the world as my parish." Indeed historians have hailed John Wesley as one of the foremost social reformers of his century. His obituary announced that "by the humane endeavours of him and his brother Charles a sense of decency in morals and religion was introduced to the low-est classes of mankind; the ignorant were instructed, the wretched relieved, and the abandoned reclaimed."[1]

Use the Road Map

God prepared an abundant life for us before we were even born. Part of His plan is for us to do good works. He has given us a road map — the Bible — as a guide to help us fulfill that plan.

One time I decided to take a guest singer from Sweden to Los Angeles's famous Farmer's Market. As we drove through Los Angeles, the visiting singer noticed that I kept getting lost. Finally he said to me, "Do you know where you are going? Don't you have a map?"

"No," I replied. "I've been this way before, and I

think I know the direction."

But I didn't. After getting lost several more times, he exclaimed, "Please, just take out your map, even though you think you've been this way before!"

It is just as important for us to use our spiritual road map. The Word advises us:

> There is a way which seemeth right unto a man, but the end thereof are the ways of death (Prov. 14:12).

Our road map can keep us from straying onto the ways of death.

God's plan for our lives is to do good works — to change our world as the Wesley brothers changed theirs. He has already given us an abundant life (John 10:10) and ordered our steps (Ps. 37:23) so that we can reach our destinies.

Then why do many people struggle to find God's plan? Some people have a lot of reasons: "It's the enemy — the devil," "It's my circumstances," "It's a lack of faith" or "It's because of my family background."

I believe the main reason people struggle is because they do not believe they are who God says they are.

Know Who You Are

> I will receive you, and will be a Father unto you, and ye shall be my sons and daughters, saith the Lord Almighty (2 Cor. 6:17b-18).

> He that believeth on me, the works that I do shall he do also; and greater works than

17

these shall he do (John 14:12).

Every person who acknowledges Jesus as Lord becomes a son or daughter of God — and has an incredible work to do for Him.

One day near the end of the Civil War, a young slave girl named Mary gave birth to a frail, weak infant whom no one expected to live. But he did live, and a few months later he and his mother were abducted by supporters of slavery.

Moses Carver, who owned Mary, was unsuccessful in his attempt to fight off the assailants. Both the baby and his mother were sold to new owners. The mother was never found, but the Carvers located the baby, brought him back to their farm and raised the boy as if he were their own son. They had no way of knowing that one day George Washington Carver would be one of the most influential men in American history.

There was something special about young George Carver. He loved nature and animals, spending long hours walking in the woods. It was a habit he continued throughout his life. He once told his adoptive mother that he wanted to know all there was to know about everything.

He accepted Christ when he was ten years old. "God came into my heart one afternoon while I was alone in the loft of our big barn." Kneeling beside a barrel of corn, he prayed for Christ to become his Savior.

Young George Washington Carver knew God loved him, and he knew the God idea for his life. His dream was to train and equip young black men and women so they could be a vital part of the American work force. He found his calling on the campus of Tuskegee Institute in Tuskegee, Alabama, where he remained for forty-seven years. He wrote, "I want [my students] to find Jesus....How I long for each one to walk and talk with the Great Creator through the things He has created."

Overcoming the severest of odds — poverty and slavery — Carver became one of the country's most respected agriculturists. He realized that the soil of Southern farms became worn out from constant planting of cotton. He suggested the farmers rotate their cotton crops with plantings of peanuts and sweet potatoes.

One day Carver asked God, "Mr. Creator, why did You make the peanut?"

With God's help, Carver discovered more than three hundred marketable products made in part from the peanut, including mayonnaise, cheese, shampoo, instant coffee, flour, soap, rubber, face powder, plastics, adhesives, axle grease and pickles. He discovered an additional 150 uses for the sweet potato.

His love for Christ, and his confidence in God's love for him, helped him to conquer the negative effects of poverty and racial prejudice. In the end, he earned the respect and admiration of his peers and the grateful acknowledgement of future generations.[2]

George Washington Carver believed, as did the Wesley brothers, that he could make it with the God idea from a God who loved him very much. Many people believe that somebody else can make it — but not themselves.

God wants you to know that *you* can make it. God has a God idea for you. You will fulfill your destiny when you believe that you can.

Believe That You Can Make It

Rahab the harlot fulfilled her destiny. She was a prostitute — everybody in her city knew she was not living a good life. But when she heard about God's people coming to her city, she grabbed the opportunity to change her life. She had enough faith to believe that God could do something great — even through her.

> And the woman took the two men [Caleb and Joshua], and hid them....And she said unto the men, I know that the Lord hath given you the land....for the Lord your God, he is God in heaven above, and in earth beneath. Now therefore, I pray you, swear unto me by the Lord, since I have shewed you kindness, that ye will also shew kindness unto my father's house....Then she let them down by a cord through the window: for her house was upon the town wall, and she dwelt upon the wall. And she said unto them, Get you to the mountain, lest the pursuers meet you; and hide yourselves there three days, until the pursuers be returned: and afterward may ye go your way (Josh. 2:4, 9, 11-12, 15-16).

She reached a point of desperation. Often this is the key to our willingness to change and follow a God idea. We must be at a point of desperation.

Near the end of his boxing career, the great boxer Muhammad Ali started doing something he called the *rope-a-dope*. When his opponent began to flail him with punches, Ali would lean up against the ropes, cover his head with his arms and let that fighter keep punching and punching as he simply blocked the punches. He called this the *rope-a-dope* because he would lean against the rope and play "like a dope."

When his opponent started to tire, Ali would do his famous *Ali shuffle* — shuffling his legs and coming out with a flurry of punches, often knocking out his opponent. I think it is time we quit doing the *rope-a-dope* in our spiritual lives and begin the *Ali shuffle!*

Maybe in 1986 you said, "This is going to be my year." The next year arrived, and again you asserted, "Well, *this* is going to be a great year for me." But the nineties are here, and you are still living the same way, facing the same defeats and coping with the same sense of emptiness and lack of purpose.

We must get desperate — come off the ropes and knock out those things that have been defeating us. With God's help, and God's idea, we can make it.

Stinking Thinking

Remember that God has already prepared a place for us — a work for us to do. Not only can God do it for other people, but He can do it for you.

There are four biblical examples of situations where God gave people a promise — a God idea — but their *stinking thinking* almost held them back from their destiny.

Gideon

And the angel of the Lord appeared unto him [Gideon], and said unto him, The Lord is with thee, thou mighty man of valour.

And Gideon said unto him, Oh my Lord, if
the Lord be with us, why then is all this
befallen us? and where be all his miracles
which our fathers told us of, saying, Did not
the Lord bring us up from Egypt? but now the
Lord hath forsaken us, and delivered us into
the hands of the Midianites.

And the Lord looked upon him, and said,
Go in this thy might, and thou shalt save
Israel from the hand of the Midianites: have
not I sent thee?

And he said unto him, Oh my Lord, where-
with shall I save Israel? behold, my family is
poor in Manasseh, and I am the least in my
father's house (Judg. 6:12-15).

When Gideon received his God idea, he did not feel
worthy to do it. His excuse was, "God, I don't think I
can do it. I am just a poor farmer, not like the mighty
warriors from my tribe of Manasseh."

Gideon came from the half-tribe of Manasseh, the
son of Joseph and his Egyptian wife Asenath (Gen.
41:51). Jacob adopted both of Joseph's sons on his
deathbed, but he gave the birthright blessing to
Manasseh's younger brother, Ephraim.

The tribe was nomadic, spreading over the wide
regions of land it had conquered rather than remain-
ing closely connected to the great body of Israel. The
men of the tribe were mighty men of war, driving out
the inhabitants of any land they chose to attack.

But Gideon's family was not one of the prestigious
warrior families. The men of his family were farmers,

secretly growing wheat at a time when the Midianites were oppressing the tribe.

Although God had called him "thou mighty man of valour" (Judg. 6:12), Gideon had replied to God, "I am the least in my father's house" (v. 15). He suffered from low self-esteem.

God's opinion makes man's opinion irrelevant. God was trying to speak His opinion into this young man — "You are a mighty man of valour." Gideon piled up excuses because he didn't believe in himself. So God took him step-by-step. God does not expect us to soar in life on our first attempt. He teaches us one step at a time.

First, we must learn to stand in faith. When Gideon gave his excuses to God, God promised He would be with Gideon, "and thou shalt smite the Midianites..." (v. 16).

Encouraged by the Lord's promise, Gideon replied, "Depart not hence, I pray thee, until I come unto thee, and bring forth my present, and set it before thee" (v. 18).

Gideon had to learn to wait for God to tell him what to do next. This requires faith. He had to discard his own ideas of failure and patiently wait for God to birth the God idea in his spirit.

Next, God teaches us how to walk out His principles by faith. When Gideon had learned to stand, God directed him to step forward on a definite course. He was instructed to tear down the altar of Baal and construct an altar to God in its place.

Gideon could not have obeyed the Lord in this step if he had not first learned to stand in faith rather than cower in fear. Tearing down the altar was a bold, aggressive affront to the Midianites. It caused an offensive attack on the part of the enemy.

> Then all the Midianites and the Amalekites
> and the children of the east were gathered
> together, and went over, and pitched in the
> valley of Jezreel (v. 33).

In other words, they were ready to strike back and
destroy the tribe of Manasseh because one young
upstart dared to believe his God's idea was better than
the lying deceitfulness of their god Baal.

Now Gideon was ready to learn to run — in victory,
not defeat.

> But the Spirit of the Lord came upon Gideon,
> and he blew a trumpet....And it came to
> pass...that the Lord said unto him, Arise, get
> thee down unto the host; for I have delivered
> it into thine hand....And the Midianites and
> the Amalekites and all the children of the
> east lay along in the valley like grasshoppers
> for multitude....And he [Gideon] divided the
> three hundred men into three compa-
> nies....And they stood every man in his place
> round about the camp: and all the host ran,
> and cried, and fled (6:34; 7:9,12,16,21).

Finally God taught Gideon to soar.

> And Gideon sent messengers throughout all
> mount Ephraim, saying, Come down against
> the Midianites, and take before them the wa-
> ters unto Beth-barah and Jordan....Thus was
> Midian subdued before the children of Israel,
> so that they lifted up their heads no more.

And the country was in quietness forty years
in the days of Gideon (7:24; 8:28).

Moses

Although he was born under adversity and raised in
a godless home, Moses remained confident in his
commitment to the God of his fathers during the early
years of his life. But he made a major mistake — he
moved ahead of the God idea for his life.

One day he saw an Egyptian slave master abusing a
Hebrew slave. In a fit of rage he killed the Egyptian
master. As a result he had to flee into the desert where
he wound up tending sheep. He spent the next forty
years of his life in that desert.

Maybe you have found yourself in a "desert experience." That experience can erode your sense of self-
worth. It may be the dryness of a broken relationship
or a divorce, or a longtime job that is suddenly lost. It
may be financial distress or an experience that is emotionally draining. Like Moses, you find yourself alone
and isolated in a desert, far removed from your goals
and dreams of success.

But God arrived on the scene in a burning bush.

> The angel of the Lord appeared unto him in
> a flame of fire out of the midst of a bush: and
> he looked, and, behold, the bush burned
> with fire, and the bush was not consumed.
> And Moses said, I will now turn aside, and
> see this great sight, why the bush is not
> burnt. And when the Lord saw that he turned
> aside to see, God called unto him out of the
> midst of the bush, and said, Moses, Moses.

And he said, Here am I (Ex. 3:2-4).

God was reaffirming His God idea to Moses. He was saying, "Now is the time for you to go and deliver the people I have called you to deliver."

Moses didn't expect this to be the moment of the rebirthing of his God idea. He was minding his own business on the back side of the desert. But God had determined that the time had come.

Remember, your God idea will happen — but it may not happen just when you want it to. God is always right on time. He said to Moses,

> I have surely seen the affliction of my people
> which are in Egypt, and have heard their cry
> by reason of their taskmasters; for I know
> their sorrows; and I am come down to de-
> liver them out of the hand of the Egyptians,
> and to bring them up out of that land unto a
> good land and a large, unto a land flowing
> with milk and honey (Ex. 3:7-8).

Just as Gideon had done, Moses responded by making excuses: "I really don't know if I can do it. God, who shall I say sent me?"

God continues by saying, "I AM THAT I AM: and he said, Thus shalt thou say unto the children of Israel, I AM hath sent me unto you" (Ex. 3:14).

Once again God led His servant step-by-step. He affirmed His presence and told Moses exactly what to say. He showed Moses the miracle he held in his own hand as He turned Moses' rod into a serpent and then back into a rod. He even showed Moses the miraculous power

He possessed by turning Moses' hand to leprosy and healing it whole again. Finally, when Moses still insisted that he was unable to speak eloquently to the people, God provided Moses' brother, Aaron, to speak for him.

God will deal with us in the same way as He leads us to move ahead with our God ideas.

The Children of Israel

In Numbers 13 God tells the children of Israel to move ahead with the God idea He had given to them.

> And the Lord spake unto Moses, saying, Send thou men, that they may search the land of Canaan, which I give unto the children of Israel (Num. 13:1-2).

There are four key points to the God idea for the children of Israel: 1) God gave them the *site* — the land of Canaan; 2) He gave them the *right* to take possession of it; 3) He gave them the *might* — strength to be victorious in their takeover; 4) they had to develop the *fight* — go in and actually take the land. Although the children of Israel had the site, the right and the might, — they were afraid to fight for what was already theirs.

It's the same with our God ideas. We have the site of the promised land. We have the right to possess our promised land. God has given us the might, or strength, but we have to develop the fight.

Moses sent out ten spies to look over the land and bring back a report to the children of Israel. Ten of the spies brought back a negative report.

> And they brought up an evil report of the

> land which they had searched unto the chil-
> dren of Israel, saying, The land, through
> which we have gone to search it, is a land
> that eateth up the inhabitants thereof; and all
> the people that we saw in it are men of a
> great stature. And there we saw the giants,
> the sons of Anak, which come of the giants:
> and we were in our own sight as grasshoppers,
> and so we were in their sight (Num. 13:32-33).

Because they used their natural sight — their good ideas — they saw only giants and failure. They looked at the enemy and saw how big it was. They should have looked at their God to see how big He is!

Because they saw the enemy as giants, they saw themselves as mere grasshoppers — vulnerable to being smashed underfoot by the enemy. Because they saw themselves as grasshoppers, the enemy saw them that way too.

There's an interesting comparison of the word *grasshopper* in the stories of Gideon and the ten spies. In Numbers the ten spies refer to *themselves* as grasshoppers (13:33). Yet in Judges, when God taught Gideon to run in victory, the Bible says it was the *enemy* who "lay along in the valley like grasshoppers" (Judg. 7:12).

Grasshoppers usually can be found in great numbers. They are prolific breeders and have been known to destroy entire crops. They do not sneak around in small numbers like spies.

The perception of the ten spies was clouded by fear. They were not the grasshoppers — the enemy was!

Only Caleb and Joshua really plugged into the God idea for that circumstance. Their report was much different from that of the ten spies. Caleb and Joshua had a different spirit. Their spirit had been renewed by what God said about them.

> And Caleb stilled the people before Moses, and said, Let us go up at once, and possess it; for we are well able to overcome it (Num. 13:30).

The children of Israel had the promised land in their sight. They had the right to it. They had the might if they went forward in the strength of God. But they were afraid to fight.

Joseph

Joseph the dreamer provides the fourth example. He came from a dysfunctional family. He had many brothers and sisters and did not get along well with them. His father possessed a character flaw, and Joseph himself often spoke impulsively, which had alienated him from his brothers.

When God did give Joseph a dream — a God idea — he immediately boasted to his brothers:

> Hear, I pray you, this dream which I have dreamed: For, behold, we were binding sheaves in the field, and, lo, my sheaf arose, and also stood upright; and, behold, your sheaves stood round about, and made obeisance to my sheaf (Gen. 37:6-7).

His arrogance incensed his brothers, and they replied,

> Shalt thou indeed reign over us? or shalt thou
> indeed have dominion over us? And they
> hated him yet the more for his dreams, and
> for his words (37:8).

From that time on their hatred grew, and they plotted to get rid of him. Finally the opportunity arose, and they threw him into a pit, then sold him to a passing caravan headed to Egypt (Gen. 37:28).

God began a step-by-step maturing process in Joseph, dealing with the immaturity and arrogance in his heart. Over a period of time in Egypt Joseph's spirit was quickened to believe that he could do what God had told him to do. He learned to follow God's process, not jumping ahead of God to follow his own good ideas.

Joseph went step-by-step. God was patient with him, even in his setbacks. And God helped him to fulfill his destiny. God restored his family to him and allowed him to rise to powerful leadership in Egypt.

God wants us to be successful. He gets more glory from our successes than from our failures. He will reverse the curse in our life. As we begin to walk in our God idea, the good works that He created us to do will be possible (Eph. 2:10). We not only will affect our own destiny — but the destiny of others as well.

We can be confident that God has a God idea for us. We can recognize the value God has placed on us — the love He has expressed for us. And by following the ten principles in this book, we can fulfill the destiny God has created for us. ❧

ONE

STOP
LOOK
LISTEN

Principle One:

Stop in the right place, look to the right source and listen to the right voice.

THERE IS a God thought for you! God has a God idea for each step we take. And the revelation of a God idea will motivate us to move forward in the plans God has for our lives.

A God idea moved Noah to build the ark. Peter walked on water as the result of a revelation from God. Paul wrote thirteen epistles which are filled with God ideas that he received and then shared with others.

A God idea catapulted me into a healing ministry. I was spiritually immature but eager to serve God in a big way when I entered Bible school in 1980. I wasn't sure what God wanted to do with me, but I knew I wanted to be ready — so I began preparing for the ministry. At first, Bible school was an exciting place to be as I heard of the miraculous power of God to change people's lives. But during my first year at school I became sick and tired of hearing about the power of God without seeing it. I knew we were supposed to be laying hands on the sick and seeing them recover; delivering the oppressed and releasing those who were bound by addictive lifestyles through the power of God.

I knew the God idea for Jesus:

> The Spirit of the Lord God is upon me; because the Lord hath anointed me to preach good tidings unto the meek; he hath sent me to bind up the brokenhearted, to proclaim liberty to the captives, and the opening of the prison to them that are bound (Is. 61:1).

I longed to be like Jesus. I wanted His Spirit to empower me to do the same things He had done. But I felt inept, powerless and ineffective.

I decided to talk to the "Man" Himself — God, the source of spiritual power and ministry. But because I was so young in my faith, I didn't know exactly how to approach Him. I had read something in the Bible about anointing oil, so I decided to go to the campus chapel, anoint myself and pray until I heard from God.

I had no idea where to get anointing oil — or if there was such a thing. So I grabbed a little can of shortening — the white stuff — hid it under my jacket and crossed the campus to the chapel, locking the door behind me to be sure I was alone. I wasn't sure anyone else would understand what I was doing there. As Fred Price says, "You can't get an FM radio station on an AM dial!"

I rubbed that shortening on my forehead, rubbed my hands together to get rid of the excess grease, put my hands up in the air and beseeched God to give me the power to do the things I knew I should be doing for Him.

Soon that shortening was dripping down my face and running down my arms. But, undeterred, I cried out to God: "God, Your Word says that You are no respecter of persons" (Acts 10:34). If You could use Smith Wigglesworth, Katherine Kuhlman, Oral Roberts and Benny Hinn, You can use me. I'm going to seek You with everything I have. I am not going to quit coming boldly to the throne of grace (Heb. 4:16) until I get what I'm after."

There, alone in that chapel with shortening dripping off my elbows and chin, God birthed His God idea into my life. I shook under the power of God, and my hands vibrated as I held them lifted up high. I left the chapel knowing that encounter had changed my life — but not sure how the change would be evident.

I had volunteered earlier in the year to be the driver for an older woman evangelist as she traveled in the area to preach at various churches. Several days after my encounter in the chapel I drove her to a meeting. As we rode together, she turned to me and asked, "Young man, what did you do to your hands?"

"What are you talking about?" I responded, holding out my hands to show her they were fine.

But she persisted: "You did something to your hands. The Lord told me that whatever you did to your hands — whatever you asked for — you got it all!"

I knew I had received the God idea for my life. Soon after that I began receiving invitations to speak at many different churches. I went from preaching to six people to large crowds of people waiting to hear from God. Signs and wonders started to happen; people were healed and delivered by the power of God. The God idea changed my life — empowered me for the work God has for me.

The God idea is not just for people who are in the ministry. In my case, I was seeking for a ministry that involved preaching and praying for people's healing because I believe that Jesus really is a healer.

But just because I am a minister doesn't mean I can hear God more than you can as a janitor, doctor, lawyer or professional football player. God is no respecter of persons — if He can speak to Moses and the apostle Paul, He can speak to anyone.

So what can we do to get the God idea? The process starts with three steps — stop, look and listen.

Stop

Many people become so busy that it is impossible to slow their minds down long enough to receive fresh revelation of a God idea. Even while sitting in church their minds are planning their next big project. Or perhaps their minds are cluttered with mundane things having to do with this life. They are sitting around thinking, "Tomorrow is the PTA meeting, then Johnny has a basketball game and the girls have to be at soccer practice. Then I must get to the store to get those new curtains, and I probably won't even have time to get all the laundry done." And on and on the mind goes.

If we are going to receive a God idea for our situations, we have to STOP. It's impossible to listen to God when we're going too fast.

In Bible times the people didn't have radios, television sets and cars. If they had a meeting in Jericho, they left their Jerusalem condos and walked to Jericho. Perhaps they had the latest model donkey to carry them instead. And as they walked or rode, they had nothing better to do than meditate.

Meditation is not a New Age phenomenon. God thought it up! It is a fantastic way to receive a God idea. The Scriptures are filled with admonitions to meditate on the Word and works of God.

- This book of the law shall not depart out of thy mouth; but thou shalt meditate therein day and night, that thou mayest observe to do according to all that is written therein: for then thou shalt make thy way prosperous, and then thou shalt have good success (Josh. 1:8).

- I remember the days of old; I meditate on all thy works; I muse on the work of thy hands (Ps. 143:5).

- Neglect not the gift that is in thee....Meditate upon these things; give thyself wholly to them; that thy profiting may appear to all (1 Tim. 4:14-15).

But today we've got car phones, fax machines and a beeper clipped to our belts. Perhaps we just need to stop.

One time I was speaking at a luncheon for successful

business people in Singapore. I was telling them how Jonah followed the good idea rather than the God idea for his life.

All of a sudden beepers went off all around the room. I watched as many people reached into their pockets to turn their beepers off. I learned later that these business people were so used to being prompt that they had set their beepers to go off at the time they were supposed to return to work. But I had gone a little overtime in my speaking. I needed to stop!

Most of my life has been very busy. I was raised in the progressive urban setting of Southern California. My ministry has allowed me to travel to almost thirty countries, including many visits to Europe. A lot of Europeans are more laid-back — more relaxed — than Americans.

One time, when I was twenty, I was trying to explain God's plan for me to some people from Sweden. At that point I was uptight and nervous about accurately discerning what God wanted me to do with my life.

Finally one of the people said, "You are only twenty years old. Why don't you just travel and relax a bit?"

It was hard for me to comprehend what he was trying to tell me. What did he mean by "relax"? But I have since learned the value of relaxation and taking time to listen to God.

There is a time to discipline yourself to *go for it* with all the persistence you have. But there is also a time to stop.

For thus saith the Lord God, the Holy One of Israel; In returning and rest shall ye be saved;

in quietness and in confidence shall be your
strength (Is. 30:15).

Retreating to a quiet place of rest and peace is
invigorating and renewing. Great ideas can be birthed
in an environment of silence. Many times you will get
God ideas just by being silent.

If I had not stopped in the busyness of my life at
Bible school for that personal encounter with God, I
would not have received my God idea. I might have
missed the opportunity to be filled with the power of
God to fulfill His plan for my life. The urgency of my
own good ideas could have crowded out the excel-
lency of His God idea for me.

Look

Second, we need to look to God. Sometimes when
a problem hits we look everywhere else but to God.
I've got good news: God knows our past and He
knows our present, but He also knows our future.
God can help us find His solution to our problems by
helping us "sense" what He knows.

> He hath made every thing beautiful in his
> time: also he hath set the world in their heart,
> so that no man can find out the work that
> God maketh from the beginning to the end
> (Eccl. 3:11).

This is an interesting verse. It tells us that God
knows our beginning and our end — and everything
in between. But it seems to indicate that God works

within us — on the interior. All the good ideas we have about the external events and circumstances of our lives will never lead us to the God idea. It has been placed within us — and we must look within to find it.

David was searching for his God idea when he encouraged himself in the Lord (1 Sam. 30:6). He looked within, to the place where his spirit communed with the Spirit of God, to grasp the God idea and pull it out to affect his external circumstances.

Listen

Finally, we need to listen to the voice of God. Perhaps some of you are thinking, *I don't hear the voice of God.*

God may never speak to us in an audible voice, although He can if He chooses to do so. We develop communion with God inside our spirits. As we spend time developing that gift of hearing God, we will learn to discern the sound of His voice.

> My sheep hear my voice, and I know them,
> and they follow me (John 10:27).

We usually hear one of three voices — God's voice, the devil's voice or our own voice. At times we have to decide — was it God's, was it the devil's or was it my own? As we learn to distinguish God's voice in that inner place of communion, we will understand the God ideas that He whispers in our ears.

That he would grant you, according to the

riches of his glory, to be strengthened with might by his Spirit in the inner man (Eph. 3:16).

Fire in His Bones

The prophet Jeremiah was called to the prophetic office at a most unhappy time. The final decline of Israel was under way. God told Jeremiah that his message was one of condemnation rather than salvation. His long ministry of over forty years dealt continually with judgment.

Yet Jeremiah clung to his assigned task through years of rejection and persecution. He had received his God idea, and he was determined to fulfill that plan of God in his life. He says,

> His word was in mine heart as a burning fire shut up in my bones (Jer. 20:9).

Was Jeremiah excited just because he was an emotional person? No! He had a God idea that God would do what He said He could do! That God idea sustained Jeremiah even though he did not have an external confirmation that his message was having any effect.

His soul had been ignited — his God idea was burning strong within his heart. That revelation had changed his life, and he was never the same again.

Nor will we be the same. As we follow the ten principles to getting our God ideas, that revelation will burn into our souls. The urgency of fulfilling God's plan for our lives will move us forward, walking in love and sharing the God idea with others.

When we are redeemed and justified, our direction changes. Jesus becomes Lord of our lives. He starts calling the shots instead of us. We desire to fulfill His plan and purpose for our lives. God picks the destination. He charts our course. And He orders our every step.

When I arrived at Bible school, I had no idea what my destination would be. All I knew was that I wanted to serve God with my life. But after that encounter with the God idea for my life, my destination was confirmed. From that moment on it was God who charted my course, and to this day He orders my every step.

As you learn to commune with God in your spirit, He empowers your life. You move from natural living to supernatural living. You develop a new ability to discern the things of God — a "sixth sense." ⍟

TWO

FIND YOUR
SIXTH SENSE

Principle Two:

A sixth sense from God is better than five other senses combined.

WHEN I was a kid, a boy named Mikey lived in my neighborhood. Every neighborhood has a Mikey. Mikey came up with the craziest ideas and was always in trouble. One day he came to my house and said, "Tim, I've got a great idea for a new game. We can go over to the rich neighborhood and play hide-and-seek."

"Big deal!" I responded. "What's so great about that?"

Unmoved by my lack of enthusiasm, he continued, "We'll go down in the sewers where it's completely dark and shine our flashlights. It's really neat. We can play hide-and-seek without anyone bothering us. It's just like exploring in caves."

Although I turned down his idea that day, a few days later he and about a dozen other guys came over to my house. "Tim," he said, "we're going to play hide-and-seek in the sewer. You've got to come — it's going to be great."

So, unaware that a storm was coming, we went

down into these big sewers — they were huge. We split up into groups of four. One guy had the flashlight and the others held onto him. We stumbled around looking for the other kids that were hiding from us.

Suddenly that storm hit Southern California with all of its fury, and water rushed down into the sewers. Before we knew what was happening, the water roared through the sewers, rising higher and higher. First it rose to our ankles, then to our knees. It kept rising until we thought we were going to drown. We became hysterical, screaming and crying.

I knew there was one person who could get us out of that drain — Mikey! He had been in that sewer so many times he knew it like the back of his hand. He knew exactly which way to go. So I stood up and yelled, "Mikey!"

He grabbed a big flashlight and came running past me like Superman, calling back to us, "Follow me!"

I yelled, "Everybody grab the hand of the person next to you." I held onto Mikey, and everyone else followed along behind as Mikey led us through the darkness. He was the sewer king. We knew we were going to make it to safety. Not one of us said, "Are you sure you know which way you're going?" When you are looking for someone who knows the way out, you're willing to go with anyone who says, "Follow me."

Mikey led us through that sewer until, before we knew what had happened, he pried open a manhole cover and we were pouring out of the belly of the earth to safety. How? Mikey had been there before — he knew that drain.

The world is looking for a Mikey today. People are perplexed. They're going through tough times. Banks are closing, major industries are folding and people are rapidly losing confidence in those things which previously brought them security. They are looking for answers. When they fail to find the answer in the natural realm, they turn to the supernatural realm.

Everywhere you look today, people are talking about the power of the supernatural. Crystals, pyramids, ouija boards, horoscopes, reincarnation, astral projection and the New Age movement are becoming household words. People want to know how to use the supernatural for their own benefit. What does God have to say about supernatural living? Do Christians truly have a sixth sense?

This move toward the supernatural is not a new phenomenon. People turned to the supernatural in Bible times too. The book of 1 Samuel provides us with a poignant example of two men's searches for supernatural answers to life's devastating problems.

A Search in the Wrong Direction

King Saul provides us with the first example. There had been a time in Saul's life when he experienced the presence of God on a daily basis. However, through disobedience and sin he had lost the presence of the Lord. "And when Saul enquired of the Lord, the Lord answered him not, neither by dreams, nor by Urim, nor by prophets" (1 Sam. 28:6).

Saul was greatly disturbed by this lack of guidance. Not only had Samuel — the prophet who had counseled and guided him in spiritual matters — died, but now the Lord refused to speak to him in any fashion.

When a battle arose between the Philistines and the Israelites, Saul was unsure how to advise his men for battle. So he told his servant,

Seek me a woman that hath a familiar spirit, that
I may go to her, and enquire of her (1 Sam. 28:7).

Saul was searching for a supernatural answer to his
dilemma, but he consulted a witch — a servant of
Satan. He sought advice in the wrong direction, and it
ultimately brought ruin not only to him but to his
kingdom as well.

The nation of Israel lost the battle, and Saul lost
many men — including his sons Abinadab, Mel-
chishua and Jonathan.

Our decisions can affect the lives of those around
us. Even Saul's decision to take his own life by falling
on his sword led to the death of his armor bearer —
who also fell on his own sword as he had seen his
leader do (see 1 Sam. 31).

The practice of consulting psychics has become
very popular. Television advertises hot-line telephone
numbers where you can call and get personal advice
from a psychic. Many people who are seeking direction
for their lives call these numbers daily.

Many nice people have gotten caught up in psychic
phenomena. It is God who gives valid direction for
our lives. But there is a counterfeit source for everything that is good.

Psychic phenomena is a form of sorcery and witchcraft.
It does not come from God. It must be avoided by anyone
who desires to find the God idea for his or her life.

A Search in the Right Direction

David searched for answers to life's problems in the
right direction. He was in much the same position as King

Saul. His people had rejected him, his enemies had gathered against him and he didn't know how to solve his problem. But David sought direction from the right source:

> And David was greatly distressed; for the people spake of stoning him, because the soul of all the people was grieved, every man for his sons and for his daughters: but David encouraged himself in the Lord his God (1 Sam. 30:6).

Just prior to this the Amalekites had crept into Ziklag, David's hometown, and burned it, taking captive the wives and children of David and his men. David's men turned against him. He found himself alone, rejected and without answers.

But he knew where to go when trouble arose. God had never failed him, and he knew he could depend on God to provide him with the help he needed now. He "encouraged himself in the Lord." David asked God,

> Shall I pursue after this troop? shall I overtake them? (1 Sam. 30:8).

God answered David and instructed him to pursue the enemy, overtake them and recover all that they had taken. When David's men saw that David had received the answer he needed, they followed him also, and a mighty victory resulted.

Once again the people were looking for a supernatural answer. David went to the right Source — to God Himself — and thus achieved a great victory for himself and his men.

We Have More Than Five Senses

We know that we have five senses — sight, touch, smell, taste and hearing. But when we are born again, something happens to us. Old things pass away, and all things become new (see 2 Cor. 5:17). We become new creations in Christ Jesus, and the Holy Spirit comes to dwell within us. Suddenly we can learn to be led by the Spirit.

Above that which is good in the physical realm, we find we have access to that which is godly. Psalm 18:28, says, "For thou wilt light my candle: the Lord my God will enlighten my darkness."

Proverbs 20:27 goes on to say, "The spirit of man is the candle of the Lord." Not only does God light our way, but we become the candle that lights the way for others.

Romans 8:14 tells us, "For as many as are led by the Spirit of God, they are the sons of God." We learn to be led by the Spirit.

The Spirit-led Christian develops a sixth sense. No longer must we rely solely on our five natural senses to find solutions to earth's problems. We can use our sixth sense — a supernatural sense — to bring supernatural solutions to natural situations.

There is a vast difference between a "good idea" — one which we arrive at through the use of our five natural senses — and a "God idea," one which requires the use of our supernatural sixth sense. I do not want good ideas for my life; I want God ideas. In this decade of the nineties the church must walk according to the God ideas. If our steps are ordered by the Lord, people will follow us because they see that supernatural answers solve life's biggest problems.

Using Our Sixth Sense

Paul had learned to use his sixth sense.

After Paul was seized by the Jews, he appeared before many Jewish officials, including Agrippa and Festus. It was then determined that he should be sent by ship to Rome, along with several other prisoners. The sailboats used in the ancient Mediterranean world were not large or sturdy enough to face the winter storms. The dangerous season for sailing began about September 14, and after November 11 all sailing came to an end for the winter. The fast to which Luke refers is the day of atonement, which fell at the end of September or early in October. Thus, they were traveling during the month of October.[1]

Paul's sixth sense caused him to express his concern. He said, "Sirs, I perceive that this voyage will be with hurt and much damage, not only of the lading and ship, but also of our lives" (Acts 27:10).

Paul had received a God idea and was telling those men, "I've got a word from God. We need to pull the ship over and stop. If we don't stop, there will be great damage to you and the ship." But instead of listening to the voice of God through the man of God, they decided to sail on.

These words from Paul are a prophetic word for the church and the world today. The church and the world are in a bad situation — a spiritual storm.

Throughout the Bible we are continually reminded that we will reap what we sow.

> Be not deceived; God is not mocked: for whatsoever a man soweth, that shall he also

51

reap. For he that soweth to his flesh shall of the flesh reap corruption; but he that soweth to the Spirit shall of the Spirit reap life ever-lasting (Gal. 6:7-8).

For they have sown the wind, and they shall reap the whirlwind (Hos. 8:7).

A World Lost at Sea

All around us we see a world that is reaping the whirlwind of certain destruction. So many people are hurting spiritually, physically and emotionally. But in the midst of the storm, God is raising up His church — men and women of God who discern, not with their five senses, but with their sixth sense. By staying attuned to God we can lead our families to spiritual victory.

If we allow the Lord to develop our sixth sense, the Holy Spirit will speak to us with a God idea: "This is how to get out of debt; this is what you should do; this is how to raise your family; this is how to get yourself out of that situation." Our success will be a supernatural victory through the Holy Spirit.

When Paul's ship reached the island of Crete, it was hit by a heavy-duty storm. The ships of that day did not use compasses. The only way they could navigate was by plotting the position of the moon and the stars. When the storm came, all navigation ceased, and the little ship tossed and rolled dangerously close to the rocks off the coast of Crete.

Surrounded by howling winds and crashing waves, the men became more perplexed because they had no idea where they were. They couldn't see the sun; they couldn't see the moon; they couldn't see the stars; they had no way of knowing which way to go.

Finally they gave up all hope of being rescued. That's how many people feel today. The world has endured the assault of the whirlwind prophesied in Hosea, and people are suffering the pain and loss that storm has brought. Through the medium of television we are continually bombarded with talk-show hosts laying wide open the pain that their participants have endured. We see worldwide disaster every time we turn on a news broadcast. We have a world that's in pain, that has suffered loss.

The result of trying to find solutions to life's problems by using our own "good ideas" is clearly seen. Much of the world is like a ship tossed at sea, crushed by the storm that has assaulted it, lost and without hope.

The man or woman of God who clearly discerns the supernatural God idea for each circumstance of life can say, "Blessed is the man that trusteth in the Lord, and whose hope the Lord is" (Jer. 17:7).

Discerning a God Idea

Paul had discerned the God idea.

> But after long abstinence Paul stood forth in the midst of them, and said, Sirs, ye should have hearkened unto me, and not have loosed from Crete, and to have gained this harm and loss. And now I exhort you to be of good cheer: for there shall be no loss of any man's life among you, but of the ship (Acts 27:21-22).

How did Paul know this? How can we know the God idea for our lives, and for the lives of those who are lost and without hope? Paul continues,

> For there stood by me this night the angel of God, whose I am, and whom I serve, saying, Fear not, Paul; thou must be brought before Caesar: and, lo, God hath given thee all them that sail with thee (vv. 23-24).

God spoke to His servant in the midst of the storm. God reminded Paul that the God idea for his life had not yet been fulfilled. And He told Paul that all those who were traveling with him would be saved with Paul.

There are many times in the lives of believers when something inside will say, "Don't do that. Watch that person. Beware of this situation." The Spirit of God lives inside believers. We can perceive with our spirit and discern supernatural solutions to life's problems. We can learn to distinguish a God idea that is greater than the good ideas of those who live their lives according to the natural realm.

These revelatory God ideas will help us to discern when to buy or sell a house or car, how to guide and care for our children, and what decisions to make in our families. Men and women in business can rely on their God ideas to direct the course of their business. We can accurately discern the work of the devil as he uses his tactics to sabotage our lives and businesses.

Our supernatural sixth sense will keep us from falling for the deceit and lies around us. God will teach us to walk according to God ideas, to use our sixth sense. The Bible says the natural mind cannot understand the things of the spirit. "But the natural man receiveth not the things of the Spirit of God: for they are foolishness unto him: neither can he know them, because they are spiritually discerned" (1 Cor. 2:14).

We can spiritually discern when the Holy Spirit talks to us. "But he that is spiritual judgeth all things....For who hath known the mind of the Lord, that he may instruct him? But we have the mind of Christ" (1 Cor. 2:15-16).

Shipwrecked, cold, without food — the world knows it is in trouble. That's why people are beginning to turn to God. They are going for the sixth sense. They know that the five senses cannot get them out of the storm.

Spiritual Light in the Storm

God always raises up people in the midst of the storm. Elijah received a revelatory God idea that drought would come and the land would see no rain for a period of years. Then he also revealed the end of the drought and prayed rain down upon the people (see 1 Kin. 17–18).

Micah supernaturally discerned the connection between the wickedness of Israel's leaders and the threatening military activities of the Assyrians. He knew that God would use the Assyrians to punish and destroy the wicked Israelites. He knew what the Lord would require if Israel were victorious:

> He hath shewed thee, O man, what is good; and what doth the Lord require of thee, but to do justly, and to love mercy, and to walk humbly with thy God? (Mic. 6:8).

Not much is known about the personal life of the prophet Haggai, but we do know he was sent by God to awaken the people and stir them from their lethargy to undertake the restoration of the temple. His message urged the people to seek for their own God ideas.

> Is it time for you yourselves to dwell in your paneled houses, and this temple to lie in ruins?...Consider your ways! You have sown much, and bring in little; you eat, but do not have enough; you drink, but you are not filled with drink; you clothe yourselves, but no one is warm; and he who earns wages, earns wages to put into a bag with holes (Hag. 1:4-6, NKJV).

The God ideas which Haggai was sharing with the people of his day are as fresh today as they were hundreds of years ago when he shared them for the first time.

The world is looking for men and women of God who will stand up and say, "Go this way!" God is raising up churches that can reveal the God ideas for the communities of people around them. We can use our sixth senses to impact our neighborhoods with truth.

Although God is raising up spiritual leaders and churches to reveal the God ideas to the unsaved world lost in a spiritual storm, He desires for every believer to receive a personal revelation from Him. The Holy Spirit will speak to us and direct us, not just in major decisions, but in every aspect of our lives. God desires to teach us how to live supernatural lives.

The Holy Spirit acts as our inner gyroscope. When we are moving in the will of God, our spirit is calm and at peace. God's voice is the *still, small voice.* We will only hear Him as we become still and quiet before Him. But as we do, the people around us will be drawn by our calm assurance and put their hope in the God who can rescue them from the spiritual storms of life.

Discernment Required

A key to this quality of spiritual lifestyle is discernment. God gives His people discernment for spiritual direction, but He also helps His people to discern situations which might bring harm or danger.

God has allowed me to discern dangerous situations as I travel in other countries. On one occasion I was conducting an evangelistic crusade in Spain. I could feel God's presence and power as I preached, but it seemed as though my words stopped in midair. I sensed heavy oppression in the service.

I had heard stories of evangelists who ministered there for over a month with only a single person responding to salvation. In many cases the evangelist would get sick or suffer terrible misfortune. I knew I was engaged in intensive spiritual warfare.

As I prayed for spiritual discernment in that situation, I stepped away from my five senses and allowed the Holy Spirit to minister to me through my sixth sense. He said, "Tim, you need to reach these Spaniards from a different angle than you do people in other countries."

As I listened to the voice of God, He gave me an idea. One night as I got up to speak, I put into practice the God idea I had been given. "The devil talked to me today," I said as I paced the platform. "He told me that he's after your families."

I watched the people as they looked at each other. Immediately I could see that this was hitting home.

Later I found out that Spanish people fear the devil greatly and have an all-consuming desire to protect and love their families.

I went on to explain the scripture which says,

> The thief [devil] cometh not, but for to steal, and to kill, and to destroy: I am come that they might have life, and that they might have it more abundantly (John 10:10).

I said, "If you want the devil to leave your families alone, bring them tomorrow night!"

The next night the place was packed; the people had returned with their families. That night I presented the message that Jesus came to give them abundant life. In the one week that I was there, 177 people were saved, and many of them were also baptized in the Holy Spirit.

It happened because of spiritual discernment — a God idea.

The same discernment is available for all believers today. God will give you discernment in the midst of the storm. God will give you a God idea for every circumstance you face. And He will allow you to share that idea with people in your life. As you walk in love and are led by the Spirit, you will make a spiritual impact on those around you. Let's look now at how that revelation of God will enable us to replace good ideas with God ideas. 𝓿

THREE

SEEK A PERSONAL REVELATION

Principle Three:

Eliminating good ideas will help you find the God ideas.

HAVE YOU ever felt that you were wandering, using up energy and time but getting no-where? I've had times like that. Some people call those times *wilderness experiences.*

The wilderness has long been a symbol of the negative things in our lives. After a tremendous experience of Sunday morning worship, we say, "I've been to the mountain." But let a good testing of our faith come our way, and we respond, "I'm in the wilderness, but by God's grace I'm going to make it through."

A wilderness experience may be a trial or persecution. It could mean a period of spiritual inactivity where doubts assail us. It could come during a period of broken hopes and dreams. As in a geographical wilderness, one characteristic is true of all wilderness experiences — spiritual growth is at a standstill!

We must understand the importance of the wilderness experiences in our lives. Many of us fear the solitary place — the wilderness times — when it seems there is no growth or vision. We would choose to be in the middle of a dynamic praise and worship service far more often than we would choose to be set aside in solitude.

Jesus sought the solitary place. Whenever He could, He withdrew alone to the wilderness to receive fresh revelation for His life.

- And when it was day, he departed and went into a desert place (Luke 4:42).

- And he withdrew himself into the wilderness, and prayed (Luke 5:16).

- And he took them [the disciples], and went aside privately into a desert place (Luke 9:10).

When the stress and pressures of ministry overwhelmed Jesus and His disciples, He advised them to go to the wilderness, saying, "Come ye yourselves apart into a desert place, and rest a while" (Mark 6:31).

Preparation for Growth

Learn to look at your wilderness experiences as preparation for great growth. After you have eliminated all of your good ideas, you are in a prime position to receive the revelation of a God idea. The wilderness is the perfect place for that revelation. You are empty, inactive, at the end of your own resources — just the right conditions for a God idea to burst forth and take root. *Emptiness always precedes filling.*

I remember the empty feeling of not having the God idea I needed for my life. I had been born and raised in Southern California, but after a vacation trip to Florida to visit my sister, I believed it was God's idea for me to attend Southeastern College in Central Florida. We had visited the campus while I was in Florida, and while there I felt it was the place for me.

Near the end of 1980, my first year at Southeastern, I was trying to make a major decision concerning God's direction for my next year. I knew my destination was the ministry, but I needed to hear from God regarding the course I would take to get there. Should I continue my college education in Florida or complete my degree in California?

I longed to be back in the familiar environment of California. Besides, I was getting very lonely. But I had made several new friends in Florida and was enjoying the school.

Although I needed to make a decision soon, I had been unable to distinguish what God wanted me to do. I wasn't sure whether I should "fleece" God for an answer as Gideon had (see Judg. 6:36-40) or check out the window every five minutes for a rainbow like God gave to Noah (see Gen. 9:12-13). I just knew I needed an answer. I needed to know God's plan for this particular situation — I needed a *God idea!*

In search of my God idea, I decided to seek the advice of one of the most spiritual young men on campus. This particular brother was known for being a little peculiar. One time he got mad at his roommate for eating potato chips and studying the Bible at the same time. He said that eating potato chips and studying the Bible didn't go together. On another occasion, after he gave a tremendous prophecy in chapel, he turned to me and winked as if to say, "See, that's how you do it!"

One morning I went to his room and said, "Brother, I have a very important decision to make, and I need to know how to get God's answer about my situation. Can you share any spiritual insights that would help me with this dilemma?"

After I explained my problem in great detail, he looked at me and said, "Don't worry, this is a very easy problem to solve."

I felt much better already. This decision had caused me many worrisome days and sleepless nights. My fleece idea had failed, and no rainbow had made its appearance outside my dorm window. But I had every confidence in the spiritual insights this man of God could share with me. I waited eagerly for his answer to the question of my future destiny.

"Brother Tim," he said, "you need to pray until God tells you what to do. Don't leave the place of prayer until God gives you a specific answer." He even offered me the use of his prayer closet.

I knew I had it made. He actually had a closet that was emptied of the usual things college students cram into their closets. There he would spend hours talking to God loudly in prayer. I was certain it would be a good place to seek God for an answer to my prayer.

"Go ahead," he said. "I have a class. You can just stay here and pray." As he left the room, he reminded me, "Now, remember, don't come out until you have a specific answer."

As he left, I peeked inside the closet — a modern day Holy of Holies. The place where God met face-to-face with man. Confidently I walked into that small place of prayer. It was completely bare except for a cushion and a baseball bat leaning in one corner. I wasn't sure what he used the bat for — surely not to threaten God for an answer. He must be one of those super spiritual types who also love sports, I decided. Just my kind of guy!

I knew enough about God to know that while some of my good ideas may come true, God ideas always come true. The Scriptures said my steps were ordered by the Lord. If I trusted in the Lord with all my heart and did not lean on my own understanding, He would direct my path.

"OK, God," I said, "I need Your idea."

I got down on my knees (I figured that must be what my friend did to get his prayers answered). I had heard him praying loudly many times, so I began praying loudly also. His last words to me echoed in my ears, "Don't come out until you get a specific answer."

After one hour I was fresh out of ideas and things to pray about. The cushion was a lot more comfortable to sit on, so I sat down and leaned against the wall. I found myself growing sleepy as I quietly listened for the voice of the Lord. Would it be the still, small voice that Elijah had heard, or would it be the audible voice I had heard Oral Roberts testify about?

The next thing I knew, I found myself waking up from a deep sleep. How much time had passed? I had no idea. I didn't have a watch, but it was too dark to see anyway. How could I have fallen asleep at such an important time in my life! Maybe I had missed God's direction. Maybe He had spoken audibly while

I was sleeping, and I had missed hearing Him.

I strained with everything I had inside me to hear His voice of direction, but there was no other voice than my own. Finally I heard some movement in the room outside. My spiritual mentor must have returned from his classes.

It was obvious that I wasn't getting any specific direction from God, but I needed to save my reputation as a man of God.

I sure didn't feel like Moses coming down from Mt. Sinai, but I didn't want to disappoint my friend. My hand touched the bat in the corner, and my mind wandered back to long-ago days of little league baseball when things seemed so much easier. I placed the bat carefully back in the closet's corner and reached for the doorknob. Putting on the best I-just-met-with-God face I could muster, I opened the door.

My eyes met the eyes of my friend as he walked toward me with a big smile on his face. "Well, didn't I tell you that was the way to get your answer?" he asked.

Not wanting to disappoint him, I replied, "Yeah! You sure did."

"Did you get your word from the Lord?" he asked.

"I really had a powerful time!" I replied evasively. Inwardly I was frustrated, fatigued and discouraged.

All I wanted was for God's perfect will to be done in my life. Already I had a good idea. I knew what I wanted to do. But the question remained, What did God want...what was the *God idea* for this situation? In my spiritual immaturity, I wished someone would tell me ten easy, foolproof steps to find my answer. I had not yet learned the principles this book gives for getting the God idea. So I remained camped out in the wilderness, with no revelation at all.

God did have a perfect plan regarding my education, but it took until the following summer for Him to reveal it, as I'll share with you later in this chapter.

A Revelation of God

Paul is a good role model of how to survive the wilderness. He says,

> But I make known to you, brethren, that the gospel which was preached by me is not according to man. For I neither received it from man, nor was I taught it, but it came through the revelation of Jesus Christ (Gal. 1:11-12, NKJV).

Paul was very zealous in his youth. He was brought up under the strictest training in the Scriptures. He trained under Gamaliel, an eminent Pharisee who was revered for his knowledge of the law (Acts 22:3). When Paul became a Christian, something changed.

Paul says, "Nor did I go up to Jerusalem to those who were apostles before me; but I went to Arabia, and returned again to Damascus" (Gal. 1:17, NKJV).

Paul received a firsthand God idea about Jesus in his wilderness experience in Arabia. Following his conversion, he did not go to Jerusalem to sit at the feet of the apostles and be discipled in the knowledge of Jesus. He went alone into the wilderness for about three years where God Himself discipled Paul. He received his revelation during his wilderness time.

During that three-year period in the wilderness, Paul discarded all his good ideas.

Paul, who came from Cilicia, no doubt had been included in the group of Jewish members of the synagogue in Cilicia who disputed the teachings of Stephen (see Acts 6:9). By the time he witnessed the death of Stephen (Acts 7:58–8:1), he had decided it was a good idea to oppose all *heretical* teachings claiming Jesus as the long-awaited Messiah. He quickly rose to the role of *Great Persecutor* of the early Christian church, convinced that this new movement which proclaimed a crucified criminal to be the Messiah could not possibly be of God. His zealous desire to compel Christians to deny their faith on penalty of imprisonment and even death had put him on the road to Damascus, where he planned to extradite that group of believers back to Jerusalem to face judgment.

But in the Arabian wilderness he eliminated all these beliefs that had hindered him from following the God idea for his life. He allowed God to radically change his perspective, his knowledge and his spirit. When he came out of that wilderness, he knew his destination. He was on a new course, and every step he took for the remainder of his life was a God idea.

Good Ideas Get in the Way of God Ideas

The children of Israel had a more difficult time listening to the God ideas during their wilderness experience. They had not completed the process of elimination — and their good ideas continually got in the way of the God ideas.

The Israelites might have been in the promised land in a matter of weeks if they had allowed God to bring revelation into their lives. Instead, they looked to their own good ideas — to the exclusion of God — and ended up stuck in the wilderness for forty years.

When God revealed His awesome, glorious presence to Moses on Mt. Sinai, the people of Israel saw the cloud of His presence (Ex. 24:17-18). But they rejected that revelation of God and sought to create their own god to worship in the golden calf (Ex. 32:2-6).

They chose the tangible, created gods of their world above the invisible Creator God of the universe. If anything or anyone is more important to us than the knowledge of God, we will not see the revelation of our God ideas.

When God longed to bring them into the promised land, the children of Israel believed the evil report of ten spies who said they could not overcome the enemy. They cried,

> Wherefore hath the Lord brought us unto this land, to fall by the sword...were it not better for us to return into Egypt? And they said one to another, Let us make a captain, and let us return into Egypt (Num. 14:3-4).

They wanted to go backward instead of forward. Unless we let go of what worked in the past, we cannot open our hands to grasp God's destiny for us.

That is the lesson I had to learn from my prayer-closet experience in Bible school. My friend's ideas of how to get an answer from God were useless to me. God wanted to give me a God idea in His own unique way.

I didn't receive the answer to my prayer-closet request until the following summer, when I returned home. When I arrived home, I was determined not to return to Florida. But for some strange reason I began to long for Florida by the end of the summer. Through my longing for my friends and studies in Florida, God spoke and confirmed to me that I was to return to Southeastern college.

Secondhand Ideas

Many believers have not yet received their own personal God idea. We may have a good idea that was passed on from our grandmother or from some other old saint who died years ago. Maybe we've received our good idea from books or tapes. These ideas may be useful to help us confirm God's will, but God wants to reveal our personal God idea in a personal way. Secondhand knowledge will not be enough to handle a wilderness experience. Only a God idea will do.

If we take another look at the example of Paul in the wilderness of Arabia, we find that sometimes God must lead us into the wilderness where there are no distractions so He can have our undivided attention. He wants us to get to know Him in the wilderness.

Sometimes the wilderness is the only place where we actually listen to Him. Paul wanted a God idea — not just a good idea. He didn't want to hear what Peter thought about Jesus. He wanted to encounter Jesus for himself. He went to the wilderness asking for a revelation of God. He said, "Jesus, who are You? I want to know You."

Another person's God idea will never work for you!

Even though Paul and Silas traveled together for some of Paul's missionary journeys, each one was following their own unique God idea. While Paul was in one wilderness situation getting a God idea, Silas was somewhere else getting his God idea.

For a time their God ideas allowed them to travel together. But the time came when God's plans for their lives led them down separate paths.

> But when the Jews of Thessalonica had knowledge that the word of God was preached of Paul at Berea, they came thither also, and stirred up the people. And then immediately the brethren sent away Paul to go as it were to the sea: but Silas...abode there still (Acts 17:13-14).

When Paul and Silas sang praises to God from the midst of the Philippian jail, it was because each man had a unique sense of the God idea for his life (see Acts 16:25).

Confidence Results

Paul's confidence in God came as a result of receiving a God idea in his wilderness experience. Later on in his life, when Paul stood before King Agrippa, he said,

> Whereupon, O king Agrippa, I was not disobedient unto the heavenly vision....Having therefore obtained help of God, I continue unto this day, witnessing both to small and great (Acts 26:19, 22).

71

That confidence was evident to Agrippa, and he replied to Paul, "Almost thou persuadest me to be a Christian" (Acts 26:28).

In his letter to the Galatians about his wilderness experience, Paul says three interesting things. First, he tells us that God had set him apart (see Gal. 1:15). His wilderness experience successfully catapulted him through the process of elimination. He removed himself from his good ideas.

Second, Paul knew that God had a plan for his life (see Gal. 1:16). Once he had eliminated his good ideas, Paul was able to grasp a sense of destiny, or calling, to a God idea.

Third, he knew that he got his idea from God (see Gal. 1:16). Just another good idea would be no good. Even if a good idea comes to us from someone like Billy Graham, John Wesley or Martin Luther, it still would not be our God idea. The most another person's good ideas can do for us is to confirm our God idea. A God idea is firsthand revelation from God.

We need personal, firsthand knowledge that God is who He says He is in our life. We need a God idea and not just someone's good idea.

Let's go on to see how our God idea will make us ready to move forward. ۞

FOUR

SAY NO
TO
KNOWING

Principle Four:

Look beyond human reason.

C AN IT be a God idea even when it doesn't seem to be a good idea? It was for me. From the time I was a little kid, I knew I was supposed to do something special.

I learned early to think big in small places. I was raised in a family that didn't have very much money, and there were few dreamers in my family background. But I dreamed big dreams.

"Up for bat — Will-l-ee-e Mays!" the announcer called over the loudspeaker. The sound echoed through the stadium as Willie Mays, the great baseball player, donned his cap and picked up his bat, striding confidently to the plate. As the first pitch crossed the plate he swung, then ran victoriously around the bases as the announcer called out, "Home run!" The crowds roared as he returned to the dugout.

I was both announcer and player, and the stadium was my living room. The game was only pretense, but the determination in my heart to *make it big* was not a fantasy. I was going to do something great. That didn't seem possible for the poor son of a steelworker father and donut shop employee mother. My dad quit school in the tenth grade, and my mother never finished the sixth grade.

Yet I knew I had a destiny to fulfill.

Recently I sat in the Maui, Hawaii, home of the mother of Christian Lassen, one of the greatest painters in the world today. His marine and ocean life paintings are sold around the world.

As a young boy in school, Christian used to doodle or stare out the window while the teacher was talking. One day his teacher told him, "You will never amount to anything if you keep this up."

The teacher finally confronted his mother with these words, "Your son has a real problem. His attention span is very short — he doodles constantly and daydreams the whole day long."

Human reasoning would agree with that teacher. But Christian Lassen received his God idea — to become a great painter. Today he is painting some of the greatest paintings in the world.

Thirst for Knowledge

Higher education throughout the ages has been sought by the socially elite, the wealthy and the powerful. Knowledge has been esteemed as the door that opens the way to upward social mobility and financial success.

The problem with man is that he takes himself too seriously. As it was at the time of the destruction of the tower of Babel (see Gen. 11), the creation is still seeking equality with the Creator. Knowledge is power, and man

is always trying to increase his power and authority.

Humanistic reasoning may believe in a higher power. But it believes that it comes from within man and not from a superior divine being. Ever since his fall from heaven because of his desire to be like God, Satan has manipulated humanistic reasoning to make reality into superstition and superstition into reality. He still wants to steal away God's rightful glory and honor and lavish it upon himself.

The truth is, there is nothing new under the sun (Eccl. 1:9). At best, all man can do is become more aware of who God is and what He has done. The evolutionists have never been able to go back to the point in time when there was absolutely nothing. Science cannot answer the question, Where did the elements necessary to begin the process of evolution come from?

Only God was able to start with nothing. He spoke the world into existence (see Gen. 1).

Humanistic reason tries to mimic this characteristic of God. If an idea is repeated enough times, and if enough people agree with that idea, it is accepted as fact. Today's advertisers know that simple labeling will often cause something to be accepted or rejected. Use the right colors, place the right models in the right poses, sing the right song and do it all at the right time, and there will be millions of dollars of profit as a reward.

But if God is involved, then not only is the thought labeled as mere fantasy of the feeble-minded, but it may even be discarded as inflammatory and illegal.

God's Ways Are Not Man's Ways

What it boils down to is this: God's ways are not

man's ways. The magnitude of God cannot be dissected or scaled down to fit within man's capacity for understanding. God is the Source of all truth and knowledge. Every fact, from the least to the greatest, is known to Him. Nothing escapes His attention. God has absolute power and authority. Whatever limited knowledge we have is the result of God allowing us to see and comprehend.

Man has dedicated himself to proving that he has complete charge of his destiny. He believes that after he has accumulated enough knowledge, all hunger, disease and war will be eliminated, and everyone will live happily ever after. But the facts don't bear this out. Newspapers and television news programs are filled with stories about starvation, disease, crime and fighting throughout the world, perhaps more than at any other time in history. Things aren't getting better; they're getting worse.

During a recent layover at the Dallas airport, I bought the morning newspaper. Settling back in my seat on the plane, I flipped through the paper looking for the sports section. But there in the local section was a story about a minister who was launching a crusade against Barney the purple dinosaur. He described Barney as a New Age leader, condemning his songs as too self-gratifying and decrying his message as ungodly. He's determined that Barney should be extinct — that no more Barney sales should be made to kids.

Sitting there in my airplane seat, I laughed aloud. The thought of a crusade against Barney in a world where terrible atrocities are occurring daily seemed somehow insignificant.

This man had reasoned out his idea for making the world

a better place. But the believer has the privilege of rising above human reason to see into the very mind of God.

I was invited to speak at a crusade which was being held in a bull-fighting arena in Monterey, Mexico. One morning while I was there I went into a local restaurant for breakfast with one of the crusade team members.

Since I am part Spanish and know a little of the language, I said a few things in Spanish to our waitress. Assuming I spoke her language fluently, she immediately began to chatter away excitedly in her native tongue.

As she was talking, I occasionally nodded my head. The person with me watched the two of us intently and couldn't believe I was so fluent in Spanish, even though I really wasn't saying anything — the waitress was doing all the talking.

After she finished talking, I nodded again and said, "*Si,*" which means, "Yes, I agree." She smiled at me and left to get our food.

"I didn't know you were so great in Spanish," my friend said.

With a laugh, I replied, "I really don't understand the language. I just nodded my head to everything she said."

There are thousands of Spanish words. Without at least an elementary knowledge of Spanish and its usage, communication is next to impossible. If I really want to communicate with someone who speaks Spanish, I must first acknowledge my inability to speak it. I will have to use an interpreter or some basic sign language to bridge my inability to speak. The few Spanish words I do know are useless in a conversation.

Just so when it comes to life, death and eternity — I must place my trust in the only One who can really speak the language. When I lean unto my own understanding, I'm going to make a lot of mistakes because I really don't understand the situation completely.

Christ Jesus, Our Bridge

Jesus is the bridge that crosses over the gulf of my lack of knowledge. He is the way, the truth and the life. No man comes to the Father except by Him (John 14:6). When the answers elude us and everything seems out of our grasp, when circumstances are out of control, we lean not unto our own understanding. We can trust the Lord even when we don't have all the answers. God has the solution; we only have to seek His solutions through our bridge, Christ Jesus.

Likewise, when we think we have all the answers, when everything is under control, then, and especially then, we must lean not unto our own understanding. Realizing how little we really know, we allow God to lead, guide and direct our lives.

How many times have you heard, "If I knew then what I know now"? The fact is: God knows now what our future holds. He'll prepare us for it, even though we might not understand the preparation at the time.

God began preparing Samuel for the work he was to do even before he was conceived.

> And she [Hannah] vowed a vow, and said, O Lord of hosts, if thou wilt indeed look on the affliction of thine handmaid, and remember me, and not forget thine handmaid, but wilt give unto thine handmaid a man child, then I will give him unto the Lord all the days of his life (1 Sam. 1:11).

As just a young boy, Samuel was taken to the temple to live with the high priest. As Samuel grew and learned the ways of God from Eli, the high priest, God spoke to Eli, saying,

> I will raise me up a faithful priest, that shall do according to that which is in mine heart and in my mind: and I will build him a sure house; and he shall walk before mine anointed for ever (1 Sam. 2:35).

Soon after that revelation to Eli, God revealed Himself to Samuel, calling him into the God idea for his life. At the moment of that encounter with God, Samuel was given his first assignment as a prophet. God continued to reveal His God ideas to Samuel, often whispering in his ear ("Now the Lord had told Samuel in his ear," [1 Sam. 9:15]). Samuel never swerved from his determination to fulfill God's plan for his life.

Our Encyclopedia of God Ideas

God will prepare us to fulfill His plan for our lives, just as He prepared Samuel. Many of the God ideas for our lives have already been revealed in His Word. The Word clearly indicates many things that the believer can know as we allow Christ to open the wisdom of God to us.

The Love of Christ

> And to know the love of Christ, which passeth knowledge, that ye might be filled with all the fulness of God (Eph. 3:19).

Growing up in a predominantly Caucasian neighborhood was difficult at times for me. Oftentimes little kids would make fun of me because of my skin color, saying, "People who look like you are probably great dancers," or, "A lot of great athletes look just like you."

I was stereotyped by my skin color. Outwardly I acted as though I thought it was cute, but on the inside it really hurt me. As I grew older I noticed more and more situations where I was treated with prejudice because of my skin color.

When I was about ten years of age, I had a friend from school whom I really liked. We played sports together in the school yard. When his parents discovered the color of my skin, they wouldn't let him spend time with me anymore.

Another time, as I walked into a friend's home, a visiting relative commented to my friend's mother, "I can't believe you are letting this young boy in your house."

Due to this kind of treatment, I developed a chip on my shoulder. As I grew older that chip on my shoulder turned into a rock.

When I decided to stand strong for God, my thinking was, God, I will love everybody, but I don't want to love prejudiced people. But that attitude doesn't go too far in the kingdom — it doesn't line up with 1 Corinthians 13.

God dealt with me about my attitude toward prejudiced people. He revealed my attitude for what it was — prejudice. As I learned to understand the heart of God, my own heart began to change.

> Thus saith the Lord, Let not the wise man glory in his wisdom, neither let the mighty man glory in his might, let not the rich man

glory in his riches: But let him that glorieth
glory in this, that he understandeth and
knoweth me (Jer. 9:23-24).

The closer I got to God by prayer and Bible study,
the more His nature changed my own. Loving people
— even those who were prejudiced and didn't really
love me — became a way of life for me.

After I preached in one Southern church, a lady
came up to me and said, "You are one of the sharpest,
cleanest, nicest colored boys I have ever seen. You are
a great speaker. You have a really good vocabulary."
(As if to say that people who looked like me usually
didn't.)

I took her face in my hands in a gentle way and
said, "You know, that is one of the nicest compliments
from this part of the country that I have ever received." I knew I had been changed!

It is God's idea for believers to be filled with a great
love for people who have not given their lives to
Christ. The love of God which spilled out from Jesus
on the cross of Calvary will spill out of our hearts.

When the Lord told me that I would be used in the
working of signs and wonders and healing of the sick,
He revealed through His Word that compassion would
be the key to open the door to the miraculous. He opened
my eyes to the different scriptures where Jesus was
moved with compassion to heal the sick.

- But when he saw the multitudes, he was
  moved with compassion on them, because
  they fainted (Matt. 9:36).

- Jesus...saw a great multitude, and was

moved with compassion toward them, and he healed their sick (Matt. 14:14).

- So Jesus had compassion on them, and touched their eyes: and immediately their eyes received sight (Matt. 20:34).

- And Jesus, moved with compassion, put forth his hand...and saith unto him...be thou clean (Mark 1:41).

One time when I was feeling tired and depressed — having a pity party with me, myself and I — I got a call from somebody who wanted me to visit a friend who was very ill and in the hospital.

Rather begrudgingly I went to the hospital and got on the elevator to go up to the person's room, but I got off on the wrong floor. I discovered I was in the burn ward. As I stepped off the elevator, a little kid holding a balloon ran up to me. His face was severely burned — he had only one nostril that apparently the doctors had carved out during reconstructive surgery.

"Hey, are you the guy that is coming to entertain us?" he asked me.

"No, I'm not," I replied.

This little guy was so happy and loving in spite of his tragic burns. I was very touched by it, and, leaning down to his height, I said, "What are you guys doing?"

"We're having a party," he said, "but we have to wait for the entertainment to get here."

"Can I see?" I asked. I walked down the hall with him. As we turned into a large room I saw a whole group of kids who were also burn victims. Many had burned faces, and some had burns all over their bodies. But these kids were happy, full of enthusiasm and love. I realized that love and enthusiasm go together. Because of God's great love for us, we can be the most loving and enthusiastic people on the face of the earth. My depression lifted, and their attitudes really touched my life.

When we begin to feel sorry for ourselves, we need to look outside ourselves. We will find many people who are facing situations much more difficult than ours.

It is God's idea that we be consumed with compassion as Christ was.

The All-sufficiency of God

> But my God shall supply all your need according to his riches in glory by Christ Jesus (Phil. 4:19).

When Paul and Silas were in jail at Philippi, they did not call out, "Hey, what time is supper? I need a mat to lie on! Can't you at least let me make my one phone call?" They had all they needed — they had their God ideas. And they were able to endure the deprivation of their imprisonment by praising God for being all they needed.

Paul knew God was going to deliver him. He had an assurance — a personal, firsthand encounter. We'll never praise God at midnight unless we have a God idea that He's big enough to do what He said He'll do.

Paul understood the all-sufficiency of God in other areas of his life as well. To the Philippians he wrote,

> Not that I speak in respect of want: for I have learned, in whatsoever state I am, therewith to be content. I know both how to be abased,

and I know how to abound: every where and in all things I am instructed both to be full and to be hungry, both to abound and to suffer need (Phil. 4:11-12).

The Power of God to Fulfill the Plan of God

Any God ideas that we attempt to share with an ungodly world must be shared through the power of God. The power of God surrounded Peter as he stood before the thousands of people gathered in Jerusalem on the day of Pentecost, (see Acts 2). That power activated him to turn his world upside down (Acts 17:6).

When Martin Luther received the understanding that justification is by faith, the power of God caused him to move out from the religious establishment. When Kenneth Hagin had an illumination of faith, he acted upon it through the power of God. That same power moved Oral Roberts into a healing ministry and Billy Graham into world evangelism.

The power of God provided me an opportunity to pray over a session of the United States Congress in Washington, D.C. God's power had even arranged the events beforehand.

A wonderful Christian lady who was working for a congressman had been healed of cancer during one of my services. She was so excited about what had taken place in her own body that she told the congressman. Through a series of events the opportunity came for me to pray in Congress.

After my prayer, I went to the floor to talk with some of the congressmen. One of them said to me, "You are a very unusual minister. You seem to have a lot of life and energy." I appreciated his comments very much.

Another congressman came up to say, "Your prayer was powerful. When you prayed, it seemed as though God actually listened."

God's power should be evident in every Christian's life. People should notice that we've been with Jesus. They should see His power demonstrated in every aspect of our lives.

Finding the God idea is so much simpler when we quit trying to use our good ideas to find it! Human reason is useless in the spiritual decision-making process.

Excluding the God Idea

In Jesus' day the Pharisees were intently zealous to carry out the letter of the law. Jesus wanted to help people see that the law was the supreme guide of life. But the Pharisees magnified each minute portion of the law to such an extent that it became a supreme nuisance rather than a supreme guide for their lives.

Jesus became very upset with this determination on the part of the Pharisees. In Matthew he says,

> Woe unto you...Pharisees, hypocrites! for ye pay tithe of mint and anise and cummin, and have omitted the weightier matters of the law, judgment, mercy, and faith: these ought ye to have done, and not to leave the other undone. Ye blind guides, which strain at a gnat, and swallow a camel....Ye are like unto whited sepulchres, which indeed appear beautiful outward, but are within full of dead men's bones, and of all uncleanness (Matt. 23:23-24, 27).

Jesus didn't mince words, did He? I can't imagine trying to swallow a camel, but when I rely on my own good ideas — my human reason — that is what He said I am doing. My good ideas just pretty up the outside until I look like a beautiful tomb, dead inside.

Letting go of human reason will allow the God idea for our lives to permeate within, building up the inner man or woman of God.

Due to the frailty of life, every decision and judgment we make could be final. There are no guarantees for a second chance. There isn't always an opportunity to undo something you have said or done.

We can make good and wise decisions if we maintain a relationship with the One who has all the answers. Our resource is the Source of all truth and knowledge.

The ability to walk in God's biggest and ultimate idea for you does not come overnight. Just as a baby begins with one or two faltering steps, we start taking small steps in the right direction.

Before we can win a thousand souls for God we must speak to one. Before God will reveal the perfect mate for your life, He may expect you to eliminate the imperfections of your own life. The prosperity of a successful career may never come unless we learn to be good stewards of the little that we already possess.

As we move forward with the God ideas we have already received, God will always be at our side, watching our every step as we learn to open our hearts to the fullness of His knowledge and truth. And, as we shall see next, He may give us a big idea in a small place. ◊

FIVE

TRUST GOD
IN
SMALL PLACES

Principle Five:

Big ideas
come in
little places.

WHEN WE find ourselves in situations that we do not like, we are in what I call *small places*. It may be a school or job you don't like. Or possibly it is a relationship that is difficult to maintain. Maybe it's a habit you can't seem to break.

God leads us to *small places* to allow us the opportunity to see His *big idea* for that place. Often that big idea does not involve you alone, but also those around you in that small place. God is not always thinking exclusively about you. Very likely He is thinking of the people you will touch as well.

When you move into a new neighborhood, you touch that entire neighborhood. When you get hired for a new job or transferred to a different department, you touch the lives of the people in that area. Everywhere you go your life affects the lives of other people.

That was true in the life of George Müller. Born in 1805 in Prussia, the son of a government tax-collector, he entered the Lutheran ministry as a young man.

Feeling a strong call to evangelism, he went to London to train as a missionary to the Jews. This became impossible when he fell ill, so he took pastoral charge of a small independent chapel in Devon.

Müller and his wife moved to Bristol in 1832, arriving just after cholera had swept through the city, leaving hundreds of poor children living in squalid, narrow streets where they foraged for food in the garbage heaps.

Müller determined to feed, clothe and educate these destitute orphan children. He believed this to be the God idea for his life and was certain the Lord would provide what was necessary — one thousand pounds to begin a home and the right people to run it. In April 1836 Müller opened a home for thirty orphaned girls. Within two years he had three homes and more than a hundred children under his care.

By 1870 more than two thousand resident children lived in George Müller's orphan homes. Yet he never made an appeal for money. The children never went hungry or ill-dressed. Never a debt went unpaid. Müller's only security was his unshakable trust that God knew their needs and would provide. God did so, though often at the very last moment when there was not a penny in the purse and no food on the tables. Müller's homes existed by a never-ending succession of miracles of faith.

When George Müller died in 1898 at age ninety-two, he had raised over 1,453,153 British pounds. But George Müller never broke his promise to God to live by faith and trust alone. He died with only 160 pounds to his name. The life work of this great Christian leader was based on the fundamental belief that trust and faith were all he needed. His commitment still challenges us today.[1]

The big idea that God gave to George Müller when he first arrived in Bristol taught him to trust God in that small place. And although that small beginning led to a great work for God among the orphaned children of England, the idea never changed. God's idea in a small place was big enough for his entire life.

Be Faithful in Little Things

You can hear God call you to full-time ministry after you learn to discern His voice in smaller things. You can trust God for a business or a nation after you learn to trust Him in the small things. The way you discern the call and have the faith for God's *big idea* is to be faithful in the little ideas.

Remember the parable of the talents? God calls you to use what you have before He gives you more. God will not call the preacher to preach to five thousand sinners until he has obeyed God's call to preach to five. God will not entrust the business owner with a million-dollar profit until that person has trusted God for the hundred dollars lacking for rent.

In his book *The Winner Within*, Pat Reilly, coach of the New York Knicks and former coach of the Los Angeles Lakers, talks about his step-by-step climb up the ladder of success.[2] He began by accepting a job as the team's traveling secretary, working for another coach. Then he moved into the position of assistant coach. Finally he became head coach.

Pat Reilly led the Los Angeles Lakers to many championships, helping them to become a dynasty. But his success did not come overnight. His rise from a kind of *fetch-it* position to that of head coach of one of the greatest teams of all time was a step-by-step process.

George Kinney, founder of Kinney Shoes, also learned to be faithful in little things. As a widower with a young son, he lost his job at a department store during a layoff time. I am sure he thought, *What am I going to do in this situation? Am I going to get bitter, or am I going to get better?*

He was able to scrape together fifteen hundred dollars to open his own store. Then, step-by-step, his store began to grow. People came from miles around to buy Kinney shoes. Now he has a multimillion-dollar company.

He didn't give up — he kept growing step-by-step. He was thinking big in small places.

I had the opportunity of meeting Dick Clark in an airplane one day. Dick Clark has been very successful, with several television game shows to his credit — including the long-running "American Bandstand."

I read the story of his climb to success. As a young boy he was very attached to his older brother. But this brother served in the military during World War II, and his plane was shot down. He never came home from the war.

Dick Clark was very lonely for his brother. He listened to the radio for hours at a time. He dreamed of becoming a radio announcer someday, often practicing his radio voice in his room.

He was thinking big in small places. He could have given up in despair, but he decided to get up and make something of himself. Step-by-step he rose to success, which he still enjoys today.

We can get on the road to God's ultimate idea for us

by starting to trust Him and His provision in every situation. Red lights, setbacks, detours — God has a big idea for you in each.

The Process of Elimination

Many Christians follow the *good idea* for their life and not the *God idea*. We sometimes fail to understand that our steps are ordered by the Lord. We are filled with our good ideas for our small places, and we miss the God idea.

I met Marty Celaya when we were both in a high school art class as struggling artists. He remains one of my best friends to this day. Marty wanted the prestige of wearing a varsity jacket around the high school campus and was determined to get a varsity letter in some sport.

Marty had trouble figuring out which sport he was best suited for. He finally narrowed it down to tennis or track. Marty seemed to have potential for track, and with the right instructor I felt he might do well, so I encouraged him to try out for the track team. But Marty couldn't decide whether to choose tennis or track. Unfortunately we had never heard about good ideas or God ideas.

Eventually Marty chose tennis. He had only been on the tennis team about ten minutes when he realized he would never be a John McEnroe. The tennis coach knew this too. Marty's good idea of getting a letter in tennis seemed unattainable.

As the tennis team practiced one afternoon, the coach suddenly realized that Marty was gone. Soon a group of cross-country runners jogged past the tennis courts. One of the tennis players yelled, "There he is!" Marty was right in the front of the pack.

Everyone on the tennis courts laughed hysterically as he ran by. Marty would be remembered forever as the guy who changed sports faster than any other athlete in high school history. Through great determination and much sweat, Marty finally got his letter in track and field and proudly walked the halls of our old high school wearing his letterman jacket.

He found the right idea through a process of elimination. Fortunately for Marty, it did not take him very long to figure out a way to reach his goal.

Sadly enough, many Christians waste a lifetime without reaching the God ideas for their lives. They fail to realize that they can only reach the God idea through the process of elimination.

Before acting upon a good idea, submit it to the scrutiny of God's Word. Does it line up with biblical principles? Is there an example from the Word of God which will show you a better response than your good idea? Would Jesus have the same idea — respond the same way?

Ask God how He feels about your good idea. Spend time in prayer, seeking God's wisdom. Perhaps journal your conversation with God so that when you face a similar decision in the future you will be able to look back and see how God responded to a good idea that you brought to Him in prayer.

As we seek God's guidance we will discover that one by one our good ideas will fall away as God's ideas are revealed. We learn this as we start trusting God in small places.

We may need to eliminate ideas which are contrary

to the revealed Word of God. There may be good ideas in our lives which are blocking the presence of God; these will have to be eliminated. Perhaps our good ideas fill our lives so completely that they hinder us from developing our relationship with Jesus Christ. These ideas will have to go.

Good ideas are things like taking on just one more extracurricular activity, spending time alone, avoiding confrontation, surprising your wife with an expensive piece of jewelry.

None of these is a *bad* idea. We may have decided they are good ideas to pursue. But God's idea may be spending more devotional time with Him rather than assuming another extracurricular responsibility. A God idea may be surrounding yourself with Christian fellowship instead of withdrawing in discouragement. He may say that confrontation is necessary to avoid sidestepping His will because of the influence of others, or that paying off that overused credit card is His idea — not using it more.

One Step at a Time

There are three components to each God idea that God has for us.

1. The destination He has chosen.

2. The course He wants us to take.

3. The steps that will get us there.

All three parts — the destination, the course and the steps — must be followed carefully. If we attempt to change or modify any of these, then we are moving out of the perfect will of God for our lives.

Maybe we'll accept the destination, but we want to get there by following a different course. Possibly we'll say yes to the destination and to the course, but on a daily basis we want to make our own choices of when, where and how we'll do our stepping. In essence we're saying, "God, You handle the big decisions, and I'll take care of the smaller ones."

Esther learned to trust God with her destination, following the course her God idea laid out for her. She discovered that step-by-step God could bring her to the fulfillment of the God idea in her life.

> And the decree of Esther confirmed these matters of Purim; and it was written in the book (Esth. 9:32).

This rather obscure verse in the book of Esther gives us the ultimate destination of Esther's God idea. God intended to use her to bring the entire nation of Israel (and its posterity) to a yearly praise celebration of God's goodness (the Feast of Purim). This feast day was to be filled with joy and generosity and would commemorate God's miraculous deliverance over Israel's enemies.

But I doubt that Esther understood her destination when she began to walk according to her God idea. Rather, she simply chose to follow the course God laid before her. It was God's idea to elevate this unknown Jewish girl to a position of honor in the Persian-Mede empire.

As we read the book of Esther, we can see the steps

that God set before Esther as He moved her toward her destination:

- She was born to a family of the tribe of Benjamin (2:5-7).

- Orphaned at a young age, she was adopted into the family of her cousin Mordecai (2:7).

- She became a part of a large group of beautiful young maidens from which King Ahasuerus would choose a new wife (2:8).

- Although Jewish, she was chosen by King Ahasuerus to be his wife (2:17).

- She became aware of the evil plan of Haman to destroy her people (4:4).

- She broke tradition by presenting herself to the king unannounced (5:2).

- She confronted the plot of Haman and told the king about it (7:3-6).

- She asked the king to spare her people and punish Haman (8:5).

- When victory for her people was secured, she asked the king to institute a religious feast day which would cause her people to remember their deliverance (9:25,29).

- She ultimately brought her people and all the people of the Persian-Mede empire into an awareness of the miracle power of the God of Israel (9:31).

Who would have thought that a Jewess — a captive, an orphan — was born to be a queen! But because Esther was willing to give up her good ideas in order to follow the God idea for her life, she distinguished herself as a spiritual leader of two nations.

God must be God every day, all the way. He is Lord of everything or He is Lord of nothing. If He is your Lord on a part-time basis, then you are not trusting Him completely and will not succeed.

I was a dreamer as a young boy. I believed that I was supposed to touch people in a big way. I used to dream about my destination. As I grew in my understanding of God, I learned that I must discover the course and take the steps God directed in order to reach my destination. Action was necessary to activate my faith.

Keeping in shape is a good example. Often as I pass a newsstand I will glance at the covers of magazines such as *Muscle and Fitness*. The covers always picture someone in excellent physical condition. I saw the work required to maintain a tremendous physical shape when I decided to work out regularly in the gym.

I knew that as I grew older my body was not going to respond the way it used to when it was younger. I began to dream about getting in shape. That was my destination — to see myself looking like Arnold Schwarzenegger.

I met a tremendous bodybuilder named James DeMello. He has become a motivational speaker and evangelist for God. "Tim," he said, "if you want to get in shape, you have to take these steps." He talked about the destination — getting in shape. Then he outlined the course and helped me to understand the steps I had to take.

First I had to learn to eat right. I would have to quit drinking Cokes and start drinking more water. I had to exercise my cardiovascular system. But I wouldn't reach my destination until I understood the course and took the steps necessary to move me forward.

After eating better, drinking the proper liquids and working out for several years, my body began to respond to the course James DeMello set out for me. It has been very fulfilling to start feeling better about myself both physically and emotionally. But it has been a step-by-step process. Inch by inch, everything's a cinch. Yard by yard — it starts getting real hard.

Trusting God in each little thing, in every small place, will equip us to reach the ultimate big ideas that God has for us. God's vision for our lives will become our own vision — we will become the people God created us to be.

When God first shared his God ideas with the people of Israel, He taught them how to observe and follow His ideas for their lives. The book of Leviticus details the observance of the laws of God. It is filled with directions from God.

Tucked away in all the details of old covenant law is a beautiful promise for us when we follow God's instruction in little things.

> If ye walk in my statutes (God ideas)...I will give you rain in due season, and the land shall yield her increase....ye shall eat your bread to the full, and dwell in your land safely. And I will give you peace in the

land...and I will rid evil beasts out of the land, neither shall the sword go through your land.

And ye shall chase your enemies, and they shall fall before you by the sword....For I will have respect unto you, and make you fruitful, and multiply you, and establish my covenant with you (Lev. 26:3-9).

The Lord concludes His promise by saying, "And I will walk among you, and will be your God, and ye shall be my people" (Lev. 26:12).

You can have a personal encounter with God. He will share His specific plan for your life — He will give you your God idea.

As we trust Him in the small places, He will lead us to a personal revelation of His will for our lives. And, as we will discover next, that revelation will get us going. 💡

SIX

GET
GOING!

Principle Six:

Get busy!
God will direct
your steps
as you go.

GOD TAUGHT the Israelites the difference between a good idea and a God idea as they fled from Egypt the morning after the Passover. They followed God's direction until they arrived at the Red Sea, but then it seemed as though their efforts were thwarted.

There was nowhere else to go. They were hemmed in on every side by mountains, and the wide expanse of water in front of them prevented them from going forward. God instructed, "Speak unto the children of Israel, that they turn and encamp...by the sea" (Ex. 14:2).

The mountains were around them, the Red Sea was before them and the Egyptians were chasing after them. What should they do now?

The best idea they could dream up was to go back to Egypt. "It had been better for us to serve the Egyptians, than that we should die in the wilderness" they reasoned (Ex. 14:12). Moses had a plan too. But was it a good idea or a God idea?

Is This Really a God Idea?

A spiritual leader needs to be able to discern a God idea in situations which affect those under his or her leadership. This is true for the pastor, but it is also true for the Sunday school teacher, the parent or the Christian young person who is trying to maintain a Christian witness among his peers.

Sometimes we think our good idea is a God idea. I think that is probably what Moses thought as he stood to counsel with his people on the edge of the Red Sea. He said to them,

> Fear ye not, *stand still*, and see the salvation of the Lord....The Lord shall fight for you, and ye shall hold your peace (Ex. 14:13-14, italics added).

That sounds like a God idea, doesn't it? And in many circumstances it would be. But God answered Moses:

> Wherefore criest thou unto me? speak unto the children of Israel, that they *go forward* (Ex. 14:15, italics added).

Moses' advice to stand still was based upon the options that the circumstances presented to the Israelites. His idea was a *good* idea only if the evident options were considered. But God's idea to go forward was based upon His omnipotent ability to alter the circumstances to bring a supernatural victory.

Moses would never have seen the God idea if He

106

had stood still on the banks of the Red Sea. God had not decided to come down and fight the Egyptians for Moses while the children of Israel stood by, bravely holding their peace. God intended for Moses to *get going!* The victory was not to come until they took the first step out of their wilderness into the waters of the Red Sea.

God doesn't want us to stand still in the midst of our circumstances, trying to come up with a good idea — a plan of action — based on the options that circumstance offers to us. He wants us to get going, to step forward in our fuzzy image of the God idea for that circumstance. God will make His directions clearer as we continue that forward move.

Don't forget that two-thirds of God's name is *Go.*

Over the years, I have enjoyed following the career of Dominique Wilkins, a star basketball player for the Atlanta Hawks.

While he was in San Antonio, Texas, to play the San Antonio Spurs, I had lunch with him. We talked about a leg injury he had received in the previous year. Many people wondered if he could come back after such a severe leg injury.

"Tim," he said as we began to talk, "there were times when I felt so depressed and down in the dumps. But I just kept pressing on. I thought about getting better. I started working out even though it was painful. I saw myself having a better year."

He told me how God helped him get motivated and get going. He relied on God's strength in the midst of his situation. Because of his persistence, his first year back in basketball became one of the greatest seasons of his career.

He could have given up in the midst of bad circumstances, but he got up and did something about it and reversed his situation.

The key is never to give up.

Jacob Riis, a nineteenth century social reformer and writer, said, "When nothing seems to help, I go and look at a stonecutter, hammering away at his rock, perhaps a hundred times without as much as a crack showing in it. Yet at the hundred and first blow it will split in two, and I know it was not that blow that did it — but all that had gone before."[1]

Good Ideas and God Ideas in Conflict

Paul learned this same lesson as he traveled with his companions on his second missionary journey. Paul began his trip by traveling through the area of Galatia, which he had visited on his first missionary journey. Twice Paul had plans to travel into Asia when the Spirit of God sent him elsewhere (see Acts 16:6-7).

Does this mean that Paul wasn't listening to the voice of God when he decided to travel into Asia? He had already spent three years in the wilderness of Arabia learning to discern the God idea for his life. God had radically changed Paul into a committed man of God — following God's ideas for his life. Had he forgotten how to listen to God's ideas and fallen back into the trap of his own good ideas?

That is not the case in this story. Rather, this portion of Scripture illustrates the principle Paul had learned: If he simply got going, God would provide the direction he needed. Paul was led by the Spirit on a step-by-step course to his ultimate destination.

Paul and his companions passed by Mysia, a province in the northwest of Asia Minor, where God said, "Don't follow your plans to go north to Bithynia. I'm stopping you and sending you to another place." So they turned south to travel down to Troas, the chief port of the province. This took them farther away from the mountainous northwest province of Bithynia. According to human reason, it seemed that Bithynia needed Paul's help more than Macedonia. The area of Bithynia hadn't been exposed to the gospel and was a very sinful place. It was under the demonic control of Satan.

Maybe at this point Paul was saying (as would many believers), "God, what on earth are You doing? I thought I knew where You wanted me to go. Why have You changed my plans?"

But as they rested at Troas waiting for God's direction, Paul had a vision. In his vision he saw a man of Macedonia standing and begging him to come over to Macedonia to help the people there.

> And after he had seen the vision, immediately we endeavoured to go into Macedonia, assuredly gathering that the Lord had called us for to preach the gospel unto them (Acts 16:10).

This became the beginning of the evangelization of Europe. As time passed, I'm sure Paul found it much easier to look back and understand why God redirected his steps, for he declared, "A great door and effectual is opened unto me" (1 Cor. 16:9).

God speaks to us every single day of our lives. He

has a God idea for every big or small circumstance we face. Although a vision such as Paul had is only one of many ways that God speaks, He will lead us in the steps of righteousness for His name's sake.

> And we know that all things work together for good to them that love God, to them who are the called according to his purpose (Rom. 8:28).

All things work together for God's perfect will to be performed in your life. It may not always seem as though God is leading you on a perfect path. Paul had a good idea, but he was rerouted into Macedonia by a God idea.

The Word of God illustrates the long-lasting benefits of Paul's visit to Macedonia. The gospel of Christ was spread throughout this country. Perhaps the best example of the fruit of Paul's labors is through his ministry to the city of Philippi, which was in Macedonia. When Paul arrived in Philippi, it resembled many of today's large cities. It was a crossroads for both sea and land travel — an important center for business, government, communications and culture. The citizens were generally materialistic pagans. It was a fast-paced, fast-living metropolitan complex.

The first church in Europe was established in Philippi, and Paul's epistle to the Philippian believers has always been a favorite of many Christians.

The Philippian church continued to support Paul financially throughout his life. It was to these generous, gentle Philippian believers that Paul expressed the vision of a man who lives by God ideas: "I can do all things through Christ which strengtheneth me" (Phil. 4:13). The dominant theme of his letter to the Philippians is *joy*.

Finding a Specific God Idea

During his time in Philippi, Paul ministered to four individuals who represented areas of ministry where believers can be directed by a God idea.

Ordinary, Everyday People

> And on the sabbath we went out of the city by a river side....and a certain woman named Lydia...heard us: whose heart the Lord opened (Acts 16:13-14).

Lydia was just an ordinary woman who lived in Philippi. She sold material to wealthy families, who used it for their clothing. Lydia was among a group of women meeting by the riverside to pray, and as she listened to the gospel story her heart was gripped with a desire to serve this Jesus whom Paul talked about.

There are men and women today who go about their jobs every day, aware that there must be more to life — maybe even seeking it among the myriad of self-help or religious meetings offered in their communities. They aren't even aware of their need for a God idea. If we will get going, God may direct us to take a God idea to them, providing them the opportunity to say, as Lydia probably said, "This is what I've been waiting for!"

Demonically Imprisoned People

> A certain damsel possessed with a spirit of
> divination met us....The same followed Paul
> and us, and cried, saying, These men are the
> servants of the most high God....And this did
> she many days. But Paul, being grieved,
> turned and said to the spirit, I command thee
> in the name of Jesus Christ to come out of
> her. And he came out the same hour (Acts
> 16:16-18).

Here was a poor, wretched, demon-possessed slave
girl who was being used by her masters to bring in
money. I can't help but wonder if deep within the
soul of this girl dwelt the hope of deliverance through
the message Paul was preaching. Day after day she
cried for others to listen to Paul. Perhaps she was
longing for this man to offer her a way out of her
miserable existence.

And he did! It was God's idea to break the hold that
Satan had on this girl, just as God desires to break the
hold that Satan has on the people of our communities
today. He will direct us to recognize and confront the
supernatural power-hold Satan exerts, breaking the
bondage for those to whom we give the message of
deliverance and salvation.

People in the Business World

> And the keeper of the prison...drew out his
> sword, and would have killed himself....But
> Paul cried with a loud voice, saying, Do thy-

> self no harm: for we are all here. Then he
> called for a light...and fell down before Paul
> and Silas...and said, Sirs, what must I do to
> be saved? (Acts 16:27-30).

The Philippian jailer who guarded Paul and Silas after they were thrown in prison for preaching the gospel is representative of people in the business world who may come in contact with the man of God. He had not come to Paul — Paul came to him. And that encounter with the man of God brought salvation not only to him but to his entire household.

Believers today can have just as great an impact on the business world as Paul had on this Philippian jailer. But first we have to move forward, allowing God to direct our steps with a God idea.

Governmental Leaders

> And when it was day, the magistrates sent
> the serjeants, saying, Let those men go....But
> Paul said unto them...Let them come them-
> selves and fetch us out....And they came and
> besought them, and brought them out, and
> desired them to depart out of the city (Acts
> 16:35,37,39).

The magistrates — civil judges in the city of Philippi — just wanted to get Paul and Silas out of their city. These governmental leaders would have preferred to turn their backs and let someone else confront these men of God.

But Paul knew that God wanted to confront these

leaders with a God idea. Paul sent back the message, "If they want to get rid of us, let them come and do it themselves." The magistrates came in person to escort Paul and Silas out of town.

God's Word does not indicate that this confrontation with a God idea had any impact on the hard hearts of these civil leaders. At times God will ask us to confront the ungodly government leaders of our day also. There is a God idea for every person alive — even those who do not know they need it. And the seed of that confrontation will take root and blossom even when we do not see it happen.

Look for God Ideas in Everything

God can speak to us about anything. It may be tithing; it may be walking in love; it may be showing grace and mercy; it may be turning away from some besetting sin; or it may be living an abundant life; but God is always speaking to His people about something.

God most often deals with me about personal issues when I'm in the middle of the wilderness. He wants me to remove myself from any person, place or thing that would divert my attention from Him so He can speak to me face-to-face as a friend. And when He speaks, He often says to me as He did to Moses, "Why are you standing there crying unto Me — *go forward*" (see Ex. 14:15).

At one time I was speaking in the Bitter Root valley of Montana. During the two-month period preceding my time in Montana, I had been traveling a lot, speaking in three different countries. I was tired and anxious to finish that portion of the itinerary.

After speaking in the evening session, I went to bed and was still exhausted when I awoke in the morning. I started to think about how I needed to cut back on my schedule, but soon my thoughts became destructive rather than constructive.

Deciding to do something about it, I got some young people to go horseback riding with me. I'm from the city and had never been around horses much, but we decided to take some trail horses up into the mountains of the Bitter Root valley.

We went up to a beautiful area filled with trees and lakes and wildlife of every sort. My mind and spirit were renewed in that environment.

If I had stayed inside, closed the curtain and felt sorry for myself, I don't think I would have been able to shake off my depressed mood. But getting on that horse and going up to that beautiful country stirred energy inside me and allowed God to minister to me. He showed me ways to cut back my schedule and do some things I needed to do.

It's probably the same way in your life. There may be times when you feel you are supposed to go in one direction, but suddenly you run into a detour. Though you know the way you are going is the only logical way to go, God directs you to turn and go a different way. Even when you turn, you encounter obstacles. Paul and Silas landed in a Philippian jail for following their God idea!

Mission Accomplished!

When Paul began his missionary journeys, he wanted to take the message of salvation to the entire world. He could have felt that his good ideas were thwarted when God prevented him from traveling into Asia and Bithynia. But he didn't. He followed his God idea to Macedonia and started a revival in that country.

Much later, as he sat imprisoned in Rome near the end of his life, he wrote his prison epistles. To his friends in the Macedonian city of Philippi, he wrote,

> I thank my God upon every remembrance of you....being confident of this very thing, that he which hath begun a good work [a God idea] in you will perform it until the day of Jesus Christ....That at the name of Jesus every knee should bow...and that every tongue should confess that Jesus Christ is Lord, to the glory of God the Father (Phil. 1:3,6; 2:10-11).

The God idea had altered his plans, and he had to give up his good ideas to follow in the path God directed. But he ended his life with the confidence that every knee would bow in submission to the Christ he served. He *got going*, and the world has never been the same since. ᕟ

Principle Seven:

When things heat up — cool off with a God idea.

SEVEN

KEEP YOUR COOL WHEN THINGS GET HOT

THERE WILL always be an opposition to your mission. The Bible tells us clearly that there is an enemy to the Christian.

> Be sober, be vigilant; because your adversary the devil, as a roaring lion, walketh about, seeking whom he may devour (1 Pet. 5:8).

Lucifer, who is now called Satan, is a real being. He opposes the things of God. He and his host of demons are the perpetrators of the evil in our world.

We need only to pick up the morning newspaper or turn on the television news to be bombarded with reports of evil — negative circumstances in the lives of people throughout the world. From the isolated incident in the tiny Midwestern town to the nation-wide genocide of an entire ethnic group, Satan actively works to destroy what God has lovingly created.

We are mindful of the enemy's devices. But,

"Greater is he that is in you, than he that is in the world" (1 John 4:4). We do not need to be afraid of him.

Satan is amazingly predictable. When things are going well and you're experiencing spiritual victories, be forewarned — Satan is preparing a pitfall.

Satan is the prince of this world (John 14:30). Satan will be the enemy of God and His children until his power is finally stripped and he is cast forever into darkness. "The whole history of the world subsequent to Christ is a struggle against the empire of Satan."[1]

But for the believer who is appropriating the power of God in his or her life, Satan is fundamentally vanquished. We can be victorious over his attacks.

Paul and Silas felt the backlash of their intrusion into Satan's territory. The slave girl's masters were enraged that Paul had cast the demons out of her. They dragged Paul and Silas into the marketplace and made false accusations against them. A crowd gathered around as the magistrates listened to the fabrications.

Caught up in the emotions of the moment, the crowd turned into a mob and joined in the attack against Paul and Silas. The magistrates, bending to the will of the people, ordered Paul and Silas to be stripped and beaten.

Paul and Silas had come to Macedonia to do good. Paul had received a vision — God spoke to him. But suddenly they were thrown into prison for doing good! The guards beat Paul thirty-nine times across the back with a whip that had little balls with barbs attached to the end of the whip. That whip no doubt pulled the skin right off his back.

The jailor was commanded to guard them carefully, so he put them in an inner cell and fastened their feet in stocks. Stocks were large wooden beams to which the feet were attached. Often the prisoners' arms would be fastened with chains attached to the ceiling so that the prisoner was left hanging in the air.

How perplexing it is when we set out to do good but find ourselves in bad situations. Paul went to prison where he was fastened in stocks, bleeding from the stripes across his back.

How Should We Respond?

Of all the Bible characters in a hot spot, probably Shadrach, Meshach and Abednego are best known (see Dan. 3). They remained cool and collected as their God idea took on bodily form and joined them in their hot spot. And because they did, an entire nation learned of the power to deliver that the God of these three Israelite boys possessed.

Paul also kept his cool in the middle of his hot spot. He was in a tough situation, but he did not despair and give up in defeat. He knew there was a God idea for every step of his life, and he simply looked for the God idea in this circumstance.

Here are some principles Paul followed when he found himself in tough situations.

Consider what God idea you have already received that applies to your situation now.

Paul spent three years in the wilderness of Arabia receiving God ideas for his life. One of the God ideas Paul had received was that Jesus was a deliverer. We know that Paul understood this God idea, for later in his second letter to Timothy he says,

> Notwithstanding the Lord stood with me, and strengthened me; that by me the preaching might be fully known, and that all the Gentiles might hear: and I was delivered out of the mouth of the lion. And the Lord shall deliver me from every evil work, and will preserve me unto his heavenly kingdom (2 Tim. 4:17-18).

So when Paul was in chains in that Philippian jail cell, he knew Jesus would deliver him. He had a firsthand understanding of Jesus, his deliverer.

He also knew God does not lie. Paul understood the *big* God idea for his life, and he knew that his mission was not yet accomplished. He had not done the things God had said he was going to do. Therefore he knew the big God idea for his life mandated that this experience in a Philippian jail would not hinder his future ministry. Although he was in prison, he was excited. Why? Because he knew there was no way he was going to die. His mission had not yet been completed. And God does not lie.

At the end of Paul's life he reiterates his understanding of the big God idea for his life. In his departing words to Timothy he says,

> I have fought a good fight, *I have finished my course,* I have kept the faith (2 Tim. 4:7, italics added).

But back here at the Philippian jail he's singing praises, thinking, *Oh, I'm in a tough spot, but somehow God's going to get me out.* When God gives us an understanding of who He is and who we are in Him, we can praise God at the midnight hour even when everything is coming against us. But without that God idea we cannot praise Him in our hearts.

We may praise Him because our pastor or a book or teaching tape said to do it. But we will not be praising Him from out of the depths of our being unless we understand that He is who He says He is.

Respond according to what you know — not according to how you feel.

Paul knew his Deliverer would deliver him and that he would finish the course God had set out for him. Therefore he could sing, "Oh, happy day! Oh, happy day!"

I think that if I were Silas, I would have responded, "Hold on! We were just beaten! They've whipped us! There's blood dripping down our backs! Yet you're singing! Get a grip on yourself! You're losing it!"

Why is it that some people can sing "Oh, happy day!" in the midst of a bad situation, while others grumble and complain, feeling bad about it? One of the secrets is to respond to our bad situations based upon what we *know* rather than upon what we *feel*. "The way of the righteous is made plain" (Prov. 15:19).

Sometimes God leads us into uncomfortable situations for reasons we may never be able to understand. But the fact remains — God led us there, and He will lead us out.

When we are in the valley and seem unable to find the way out; when we find ourselves in tough places which never seem to cease, then we know the Word says,

- I will instruct thee and teach thee in the way which thou shalt go: I will guide thee with mine eye (Ps. 32:8).

- Thou shalt guide me with thy counsel (Ps. 73:24).

- He keepeth the paths of judgment, and preserveth the way of his saints (Prov. 2:8).

- Trust in the Lord with all thine heart; and lean not unto thine own understanding. In all thy ways acknowledge him, and he shall direct thy paths (Prov. 3:5-6).

- Fear not: for I have redeemed thee, I have called thee by thy name; thou art mine. When thou passest through the waters, I will be with thee; and through the rivers, they shall not overflow thee: when thou walkest through the fire, thou shalt not be burned; neither shall the flame kindle upon thee (Is. 43:1-2).

Resist saying, "Why me?"

Paul changed his plans to go where God directed and was beaten and thrown into prison as a result. Sometimes the Lord will tell us to do something, and we'll find ourselves in a prison experience. At that point we may be tempted to respond, "God, why me?"

When Paul found himself in a prison experience, he sang praises to the Lord!

We've all heard sermons using this portion of Scripture to encourage us to praise the Lord in all circumstances. Yet many times I have discovered that it is easy to praise the Lord during the first few moments of a bad situation, but very hard to praise Him as the weeks and months drag on.

How could Paul continue to praise God in a situation that just got worse and worse? In a later letter Paul encouraged the Philippians to "Rejoice in the Lord alway: and again I say, Rejoice" (Phil. 4:4). Do you think he repeated himself because he was aware of the fact that we might not get it the first time?

Then to the Ephesians he advised, "Giving thanks always for all things unto God and the Father in the name of our Lord Jesus Christ" (Eph. 5:20).

We can praise the Lord at all times, even in the midst of a bad situation, by looking beyond the situation to see Jesus. We praise Him because He has personally revealed Himself and His nature to us.

We can respond the way Paul and Silas did in jail. We may not be in stocks; maybe we haven't received stripes on our backs; but we will be in uncomfortable situations as we follow God's directions for our lives. God is who He said He is. He is the deliverer. He is the restorer. He's a miracle-working God. And for that we can praise Him.

> Your attitude should be the same as that of Christ Jesus:
> Who, being in very nature God, did not
>   consider equality with God something to
>   be grasped,
> but made himself nothing, taking the very
>   nature of a servant, being made in hu-
>   man likeness.
> And being found in appearance as a man,
>   he humbled himself and became obedi-
>   ent to death — even death on a cross!
> Therefore God exalted him to the highest
>   place and gave him the name that is

above every name,
that at the name of Jesus every knee should
bow, in heaven and on earth and under
the earth,
and every tongue confess that Jesus Christ
is Lord, to the glory of God the Father
(Phil. 2:5-11, NIV).

Let God ignite your spirit.

How do you know if you have a God idea? Paul got
an understanding that Jesus was a deliverer, so when he
was in the stocks, weighed down with chains, something inside him said, "You're not going to stay in
these chains, son; I have too much for you to do."

God ignited his spirit, and he started singing. God
ideas will always ignite our spirits.

Acts 16 has ignited my spirit with a burning desire
to follow the example of Paul. Paul could be locked in
prison and still praise God, while I can't even praise
God in the comfort of my own home sometimes. I
love this story of the apostle Paul because even
though he was in chains, he was still dreaming big.

I can remember driving up to Big Bear Mountain in
the San Bernardino mountains with my family when I
was a young boy. As we drove along in our beat-up
old station wagon, my sister asked, "Dad, why do we
just watch other people ski? Why can't we ski too?"

"People like us don't ski," my father answered matter-
of-factly. But even in the midst of knowing we had
nothing, there was a fighting, burning desire inside me
that I was supposed to have a special place in this world.

As an elementary student I could not read very well.
Often I would deride myself, saying, "Here I am, the star

athlete of my class, yet I'm in the worst reading group."

Then something inside me would say, "You have to train, Tim, because someday you are going to affect a lot of people." I determined to learn to read, and reading became one of my passions. Since the time I was in the fourth or fifth grade, I have loved to read.

Even though I was bound by the confines of my personal situation, I learned to think big in small places. God gave me a passion to help other people.

When we are stuck in a bad situation, we have several options:

- We can *nurse* our problems.

- We can *rehearse* our problems.

- We can *curse* our problems.

But I would rather *disperse* my problems and let God *reverse* my problems.

So I allowed God to reverse my situation. Although I was locked in the prison of poverty, living in a family of five generations of alcoholics, I envisioned myself helping other people.

It started with a dream of being on television some-day. I wanted to be like Bryant Gumbel on "NBC Today" — the host of a television program. I've always enjoyed humor and thought perhaps I could be a comedian. But I seemed to know instinctively that was not the God idea for my life.

Because I loved sports, I thought about being a sports agent. But that wasn't the God idea either. I envisioned myself as part of the entertainment field. But as I learned to understand the voice of God, I realized that the God idea for my life was to be a minister. Yet God has faithfully brought to pass the words of Psalm 37:4 in my life:

> Delight thyself also in the Lord; and he shall
> give thee the desires of thine heart.

As a minister I am able to do many of the things I dreamed of doing when I was a young boy. I have spoken in the chapel services of some of the world's greatest athletes. I teach a Bible study for many members of the entertainment field. I am able to use my personality and sense of humor in the way I present the gospel message. My television program, *Miracles With Tim Storey,* is seen in forty-two different states.

The dreams we dream in our pit experiences can become the stepping-stones to our future destinies. I have touched the lives of celebrities and down-and-outers alike. I have ministered to great athletes, but I have also been involved in programs that help kids get off drugs, off the street and out of gangs. God has allowed me to touch the hurting by reaching out to people in the LA projects that I was so familiar with as a boy.

The revelation of God's idea for my life has ignited my spirit with a passion to complete the course He has laid before me. My great desire is that as I follow that course my life will help others to find the God idea for their lives. But, as the next chapter shows, I had to learn to trust God supremely. ۞

EIGHT

REGAIN
CHILDLIKE
TRUST

Principle Eight:

Good ideas *may* come to pass, but God ideas *must* come to pass.

MY DAD was a big man, standing almost six feet, two inches in height. He had huge, strong hands. As a youngster I loved to run to meet him, often throwing myself off a step into his waiting hands. He would swing me high above his head, then let me go, catching me in his arms and gathering me to him for a great big bear hug. He has now gone to be with the Lord, but while he was on earth he was always a tremendous friend.

A little baby is born into innocence with complete trust in his parents. They feed him when he's hungry and change him when he's wet. If he begins to fall, they are right there to catch him and keep him from getting hurt. Parents have been placed on earth to take care of these little ones.

For years a baby may believe that his or her parents are infallible and invincible. Just as little babies trust their parents supremely, so we can learn to trust our heavenly Father. As we do, our God ideas will come to pass.

It must be a wonderful feeling to be a baby who has never experienced the pain of disappointment in the human race. A baby doesn't comprehend that there are liars who will deceive him, or greedy opportunists to take advantage of his trust.

The world of an infant is secure because of the faith and trust that little one has in his or her parents.

I have seen a painting that illustrates such trust. A mother sparrow had built her nest on a tree limb that stretched out over a raging waterfall. The branch rose only inches above the spot where tons of water surged over the rocks and fell many feet to the pool below. Yet safe within that nest sat five little baby sparrows, quietly nestling together under the protective watch of the mother sparrow, who perched on the edge of the nest. Those little birds had absolute trust in the care and safety their mother provided. In the midst of the storm they were secure.

Likewise, the believer can rest in perfect safety provided by our heavenly Father.

The newly saved believer is the child of God. He is born of God just as each of us is born of the two specific people God chose to be our earthly parents. Matthew tells us that becoming a Christian is like becoming a little child.

> Except ye be converted, and become as little
> children, ye shall not enter into the kingdom
> of heaven (Matt. 18:3).

The child of God can have the same kind of child-like trust in his heavenly Father that the child of man has in his parents.

It doesn't take the little baby long to learn that people will let him down. Friends will break their promises. Family members may not be there when that little child needs them the most. But God will never leave us nor forsake us. He is a "friend that sticketh closer than a brother" (Prov. 18:24).

We had five children in our family with a variety of personalities and temperaments. Even though my parents were very busy raising all of us, my dad always made sure to spend time alone with each of us. Those times with my dad were very special to me.

I loved to play baseball. For many years one of my favorite pastimes was playing third base and pitcher in Little League baseball. Many of the games were played on weekdays when my father worked. He always made a great effort to come to every one of those games. He would fight the grueling, smog-filled rush-hour traffic of Los Angeles, rushing to the baseball field as fast as he could. He always made it there before the game was over.

I would stand at third base watching the crowd eagerly and waiting for the sound of his car as it pulled into the parking lot. When I heard a car squeal to a stop on the gravel stones, I knew without even looking that it was Dad. A few seconds later a yell would come from the sidelines, "Come on, Storey!" and I knew everything was all right.

My father demonstrated the love of my heavenly Father — an even more giving Father whom we can trust completely.

The Scripture says to "trust in the Lord with *all* thine heart" (Prov. 3:5, italics added). The word *all* doesn't leave any room for compromise or doubt. *All* means "completely, 100 percent, every moment of every day." Trust Him completely — supremely — because He's supremely trustworthy.

The circumstances of our lives often rob us of the ability to trust God supremely. When that trusting, innocent little baby is disappointed by people around him, he often thinks, *I'll just do it all by myself.* With each success he becomes more and more self-reliant and less trusting of others.

By the time most believers turn their lives over to God, they've become so independent that childlike trust must be relearned.

Trust cannot be demanded; it is earned. The people in life that we trust the most are those who have been trustworthy in the little things and the big things. A stranger is not easily trusted. How many times have you rolled your eyes when a salesman at your door said, "Trust me!" as he showed you his wares?

As we regain the ability to place childlike trust in God, the struggles we experience because of our independence and inability to trust will cease. As the child who places complete trust in his earthly father, we will trust our heavenly Father.

God is no stranger to believers. He has proved His trustworthiness to us over and over again. He has a proven track record! The record of His trustworthiness to mankind is available for every believer to know.

We need only talk to someone who has walked with the Lord for many years. They will be able to relate how the hand of God was guiding them — sometimes when they weren't even aware of it. And look at His faithfulness to men and women throughout the Word.

Moses had placed his supreme trust in God for his

entire life. Through forty years of leading the Israelites to the promised land he had exhibited trust again and again. In his final message to the Israelites before he went up into a mountain to die, he reminded the people of God's trustworthiness: "The eternal God is thy refuge, and underneath are the everlasting arms: and he shall thrust out the enemy from before thee....Israel then shall dwell in safety alone" (Deut. 33:27-28).

The Psalms are filled with evidence of God's trust-worthiness, particularly to King David. Psalm 91, believed to have been written by David, is a noble song of trust. The depth of trust and the quiet confidence it expresses suggest that it is the private meditation of David, showing his childlike trust in His God. It tells us eight areas of our lives where God has already proved to be worthy of our trust:

> There shall no evil befall thee, neither shall any plague come nigh thy dwelling....He shall call upon me, and I will answer him: I will be with him in trouble; I will deliver him, and honour him. With long life will I satisfy him, and shew him my salvation (Ps. 91:10,15-16).

Protection From Evil

Our Father promises "there shall no evil befall" us. We can trust God's protection in the circumstances of life that threaten us with evil.

Protection for Our Families

Webster's dictionary tells us that the word *plague*, used in verse 10 of this psalm, means "disastrous affliction or calamity." Our Father has promised to protect the believer and his or her family from physical calamity.

If We Call — He Will Answer

Our Father answers our spiritual 911 call. I can remember times of scary childhood fears when my own father told me, "Son, I will be right here if you call!" What a relief that was to me. God promises the same benefit to the believer. At any moment, in any situation, all we need to do is call, and He will instantly answer.

He Is With Us in Trouble

We do not face the troubles and trials of life alone. God our Father is right in the middle of our troubles with us — even if we can't sense His presence. David's life provides many examples of God's intervention in times of trouble. He was spared from the jaws of a lion and a bear. When all the army of Israel cowered in fear from the giant Goliath, David picked up his five smooth stones and exclaimed, "Big man, look out! I'm not sure what God is going to do, but I trust Him completely, and I'm ready to do whatever He tells me to do."

His childlike trust in God saw him through his years as a fugitive from King Saul and led him to become a victorious warrior against the enemies of Israel. It is David who sang: "Unto thee, O Lord, do I lift up my soul. O my God, I trust in thee: let me not be ashamed, let not mine enemies triumph over me" (Ps. 25:1-2).

He Will Deliver Us

Not only is He with us — He will get us out of trouble. *Webster's* defines the word *deliver* as "to send (something aimed or guided) to an intended target or destination." God will take us *out of* our troubles, but He also sends us *to* a better place.

> For I know the thoughts that I think toward you, saith the Lord, thoughts of peace, and not of evil, to give you an expected end (Jer. 29:11).

He Will Honor Us

Honor is the expected end of Jeremiah 29:11 (see Ps. 91:15). God our heavenly Father, the Creator of the entire universe, will honor *me*, His child, if I will only trust Him. *Webster's* dictionary says the word *honor* means "reputation, recognition, credit, purity and integrity." Those characteristics will be given to the believer who trusts God.

He Will Give Us Long Life

The Scripture says, "With long life will I satisfy him" (Ps. 91:16). This indicates that life will be fulfilling and satisfying — the abundant life He promised in the Gospel of John.

I am come that they might have life, and that they might have it more abundantly (John 10:10).

He Will Show Us His Salvation

The final area of our life in which God has proved His trustworthiness is our ultimate salvation to an eternity with Him. He really can be trusted never to leave or forsake us. In fact, He will bring us into His presence to spend eternity with Him. We can trust Him not only with our lives, but with our forevers also.

As an old man who had placed his trust in God for his entire life, George Whitefield said in a sermon preached around 1766:

> But see how faith triumphs in the midst of all. No sooner does unbelief pop up its head, but faith immediately knocks it down. A never-failing maxim is there proposed: "Hope thou in God." Trust in God, believe in God; for I am sure, and all of you that know Jesus Christ are persuaded of it too, that all our troubles arise from our unbelief. O unbelief, injurious bar to comfort, force of tormenting fear! On the contrary, faith bears everything. "Put thy trust in God."[1]

When we trust, it's easier to see the God ideas that He has for us. He has already earned our trust — He has proved His trustworthiness.

Trusting my heavenly Father has become as natural for me as trusting my earthly father was as a young boy. But I had to learn to trust, just as each believer learns.

As a result of my background, I always felt as though I had to do everything myself. When you are between a rock and a hard place, it is difficult to learn to trust. You believe that if somebody has to get you out of your situation, it might as well be you.

Such an attitude of self-sufficiency can be a hindrance to our ability to see God as the source of our strength. Just as Moses needed the reassurance from God that "I AM is with you" (see Ex. 3), I needed to be reassured by God that "I will be with you in every situation."

After my father's death when I was ten years old, I would get very lonely at times. When I did, I would go to Rose Hills Memorial Park in Whittier, California, where I would sit for hours by my father's grave. I would think about the times he roared into the parking lot of my Little League baseball field, shouting, "Come on, Storey. You can do it!" He always made me feel like a champion.

I still needed his encouragement, but it was very hard to find. I had not yet learned to look to God as my source of encouragement. I was still looking to my father because I knew that I could trust him. Somehow I felt better just being at his grave.

One day I read these words from my Bible,

> A father of the fatherless....God setteth the solitary in families; he bringeth out those which are bound with chains (Ps. 68:5-6).

My relationship to God slowly began to develop. As I drove along in my car I talked with Him, just as I would have talked with my earthly father if he had been in the car with me.

Soon I was talking to Him while I was getting dressed, praying as I worked and spending time just thinking about His goodness to me. Relating to Him in my daily life was becoming as natural as relating to my earthly father had been.

Over a period of time I grew in my relationship to Him and learned to trust Him. I could see the difference. When trials hit, I no longer thought about going to my father's grave at Rose Hills cemetery. I started thinking, *OK, Tim, all you need to do is talk to God your Father.*

My relationship to my heavenly Father is still developing. There are times in my life when I want to go forward or sideways or backwards to look for answers. But I've learned to go upward and trust in the Father.

In one of his sermons, Dwight L. Moody related the story of a man who had learned to place supreme trust in God in spite of tragic circumstances:

> One of the happiest men I ever knew was a man in Dundee, Scotland, who had fallen and broken his back when he was a boy of fifteen. He had lain on his bed for about forty years, and could not be moved without a good deal of pain. Probably not a day had passed in all those years without acute suffering. But day after day the grace of God had been granted to him, and when I was in his chamber it seemed as if I was as near heaven as I could get on earth. I can imagine that when the angels passed over Dundee, they had to stop there to get refreshed.

When I saw him, I thought he must be beyond the reach of the tempter, and I asked him: "Doesn't Satan ever tempt you to doubt God, and to think that he is a hard Master?"

"Oh, yes," he said, "he does try to tempt me. I lie here and see my old schoolmates driving along in their carriages, and Satan says: 'If God is so good, why does He keep you here all these years? You might have been a rich man, riding in your own carriage.' Then I see a man who was young when I was walk by in perfect health, and Satan whispers: 'If God loved you, couldn't He have kept you from breaking your back?' "

"What do you do when Satan tempts you?"

"Ah, I just take him to Calvary, and I show him Christ, and I point out those wounds in His hands and feet and side, and say, 'Doesn't He love me?' and the fact is, Satan got such a scare there eighteen hundred years ago that he cannot stand it; he leaves me every time."[2]

Despite how bad things may seem or how crazy our world becomes, our trust in the Lord will never be shattered or disillusioned by God. In the midst of his devastating external circumstances, Job said, "Though he slay me, yet will I trust in him" (Job 13:15).

Everything around us may change, but our trust is in the One who changeth not. He is the same yesterday, today and forever (Heb. 13:8). Our trust in Him transcends the condition of our bank account or our medical report. Regardless of the facts or how we feel, despite what the doctors say and how friends advise us — trust in the Lord!

God made the world and all that is in it. He breathed life into our lungs after forming us with His hands. And He alone is able to do all that He promised. There are no circumstances beyond His control. No person, place or thing can separate us from the love of God (Rom. 8:38-39). In fact, as we shall see now, God is always looking out for us.

> I will say of the Lord, He is my refuge and my fortress: my God; in him will I trust (Ps. 91:2). ☙

NINE

REMEMBER
WHO'S
WATCHING

Principle Nine:

Remember that
God is always
looking out for you.

THE YOUNG Iroquois boy was approaching the age of manhood. He had successfully passed all the tests of manhood but one. He must be taken far into the deep forest to pass an entire night at a spot determined by the tribal fathers — and he must do so alone, with no weapons and no campfire to light the dark night.

On the night of his final test he was brought before the chief. His weapons were taken from him, and with only his blanket for warmth, he was led blindfolded to the spot deep in the forest under a tree. After his blindfold was removed he was left alone.

At first the brave young boy sat tall and straight, even enjoying the moonlit night as he gazed heavenward through the trees. But soon the darkness crept in closer, and the sounds of the forest seemed louder and closer with every passing moment. The owls hooted in the trees above him, and the crickets and katydids pierced the darkness with their shrill calls.

Familiar with these sounds, he welcomed them, communing with nature as he had been taught by the tribal fathers. Soon other more ominous sounds moved toward the boy. A coyote howled, and from just to his left he heard the answering cry of a wolf. To the right he heard the snap of breaking twigs as something moved toward him through the underbrush.

Soon fear pushed its way through his confidence. He pushed his back against the tree behind him and fastened his jaw into a determined pose, crossing his arms on his chest as he had seen the brave warriors in his tribe do so many times.

He thought he heard the breathing of a bear, and strained his ears to listen. He could almost feel its warm breath on his neck as he watched the sky above for the first sign of daybreak.

The long night passed, and finally the morning sunrise cast its first rays into the forest. Stiff with fatigue, he slowly rose to his feet. As he turned to straighten his back, he suddenly saw a figure in the shadows. Standing close behind the tree, his left hand grasping his bow and his right hand holding an arrow in place ready to use, stood his father.

As we progress through the spiritual tests of manhood and womanhood, our heavenly Father is always watching us. I once saw a plaque in a bookstore that read, "God loves you so much that He can't take His eyes off of you." The book of Job, the record of one man's greatest spiritual trial, tell us, "Behold, God is mighty, and despiseth not any....He withdraweth not his eyes from the righteous" (Job 36:5,7).

Remember, God is always looking out for you. Whether you're by yourself or with your closest friend; at work or driving down the highway; in the midst of your conversations with your family, friends or people you're trying to impress; in church or at the mall; whether people are accusing you or praising you — God is watching you. If you face prosperity or poverty — regardless of the situation — through it all God is watching.

Understand Who We Are In Christ

One constant remains in each of the above circumstances — who we are in Christ. We are His forgiven, blameless heirs — the children of God. He is our Lord and King.

Remember when you were a kid and wanted to do something you weren't sure would meet with the approval of your father? You'd ask, "Is Daddy watching?"

There are times when it's comforting to know that our Father really is watching.

A friend of mine asked me to go hunting with him in Calgary in the Canadian province of Alberta. As a city slicker, hunting is really not my passion — especially as we were going bear hunting with only bows and arrows.

I was instinctively aware of the fact that this was definitely not a God idea. But my friend, a motivational speaker, is very persuasive. He outfitted me with a bow and the arrows and even arranged for lessons to teach me how to shoot. Then we departed for Calgary, Alberta.

Now, I don't mind bears as long as they are in the zoo behind a giant fence. But I'm not much into seeing bears up real close while I'm out in the wilderness all by myself only with a bow and arrow.

When we arrived, my friend and the guides with us

tried to reassure me. "Oh, don't worry about it," they told me. "When you go out to hunt the bear, you will be fifteen feet high in a tree stand. And there will be somebody up there with you with a rifle. You are completely safe."

But on the first day of hunting the highly-paid guide took me two or three miles deep into the forest and said, "Now, all you have to do is climb up in this tree and wait. I'll be back for you in about three hours. We haven't seen any bears around here in a long time. You are going to be completely safe."

Then he left me alone — with no backup rifle!

I climbed up into the tree stand nervously, fastened myself in that tree and stood there waiting for a bear. To reassure myself I thought, *Now I know God loves me. He is not going to let me see a bear because He knows how much it would frighten me.*

At first every noise I heard terrified me. I jumped when a squirrel scurried along on a branch near me and nearly fell out of the tree when a bird landed just above my head. I was sure Not-So-Gentle Ben would come striding up to my tree at any moment.

After about an hour I relaxed. *This is really nice,* I thought. *Maybe the Lord has me out here just to commune with Him and spend a little time in prayer.*

But all of a sudden the whole forest was completely quiet. The king of the forest was about to show up. Instantly alert, I saw a giant bear moving toward me very slowly. The ground creaked as he broke the branches underneath his giant paws. My heart beat in double time. It was the kind of feeling I used to have as a little kid when I was home alone and thought a burglar had broken into my house.

Earlier we had baited the area under my tree with donuts hid under a pile of sticks. This big bear had a keen sense of smell and was heading straight for my tree. He was very large and didn't get that big by being stupid. With a flick of his giant paw he lifted those sticks off the pile of donuts, looked them over and then looked up in the tree right at me.

I was covered with camouflage clothing and had even smeared camouflage paint on my face. But I could read his mind as he stared at me: "Now that looks like a fantastic chocolate long john right up there."

I was petrified. But he turned back and began to take some donuts out of the bait. After a few bites he ran away. Soon he returned to eat more donuts and then lumbered away again.

I didn't know where to turn. Out of desperation I turned to God. "God," I pleaded, "if You get me out of this one I'll really serve You." I knew when those donuts were gone he would be thinking about eating me next.

It's a comforting thing to know that God is with us in every situation. Whether we are in a trial, have experienced a broken relationship or a divorce, have been told there is something wrong with our children, have rebellious teenagers or see a bear eating donuts just a few yards away from us — God is with us.

When that bear returned again, he finished the donuts and started shuffling in the direction of the tree where I was hiding. I knew it was either him or me. With my first shot I hit him and he fell to the ground. I shook with relief! To this day I am sure God guided that arrow to its target. It wasn't the little bit of Navaho blood I possess but the grace of God that got me out of that situation.

You Can Do It!

As children we soon learn that our parents have behavior expectations for us. Most children will go to great lengths to please their parents and measure up to their expectations. As children of our heavenly Father, we try to make our conduct and attitude pleasing to Him. Our successes are His successes. Everything we are, everything we have, everything we will become brings glory unto Him.

In the book of Matthew we see the story of a man who knew he was going on an extended trip to another country. Before he left he gathered his servants together and gave them each some money as an investment for them to use while he was gone.

> And unto one he gave five talents, to another two, and to another one; to every man according to his several ability (Matt. 25:15).

But the servant who had received only one talent dug a hole in the earth and buried it. He left it there the entire time his master was gone. When the master returned, he called his servants before him once again.

> Then he which had received the one talent came and said, Lord, I knew thee that thou art an hard man...and I was afraid, and went and hid thy talent....His lord answered...Thou wicked and slothful servant...thou oughtest therefore to have put my money to the exchangers, and then at my coming I should have received mine own with usury (Matt. 25:24-27).

This servant forgot that he would have to answer to his master for his actions. His master would be looking for an answer about the money he left. His master's words are a revelation to us: "Thou wicked and slothful servant." This *wicked* servant reminds us that we will be asked to give an account of our use of the God ideas that our heavenly Father has given to us.

God is watching us — standing on the sidelines as my father did at my baseball games. He yells, "Come on, believer! You can do it!" Cast off the unbelief that would hinder you, stretch your spiritual mitt high into the air to catch your God idea and then run the course with all your might.

The servant of Matthew 25 was also called *slothful.* The word *slothful* means "lazy, inclined to sloth (which is a disinclination to action or labor)." It's a refusal to grasp the God idea for our lives. It's the paralysis often caused by our good ideas — "I'll just sit here and keep my pew warm until Jesus comes and gets me out of this place!"

The words of the master were, "Thou oughtest therefore to have put my money to the exchangers, and then at my coming I should have received mine own with usury."

In other words, it is not God's idea for us to warm the pew and hide what He has given us. God wants us to use the God ideas He has given each of us to bring more souls into the kingdom. Then at the coming of our Lord we can say, "I brought some more, Lord. Here are those who came with me because I used my God idea to take Your salvation to them also."

There is another side to the thought that God is watching us. When I stepped up to bat in those Little

League baseball games of my youth, I was so glad my Dad was sitting in that grandstand watching me hit the ball into right field! I wanted to make him proud of me. I felt his encouragement. I was motivated by his pride in me. I took courage when I heard him call, "You can do it!"

I knew who I was. I was Anthony Storey's son! He believed in me. He had dreams and goals for what he knew I could be and do. And those dreams and goals became my own.

Even when we have no earthly father to believe in us, we have a heavenly Father who will always care for us. Although my father died when I was still young, my heavenly Father has been right beside me, urging me, "Come on, son. You can do it!" In fact, I think I heard him whisper that to me that day in the tree above the bear.

Ishmael was an Old Testament boy who lost his father. He and his mother, Hagar, were sent away from his father, Abraham (see Gen. 21). This was a devastating time for Ishmael, and it wasn't long until Hagar and Ishmael collapsed in the middle of the desert — lost, alone, homeless and without hope.

But God was still looking out for Ishmael. As he and his mother lay there in the sand, God intervened.

> And God heard the voice of the lad; and the angel of God called to Hagar out of heaven, and said unto her, What aileth thee, Hagar? fear not; for God hath heard the voice of the lad where he is. Arise, lift up the lad, and hold him in thine hand; for I will make him a great nation (Gen. 21:17-18).

God wanted to be the heavenly Father who could care for and nurture young Ishmael. He had a God idea for that boy. Although Ishmael never allowed that God idea to take root in his life and grow, God was still with him, looking out for him:

> And God was with the lad; and he grew, and dwelt in the wilderness (Gen. 21:20).

Ishmael failed to recognize his heavenly Father. He never knew who he could be if he simply sought the destination God had for him. He didn't get on the right course. We must know — really *know* — who we are in Christ Jesus. That knowledge will motivate us to take courage and to find the God idea for each circumstance we face.

The first three chapters of the book of Ephesians give us a profound look at who we are in Christ. Our position is awesome. It assures us that we:

- have been blessed with all spiritual blessings in heavenly places (1:3).

- were chosen in Him before the foundation of the world to be holy and without blame (1:4).

- are the adopted children of God (1:5).

- are accepted in the beloved (1:6).

- have redemption through His blood (1:7).

- know the mystery of His will (1:9).

- have obtained an inheritance (1:11).

- can have the spirit of wisdom and revelation in the knowledge of Him (1:17)

- may know the hope of His calling and the riches of the glory of His inheritance (1:18).

- can know the greatness of His power (1:19).

- sit with Christ in heavenly places (2:6).

- are His workmanship, created unto good works (2:10).

- are the habitation of God through the Spirit (2:22).

- are rooted and grounded in love (3:17).

- can comprehend the love of Christ (3:19).

- are filled with the fullness of God (3:19).

- have a Father who can do exceeding abundantly above all that we ask or think (3:20).

God is watching us! Hooray! — my Father's watching me. Therefore:

I can do all things through Christ which strengtheneth me (Phil. 4:13).

Because our Father is watching us, we can trust Him to be with us in the big — and small — things of life. We can press in to God with persistence, as we shall see next. 🕯

TEN

PRESS
IN TO
GOD

Principle Ten:

Be persistent in seeking your God idea.

E ARLY IN Jesus' ministry a wedding took place in the mountainous city of Cana in Galilee. Jesus and His disciples, along with His mother and other family members, attended the wedding. During the festivities Mary hurried over to Jesus to tell him, "They have no wine" (John 2:3).

It was a cultural faux pas to run out of wine at a wedding. Mary, who probably believed that Jesus would respond with a miracle, was surprised by His response, for He said, "Woman, what have I to do with thee? mine hour is not yet come" (John 2:4).

Jesus called her "woman," not "mother." He was gently yet firmly reminding her that He listened only to the voice of His heavenly Father. Though Mary had a good idea of helping her friends find a solution to their problem — it was not a God idea, and Jesus did not respond to it.

Jesus wanted His mother to understand that the former relationship between the two of them was at an end. She was not to interfere in His mission.

The reason He gave to Mary for His lack of response was, "Mine hour is not yet come."

It was not yet time for Jesus to show Himself as the miracle worker — the Messiah — through signs, wonders and miracles. He had not yet performed a miracle and had not received a God idea saying it was time to do so now.

But Mary persisted in her mission to get Jesus to meet the need for more wine. She, better than anyone else besides Jesus Himself, knew the power He possessed to bring a supernatural answer to this earthly problem. When the angel had appeared to her years before to announce the coming of Jesus, he had said,

> And, behold, thou shalt conceive in thy womb, and bring forth a son, and shalt call his name JESUS. He shall be great, and shall be called the Son of the Highest: and the Lord God shall give unto him the throne of his father David (Luke 1:31-32).

Mary wisely did not argue with Jesus. But she knew if she could not command Him, she could instruct the servants to obey His directions. So she persisted by saying to the servants, "Whatsoever he saith unto you, do it" (John 2:5).

Mary wanted a solution to the problem — a God idea — and by faith she pressed in to God for that answer. By doing so, she changed the course of history. She tapped in to the Father and His resourcefulness, and because she did, I believe the Father decided to speed up the destiny and time of Jesus' ministry. "The effectual fervent prayer of a righteous man availeth much" (James 5:16).

God answered Mary's persistence and seemed to speak a God idea to Jesus: "All right, My Son, the time has come. You can become the answer to this need — You can make more wine — and at the same time I will allow You to reveal Yourself as the Messiah who can answer every need for anyone who will believe. Step forward into the destiny for which You were brought to earth."

Our persistence in seeking for the God ideas for our lives can move us forward in the destiny God has for us. As we persist — press in to God for His revelation for our lives — He will respond by speeding up our destiny and moving us forward toward the destination for our lives.

After my Bible school experience in the chapel, God sped up the plan He had for my life. During that first year of school I moved ahead in ministry, preaching and evangelizing. I used to do anything that I could to serve. I ushered and sold product at Benny Hinn meetings.

I was also helping a seventy-year-old evangelist, driving her to different meetings and assisting her in every part of her ministry. I was also teaching a Bible study for the ROTC program for the Army. I wanted to prosper where I was planted. I did anything I could to be a servant.

Some of my friends and acquaintances did not understand this plan of God to thrust me into early ministry opportunities. They struggled with their feelings about me and finally confronted me.

Three of them, whom I will call Dumpy, Jumpy and Lumpy, approached me with their feelings. "Tim, we've got a problem with you," one of them said to me.

I had picked up on some of their negative feelings about me, so I was not too surprised to hear them say this. "What is the problem?" I asked.

"Actually it's three problems," they continued. Then, almost as an afterthought, they added, "We're saying this because we love you." They elaborated on the three points of misunderstanding.

"We don't know if we like the way you dress," my friend Dumpy told me. "I know you come from California, but this is Bible school in Florida. We just aren't into California styles here. It's not humble to dress the way you do."

His comment caught me off guard. I didn't have any money and certainly didn't consider myself to be *stylish*. Most of my clothes had been purchased in thrift or secondhand stores. But I had always believed that whatever I had could be clean and ironed. If my clothes looked good, it was simply because I took care of them.

Jumpy burst into the conversation. "And we don't like the way you walk."

I couldn't help grinning a little on this one. "Well, how do I walk?" I asked.

Jumpy stood up to demonstrate. "Here, let me show you," he said, and he half-strutted, half-pounced across the room. "You kind of walk like a tiger. A lot of us have been talking about it. It draws attention to yourself."

"Well, how should I walk?" I asked. I certainly

hoped I didn't look the way my friend had demonstrated. Not even a tiger would want to be identified
with that walk.

Jumpy replied, "A little more humble," and stood
once more to demonstrate. This time he sort of slunk
across the floor, his chin touching his chest.

But they hadn't finished yet. Now Lumpy spoke up.
"And we don't like all this stuff about your visions and
dreams. You know, that sign you have up — that's a
sign of pride."

He was referring to a sign I kept over my bed which
read: "Yes, you can — three million souls." That sign
was the result of another God idea. One day as I
prayed I had said to God, "Wouldn't it be great if three
thousand souls could be saved through the ministry
that You give to me?"

But God had replied, "That's not enough!"

"Well, how about three hundred thousand?" I suggested.

Again He had spoken to me, "No, that's still not
enough."

With a sudden burst of faith, I shot back, "OK, how
about three million?"

God said, "That's a good start!"

Now my friend continued, "That sign shows how
proud you are. Who do you think you are?"

I thought about who I was. I came from a poor
family and could barely afford to attend Bible college.
I wore secondhand clothes and carefully budgeted
what little money I had. I was grateful for every little
thing God sent my way.

My friends were judging me by external appear-
ances, but they knew nothing about who I was.

I had done nothing but press in to God for the God

idea for my life. And because I did, He favored me with opportunities to speed up His destiny for my life. I had already begun to move into ministry while still in Bible college. My friends did not understand God's move in my life.

I called my mother and said, "I'm thinking of quitting Bible school. Maybe I'll go into broadcasting — work at NBC like Bryant Gumbel does." All at once I wanted to use my energy and the gifts God gave me for something else.

My mother counseled me, "Tim, don't leave until you talk to God."

I respected my mother, and I knew her advice was right. When we finished our conversation, I walked to the chapel and knelt before God once again. "God," I cried out, "maybe I am full of pride. Maybe I don't walk in humility. Maybe I am too interested in my personal appearance."

But there in that chapel God whispered back to me, "It's all foolishness. You are fearfully and wonderfully made. I made you to be Tim Storey — now be Tim Storey! I've called you to be a champion." And as I knelt there before Him, God began to fill me with new God ideas — bigger dreams and visions of His plan for my life.

There may be times in your life when nobody believes in you but you; times when people do not really know your spirit — and fail to understand your spiritual motives. But if you have a God idea, keep moving forward in it.

In his book *All You Can Do Is All You Can Do, But All You Can Do Is Enough*, A. L. Williams includes a list of "Reasons Not to Quit."

You may not notice it in the tough times, but chances are you've already come a long way from where you were when you started out on this new course.

- You've learned a lot; your experience has developed you into someone with a better chance of success than you had before. If you quit now, you've made that progress for nothing.

- You've paid a price. Think of all the sacrifices you've made trying to *go for it*. If you quit now, all that you worked so hard for and suffered for will mean nothing.

- You've set goals and made plans that involved your whole family. Can you live with yourself if you fold up your tent and go home?[1]

The devil will bring people into our lives to push us, prod us and try to knock us down. But God is waiting to birth His God idea into our lives. We must press in to catch the vision He has for us.

When Paul persisted with God in the desert of Arabia, he got a revelation. He met with God and received his God idea. Persist for yours.

In my desperation I said, "I'm going to find God. I'm going to get to know Him and His plan for my life." I began to seek the Lord with everything I had, and out of that desperation God brought forth a greater destiny in my life.

Go to Your Daddy!

My father and I had a great relationship when I was a young boy. But when I was just ten years old, my father died. As I grew, I was always looking for a role model — someone to encourage me with, "Come on, Storey, you can do it!"

I knew the Bible said that God was "A father of the fatherless" (Ps. 68:5). But somehow that just didn't seem *enough*. My father was not only my father — he was my *daddy!*

Then I discovered that God was my *Daddy* too.

> But ye have received the Spirit of adoption, whereby we cry, Abba, Father (Rom. 8:15).

The word *abba* is an Aramaic word which is similar in meaning to our word *daddy*. I can run to Him and throw myself into His arms just as I threw myself into my daddy's arms. He is my heavenly *Daddy!*

We have a Daddy that really cares. His love is everlasting.

> Yea, I have loved thee with an everlasting love: therefore with lovingkindness have I drawn thee (Jer. 31:3).

His love is accepting.

> To the praise of the glory of his grace, wherein he hath made us accepted in the beloved (Eph. 1:6).

Sometimes, in the midst of wilderness experiences, we don't even accept ourselves because of failures and mistakes we have made. But God's love is everlasting, accepting and intimate. He is a Daddy who cares, who hugs and holds us in His great big arms.

When I was a boy growing into a young man, I needed the intimacy of the Lord — and I still do.

God does not mind if we come to Him. That's why the Holy Spirit draws us to the Father. The Scriptures illustrate God's love for His children by saying,

> "When Israel was a child, then I loved him, and called my son out of Egypt....I drew them with cords of a man, with bands of love" (Hos. 11:1,4).

Persistence Pays Off

My persistence in pressing in to God when my friends confronted me with their misunderstandings resulted in a bigger vision of the God idea for my life. That bigger vision has enabled me to move forward in God's plan, and with God's help I will be able to reach my goal of three million souls saved.

That vision God gave me when I persisted in the wilderness was His unique God idea for my life. But it wasn't meant just for me — it was meant to touch the lives of others too.

In his twenty-nine years of life and six years of ministry, David Brainerd (1718–1747), a pioneer missionary to the American Indians, inspired millions of Christians to a deeper devotion to Jesus Christ and sent hundreds of young people into the mission field.

A somber young man, Brainerd was frail and sickly. Yet he chose to take on the incredible hardships of travel beyond the frontier, the difficulties of communicating with primitive, unlettered tribes.

He also had to battle a nagging sense of failure and injustice resulting from his expulsion from Yale College. Yet there is no doubt God was at work in David Brainerd's life.

We can learn much about the God idea in David Brainerd's life from extracts from his diary. The birth of a great desire to reach the American Indians with the gospel message can be seen in his entry for Monday, April 12, 1742:

> I was specially assisted to intercede and plead for poor souls, and for the enlargement of Christ's kingdom in the world, and for special grace for myself, to fit me for special services. It was no matter when, nor where, nor how Christ should send me, nor what trials He should still exercise me with, if I might but be prepared for His work and will.[2]

Soon after that, Brainerd's unique calling to the Indians became a reality.

> Thursday, August 12 — This morning I had in a great measure lost my hopes of God's sending me among the heathen afar off, and of seeing them flock home to Christ. It

seemed as though I never could nor should preach any more; yet about nine or ten o'clock the people came over and I was forced to preach.

And blessed be God, He gave me His presence and Spirit in prayer and preaching, so that I was much assisted, and spoke with power from Job 14:14. Some Indians cried out in great distress, and all appeared greatly concerned.[3]

From that time on David Brainerd never swerved in his understanding of the God idea for his life. At great peril and ultimate loss of life he sacrificed everything to reach *his* Indians with the gospel. On June 28, 1744, he wrote:

Spent the morning in reading several parts of the Holy Scripture, and in fervent prayer for my Indians, that God would set up His kingdom among them, and bring them into His church. I could freely tell the Lord, He knew that the cause was not mine which I was engaged in; but it was His own cause, and it would be for His own glory to convert the poor Indians.[4]

Although his health was ruined by his rugged life, David Brainerd gave his life to the Indians God had given him to nurture spiritually. His message was one of love — the love of God, the love that Christ displayed on the cross of Calvary and Brainerd's own heart of love.

David Brainerd understood the God idea for his life. Just like the apostle Paul, he exhibited the characteristics of those who are willing to use their God idea to help others.

Like these ordinary men who were used greatly by God, we can learn to share our God ideas with those around us — thus fulfilling God's ultimate purpose for each believer (see Mark 16:15). ✿

CONCLUSION

GOD-IDEA
PEOPLE

A S THE God idea becomes real in your life, God will develop some character traits in you that will help you take the steps, follow the course and reach the destination He has planned for you.

The life of Paul demonstrates five qualities of God-idea people.

1. They are open to change.

Paul knew he'd heard from God even when he found himself in prison. His circumstances had changed, but his God idea had not changed.

Paul was open to a change of direction. The change of response from those to whom he ministered did not discourage him, even when that change threatened his safety and security. He saw an opportunity to share his God idea — and he was ready.

2. They are unshaken by difficult situations.

Paul was an apostle, the first missionary of the early

Christian church. His letters to the early congregations make up much of the New Testament. Paul had a very important role to play in the establishment of the church and in the record of our doctrine and Christian behavior for today. These roles were part of the large God idea for his life.

But there was a Philippian jailer who needed a word from the Lord. He was just an ordinary person like you and me, but he was important to the Lord. He, too, was part of the large God idea for Paul's life. He was one of the reasons why Paul's plans had been changed by the Lord. And Paul was willing to share that idea with the jailer. Not even imprisonment and an earthquake could cause Paul to leave Philippi without completing his ministry to that jailer.

3. *They do not run at the first opportunity.*

About midnight Paul and Silas were praying and singing hymns to God. Suddenly there was such a violent earthquake that the foundations of the prison were shaken. All the cell doors flew open, and the chains fell off all the prisoners.

The jailer, who had fallen asleep, woke up. When he saw the cell doors open, he was sure all the prisoners had escaped. He drew his sword and was about to kill himself, but Paul shouted, "Don't harm yourself; we are all here!" (see Acts 16:28).

The jailer called for the lights and rushed into the cell, expecting to find it empty. His life was probably passing before him. He knew his prisoners would be gone. He knew he would have to pay for it with his own life.

But Paul and Silas were still there. He fell trembling

before them. He was shocked. He was dumbfounded. He couldn't believe his eyes. In deep gratitude and with great awareness of his own need for salvation, he brought them out and asked them, "Sirs, what must I do to be saved?" (v. 30).

Paul and Silas talked a convincing gospel, but so did other "religious" zealots. Paul and Silas seemed to possess supernatural powers, but many magicians and mystics could perform tricks. The difference for the jailer wasn't in what they preached or in the wonders they performed. For the jailer, the greatest miracle of all was that these men stayed when they could have run away. I dare say most of us would have fled from the prison, rejoicing in how the Lord had provided a way where there had been no way.

4. They have no desire for earthly fame or possessions.

It was Paul who stated,

> Yea doubtless, and I count all things but loss for the excellency of the knowledge of Christ Jesus my Lord: for whom I have suffered the loss of all things, and do count them but dung, that I may win Christ, and be found in him (Phil. 3:8-9).

Paul never sought for big honorariums for his speaking engagements; he didn't build a mansion next to the ocean or drive a Mercedes-Benz. He had no desire for things of earth. The only possessions he desired were the souls of those to whom he brought the good news.

5. *They are content with a future heavenly reward.*

Herein lies the crux of the matter. Jesus is the author and finisher of our faith, and He has gone ahead of us to prepare a heavenly reward for those who finish the course of their God idea.

I've met many tremendous people. I've been in some of the greatest homes throughout the world and dined in some of the greatest restaurants. But one person who has exhibited tremendous spiritual leadership in my life is Ron L. Prinzing, the pastor of First Family Church in Whittier, California. He has pastored that church for over thirty years. When I was about four years old, my family started attending his church.

Even though our family was one of the few minority families in that church, he really loved us. Whenever there was a crisis in our family, he was there. He was the one who was there for us when my father passed away. He was there when my sister was killed in a car accident at age nineteen. He was there with us through thick and thin.

In my opinion, Ron Prinzing represents the *Jesus style*. He is not as well-known as some ministers I know, but he is consistent in the God idea for his life.

He is not looking for earthly rewards but realizes a much greater reward is laid up for him in heaven.

Champions

Accept your idea from God and then God will be open to work miracles in your life. And as a result of your personal encounter with Him, you'll be equipped to minister the reality of that idea to others who need to hear it.

> Trust in the Lord with all thine heart; and lean not unto thine own understanding. In all thy ways acknowledge him, and he shall direct thy paths (Prov. 3:5-6).

> The steps of a good man are ordered by the Lord: and he delighteth in his way. Though he fall, he shall not be utterly cast down: for the Lord upholdeth him with his hand (Ps. 37:23-24).

Don't forget that a small acorn grows into a great oak tree. So grow the seeds of greatness in your own life. It takes work and discipline and proper nurturing. It also takes time — it may not happen overnight.

We may not be what we want to be, but thank God we are not what we used to be! Continue walking in the God ideas He has given to you. Be the champion God has called you to be. Be a God-idea person! ॐ

NOTES

Introduction:
God's People Need God Ideas

1. John D. Woodbridge, ed., *Great Leaders of the Christian Church* (Chicago, Ill.: Moody Press, 1988), pp. 289-294.
2. "Why Did You Make the Peanut?" *In Touch*, January 1994, pp. 8-9.

Chapter 2:
Find Your Sixth Sense

1. *The Wycliffe Bible Commentary* (Nashville, Tenn.: The Southwestern Company, 1962), p. 1174.

Chapter 5:
Trust God in Small Places

1. Woodbridge, *Great Leaders*, pp. 322-324.
2. Pat Reilly, *The Winner Within* (New York, N.Y.: Putnam Publishing Group, 1993).

Chapter 6:
Get Going!

1. A. L. Williams, *All You Can Do Is All You Can Do, But All You Can Do Is Enough* (New York, N.Y.: Ivy Books, 1989), p. 157.

Chapter 7:
Keep Your Cool When Things Get Hot

1. Merrill F. Unger, *Unger's Bible Dictionary* (Chicago, Ill.: Moody Press, 1957), p. 973.

Chapter 8:
Regain Childlike Trust

1. Sherwood Eliot Wirt, ed., *Spiritual Awakening* (Westchester, Ill.: Crossway Books, 1986), p. 31.
2. Roger Lundin & Mark A. Noll, eds., *Voices From the Heart* (Grand Rapids, Mich.: William B. Eerdmans Publishing Company, 1987), pp. 213-214.

Chapter 10:
Press in to God

1. Williams, *All You Can Do,* p. 167.
2. Wirt, *Spiritual Awakening,* p. 125.
3. Ibid., p. 126.
4. Ibid., p. 128.

For information concerning other books,
videos and cassettes by Tim Storey, write to:

Tim Storey
c/o Tim Storey Ministries
P. O. Box 1428
Whittier, California 90609

If you enjoyed *Good Idea or God Idea?*, we would
like to recommend the following books:

Hippo in the Garden
by James Ryle

Author James Ryle says that God speaks to us at unusual times
in unexpected places. Through his humorous personal
anecdotes and references to the Old and New Testament
Scriptures, you will discover that every circumstance of life
becomes an opportunity to converse with God.

Keeping Your Dreams Alive When They Steal Your Coat
by Doug Murren

Author Doug Murren will inspire you to see your dreams to
fulfillment — no matter what happens to you along the way.
With a dash of humor, he shows how the life of Joseph
is a practical model for today's dreamers.
You don't have God's dreams — they have you!

The Sound of His Voice
by Kim Clement

Author Kim Clement shares that prophecy did not end in Bible
times and that it has been the forgotten ministry of the church. He
gives practical principles for hearing the voice of God. *The Sound
of His Voice* is a call for prophecy to come alive in every believer.

You're Born an Original — Don't Die a Copy!
by John L. Mason

In this above-average sequel to his national best-seller *An Enemy
Called Average*, John Mason writes fifty-two powerful nuggets of
truth. You will be inspired to be the original person God created
you to be, using the unique gifts and talents He has given you.

Available at your local Christian bookstore or from:

Creation House
600 Rinehart Road
Lake Mary, FL 32746
1-800-451-4598